Penguin Bool

PRESENT TI.

David Storey was born in 1933 and is the third son of a mineworker. He was educated at the Queen Elizabeth School at Wakefield and the Slade School of Fine Art. He has had various jobs ranging from professional footballer to school-teaching and showground tent-erecting. He is now both a novelist and a dramatist.

His novels include *This Sporting Life*, which won the Macmillan Fiction Award in 1960 and was also filmed; *Flight into Camden*, which won the John Llewelyn Rhys Memorial Prize and also the Somerset Maugham Award in 1963; *Radcliffe*; *Pasmore*, which won the Faber Memorial Prize in 1973; *A Temporary Life*; *Saville*, which won the Booker Prize in 1976; and *A Prodigal Child* (1982). He has received numerous drama awards including the New York Critics' Best Play of the Year Award in three years out of four. His plays include *The Restoration of Arnold Middleton*; *In Celebration*, which has been filmed; *The Contractor*; *Home*; *The Changing Room*; *The Farm*; *Life Class*; *Mother's Day*; *Sisters* and *Early Days*. Several of David Storey's novels are published by Penguin as are three volumes of his plays.

David Storey lives in London. He was married in 1956 and has four children.

David Storey

PRESENT TIMES

PENGUIN BOOKS

Penguin Books Ltd, Harmondsworth, Middlesex, England
Viking Penguin Inc., 40 West 23rd Street, New York, New York 10010, U.S.A.
Penguin Books Australia Ltd, Ringwood, Victoria, Australia
Penguin Books Canada Ltd, 2801 John Street, Markham, Ontario, Canada L3R 1B4
Penguin Books (N.Z.) Ltd, 182–190 Wairau Road, Auckland 10, New Zealand

First published by Jonathan Cape 1984
Published in Penguin Books 1985

Copyright © David Storey, 1984
All rights reserved

Made and printed in Great Britain by
Richard Clay (The Chaucer Press) Ltd, Bungay, Suffolk
Typeset in Bembo

I

'He's brok' his shoulder.' The pug-nosed, the pug-eared Morgan tapped his fingers at the typewriter keys with insufficient pressure to print a letter then, pausing only to gaze out to the mist-shrouded figures gathered around the referee, tapped the keys more firmly and committed to paper, 'Stephenson received an injury in the thirty-third minute of the second half which resulted in his leaving the field just when his presence,' his dark eyes gazed down to where a player stepped back to take the free kick, 'was being appreciated by a capacity crowd.'

'That should do it,' the stockily-built, the tousle-haired, the pugnaciously-featured Attercliffe said.

Morgan looked at the pen in Attercliffe's hand: 'Not learnt to bloody well type yet, Frank?'

'I write half of it up before I come,' the one-time player said.

'Thy ghost-writer not coming today, then, is he?'

'He isn't.' Attercliffe scribbled with his pen.

'He wa're in the bar half-time, tha knows.'

Attercliffe forgot to restart his watch and, having written up the goal as the ball curled over the bar, leaned across Morgan's arm and asked, 'What time is it?'

'By God.' Morgan laughed. 'Why they keep you on I've no idea.' He picked up his binoculars, leaned over Jenkinson on his other side, and said, 'Was that Havercroft or Audsley?'

'Audsley.'

The communal desk-top shuddered.

Stephenson, Attercliffe observed, and not the substitute, had got up from the players' bench, his head emerging above the concrete bunker into which, only seconds before, he'd been drawn down: a blanket, however, was wrapped around his shoulder and a hand was laid across his back, for the substitute was taking off his track suit and now stepped out in his black-plasticated, white-laced boots – his striped green and yellow jersey and his clean white shorts – and did a knees-bend and one or two stretches: a moment later, after Stephenson had gone – disappearing into the tunnel-mouth, a red-track-suited figure beside him – the substitute waved his arm and, to a cheer from the crowd, ran on, his clean limbs and costume conspicuous before, stooping, he was absorbed inside a scrum.

'Who was it?'

'Patterson,' came along the row of typing figures as the loud-speaker announced his substitution.

'Thirty-third minute.'

'I made it thirty-eight.'

'Injury thirty-third, replacement thirty-eight.'

Attercliffe made a note on his pad, wrote, 'Patterson replaced Stephenson in the thirty-eighth minute' – wondered if he'd got all the 'h's and enough 't's in 'eighth' – when the press box door was pushed open behind his back and a gnarled hand was clasped about his shoulder. A voice – accompanied by a breath redolent of whisky and chicken vindaloo (a favourite dish) – said, 'How are we, Frank?' and Fredericks's small, close-cropped head was placed beside his own; a fissured face, inset with pale-blue eyes and overtopped by bushy brows, peered past him to the pitch below. 'A score?'

'An injury.'

'Got it down?'

'That's right.'

'Be making a hack of you yet, like Morgan here, or Wichita-Jones.'

'Davidson-Smith,' said Morgan.

'How are you, Jake?' Fredericks addressed an overcoated, deerstalker-hatted figure further along the row who, having looked up, turned back to the pitch. 'No heating in here? I thought they had.'

'It's brok'n, Freddie,' Morgan said. He, too, Attercliffe assumed, must have been taking in the fumes but, apart from an averted head, his gaze remained fixed on the pitch below.

6

'"Sharp sidestep" is better than "quick sidestep",' Fredericks said.

'I don't like alliteration,' Morgan said and, as another move occurred on the pitch below, he glanced at his watch, typed, pressed the stop-watch button and, raising his binoculars, one-handed, gazed to the rows of figures directly below and added, 'Phyllis Gardner is in the stand.'

'I've seen her,' Fredericks said. 'First place to look when Dougie is playing.' Stooping to gaze at the fur-hatted, fur-coated figure towards which Morgan's glasses were still inclined, he added, 'It's not alliterative, or only half.'

'What isn't?' Morgan raised his glasses to the field and, just as quickly, put them down to recommence his typing.

'"Quick sidestep" sounds like Victor Sylvester, though you won't remember him, however.'

'How about Ginger Rogers?'

'Fred Astaire.'

'Phyllis Gardner.'

A roar went up from the crowd.

Attercliffe jotted down one or two names and amended the paragraph describing the last quarter of the match and asked, 'Who's Phyllis Gardner?'

The typewriter clicked briskly to his right and Fredericks, his hand on Attercliffe's back, straightened.

'An actress.'

'Like hell.' Morgan, a pencil in his mouth, gazed at the mass of words before him.

'I thought she'd been in a film.'

'One.'

'Well.'

'Hardly an actress, sport, old friend.'

A trumpet blared from the ranks behind one goal.

'I've been in a film,' Morgan said. 'I wouldn't say I was an actor.'

'She's more than a bloody hiccup.' Fredericks leaned across Attercliffe's shoulder. 'Got the first try?'

'More or less.'

'A good 'un.'

'It was.'

'Been nought since then.'

7

'Not that he'd see it.' Morgan removed the pencil from between his teeth. 'The bar window only looks out on the twenty-five.'

'T'alf that bloody counts,' Fredericks said. 'Any silly bugger can look at nought.'

A whistle blew.

Figures stooped: the ball was kicked towards them from across the field.

'Still wi' Dougie Walters,' Morgan said. 'That's why she's here. Last three homes and one away.'

'Any ideas, Frank?' Fredericks asked.

'None,' Attercliffe said.

'Should have. Your age. You're still a young man.'

'Forty-seven.'

'Near sixty,' Fredericks said, 'yet I still have one or two pretensions.' He stooped to Attercliffe's pad, screwed up his eyes to read without his glasses, put his hand in his inside pocket, took out a pen, drew the pad towards him, wrote for several seconds, then set the pad once more beside Attercliffe on the desk.

Barry Morgan would like to fuck Phyllis Gardner but his wife wouldn't let him so in his report tomorrow morning he will indicate that Dougie Walters' prick isn't long enough to stuff a chicken.

'Something along those lines,' he said.

'Genius, this man,' Morgan said. 'Can write a report from the back of the bar and even get the full-back's second initial.'

Phyllis Gardner had red fingernails, red lipstick, and a touch of brown rouge along each cheek which accentuated the slenderness of her cheekbones and gave her pale-blue eyes, which were drawn out laterally by eye-liner and mascara, an oriental look. Morgan, in his astrakhan hat and fur-collared overcoat, and his white and black-plasticated, buttoned-down driving gloves, having phoned in his match report, approached her across the bar and inquired in a voice loud enough to be heard the other side, 'How are you, Phyl?', to which the fur-coated figure replied, 'I'm waiting for Dougie,' her head turning to the players' entrance from where, on cue, Dougie Walters appeared, his hair, wet from the bath, combed smoothly down, his face gleaming, his twice-broken nose

8

conspicuous, his jaw pronounced and accentuated further by the strands of beard thrust out by the collar of his overcoat.

Fredericks lifted his glass, bared his teeth, said, 'Here's to it,' and drank.

Emptying his glass, he set it down: his gaze went over to the figure of Dougie and, saying to Attercliffe, 'I shan't be a minute,' he crossed the floor and, breathing his liquored breath in Walters's face, said, 'A blinder, Dougie,' at the same time his arm displacing Morgan so that the astrakhan-hatted figure was standing a moment later behind his back.

'Phoned it through.' Davidson-Smith sat down, his overcoat buttoned, adjusted his tie within his collar and, having done so, ran his finger over his rectangular, grey- and orange-tinged moustache and added, 'Two hundred and fifty goldies cut down to twenty by tomorrow morn.'

'Do you fancy a drink?' Attercliffe asked.

'No thanks.' He glanced at the one in Attercliffe's hand and added, 'I see Freddie's sticking his thumb up Morgan's nose,' and, exuding a tang of male deodorant, continued, 'Does Fredericks do much of the composition these days, Frank?'

'His share.'

'Used to do all of it at one time, didn't he?' His eyes drifted up to where Fredericks and Walters and Morgan and Phyllis had formed themselves into a single group and he added, to Attercliffe's surprise, 'She's coming this way.'

'Frank?' a voice inquired with such a musical intonation that Attercliffe was already standing before the voice had time to add, 'You don't mind my intruding?'

Blue, mascaraed eyes, long-lashed, glanced from him to Davidson-Smith and back again: she smiled; pearl-buttoned teeth appeared between brightly-fashioned lips.

'Miss Gardner.'

'Mr Fredericks sent me.'

Attercliffe didn't glance in that direction, neither did he glance at Davidson-Smith who, having risen, had manoeuvred himself around the table, his right hand half-extended.

'He said you were diffident.' She frowned. 'About approaching me.'

'I am.'

Her smile returned.

9

'I'm free,' she announced, 'the first half of next week.'

'Fine.'

Attercliffe caught a glimpse of Fredericks's face – eyes distended, brow puckered, nostrils dilated, mouth contorted – juxtaposed against the astrakhan-hatted head of Morgan.

'Mornings are a better time for me.'

'Mornings.'

'Will Tuesday be all right?'

'Fine.'

'Eleven o'clock.'

'Good.'

'I'll give you my address.'

From her handbag she took out a piece of paper; her fingers were slender, the nails long and drawn to a point. She unscrewed a gold-topped pen and wrote.

'Can you read it?'

He examined the scrawl.

'"Thirty-six Queensgate. Flat seven."' She read it for him. 'Eleven o'clock.' She held out her hand.

Beyond her head he saw Dougie Walters coming across, Fredericks talking by his shoulder.

'Goodbye,' she said.

'Goodbye,' Attercliffe said.

'Goodbye, Miss Gardner.' Davidson-Smith raised his hand to his deerstalker hat.

She was already halfway across the bar before she re-encountered Walters who, interrupting Fredericks's conversation, took her arm and, without any further acknowledgment of Fredericks, or Attercliffe, or Davidson-Smith, or Morgan, led her to the door.

'A charming girl,' Fredericks said as he took his seat at the table.

'Very,' Attercliffe said.

'Beautiful features.'

'Lovely.'

'Fancy a drink?' Davidson-Smith inquired.

'I'm off it, presently,' Fredericks said.

'Meeting the fiancée for dinner.' Davidson-Smith got up. 'I'd better make a start.'

His overcoat was fastened as he crossed the bar; his hatted head was nodded either side and at one point he paused, listening, before, with a wave, he reached the door.

'What was that about?' Attercliffe asked.

'Do you fancy a drink?'

'No thanks.'

'I'll get another.'

Already Fredericks was on his feet.

By the time he came back Attercliffe was standing, pulling on his coat, and when Fredericks said, 'One for the road,' and handed him a glass he shook his head. Fredericks appealed, 'Can't let it go to waste,' taking it from him as he finished his own.

Attercliffe preceded him to the door, but even then, having cleared the way, it was several minutes before Fredericks joined him on the steps outside.

'What do we do from now till then?' He waited for Attercliffe to open the car door.

'I'll take you home,' Attercliffe said.

'The Buckingham might be better.'

The crowd had gone; only the players' and the committee's cars and the visiting team's high-windowed coach remained.

They drove in silence towards the town.

'She's very pretty.'

'Since when,' Attercliffe said, 'have you gone in for made-up women?'

'I thought you might.'

'What do I do at eleven o'clock?'

'Morning or evening?'

'Morning.'

'Which day?'

'Tuesday.'

'Make something up.'

'What did you tell her?'

Fredericks concentrated for a while on the road ahead: there wasn't a great deal to see but the opalescence of their own lights in front of the bonnet.

'I said you wanted to do an interview but were too diffident to ask.'

'I bet Dougie was impressed.'

'Not as much as Morgan. He didn't believe it for a second.'

'What do I do?'

'Use your imagination.'

'I don't know anything about her.'

'Look it up.'

'Where?'

'Ask Cornforth. He does entertainment.'

'What happens when this interview doesn't appear?'

'She'll never notice.'

'She's bound to.'

'Training at Morristown on Tuesday evenings. Pity you didn't make it then.'

'Do you think Walters will be there?'

'Do you want my frank opinion?'

He looked at Attercliffe directly.

'Give it to Booth. He's open to novelties. Then again, if it isn't used, you can always blame yours truly.' He shifted his position. 'Seize the chance.'

The lights of the town appeared; within minutes they were passing through the city centre.

'See you,' Fredericks said as he got out at the Buckingham Hotel, and added, 'Do you want to bring it round to my place before you hand it in?'

'Sure.'

'Don't come till late.'

'I shan't.'

'Make it ten. I'll be awake by then.'

'Right.'

As he drove off he could see Fredericks's figure, swaying, making for the Brasserie Bar.

2

He turned into Walton Lane as the last vestige of light was leaving the western sky – far, far away, close to the gorge-like crest of the valley – and braked to avoid a group of children darting from one side of the road to the other. As he turned into the gateless drive of the third, detached, 'executive' dwelling on his left, he sounded the horn.

Through the uncurtained side-window he saw Elise, his eldest daughter, look up from the kitchen sink: her dark hair hung in straight strands, accentuating beneath the overhead light the slimness of her features.

He banged the car door, and saw her, hurriedly, begin to dry her hair, rubbing it inside a towel.

In order to delay his arrival he went round to the front; through the glazed panels of the door he could see a figure, a towel around its head, mount the stairs. When he unlocked the door, however, and opened it, a second figure darted out: black-skinned, woolly-hatted, zip-jacketed, jeaned, it ran past him to the road. The padding of its plimsolled feet, first across the lawn, then across the drive, then along the road itself, was obscured finally by the whine of music from the living-room.

Watching television, lying on the floor – when he stepped inside the room – was his second-eldest daughter, Catherine.

She, too, had long dark hair only, in this instance, it was fastened in a series of tiny plaits, each secured by a rubber band. As he entered, she looked up and said, 'Mummy rang.'

'Who's that?'

'Who's who?'

'Somebody ran out when I came in.'

'That's Benjie.'

'Benjie who?'

'Benjie,' she said.

'Why didn't he stay?'

'He wanted to leave.'

'He never said hello.'

'That's right.'

Attercliffe realised, from Catherine's pigtails, that she too had washed her hair and drew the conclusion that she and Elise were going out.

'She's not very happy.'

'Who isn't?'

'Mummy.'

'Why not?'

'Gavin is always leaving her alone.'

Elise – her jeans stained damp, her plimsolls damp, her T-shirt damp ('Sucker' stamped across the breast) – descended the stairs – as if from the bathroom – and, towelling her hair, surveyed Attercliffe from the living-room door.

'Who's Gavin?'

'Her boyfriend.'

'What happened to Maurice?'

'Oh, *Maurice*.'

From the television came a series of yells, followed by a blare of music. Having glanced up at his eldest daughter, Attercliffe surveyed her sister: jerseyed shoulders, pleated skirt, pigtailed head.

'Maurice isn't interested in Mummy any more.'

'Since when?'

'Honestly, Dad, you never keep up.'

Silhouetting his daughter's head, the television screen was incandescent.

'In any case,' Attercliffe said, 'who's Gavin?'

'A friend.'

'How old is he?'

Elise pushed past him, gazing at the screen from a position which obstructed Attercliffe's view completely.

'Is he young, old, or medium?' he added.

'Younger than you.'

Catherine tossed the remark across her shoulder.

'How much younger?'

'Lots.'

'He's twenty-six.' Elise turned, the towel knotted round her head.

'That's young.'

'Sounds old to me.'

'Your mother's forty.' Attercliffe paused. '*Sheila* is almost forty-one.'

'She was thirty-nine last year.'

He went through to the kitchen: the floor was wet, the draining-board was wet, the wall was wet; Elise's footprints led out to the hall. Clots of hair hung in the plughole. A comb and a hairbrush, also wet, stood on the kitchen table.

'How did it go?'

Elise watched him from the door.

For a moment he thought she'd come in with the intention of clearing up the sink.

'All right.'

'Get everything down?'

'I think so.'

'We saw the result on television.'

'Good.'

'Mr Fredericks there?'

'He was.'

'He rang up after you left.'

'What about?'

'He said he'd be late.'

'So I discovered.'

'Why don't you work on your own?'

'I do.'

'You always work with him.'

'We write this column together.'

'He doesn't do any of it, Sheila says.'

'What else has she told you?'

'He leaves most of it to you.' She ran the comb through the bristles of the brush, collected the strands of hair, opened the lid of the rubbish bin, and dropped them in.

'Did you answer the telephone, or Cathy?'

'Cathy.'

'What did Sheila say about being unhappy?'

'Cathy asked her how she was and she said she wasn't feeling well.'

'That doesn't mean unhappy.'

'She asked her what the matter was and Mummy said, "Everything, really," and when she said, "What's everything?" she said she hardly ever sees Gavin.'

'I've never even heard of Gavin.'

'You don't have to hear of everyone.'

In many respects, Attercliffe reflected, it was as if Elise were the child of another father, one who seldom showed up and who, when he did – distressed at what his daughter had become – only succeeded in bawling her out. Also, he reminded himself, living in the circumstances that they did, she had to keep up her guard against encroachments: anything close was fraught with pain.

'Are you going out tonight?'

'With Sandra.'

'Is Cathy going out?'

'I think so.'

'Isn't she going out with you?'

'No.'

She turned to the door.

'Have you got a lift home?'

'I think so.'

'If you're staying at Sandra's could you give me a ring?'

'Sure.'

She went out to the hall; the living-room door was closed; the murmur of voices ('What did he say?') was interrupted by the sound of singing.

Attercliffe took off his overcoat and carried it upstairs.

A bedroom at the back, once occupied by his youngest daughter, now contained a desk as well as a bed: on the bed he placed his coat and on the desk his notes.

Through the window the lights of the estate stretched up a slope to a field which interceded between the last of the houses and the silhouetted hulk of a ruined castle: a mist hung in the air, turning each patch of light into a liquid blur.

In the uncurtained window of the house across the wattle fence at the end of his lawned back garden he watched a woman whom he had watched on numerous occasions before seated in the kitchen talking into a wall telephone.

'Dad?'

It was Catherine's call from the foot of the stairs.

The hair stood up on the back of his neck.

'Do you want a cup of tea?'

'I wouldn't mind.'

'Shall I bring it up?'

'All right.'

He lifted the typewriter off the floor, got out the Tipp-Ex sheets and a carbon, rolled in the paper, and sat down at the desk.

'Shall I come in?'

The features of an inquiring child, its head enclosed in a halo of plaited hair, appeared around the door.

' "Shall", or "can"?'

She came inside with a cup and a saucer.

'Anything to eat?'

'No thanks.'

'You'll have drunk a bit already.'

'Not much.'

She rubbed her feet against the carpet. 'All right if I go out tonight?'

'Usually you tell me,' Attercliffe said. 'Not inquire.'

'I might be late.'

'How late?'

'Two or three.'

'In the morning?'

'I could stay at Benjie's.'

'Who is this Benjie?'

'A friend.'

'Why did he run away?'

'He was frightened.'

'What of?'

'You.'

'I'd like to have met him,' Attercliffe said.

'Another time.'

'I'd prefer you to come back, nevertheless.'

'I've stayed at Benjie's before.'

'When?'

'When I've been staying over at Mum's.'

'She never told me.'

'She doesn't have to tell you everything.'

17

'Isn't it late for a girl of fifteen?'

'I'm in my sixteenth year, Dad.'

He paused. 'Do you have a separate room at Benjie's?'

'Of course.'

'Don't Benjie's parents think it odd their son bringing a girl to spend the night?'

'They've invited me to come.'

'Tonight?'

'Often.'

She dug her foot at the carpet.

'Where are you going?'

'A party.'

'Same one as Elly's?'

'No.'

'Whose?'

'You don't know them.'

'Are they black?'

'Why do they have to be black?'

'Benjie's black.'

'So what?'

'What does he do?'

'Nothing.'

She lowered her head.

'Is he still at school?'

'No.'

'He's out of work,' Attercliffe suggested.

'He may have to go into Borstal soon.'

'What for?'

'Because he's been charged.'

'What with?'

'Attacking a white man.'

Attercliffe returned his gaze to the window; he examined his daughter's reflection: dark eyes seethed within a pigtailed head – pale-cheeked, slim-necked, broad-browed, sharp-nosed – pugnaciously featured, he concluded, like himself.

'Why?'

'He insulted his brother.'

'Whose brother?'

'Benjie's.'

'Where?'

18

'At a dance hall.'

'Were you there?'

'No.' She shook her head.

'What happened?'

'There were eight, including Benjie and his brother. They attacked this man in the car park.'

'What with?'

'A knife.'

She added, 'They were originally charged with attempted murder, then with grievous bodily harm with intent, but it'll only be G.B.H., in the end.'

Attercliffe's hand, on the one side, gripped the desk; on the other his hand encountered first the edge of the chair and then its back. 'Why?'

'Because of the provocation.'

'What provocation?'

'He called them names.'

Attercliffe returned his gaze to his daughter: he examined the division of her hair into plaits.

'Has he been to Borstal before?'

'Only once.'

'What for?'

'Stealing.'

'Where from?'

'Shops.'

'Anywhere else?'

'Houses.'

'Does Sheila know?'

'I've told her.'

'What did she say?'

' "You have to take everyone as you find them." '

Attercliffe laughed; the sound was sufficient to prompt Catherine to raise her head.

'It's nothing but racial prejudice, Dad.'

'What about his friends?'

'The whole of society's against them. You don't know what it's like to be black.'

'Sticking a knife into someone is a cause for legitimate complaint,' he said.

'It was Benjie's brother who stabbed him.'

'Do the police know that?'

'No.' She dug her foot at the carpet again.

'I was brought up in far greater poverty than Benjie's had to endure. I've had to fight harder, and longer, and against greater odds,' he said.

'Have you had to fight,' she said, looking up, 'against the colour of your skin?'

'I've fought for what I am,' he said.

His own father used to tell him that: an employee of the London and North-Eastern Railway Company, with his furtively acquired supplies of railway coal, his frost-bitten hands, his Neanderthal stoop from standing so many hours of his adult life on the open platform of a steam locomotive. 'I'd have more sympathy for Benjie if his energies were directed to changing the world he lives in, instead of stealing from shops, breaking into houses, and stabbing a man at the back of a dance hall.'

'He only kicked him once.'

'After he stabbed him?'

'There are other sides to his nature.'

'What sides?'

'He gave me this jersey.'

'How could he afford it?'

'He stole it.' She added, 'He cared about me. He wanted me to have it. You're such a conformist.'

Attercliffe's gaze went back to his daughter's hair: he examined once more its fusillade of plaits, each secured by a check-patterned ribbon.

'What room do you sleep in when you stay overnight?'

'His sisters'.'

'His sister's, or his sisters'?'

'His sisters'!'

'How many has he got?'

'Eight.'

'Eight!'

'Five of them don't live at home. Doreen and Sheba share a bed when I go there and I sleep in Sasha's.'

'How old's Sasha?'

'Sixteen.'

'Does she steal and mutilate?'

'Not that I know of.'

20

'She earns a living.'

'She's still at school.'

'An intellectual.'

'She leaves at Easter.'

'How many brothers?'

'Two.'

'Ten children.'

'You've got five.'

'You don't have to remind me,' Attercliffe said. 'When you were born I thought I was responding to a God-given gift. I thought I was showing an appetite for living.'

'In any case, Mr Foster has two other wives.'

'*Two* other wives?'

'He has one in Jamaica.'

'My God.'

'Sheila has got two husbands. Three, if you count Gavin.'

'Jesus Christ.'

'He's a Moslem.'

'Gavin?'

'Mr Foster.'

'How old is he?'

'Older than you.'

'How much older?'

'He looks younger, but is five years older.'

'Jesus.'

'In any case, I don't see the point of all these questions.'

'I'm trying to look, Catherine, for something to tell me when you go out at night that I don't have to worry, that you'll be in the hands of people who intend to return you to this house in the same shape, the same physical and mental shape, in which you left it.'

'They will.'

'You see my concern?'

'You never get on at Elise.'

'She spends the night at Sandra's.'

'And Sandra's white.'

'Sandra is not a homicidal maniac.'

'Neither is Benjie.'

'His brother is. Benjie has still to prove his potential.'

'If Christ were on earth he'd love Benjie, and he'd love his brother and he'd love the Fosters.'

'They don't believe in Christ, they're Moslem.'

'They believe Jesus was a prophet.'

'Have they told you that?'

'I've read it in a book.' The plaits were shaken: it was getting close to the time she would have to go out. 'Don't you see that Christ would love Benjie *because* of his sins? He would see him as a human being, and not through the eyes of racial prejudice.'

'Benjie is like he is, and I react like I do,' Attercliffe said, 'because of racial prejudice?'

The tone of incredulity in his voice was heightened by the ordeal of his having had to compose a match report on his own and because he knew he would have to have 'Pindar's Weekend Round-up' in the hands of the compositors by this time tomorrow.

'You don't even know him.'

'I've seen him.'

'For five seconds.'

'That's all he'd allow me.'

'He despises the way you live.'

'What does he despise about it?'

'Its emptiness. Its lack of joy. Its lack of meaning.'

'Sticking a knife into somebody outnumbered eight to one is a better advertisement for living?' Attercliffe asked.

'I wish I hadn't told you.'

'I'm glad you did. Even if it's something Benjie doesn't believe in, telling the truth with me is all that counts. At least when we have the truth we can live like human beings. It's the truth,' Attercliffe said, 'I'm always keen on.'

'In that case, he didn't stick in the knife.'

'Stealing from shops is a better bargain.'

'He doesn't know better.'

'He's a shifty creep.'

She didn't answer.

'I hate him. I can't deny it. Not because he's black, but because of what he's doing to you.'

'If you're worried I'll get pregnant, I'm taking the pill.'

'At fifteen!'

'I'm in my sixteenth year.'

'You never told me,' Attercliffe said. 'Haven't I to be consulted?

Doesn't the doctor have to *inform* me, if you're under age?'

'I've told Sheila.'

'She never told me.'

'That's up to her.'

'We live under the same roof, Cathy,' Attercliffe said. 'I'm not only responsible for your material welfare but I'm trying to cater for your moral being as well.'

'The way *we* live?' his daughter said.

'Do you know the effect of all this chemical ingestion? If you're imbibing these pills at fifteen, what are you going to look like,' he said, 'at the age of forty-five?'

'Elise takes them.'

'She asked her mother. I had no choice. She's two years older.'

'I care about you,' his daughter said. 'So does Elise.'

'I'd prefer you not to go out with Benjie,' Attercliffe said, after a very long pause.

'That's blackmail. You only care about your own feelings, I love Benjie.'

'At fifteen?'

'What has age got to do with it? A child can love. I'm older than a child.'

She paused. 'Do you want anything else?'

'Will you be coming back?' he asked her.

'That's right.' She turned to the door.

'Is Elise coming back?'

'I've no idea.'

Her feet thudded along the landing; her voice, singing, came from the bathroom: she was standing in front of the mirror, he imagined, taking out her plaits.

What did it matter, Attercliffe reflected, as long as he loved her? (Love encompasseth all things, Dad.) Can anything in life be stronger than that – the pain she caused, the anxiety he felt, the torment of knowing she was in other hands (criminality countenanced by race)?

If Christ loves Benjie why can't I?

He sat at the typewriter and tapped the keys; Elise, too, was getting dressed: at some point during the argument she had come upstairs, for he could hear her voice calling from her bedroom, describing the merits of a record she had bought that afternoon.

23

They (he) had brought up their (his) daughters without a hint of sexual prejudice, only to see them take to dolls almost before they were able to walk, to pass on to lipstick, rouge and dresses, squirming, giggling, digging in their toes, transferring their affections from horses to men, from men to pimply youths.

Boys were different (he had two sons – eleven and thirteen – and one remaining daughter – seven): boys were not inclined to come home pregnant, to dissolve in tears when things went wrong – though they were, he recalled, in other families, inclined to thieve, to mutilate, and to make their lovers, wherever possible, accomplices after the fact.

'Are you ready, Elly?'

'I shall be in a minute.'

Suspicious that, if one of them were left behind, Attercliffe might be tempted to change his mind, they were going out together.

'Do you want some of this?'

Hallucinogens, narcotics, deodorant?

'No thanks.'

Had they taken their pills? How many times had he passed Elise's bed only to see 'sun''s pill untouched on 'mon' morning, or 'fri''s still there on 'sat' afternoon? Was this too intimate a part of the feminine mystique to permit intrusion, incurring the same displeasure as if, for instance, he had inquired about the goings-on of the previous night?

Having tapped the typewriter keys he went downstairs; he gazed at the television set, and turned it off.

He sat in the living-room for several seconds – broad window to the front, narrower to the back – then went into the kitchen and looked in the fridge: yesterday's lunch was still intact, as was yesterday's supper and the afternoon's tea.

'Are you ready, Elly?'

'I shall be in a minute.'

'Are you catching the twenty-one?'

The answer was lost amidst the whine of electronic music.

In a pan, on the electric stove, stood the remains of that day's lunch.

Having turned the electricity on, Attercliffe turned it off and gazed at his reflection in the yet uncurtained kitchen window.

Not only grey, his hair was white, in two broad swathes, one

24

above each ear: dark eyes, black-lashed, gazed out from beneath brows thickened by scarring over the years; the cheeks looked beaten-in, the outward-glancing cheekbones sharp, the jaw pronounced, the mouth full-lipped, the teeth irregular (the lower set his, the upper not) – the whole overhanging a square-shaped chest, broad, thick-shouldered, sturdy.

'Ready!'

'Right!'

Feet pounded on the stairs.

The house shook; the kitchen trembled.

A white Negro came in the kitchen door and looked at Attercliffe with coal-black eyes; white paint had been applied about the face within which a purple orifice glistened: cannibal or aboriginal relic, it gazed at him for several seconds.

'We're off.'

'Got your key?'

'That's right.'

'Who's seeing you home?'

'No one.'

Elise appeared in the hall behind: hair plastered down, nostrils distended.

'Are you walking back from town by yourself?'

'I have done before.'

'What about Benjie?'

'I can't expect him to walk out and walk all the way back again.'

'Why not?'

'It'd be unfair.'

'I'd have thought, if he cares about you as much as you say he does,' Attercliffe said, 'it would be his prime concern. Doesn't he care if you get attacked?'

She turned to the door.

'Can't he steal a taxi?' he asked.

'He hasn't learned to drive.'

'Can't he mug someone to pay for the cab?'

Attercliffe felt in his pocket.

'We'll manage.'

'What if someone attacks you?'

'They have.'

'When?'

25

'The other night.'

He stepped out to the hall. 'What did you do?'

'I screamed.'

'Jesus.'

'It's quite nice walking back on your own at night.'

'Yeah,' Elise said behind his back.

'Good night, Dad.'

'Good night,' Attercliffe said, and called, 'See you in the morning,' as she opened the door.

'Will you be all right on your own?' Elise paused on the step.

'I've been on my own before,' he said.

'See you in the morning, Dad.'

'See you.'

He closed the door after her and her sister's forms had disappeared between the gateless gateposts. A whiff of perfume lingered in the hall: he went back to the bedroom and sat at the desk.

Holder – try, 18th min. Bennett converted. Watkinson try, 57th min. Bennett failed. Audsley free kick, 83rd min.

He had to ring up to get the full results in one or two minutes (three other matches today, the rest tomorrow), only, he gazed at the notes and the cover of the programme and tapped his fingers on the typewriter keys and, finally, got out the scrap of paper and looked at the address, '36 Queensgate, Flat 7', and noticed for the first time she'd added her name, 'Phyllis Gardner', in brackets.

The doorbell rang.

He got up, thought, 'Forgotten their keys,' and went downstairs.

He could see through the frosted panels of the door that the figure standing there was of neither of his daughters, and speculated that it might even be that of Dougie Walters interpreting intention for accomplished fact.

Turning the latch and lifting the sneck he found, however, with some alarm, that he was gazing at his wife.

3

Her hair was concealed beneath a headscarf and the collar of a fur-lined coat was raised around her neck.

Her face had the slenderness of his daughters', but the eyes were grey, not brown, and the nose, if anything, was slimmer, the mouth more broadly formed: she looked considerably younger than forty; it was only when she came into the hall that the lines were apparent around her mouth, and the thin traceries evident at the corners of her eyes. She wore no make-up and looked as if, moments before, she might have been crying.

'You've just missed Elise and Catherine.'

'I've seen them.'

'Up the road?'

'On the way to the bus-stop.' She glanced past him. 'I'm not disturbing you?'

'Come in,' he said, and closed the door.

'I thought they looked attractive.'

'Could you see them in the dark?'

'They were passing under a lamp.'

He showed her into the living-room – their living-room: they had lived here sixteen years as man and wife – and though he had redecorated it once since her departure, it looked very much as it had done when they'd first arrived, with its 'executive' stone fireplace, its beige walls, its 'executive'-framed windows, its three-piece suite, and its 'executive' bookcase crowded with the children's magazines, records, bags of make-up and unironed clothes.

'How's Bryan and Keith?' (Their sons.)

'All right.'

'And Lorna?' (Their one remaining daughter.)

'She's well.'

'I was hoping to pick them up tomorrow. I've just got in. I haven't had time to ring.'

'That's all right.'

She sat by the fire.

The prospect of seeing his wife in her fur-lined coat sitting in front of their domestic fire as she might have sat in a doctor's waiting-room was not Attercliffe's vision of an inspiring evening and, after regarding her for several seconds, he asked, 'Shall I take your coat?'

'It's all right.'

They gazed at the fire together.

'Want a drink?'

She glanced up. 'You go ahead.'

'I've had one.'

'Are the girls all right?'

'I've no idea.'

She glanced across.

'Girls, these days.' He passed his hand above his head. 'You never mentioned Catherine was taking a contraceptive.'

'If she'd have wanted you to know she'd have told you herself.'

'She consulted you instead.'

She shook her head. 'You've never understood the great strides liberation has taken for women. It affects,' she continued, 'their daughters as well.'

'So I've noticed.'

'How was the match?'

'All right.'

Attercliffe shifted himself to a more formal position.

'Has Maurice sent you?'

In addition to being the man she had 'gone to', two and a half years before, Maurice was the proprietor of a motor-car show-room – of several car showrooms, come to that – a racing and rally driver in his youth, he was now a thin-haired, harsh-featured roadhog of gargantuan proportions who had, by all accounts, in a long and successful career, killed three people in road accidents. Presently the owner of a Rolls-Royce, a Bentley and a Jaguar, he was also the owner of a house which, by comparison, relegated 24 Walton Lane, Walton, Near Morristown – a four-bedroomed, one bathroomed, one living-roomed (dining-annexed), one-kitchened 'executive' dwelling – to the status of a garden shed.

'How about Gavin?'

'Who?'

'I wasn't told his second name.'

'He has two children, as a matter of fact.'

'Has he got room for you in his house, or is he moving in with Maurice?'

She didn't answer.

'Elise and Catherine said you weren't feeling well.'

Having glanced in his direction, she looked back to the fire: she was sitting on the edge of the settee, her knees together, her hands in her lap; a handbag and a pair of gloves were trapped beneath her fingers.

'I'm not.'

'Anything to complain about?'

'Nothing in particular.'

'Did you happen to be passing?'

'I came on the bus.'

'I thought you had a car.'

'I left it at home.' (A Rover: one bracket up from Attercliffe's Cortina.) She paused. 'I went for a walk, then caught a bus. I wasn't expecting to come this far.'

'Who's looking after the children?'

'Hazel.'

'Who's Hazel?'

'The au pair.'

'Could do with her here, if she's not too busy.'

'She has her hands full at present, thank you.'

Her flat-heeled shoes were positioned side by side.

'Unpleasant night.'

'It is.'

'Have you come to check the Pools?'

The fingers were raised above the handbag and the pair of gloves – all in matching leather.

'I've been thinking of coming back.'

'Where?'

'Here.'

'To this house?'

'I don't know where else I can mean.'

'How about Maurice?'

She didn't answer.

'Or Gavin?'

She didn't answer again.

'I'm not free to take you back.'

'Why not?'

'I'm getting married.'

'Who to?'

'A friend.'

She snorted, got out a handkerchief from her handbag and blew her nose, delicately, for several seconds.

'I don't think anyone's heard of her,' she said.

'I don't broadcast it around at the paper. Nor,' Attercliffe said, 'do I have it pinned up in the Buckingham Brasserie Bar.'

'Have you told the children?'

'Not yet.'

'Why not?'

'There's a time and place for everything.'

'If marriage were on the cards, Frank,' she said, 'you'd have mentioned it already.'

'We lead independent lives,' Attercliffe said. 'Cathy didn't tell me she was on the pill, I don't tell her I'm getting married. We don't sit here,' he added, 'each evening, discussing your extramarital affairs.'

'It sounds as if you do. At length.' The handkerchief was clasped more tightly.

'It was reported on the phone. We don't even think of you,' he added, 'from one day to the next.'

'It's not what Freddie tells me. I met him in the street.'

'He never mentioned it.'

'Too drunk, I suppose, to remember.'

'I doubt it.'

'He was never very fond of me.'

'Why did you speak to him?'

'He stopped me.'

'What did he say?'

'You were under the weather.'

Her eyes glanced up, then away, and he bowed his head and said, 'I'll get a drink. Do you fancy one?'

'No thanks.'

He went through to the kitchen, delved amongst the tins in the fridge, and poured himself a beer.

When he went back to the living-room she'd taken off her coat.

'I'm finding it hot.'

'It is hot.' He sat down. She was wearing a skirt, a blouse and a jacket. He indicated the fire. 'The girls have lit it. They often do at the weekend. A fire and the central heating together.'

'Cosy.' She had resumed her position, her hands in her lap: the gloves and the handbag were with the coat over the arm of the settee.

'Did you tell the girls you were calling at the house?'

'They seemed to feel I'd planned it.'

'They must have been surprised.'

'Not much.'

'What did you tell them?'

'I was coming to see you.'

'Did you tell them what about?'

She shook her head.

'Does Maurice know you're here?'

She didn't reply.

'What about Gavin?'

'Gavin I haven't seen,' she said, 'for several days.'

'Who is he?' Attercliffe asked.

'Someone I talk to.'

'I thought you talked a lot to Maurice. All those parties. And the way, you said, he mixed with the world.'

'I still like parties.' She gazed at the fire. 'And the world as well, as a matter of fact.'

'Gavin's a better conversationalist,' Attercliffe suggested.

'He's an extremely articulate and thoughtful man, sensitive, kind and forward-looking.'

'Jesus.'

'He doesn't want to injure his wife. That's why he doesn't see me.'

'You do, on the other hand?' he inquired.

'I don't want to injure her either.' She looked at him directly – the grey eyes – and he saw – though it had no effect upon him whatsoever – that she had begun to cry.

'There is so much suffering in the world that I don't see the point of creating more. Even if it means,' she went on, 'depriving yourself of what you want.'

'You like Gavin,' Attercliffe suggested.

'If you think it's promiscuity, Frank, we've been through that before. I've always believed in freedom. It was on that basis that I broke up this.' She gestured round.

'Why come back?' he asked.

'You thought that because I'd had five children my commitment to you was unalterable. It isn't. I feel as free to come back as I was to leave.'

'I too feel free,' Attercliffe said. 'I feel free to have you back or not to have you back, as the case may be.'

'We're still married, Frank,' she said.

'That's an imposition we can soon get rid of.'

'I don't see it as an imposition.'

Attercliffe was conscious of a cold sensation at the back of his neck: she was wanting to come back whether he agreed to it or not.

'You'd like to live here on your own?' he asked.

'You do.'

'Because you left.'

She glanced from him to the fire. 'Why should I be the one to suffer merely because I wish my life to expand, while you retain all the benefits of our life together, merely by standing still?'

Determination was, in fact, the one quality which, from the beginning, had drawn Attercliffe to her; she had been, for instance, as determined on having five children as she had been on not going out to work while she had them – and, having had them, on deciding that she had had not only enough of her married life but of marriage altogether.

'We can sell the house,' he said.

'I don't wish to sell the house.' She paused. 'With only half I couldn't buy anywhere as convenient as this.'

'Where do I live?'

'You only need a room and a kitchen. You can visit the children here.' She examined his look. 'It's only fair.'

'You chose to leave. I didn't.'

'I choose to come back.'

'You're living with Maurice.'

'I don't wish to any longer.'

32

'Why not?'

'That's my problem.'

'Mine, too, if it involves me moving out. Assuming that I do move out. I don't see why I should accommodate another whim.'

'Remarkable how you see everyone's aspirations, but your own, as whims. We're not all stuck in a rut like you.'

'Seems you are,' Attercliffe said. 'One that runs from here to Maurice.'

'Maurice,' she paused, 'has other friends.'

'What friends?'

'His secretary. But Veronica,' she added, 'is of no greater consequence to Maurice than Gavin is to me.'

'Gavin doesn't see you.'

'He doesn't wish to hurt his wife.' She added, 'I never anticipated Gavin's and mine being a prolonged relationship. I don't anticipate Maurice and Veronica's friendship to be one either.'

'Possession,' Attercliffe announced, 'is nine points of the law. Having left of your own free will there can't be many grounds for insisting that I have to take you back. I don't want you back.' He waved his hand. 'You can insist,' he added, 'but I'm buggered if I'll have you.'

'You'd resort to the bigotry of a male-dominated legal system in order to protect yourself?' she asked.

'Just as I would if a lunatic got inside the house and tried to burn it down. Or as you would, no doubt, if I'd wandered off with a Rolls-Royce-driven scrubber and came back two and a half years later and insisted that you let me in.'

'You're old. You're older than Maurice. Even he doesn't talk about security and pride.'

'I'm talking about common sense.' He got up, beer swilling from his glass. 'Try the same line with Maurice and see how far it gets you.'

'I'm not married to Maurice.'

'He's seen to that.'

'You're behind the times. You don't understand the first thing about freedom.'

She, too, stood up, though it wasn't to leave, for she moved to the door and out to the hall.

She went to the bathroom.

When she came down she said, 'Maurice bought his wife a house when they divorced.'

'We'll do the same for you,' he said.

'Half of this would buy a terraced house, which is where I started, Frank, but not where I mean to end, in the back streets of this town.' After a while, she added, 'Like you.'

'I have to go out,' Attercliffe said.

'I'm not stopping you.'

'I'd like to lock up before I leave.'

'It's amazing how trivial your interests have become.'

'Basic, I'd describe them.'

'A column in a local rag.'

'I started off with less.'

'You started off a very big man. So I was told. I never saw you in your prime and if I had I doubt if I or anyone else would believe it now. No wonder Elise and Catherine have turned out as they have.'

'Get yourself a drink,' he said, going to the door.

'Where are you going?'

'To make a call.'

'Your future wife.'

'It could be.'

He went upstairs and closed the bedroom door.

On the walls of the room he had hung at one time the trophies of his past career – photographs, chiefly – cuttings, match programmes, medals mounted in a felt–covered tray. With the advent of the children he had taken them down. The discoloration of the paintwork, however, remained – odd patches on the walls which, if not covered by the children's posters, marked off an area of his life which had no significance for him now at all.

He rang the bar at the Buckingham Hotel: Fredericks had left. When he rang his flat there was no reply.

He tried the York Arms, then the Devonshire, then tried the Cavendish Grill.

Fredericks came to the phone.

'Can you collect the copy?' Attercliffe asked.

'What for?'

'I can't get in this evening.'

'Not the baby–sitter again?'

'Not this time.'

34

Fredericks paused. 'Why not bring it round tomorrow night. After the results.'

'I thought you preferred to see the copy.'

'You can write "Pindar's Round-up" singlehanded. I shan't be going to watch tomorrow.'

'Anything happened?'

'Celebrating,' Fredericks said.

'Anything special?'

'I shall think of a reason,' he said, 'tonight.'

The phone was put down the other end.

'Who was it?' Sheila said when he went back down.

'Didn't you recognise the voice?'

'You don't imagine I'd be listening to your private calls.'

'I thought you were.'

'I knocked the telephone in the hall on my way from the door.' She indicated a glass of water in her hand. 'What a prescribed existence you lead.'

'It is.'

Having drunk from the glass she set it by her feet.

'We've come to a dead-end, Frank.'

'On your part,' Attercliffe said.

Having picked up his glass of beer he finished it and set it on the bookcase beside a pile of Cathy's and Elise's records.

He added, 'I'll take Bryan and Keith back here. Lorna, too, if it'll be any help.'

'You'll take all the children, as well as the house?'

'I'll sell the house,' he said.

'And find a terrace.'

'That's right.'

'The world at his feet at twenty-one, and on his knees at fifty.'

'Three years to go.'

'Martyrdom as well as sainthood.'

'If it's freedom you want, you can have it.'

She reached for the water, sipped it, then said, 'You said you wanted me back.'

'That was two and a half years ago. I've moved on since then. I'm not going back, just as you're not coming back.' He stood by the fire. 'Has Maurice kicked you out already?'

'People don't work along those lines.'

'Do you want me to have the children?'

'Half of them are mine.'

'That's right.'

'All of them are mine.' She added, 'You'll not use them as pawns between us, Frank.'

'I'm not allowing you to disrupt their lives, more than they've been disrupted already,' Attercliffe said. 'I've had a rough time with Elise and Catherine, and no doubt you've had your problems with Keith and Bryan.'

'Not to mention Lorna.'

'She can stay with her sisters. Otherwise, you're free to choose, as you have been all along.'

She clapped her hands, so slightly, they scarcely made a sound. She bowed her head.

'How kind.'

'Take it or leave it, Sheila.'

He added, 'Half this house is mine.'

'I'll talk to Elise and Cathy.'

'All right.'

'Try and convert them to a woman's way of thinking.'

'Convert, or pervert?' Attercliffe asked.

'Direct them,' she said, and rose.

She picked up her gloves, her handbag, set them aside, then picked up her coat.

She drew it on.

'Do you want a lift to the bus-stop?'

'No thank you.'

'Or into town.'

'No thanks.' She drew out her headscarf from a pocket of the coat. 'Trust you to think of the minimal gesture first.'

'Trust you,' he said, 'to try it on.'

'This isn't a try-on, Frank. I intend to move back. It'll take more than the law, as it stands, to stop me.' She drew on her gloves. 'You're quite capable of purchasing a flat. I've cost you nothing the last two years.'

'I'm on an overdraft at present, and we have another nine years to run on the mortgage. We'll own this house by the time I'm nearly sixty,' Attercliffe said.

'You could find the means, and leave me here to live with the children.'

He gazed steadily into those greyish eyes and it was significant,

36

he thought, that, in gazing back, they wavered.

'I'll see you soon,' she added.

'Right.'

'I'll talk to the girls tomorrow.'

'Here, or on the telephone?'

'I'll ring.'

'I'll pick up the children as usual,' he said.

'I'll keep them with me tomorrow,' she said. 'They should have been with you tonight. Because of the match I did you a favour. Elise didn't want to baby-sit. Nor did Cathy. I'm not very fond of these weekends,' she added, 'with your Sunday and sometimes Saturday afternoons away. I never know whether there's someone here I can trust.'

'I have the girl from next door,' he said. 'If Elise and Cathy are going out.'

'The girl from next door is not their mother. Nor is she old enough to cope.'

'Her mother comes in.'

She laughed. 'Frankly,' she said, 'I'd be surprised if a court would give you custody at all. It's not your fault. It's the nature of your job. But your job, of its nature, prevents you from being a proper father.'

She went to the door, opened it, and stepped out to the drive: pausing on the path, she glanced back and, after a further hesitation, called, 'Good night.'

A moment later, straight-backed, she passed beneath the lamp beyond the gateless gateposts.

He closed the door, went back to the living-room, picked up her glass and, together with his own, took it back to the kitchen.

Benjie, for some reason, he realised, he'd omitted to mention at all.

4

There was a pause between his ringing the bell and the sound of Fredericks's voice from the incongruous-looking intercom beside the former vicarage door – an interval during which Fredericks, no doubt, had put his head out of the top-floor window to see who it was – then Attercliffe heard the click of the lock and, having entered, looked up in time to see the grizzled head stooped over the banisters and recognise what, having sat so close to him the previous afternoon, he must have missed: his friend was ill.

'Been for a walk,' Fredericks announced as Attercliffe reached the top-floor landing.

'Late closing, aren't they?'

'Stayed till early opening.' He winked; dark pouches underlay each eye. 'Know the landlord. Ought to.' He indicated his door. 'Kept him in luxury the past twenty-five year.'

The hall of the flat was made up from the original landing; a living-room looked out to a square of terraced Victorian houses: in the centre of the square stood a church, a tall, rectangular building with round-headed, clear-glass windows and a tower topped by a soot-encrusted cross.

The floor of the living-room was littered with papers; two old upholstered chairs confronted a gas-mantled fire: opposite the fire stood a desk and, behind the door, its lid raised, an upright piano. Sheets of music were propped on the stand.

'Booze?'

'Tea,' Attercliffe said.

'You'd better make it, Atty.' Fredericks took the copy and slumped in one of the two armchairs facing the fire. 'Light it afore you go,' he added and, feeling in his jacket pocket, produced a pipe and, after the pipe, a box of matches. He tossed them across. 'Sorry about this afternoon.'

'That's all right.'

'I heard the results.'

'I've done the round-up,' Attercliffe said. 'And featured yesterday's match.' He indicated the copy then, having lit the gas-fire, went through to the kitchen.

It overlooked a garden – much overgrown – with the bowed shapes of several fruit trees leading down to a tall brick wall; beyond – the slope subsiding sharply over the roofs of a row of recently-constructed houses (facsimiles of his own in Walton Lane) – lay a vista of the moors to the west of the town: in the furthest distance stood the television mast at Hartley Crag.

The kitchen was cramped; originally the vicarage bathroom, the lower half of its window was frosted glass: a cooking-stove and a narrow table left scarcely sufficient space to stand sideways at the sink.

Attercliffe lit the gas beneath a kettle, found a teapot, put in a couple of teabags – reflected that his activities here were much the same as they were at home – set a tray and when, finally, everything was ready, carried it back to the living-room.

Only after he had poured the tea did Fredericks raise his head, and say, 'F'und everything, have you?'

'Fine.'

'There's a bottle on the shelf, if you'll pass it down.'

He picked up the copy which had fallen by his feet and when Attercliffe handed him a glass he added, 'Pour it, man, don't dribble it,' and when Attercliffe sat down and drank his tea Fredericks looked round at him and asked, 'You're not getting censorious like Pippy Booth and Attwood?'

'Have you read it?'

'I've read it.'

'Any suggestions?'

'It's fine.' He drew the copy up and, after squinting at it, took out his glasses: he drew them – between thumb and forefinger – from the top pocket of his jacket and since, plainly, he hadn't taken them out until then, and therefore couldn't have read the copy, Attercliffe got up from his chair and crossed to the window. 'Champion. Couldn't be better,' Fredericks said behind his back.

'You don't need me on this. Never have. Never will. You're a natural.'

The copy was already lowered and the glasses removed by the time Attercliffe turned round.

'You look ill, Freddie.'

'I am, lad.'

'What with?'

'One of these newfangled things.' He swallowed. 'Four consonants and three vowels afore they gi'e you a word about ten feet long. I have it i' the bowel.'

'Are they going to operate?'

'O'er my dead body.'

'What treatment have you had?'

'A bloody good 'un.' He raised his glass. 'I could carry a portable container, tha knows, if they cut it out, and though the offer's tempting, particularly wi' the company I have to keep at present, I turned it down. I'll go i' one piece, if I go at all.' He drained the glass and held it out.

'You've had enough,' Attercliffe said.

'Not half,' he said, yet added nothing further when Attercliffe took the glass and set it on the mantelshelf beside the bottle.

'Shouldn't you do what they ask?' he said.

'They ask for nought less than half a bowel and don't give me much chance with the half that's left.'

Attercliffe sat in the other chair before the fire.

'Bit of a liability,' Fredericks said.

'Not much.'

'Not half.' He shaded his eyes: the glow from the fire illuminated his figure. 'Trouble with the missis?'

'She wants to come back.'

'Inclined to let her?'

He shook his head.

'Want my advice?'

'No thanks.'

'Thank God for that.' He reached for the copy, and added, 'Get out of this racket. Tek up wi' summat else.'

'Like what?'

'Phyllis Gardner.'

Attercliffe laughed.

'Dafter things have happened.' He dug his finger below his

40

paunch. 'When the saints used to say, "Thy will be done", they couldn't have said it more sincerely than me. Mine's a secular "will be done".' He ran his hand across his stubbled scalp.

'I can't believe it,' Attercliffe said.

'Don't want to, lad.' He glanced across. 'You look like a bloody lost weekend.' He laughed. 'Before this happened I had a dream. I wa' sitting i' this chair. It wa're i' the middle of the afternoon. My faither wa' standing afore me. I hadn't thought of him for fifteen years. There he was, as large as life. Just behind him stood my mother. Their faces glowed. I thought, "This is a dream," and tried to wek up. I thought I had. Yet there they were. Still glowing. My father looked down at me and said, "It's beautiful, Freddie," and when I said, "What is it, Father?" he said, "It's beautiful, lad. Don't worry." Then I woke. Two weeks later I had such a gut-ache I went to see the doctor. He put me up to the County General and they pumped me up like a bloody balloon and spun me round on an X-ray table, and sat me in a room where this feller came in and said, "There are one or two patches: nothing we haven't seen afore," and gave me six months if I did nought about it.'

'How long ago was that?'

'At least five.'

'Why didn't you tell me?'

'I have.'

'You should have let them operate, Freddie.'

'I'd have been a shitless wonder for one or two weeks. Even wi' a plastic bowel I mayn't have lasted much more than a year. On top of which,' he gestured round, 'my heart isn't up to a big operation.' He added, 'I've been looking at all this stuff you've written.' He indicated a pile of newspapers, back copies of the *Northern Post*, already yellow, on the floor. 'Don't let it rot.'

'You're letting it rot when you could have had it out.'

'I've had my shot.' He tapped his chest. 'Be what you were when you started.' He laughed. 'In the next twenty years you'll come into your own.'

He fell asleep, so swiftly that, for several seconds, Attercliffe imagined he'd suffered an attack.

He got up from the chair, reassured himself of Fredericks's breathing, and retrieved the copy.

For some time he wandered round the flat, gazing into the kitchen, into the bathroom, cluttered up with clothes drying on a rail above the bath, into the bedroom with its oak-ended double bed: by the time he returned to the living-room it was growing dark.

'Do you want to go to church?' Fredericks said, suddenly, without turning his head.

'If you want to.'

'I'd like to.'

He got up as if he'd been awake for some time.

'I had a coat.'

Attercliffe found it for him.

'And a pair of shoes.'

These, too, Attercliffe looked for, and finally found in the kitchen.

One or two other groups of people were crossing the road to the church when they went out to the square: lights glowed from the clear-glass windows.

They sat in a pew at the back; Fredericks hadn't shaved and his stubbled features appeared more ashen still in the overhead light: his hands were clenched together.

They stood, fifteen, perhaps twenty people in all: the choir, followed by the priest, climbed into the stalls. As the service proceeded, and the light glistened from the chandeliers down the centre of the aisle, and the tolling of a bell receded, and their voices echoed in the chambered recess of the timbered roof, he recalled Fredericks saying, only weeks before, when he might have been considering ways of telling him he was ill, 'Start again. You're not too old. Think of the past. You were nothing short of a genius then,' and as he glanced across and speculated on why Fredericks had invited him to come to the church he was aware that it had as much to do with his past as it had with his illness. 'Like a traveller, looking back along the road,' he thought. 'This far have I come. Tomorrow I go farther.'

'Amen,' Fredericks said and, as they rose from a prayer, added, in much the same tone, 'Have you seen enough? I think I have.'

They retreated to the aisle, opened the glass-panelled doors, and stepped out into the darkness of the square.

'Think I'll go back home,' Fredericks said.

'Do you want me to come with you?' Attercliffe asked.

'Better get down to Benton Lane,' he said. 'They'll be wondering where we've got to.'

He left him at the vicarage door.

'Know where the present incumbent lives?' He indicated the dark Victorian building. 'In a place like yours: garden, central heating, tool-shed and a garage.' He laughed, 'Executive dwelling!' stepped to the door, unlocked it, and disappeared inside.

The entrance to the *Northern Post* offices stood at the apex of Benton Lane and Norton Square. At the top of Benton Lane stood the most prominent building of the town, the large, sandstone hulk of All Saints Church: as Attercliffe drove past, coming from the direction of the Buckingham Hotel in the city centre, the sound of an organ playing and of singing came from its open door.

Lights were on in the offices; the hallway was deserted. The room Attercliffe occupied with Fredericks and two other colleagues was located in 'The Sump', a corridor which, marking the steepening descent of Benton Lane, to the river, was approached by a flight of concrete steps, above which, to the angled ceiling, was attached a notice reading 'Duck Your Head', and on which, Attercliffe observed that evening, the 'D' had been changed to an 'F'.

A man with a bald head, large, thickly-framed spectacles, and a broad, thickly-fleshed nose was typing at a desk.

'York Arms, Buckingham, or the Devonshire?' he said.

'At home,' Attercliffe said.

'Just got back or stopped on the way?'

'I'll leave it here,' Attercliffe said.

'Will you?'

Pippy Booth returned to his typing.

'Have they been in to take it up?'

'They haven't.' His fingers rippled on.

Attercliffe laid the copy on the desk and, through the only window in the room, high in the wall, observed a light in the old hay-loft above the site of an abandoned stables across the road: a man was standing at an easel, painting.

'How long has Holford's Loft been used?'

Pippy Booth looked up. 'He was there this afternoon.' The telephone rang: Booth picked it up, listened, put it down, and added, 'Fairy, going by the way he stands.'

'Seen him before?'

'Never.'

'How are you fixed for features?'

'Pug-eared footballer tells how he did it all on Bennies?'

'A different activity altogether.'

'The City's not being sued by the Equal Opportunities Commission?'

'Not quite.'

'Front-row forward says the lads at the club won't give her a chance.'

'That's right.'

'Want a photographer?'

'I'll ask Billy.'

'How soon can I have it?'

'End of the week.'

'All right.'

The typing recommenced.

'Is "referred" with two "r"s or one?'

'Two.'

'Amazing.' He corrected the sheet before him. 'On a Sunday neet every word looks different.'

Attercliffe said, 'I wonder how he earns a living.'

'Wonder on.' Booth, to indicate his concentration, drew his chair to the desk.

The artist's look went back to the easel: a brush was dabbed at a palette.

Attercliffe went back up the steps and, drawing his overcoat about him, stepped out to the street. As he reached the car he glanced at the window again: from this perspective all that could be seen were the upper edge of a canvas, the stem of the easel, and the top of the painter's head.

5

36 Queensgate was, he discovered, a block of flats which stood in a sidestreet off the main thoroughfare of the town; the bell for number 7 had two names beside it, 'Gardner. P.' and 'Willis. H.', and, when he rang, a woman's voice sounded over the intercom and said, 'It's for you, Phyl,' and then, 'Come up.'

The latch was released and as he entered the hall a door closed above his head; a moment later a tousled, red-haired figure, in jeans and a sweater, a suede jacket over its arm, ran down a flight of stairs and announced, 'Second floor up. I'm Heather.' A round-cheeked, green-eyed face gazed out from beneath the mop of ruffled hair. 'Got your notebook?'

Attercliffe said, 'That's right. I have.'

'The photographer got here before you.'

The figure darted off; the outer door banged: when Attercliffe reached the second floor the door to the flat had been reopened.

He stepped inside a narrow hall and closed the door behind him.

At the opposite end of the hall he entered a living-room which looked directly to the street below.

A short, balding, square-shouldered figure, dressed in jeans and a leather jacket, with a bag slung across its back, was taking photographs with the aid of a flashlight.

A ball of light exploded.

'Shan't be a sec, comrade,' this figure said while, attired in a sweater and neatly-pressed trousers, her hair drawn back by a ribbon, a second figure, framed against the window, said, 'There's coffee. If you'd like it. Help yourself.'

A tray stood on a table. Turned towards the fireplace was a three-piece suite.

Attercliffe poured out some coffee. 'Talk, comrade,' the photographer said. The camera clicked for several seconds.

Attercliffe moved his head in line with the crouching back and said, 'I met a girl called Heather.'

'We share the flat.' The cheeks were rouged, the lips painted. 'We've been here several years.'

'Same line of business?' the photographer said, winding on his film.

'Has been. Though now,' she went on, 'she works in a shop.'

'What sort of a shop?'

'A florist's.'

'Hard life.'

'Very,' Phyllis said. 'Had difficulty finding it, Frank?' she added.

'None,' Attercliffe said.

'In a central location.'

'It is.'

'I had to give up an appointment to be here,' she said.

'Nothing important?' Attercliffe asked, at which she said, 'It could be. Still. Prior commitment.'

'That should do it.' The photographer straightened, picked up a cup of coffee, drank, set it down, drew his bag across his belly, picked up a roll of film from the table, turned to the door, called, 'Mine not to reason, mine but to shoot and fly,' and, with a wave in Attercliffe's direction – 'See you at the office, comrade. Charmed, Miss Gardner' – he was out of the door.

The flat door banged.

'He's very jolly.'

'Isn't he?'

'Communist?'

'Far from it.' Attercliffe shook her hand.

'Billy.'

'That's right.'

'Quite a card.'

'He is.' Having released her hand, he waited for her to sit down in an adjoining chair.

'Dougie is a great fan of yours.' She smiled again.

'I didn't know he knew me.'

She said, 'He told me of one game where, when you were sent

46

off, the crowd invaded the pitch. You were quite a hero.'

'Those were the days,' Attercliffe said, 'when the game was played exclusively by miners.'

'Really?'

'Almost.'

'How did you get into reporting?' She leaned back, her hands, clenched loosely together, wrapped around one knee.

'Fredericks was a commentator on television and took me on as his assistant. I was one of the few footballers at that time who'd had an education.'

'What school did you go to?'

'King Edward VI Grammar. The week I signed on the headmaster sent me a note which read: "Attercliffe, you have let the school down." It was a rugby union school and believed in amateur sport and had no time for professionals.' He added, 'I see by the file your agent sent you're appearing in a play at the Phoenix.'

'I'm scheduled to do a series for television and wanted something to do for the next six weeks. The part I have is the eldest of three unmarried sisters. Previously, I've only played tarts so I thought, for six weeks, it ought to be worth it.' She smiled. 'Mr Fredericks said you write.'

He indicated his notebook, now on his knees, and the ballpoint pen in his hand.

'Other than that. A play.'

'What else did he tell you?'

'Not much.' She paused. 'He says he admired the film.'

'I didn't see it,' Attercliffe said. 'He says it's very good.'

'It's the area I'm hoping to move into. The cinema is dying in Britain. And the bit that isn't, like television, is so parochial, it has no meaning anywhere else. It doesn't,' she continued, 'turn to the larger issues.'

'What are the larger issues?'

Attercliffe wrote for several seconds.

'The political issues.' She added, 'I'd like to get to London.' She gestured round. 'This is merely an interregnum.'

'How many "r"s in that?'

She laughed. 'Since it'll be seen all over I'm hoping this film will give me the break I want.' She added, 'I'm only waiting for it to be shown in New York. I could even,' she went on, 'get out of the series. I haven't signed the contract yet. It means, if it were successful, committing myself to two years in this country, though I could, if I were abroad, come back for three or four months.'

She crossed her legs; he saw, in the diagonal light from the window, how much care she'd taken with her make-up: the rougeing beneath the cheekbones, the rendering of the corners of her mouth – wasted, he reflected, on the bushy-bearded Walters.

'Was the appointment you gave up for another part?'

'It could have been.'

'Television?'

'The theatre.'

'Do you prefer the theatre?'

'Can't make a living at it. Not round here. Nor in London. Really,' her hands were clasped again, 'if this film were a success I'd stand a chance to get out of the country.'

'Do you want to get out?' he asked.

'Don't you?'

'The problems,' he said, 'I have to cope with are more than enough to keep me going.'

'Dougie says you and your wife are living apart.'

'That's right.'

'I know the man she's living with.'

'Really?'

'He's a lecher.'

'I understood he sold motor–cars.'

She laughed. After a moment she said, 'He's been round here.' She glanced across. 'Dougie threatened to throw him out.' She added, 'On the other hand, I'm surprised you'd want to go on living here. Don't you believe this country is finished? I don't want to sit in a place like this pecking at the crumbs.'

He had the impression of a presence other than her own not so much inhabiting as standing over the room: she looked to the door.

'If I had a choice I'd leave tomorrow.' She thrust herself back in her chair. 'This place is so devitalised. It's the backwater to a backwater that's already silted up. You can hardly breathe. We live like rats, scrabbling at the refuse. One or two rich ones, like Pickersgill, but most of them the sleazy variety you get in any ordinary sewer.'

He wrote again, not sure how much of this he ought to record.

'You don't use a tape-machine?'

He shook his head.

'Have you done many interviews before?'

'Not many.'

'Usually of the Dougie variety.'

'That's right.'

'If I send you two tickets will you come to the opening on Thursday?' She laughed. 'You won't have to write a review. And I won't,' she concluded, 'hold you to this.'

'This'll be in next week,' Attercliffe said.

'In time for the reviews.'

'That's right.'

'Do you want some more coffee?' She got up from her chair, took his cup, saw he hadn't drunk a great deal, and added, 'I'll get you another.'

She went out of the room. Her voice called, 'Anything to eat?' and when she reappeared she added, 'We could always go out.'

'It's quieter in here,' he said.

She filled a fresh cup from a percolator standing by the window; having set it down she said, 'It'd be possible to join one of the subsidised companies if I went to London. I've one or two friends, directors, mainly. Do you go to the theatre much?'

Having retaken her position in the adjoining chair, she propped her hands beneath her chin.

'I don't.'

'What's this play you've written?'

'When Freddie was in television, years ago, he suggested I write one. He had visions of becoming a director himself.'

'Why didn't he?'

'He's really a newspaperman and found it frustrating to comment on pictures.'

'What happened to your play?'

'I never did anything with it.'

'Why don't you send it to someone who could give you a judgment?'

'I doubt if I've even a copy.'

'Is that why Freddie describes you as diffident?'

'I've no idea.'

She gazed at him for several seconds. 'My father was a fan of yours. When I was young he used to watch you play a lot.'

49

She got out of the chair and crossed to the window.

'I get so tired of this place at times. I lived for a while in London. I was more out of work than in it.' The slender shoulders and the more slender waist, the jerseyed hips and the trousered thighs were silhouetted against the light from the window: her figure, standing there, half-darkened the room; after a moment he realised that, with a peculiar vehemence, she had begun to cry, not sharply, but with a curious self-possession. 'I get so furious at times. There seems no hope for a woman.'

'Times are changing,' Attercliffe said.

'Scarcely at all. One type of tyranny is replaced by another. Because we live in an age which has a primitivist view of man the inequalities go unnoticed.'

Having written this down, without the slightest idea what he might do with it, Attercliffe stood up.

'I'm sorry.' She turned. 'Half the people you meet don't understand a fraction of the things you say, let alone the most minuscule portion of the things you feel.'

'Tell me how you started,' Attercliffe said.

'At school. Played Lady Macbeth and Julius Caesar. Morristown High: all girls. After that I went to college. Worked in London, then in television. Knew a chap who knew another. Appeared in a play. Auditioned for a film. Got the part. Am about to appear in another play. Have a series.'

The irrelevance of this information caused her, finally, to glance in his direction.

'Will it be a profile, or an interview?' she asked.

'I'm not sure,' he said, 'until I write it.' She reminded him, he reflected, of his wife: despair might be a species of idleness but vanity was scarcely a prerequisite for unburdening yourself to someone who, even though he might be receptive, could do little if anything about it.

'I'm not sure why you asked me to be interviewed,' she said.

'It was Freddie's idea,' he said.

'Doing me a favour.'

'Correct.'

'Makes a change from your usual line.'

'Like you,' he said, 'I, too, am looking for something different.'

'Involved with football all your life, you're looking for something more expansive.'

She laughed.

'My natural instincts,' she went on, 'are to live from minute to minute. It's why I don't mind Dougie, for all the limitations of his friends, and why I ignore the scenery, keep my head down, and concentrate,' she concluded, 'on what I'm doing.'

'I've been very much the same,' Attercliffe said. 'Circumstances don't allow you,' he continued, 'to do much else.'

'Will you stay in a place like this, or leave?'

'I've five children,' Attercliffe said. 'The youngest only seven.'

'The Vikings roamed the world for two-thirds of the year, and went back home for the winter.'

'I assume that the Vikings,' Attercliffe said, 'cared less for the woman than the man. The impetus, in my case, has swung the other way.'

She laughed.

'She must have peculiar taste.' She paused. 'Choosing Maurice Pickersgill.'

'None of us,' he said, 'shows a great deal of discernment when we choose the people we love.'

'We're controlled by forces,' she suggested, 'beyond our comprehension.' Having crossed from the window to the fireplace, she leaned against the mantelshelf.

'It may,' Attercliffe said, 'be the nature of the exercise.'

She laughed again.

'I've told you about my career. I've told you about my present plans. I've told you about my future. Is there anything else you need to know?' she asked.

'If I can't write anything now,' he said, 'I don't believe I ever shall.'

'Do you syndicate any of your material?'

'To Australian newspapers.'

'How about a national?'

'It's not allowed.'

'You don't have to work in this place for good.'

'That's what my wife has often said.'

'If you're free tomorrow come to a rehearsal. I have a call at two o'clock.'

She took his pen and, in much the same manner as she had written her address, selected a clean page in his notebook and wrote another.

'We're in a church hall. I'll talk to the director. Any publicity is welcome.'

'What's Heather's views on your profession?' he asked as, having handed back the notebook and the pen, she led the way to the door.

'She's more of an activist than I am. Dougie thinks her only aim is to put him down. She's the sort of woman who feels she's right and wants everyone to know it.'

She came out to the landing, shook his hand, and added, 'I hope you'll come tomorrow. Otherwise I'll leave two tickets at the theatre. We kick off seven o'clock on Thursday night.'

When he reached the hall he heard the flat door close and, a moment later, when he reached the street, he saw her figure at the second-floor window where, waving, she drew down a blind.

6

'How do you mean you wouldn't mind Sheila coming back?'

'She has a right.' Elise dug her heel at the carpet, her legs extended, her head thrust into the cushions which, purloined from the other chairs, she had laid in the easy chair behind. 'I don't see why women shouldn't have a right.'

Attercliffe had just returned from the City ground (frost-bitten fingers, frost-bitten toes: an air of hostility from the paranoid coach at having his latest moves observed), to find his eldest daughter sprawled on her back watching television in the living-room. Catherine, he gathered, from the rush of footsteps preceding the insertion of his key in the front door, had scampered upstairs to create the semblance, should he ascend, of someone engrossed in her homework: the position of the other easy chair and its one compressed cushion indicated where, only moments before, she must have been sitting. It was in this chair that Attercliffe sat and felt his daughter's warmth rise into his frozen limbs.

'Did she ring tonight?'

'She rang at the weekend.'

'You never told me.'

'You were out at the paper.'

'On Sunday?'

'On Sunday.'

He hesitated to turn off the television in case this would provoke her into leaving the room.

'The least you could do,' he said, 'is to let me know what's going on.'

Children's footsteps rushed up and down, padding, on the concrete road outside: their screams and shouts (years ago, those of his own children, reassuringly, would have been amongst them) echoed amongst the detached 'executive' dwellings – echoed, too, no doubt, across the field, to the ramparts of the castle, and out, too, in the opposite direction, to the dark bulwark of earth, of rock, and shale, at the open-cast mining-site between Walton Lane and the river.

'I have let you know.'

'It's two days since your mother rang.'

'Why don't you call her Sheila?'

'I see her in terms of your mother at present.'

She eased herself into a sitting position.

'You can't see her as a person.'

'I see her as someone who is using you in order to lay claim to things she has no right to.'

'That's the problem with men of your generation. Women have no life except as a function of male fantasy.'

Elise was studying 'A' Levels at the Morristown Sixth-Form College; having failed to have found anything of interest in any of her other subjects during her earlier five years at Walton Middle School (Mixed), she was presently studying Sociology, Political Science and Home Economics. Art, for a short while, had attracted her attention but that, too, she had discovered was dominated by masculine preconceptions. Recently she had relaxed into a subjectivist view of human nature derived, he understood, from Marx, in which humanity was seen as a blank page upon which society wrote its incorrigible message – forgoing, he was surprised to discover, the initial step that indicated society was created by people in the first place. Now, her gaze fixed on the pulp of someone's beaten head, she said, 'It's the reason why she left.'

'In that case,' he said, 'why is she coming back?'

'I don't see why she should have to live in squalor just so you can assert your rights. Why,' she glanced in his direction, 'you'll be telling her next she was wrong to leave. I don't see why she shouldn't be as free as you are, to come and go as she chooses.'

'I wouldn't describe living in a six-bedroomed house, with servants, four cars and holidays in the Canaries at the summer and winter solstices as living in squalor,' Attercliffe said.

'I'm talking about the time when she is no longer interested in Maurice.' Once more she allowed her eyes to drift from the screen: like her mother, she was morbidly fascinated by successful men –

particularly those who had been successful in areas she affected to despise – and, but for Sheila's qualms about having her teenage daughters living in close proximity to her promiscuous lover, both she and her sister would have been living at Maurice's two and a half years before, a natural enough arrangement, he had assumed, on Sheila's departure, the two boys and Lorna remaining at home with him.

'Even Maurice,' she went on, 'has had his prejudices formed for him by society at large. If anything,' she continued, 'Mum has more right than you have to come back here. At least you can earn a living, whereas Mum, after five children, is debarred from supporting herself in a style to which she might have grown accustomed, and to which, incidentally, in the light of everything she has, in the past, put into this house, she fully deserves. Why should she be punished because of her sex?'

'You think I ought to move?'

'Why not?'

'It happens, half of it, to be my house.'

'You could, should you wish, have another family. Mum can't. Not after the menopause.'

'Would you mind if I turned the television off?'

'If you have to.'

She got up, turned it off, and added, 'It had just reached, as a matter of fact, a compassionate moment,' and went out to the kitchen.

He heard her filling the kettle.

Simultaneously, a door banged overhead and Catherine's feet tumbled down the stairs.

'Do you want a cup?' Elise's voice inquired and Attercliffe was about to respond when Catherine answered, 'Yes,' and, a moment later, appeared in the living-room door. 'Back, Dad?' she added.

'Just before you went upstairs.'

She, like her sister, was dressed in jeans and her hair, once more, was fastened in plaits. Coming further into the room, she announced, 'I've been up there all evening.'

'I thought you'd been down here.'

'Do I have to work all night?'

Catherine would take her 'O' Levels this year; eight of them, in six of which she was expected to excel: having no complaint with her in this respect, Attercliffe gazed at the fire (the weekend ashes still intact), and said, 'I hear Sheila rang.'

'Why don't you call her our mother?'

'I've been instructed not to.'

'I don't see why you can't acknowledge her as the mother of your children. I mean, we haven't been fathered by someone else?'

'With your mother,' Attercliffe said, 'you could never be sure. She was always attracted by other men. Particularly those,' he added, 'with money.'

'According to the father of a girl at school you were one of the most highly-paid footballers of your time.'

'I never earned much more than the down-payment on a house like this. And that was a feat,' Attercliffe said, 'considering how I started.'

'Maurice started with nothing.'

'He had more initiative than me.'

'More everything.'

'He didn't have more children, that's a fact.'

She sat on the arm of the settee and said, 'Why didn't you beat him up?'

'I was told it was insulting to your mother. I was told it was an expression of pride. I was told I'd be hitting an older man. I was even told it wasn't enlightened.'

'Who by?'

'Your mother.' A figure had come in with two swilling mugs of tea and – about, Attercliffe thought, to give one of them to him – walked past him, retaining one herself and handing the other to Catherine. 'Did you want one?' she asked across her shoulder.

'No thanks.'

'I'll get you one if you like.'

'No thanks.'

'No need to sound martyred.'

'I'm not.'

'I think he's being unfair to Mum. She has as much right to live here as he has.'

Catherine made no comment.

'You might,' Attercliffe said, 'have told me she'd rung.'

'She asked us not to,' Catherine said.

'You approve of her coming back?'

'I don't see why she should. You'd only have rows. Seven of us.' She gestured overhead. 'It'd be just as bad as it was before.'

'Was it bad before?' he asked.

'Terrible.'

Elise said, 'I don't remember it being bad. It only got bad,' she continued, 'after Sheila left.'

'You don't support her coming back?' he asked.

'I'd love to have Lorna,' Catherine said. 'I'm not very keen on Keith and Bryan.'

'They won't mind,' he said, 'as long as their mother is happy.'

'I can see you're going out of your way to spoil it,' Catherine said.

'I can't see that I have much choice,' he said.

'You don't have to leave home,' Elise said.

'They can hardly share the same bedroom,' her sister said. 'In which case,' she added, 'we'll be back to sharing.'

This was a facet of their mother's independence which Elise had not considered: not only would she have to share with Catherine, but, if Attercliffe were to have a separate room as well, with Lorna: no more records late at night, no more pouting, painting, primping, posing, gazing at herself in her full-length mirror.

'Dad wouldn't want to stay.'

'He's got as much right to stay as she has.' Spilling tea, Catherine sat down in the well of the settee.

'I don't see, just because he has an economic superiority, he should have priority over someone else. Sheila has more rights, if anything. After all, it's out of her *body* we were born.'

'He has kept us,' Catherine said.

'That's his privilege,' Elise said. 'It doesn't,' she continued, 'give him rights. After all,' she concluded, 'the world is on his side.'

'You make it sound,' Attercliffe said, 'as if I'm redundant.'

'When babies can be born by the transference of cells, men will be dispensable,' Elise replied.

He wondered what heading this information came under in Elise's studies at the Morristown Sixth-Form College – Political Science, Sociology or Home Economics. 'What about things like love?' he asked.

'A conditioned reflex based on biological necessity,' Elise replied.

Cathy picked her teeth: her gaze, abstracted, was focused on the hearth.

'It creates a pretty horrific picture. Self-propagating individuals wandering around in a world where no one, in any real sense, needs anyone else.'

'Need to you,' Elise said, 'is subservience for a woman. A world where reproductive necessity is no longer required of women is a world where everyone can be free of the false mystique of marriage, free of subservience to parents, free of domesticity based on the ascendancy of one sex over the other, free of the hypocrisy of love.'

'In other words,' Attercliffe said, 'I should leave you and your mother to get on with it, while I go on paying the mortgage and financing your education, as well as,' he continued, 'my wife's infidelities with Gavin.'

'Infidelity is one of the old taboos, so primitive, Dad,' Elise replied, 'I'm surprised you should even mention it.'

He was growing old: so old he could scarcely remember the vicissitudes of his youth – the austerity, the circumspection, the deprivation, the challenge – even the fervour linked to enterprise, initiative and aspiration. He examined his daughter – propped on the arm of the settee, beside her sister, massaging her cup of tea – and wondered (a) if he had had anything to do with her education whatsoever, and (b) if he played any organic part in her life at all. Perhaps even that one immemorial fuck was an aberration, a conditioned reflex, a residual spasm.

'Dad's a dinosaur,' Elise continued. 'Certainly Sheila,' she went on, 'has left him behind. As for the children: do you remember all the stories he used to tell us? All that fighting for "what was right".' She laughed. 'All that fighting "merely to survive".'

'What,' Attercliffe said, 'if it happens to be true?'

'Where has it got you?'

'It's got you to where you are at present. It's got Cathy. It's even got Sheila. As for myself, I do get satisfaction out of having fathered you. I do care about you and it's largely on those grounds that I'll insist on giving your mother, as I've offered to already, half the value of this house.'

Elise got up from the settee and, placing her cup on the bookcase, yawned: she glanced at her records, picked one up, was about to make an inquiry of her sister, when she looked at Attercliffe and said, 'She's given up her prospects of a career so that you can have a place like this, and when, finally, she behaves like a human being all you see in it is not equity but possession.'

'I ought to have nothing.'

'You have nothing, Dad, other than what Sheila has provided She has no chance to acquire possessions, other than those allowed to a woman of her age and prospects. The world is receptive to the assertiveness of a man, but it's not to a divorcée approaching the age of fifty.'

'She's forty.'

'Even thirty. Women don't initiate the way a society is run and, until they are freed from biological necessity, they never will.'

Catherine kicked her heels at the rug; having placed her cup on the floor, she thrust her hands in the pockets of her jeans and pressed her chin against her chest: she jarred her teeth together, her lower jaw tensed, her lips apart.

Attercliffe glanced at Elise. 'I should start again,' he said, 'from scratch.'

'You've still got us. You're financially responsible. It's understandable you should turn our dependency into moral blackmail Sheila's resisting it as much as she can. I want to help her. It doesn't mean I want to cut you off. I'll come and see you whenever you like. But you have no right to insist on staying here if Sheila says she wants to come back.'

'What do you think, Cathy?'

'You won't wriggle out of it,' Elise said, 'by asking Cathy.'

Catherine dug her heels at the floor more briskly. 'Don't you realise,' she said, 'that Dad has to forgo freedoms just as much as Mum? It seems to me they have more in common than sets them apart, except that Mum can't control her appetite for men. It's because Dad was manly that she married him.' She flushed a deeper shade than had Elise, who was reacting silently at present to this sisterly confession. 'Mum exploits her opportunities and turns them – as she always has – to her advantage, whereas Dad has always given us a chance. All you're saying,' she concluded, 'is that he should allow her to walk all over him.'

Elise leaned on the mantelpiece and examined her sister with an expression – raised eyebrows, flushed cheeks, glaring eyes, a turned-down corner of her mouth – which was intended, Attercliffe imagined, to signify contempt.

'Men provide one sort of freedom for women, just as women provide another sort for men. It's a reciprocal relationship, whereas all you're saying is men should forgo their right to breathe.'

It was a blessing, Attercliffe knew, to have two contentious daughters whose education, to a large extent, was superior to his own. Superior in looks, superior in intelligence, superior in sex, his daughters – if evolution had anything to look forward to – were a credit to him and a recompense for the anguish involved in bringing them up.

'You spend too much time with Benjie,' Elise replied. 'You want to find out what it's really like. And,' she swept her arm at the room, 'if you don't think men abuse their freedom, and use the tyranny of *their* economic servility to exact an even more onerous tyranny on the next in line, you don't know what you're talking about. Look around you.' She swung her arm back. 'Refusing Sheila a home because she revolted against the tyranny of being a wife and mother.'

Cathy kicked her heels again; she picked her teeth, jarred her jaw against her chest, flushed more deeply still, and said, 'If you turn everything upside down, then it's bound to look as silly as you say it does.'

'How is it upside down?' Elise picked up a record, contemplated the design on the sleeve, and put it down.

'We're just studying,' Catherine announced, 'how women were discouraged in the last century. The odd thing is the majority of the best novelists in this country in the nineteenth century were women, because, rather than men, they were the ones who led a more privileged life. Even if there were a bias against them, it wasn't one which, in real terms, and specifically in terms of their novels, did them any harm. For instance,' she raised her head, 'the art schools for over a hundred years have been populated principally by women students yet, for all their freedom of expression, there never has been and most likely never will be a woman painter of any interest. It's something to do with their natures.'

'What's to do with their natures?'

'The fact that women don't paint great pictures, compose great music, design great buildings, conceive religions, think up new philosophies. It's not,' she continued, 'in a woman's nature.'

'You've learnt all that from school.'

'I've learnt it from reading Virginia Woolf who says in this half-baked middle-class fashion that women have never had a chance. "Give me five hundred pounds a year and a room." What's she want: icing on it?'

'I've acquired my experience,' Elise glanced at Attercliffe, 'from life.'

'All you're spouting at me are fashionable ideas thought up by a lot of well-heeled women, the majority of whom, in their private lives, turn out to be nothing less than tarts.'

'You should know. Look at your boyfriend,' Elise responded.

'What's Benjie got to do with it?' Catherine inquired.

'Two generations out of the jungle.'

'Abusing Benjie is not any kind of argument,' Catherine said.

'You told me he's a moron.'

'I said he wasn't intelligent. Not our kind of intelligence. He's intelligent in different ways.'

'In thieving from shops and using knives.'

'You said you liked him.'

'I do like him. He's full of spirit. Spirit,' she concluded, 'and stupidity.'

'There are other qualities in life, apart from intelligence,' Catherine said.

'Such as?'

'A capacity to give pleasure, to entertain, to live. Simply to be what he is. That's more than can be said for your stuck-up snobs.'

'Alex,' Elise said, mentioning a name Attercliffe had never heard before, 'happens to be a socialist.'

'Precisely.'

'What's that supposed to mean?'

'Who's Alex?' Attercliffe inquired.

'Benjie can't help it if he reacts against oppression,' Catherine said.

His eldest daughter, still leaning against the mantelshelf, glanced at Attercliffe again.

'I approve of him,' she said. 'I believe in the instinctual life. It's what the future is moving us towards. All I'm asking is that you don't use the rationality of male aggression against someone of your own sex. There's enough on their side, without fighting their battles for them.'

'Who's Alex?' Attercliffe inquired again.

'Alex,' Elise said, 'is a friend.'

'A close friend?'

'A friend. How much friendlier does he have to be?'

A car went past in the road.

'Which doesn't resolve our argument,' Attercliffe went on.

'We'll be going soon ourselves,' his eldest daughter said.

'Where?'

'To university.'

'Do you still intend to go?'

'What else could we, as women, do?'

'There are still three years before I go,' Catherine said. 'It affects me whether Mum comes or not. If she does, I can't see it being very pleasant if Dad insists on staying.'

Attercliffe got up and went out to the kitchen; he filled the kettle, plugged it in, got out a tea-bag, dropped it in a mug, and gazed out, past the garage and the wattle fence, past the lights of the other houses, past the dark enclosure of the field, to the silhouetted bulwark of the castle.

'What are you thinking?'

Elise came in the door.

'I'm wondering if, in refusing your mother permission to come back here, I'm acting in her and your best interests,' Attercliffe said.

She said, 'You're acting, surely, in your own.'

'Despite your biological necessities, and economic tyrannies, I think it would be wrong for Sheila to come back. In the long run, it could only make her worse,' he said.

'How can she be worse when what she's done only makes her better?'

'Her coming here, under my domination, even if it's only an economic one, isn't going to do anything for her except take her back to where she was before. Far better,' he went on, 'to sell the house. The division, at least, will be more honest.'

Looking past him, she smiled, shook her head, then said, 'Cathy's upset.'

The kettle behind his back began to boil.

'I'll make you a cup of tea,' she added.

He went back to the living-room.

'Anything the matter?' he asked, and when he saw his younger daughter sitting, crouched, her head buried in her hands, her slender shoulders shaking, he took his place beside her; it had been a long time since he had embraced either of his daughters – already, before their mother had left, they'd insisted that he shouldn't – it was 'out of date', 'self-conscious' (not allowed) – and now, when he placed his arm around her, she rested her head against his chest. 'Anything the matter?'

'Everything,' she cried.

For a while there were no other sounds but the bellowing against his chest and of Elise preparing tea in the kitchen.

'We're always arguing,' she added.

'This is what families are like,' he said.

'Not all of them.' Her head was stooped; all he could feel was the warmth of her brow against his chest, and the pressure of her hair beneath his chin.

'We still love one another,' Attercliffe said.

'When everybody is only out for what each of us can get?'

'We're not all out for that,' he said.

'It's only hatred,' she said, 'that keeps us together.'

'Hatred of what?'

'You hate mother.'

'All I want is the best for all of us,' he said.

'You hate Benjie.'

'I don't even know him.'

'You hate Elise.'

'What you call hatred is trying to find a proper course of action. Someone,' he said, 'has to look ahead.'

'All it comes down to, Dad, is duty. You never live.' She added, 'Benjie and his family are all alive.'

'Anybody can be alive if it costs them nothing,' Attercliffe said.

'You don't understand. You never have. The whole world,' she continued, 'is full of hate. Like Elise says: no one cares about anybody except themselves.'

'That's not what Elise was trying to say,' he said.

'What's the point of anything? It all comes apart. And if it all comes apart, then all you are left with is selfishness.'

'You care about other people,' he said. 'So does your mother. So does Elise. So do I, though as you say, I have very little chance to show it, except by worrying how you are.'

'That's selfishness in itself!' she cried.

Elise came in the door; she set a cup of tea by Attercliffe's feet.

'Anything I can get you?' she asked.

63

Attercliffe shook his head.

'I'll be upstairs.'

The door closed; moments later came the sound of a record playing in her bedroom.

'It all comes down to nothing, Dad.'

'It doesn't.'

'Mum'll see there's nothing left.'

'Why do you think that?'

'She hates you. She says you've given her nothing.' She paused. 'You don't even like the things I do.'

'I don't dislike,' Attercliffe said, 'all of them.'

'Most of them.'

'Most of them,' he said, 'I don't understand.'

All she wanted to do was cry.

'Do you want your mother and me to come together?'

'You'd only quarrel.'

'You're feeling disturbed,' Attercliffe said, 'at the thought of her coming back.'

'She doesn't care,' she said. 'All she can see is what she wants.'

'I suppose you're asking me,' he said, 'to reassure you I won't be upset and won't come to any harm, and that your mother coming, and my leaving, mean nothing to me in the long run.'

'Why don't you marry again?'

'Do you think I should?'

'Mummy says you're going to.'

She drew her head up.

'Do you fancy the idea of my getting married?'

'Who to?'

'That's for me to decide.'

'Why can't you give a straight answer?'

'I'm trying,' Attercliffe said, 'to keep your mother out of it.'

'Is that why she decided,' she said, 'to come back home?'

'She'd decided to come back,' he said, 'before I mentioned it. She wants the whole of this house, as Elise suggests, and thinks I should leave it and start again.'

He got out a handkerchief: she wiped her cheeks, frowned, handed the handkerchief back, and said, 'Is there someone you're in love with?'

'I wanted your mother to be aware that I'm not as ancient as I feel at times.'

The small teeth glimmered through the puckered lips: tears, having been removed, reappeared at the corners of her eyes.

'I don't want Sheila to feel you're something she can use, indefinitely, and to her advantage. Otherwise,' he added, 'I'll end up like you.'

The uneven teeth were revealed again.

'You don't have to worry about my getting married.'

'I shan't.'

She wiped back her hair: thin wisps adhered to her cheeks and temples.

'It's not my experience that everyone is out for what they can get.'

She shook her head, leaned away from the pressure of his arm, and slowly got up.

Another car passed in the road outside.

'Is there anything else I can tell you?' he asked as she began to look amongst the unironed clothes.

'No thanks.' She shook her head.

'You mustn't allow Sheila to disturb you. There's a mischievous side to her which she can't control. When you see it showing itself you ought to point it out.'

She turned, picked up a handkerchief, and went to the door.

'I'm sorry I've made a hash of it,' he said.

'I don't feel badly done to,' she said.

The door was closed.

He picked up his tea, now cold, and drank it.

7

The glass-panelled doors divided to reveal a dusty hall: metal-framed chairs and a wooden table were set across a parquet floor. A woman in blue overalls was sitting at the table; on the floor itself the movements of several figures were being co-ordinated by a man in corduroy trousers and a Fair Isle sweater – and wearing what, at first sight, looked like a sailor's cap; only, as the doors closed behind Attercliffe's back and the figures turned he discovered it was in reality a bandage: secured by a safety-pin above one ear, it swept across the man's brow to cover one eye.

The woman in overalls got up and, taking a pencil from her mouth, crossed to where Attercliffe was standing and asked, 'Anything I can do to help?'

'I was invited by Phyllis Gardner,' Attercliffe said.

'Oh, Phyl.' Scarcely older than Elise, she added, 'Her call's been put off until tomorrow.'

'What is it, Meg?' the figure with the bandaged eye called out.

'Someone looking for Phyl.'

'Phyl's not here.' The figure smiled, the one eye still turned in Attercliffe's direction. 'You're not the chap she was on about?' and, turning, before Attercliffe could answer, he called, 'Back to your positions,' glancing at the figures behind him, extending his hand, coming forward, still glancing behind him, and adding, 'Your previous positions. The present ones we haven't worked out.'

A soft, square-shaped hand clasped Attercliffe's and the man announced, 'I'm Harry Towers. Sit in and watch,' nodding to the girl who returned to the table, and calling, 'Get them into their positions, Meg.'

Taking Attercliffe's arm, he directed him to a chair beside the table, and added, 'This is Megan, my assistant,' and as a second, even younger figure – also dressed in overalls – approached and handed him a plastic cup, continued, 'Would you like a cup of coffee? Have mine. Jenny here can get another.' The younger overalled figure moved off: a coffee-dispensing machine stood on a counter in an alcove at the side of the windowless hall. 'We're underground. It tends to get claustrophobic by the end of the day.' The face, like the hand, was large and soft, with the single eye, reddened around the pupil, enclosed within an envelope of bluish skin which, at the inception of a smile, obscured the eye' itself completely: the nose was round and fleshy, the lips full, the mouth narrow, the chin subtended in sheaths of fat. 'Just take it in. Ask any questions. We're near the end of rehearsals but, apart from my saying so, I'm sure you couldn't tell.'

He stepped on to the floor beyond the table; the parquet was marked out with coloured tape: the actors, four of them, took up their positions. A speech began; action followed: the girl sitting at the table called out a line.

The doors behind Attercliffe had opened; he heard a wordless exclamation, and the jacketed figure of Phyllis Gardner touched his hand, sat beside him and, indicating the coffee, said, 'I called your office and left a message. I thought I'd come down in case you hadn't heard.'

She acknowledged three of the actors, who waved, then Towers turned, caressed his bandage, and called, 'We can use you next. The calls, at the present, are all to cock.'

'This is the scene,' she said to Attercliffe, 'before the end. The penultimate,' she concluded, 'before the climax.'

They sat in silence as the scene progressed, her presence marked, finally, by the sharp intake of her breath as, reaching over to the table, she removed a script, opened it, whispered, 'I didn't bring mine. Do you mind if I mark it?' – whispering, once again, inaudibly, beneath her breath, her voice a steady murmur.

The bandaged head took on a hallucinatory significance in the artificially-illuminated room: the pneumatic-looking figure, its trousers crumpled, a line of skin visible below its sweater, moved around the dusty floor with a minimum of effort and a maximum display of facial expression – reinforced, rather than dissipated, by the presence of the bandage. Someone laughed: a line was repeated, retracted, then tried again.

'You didn't get the message?'

Attercliffe shook his head.

'Just as well.' The almond-fashioned eyes, without their usual make-up, were outlined in black: her face was fuller, less mature, the eyes wider, less abstracted. 'Have you made much progress?'

'I've made a start.'

'Quiet, please,' the pneumatic-looking figure called and the repetition of lines began again.

'I'll go and get some coffee.'

She got up from the chair, crossed to the alcove, filled a plastic cup at the urn and, finally, on tip-toe, returned.

She was wearing, beneath her jacket, a tweed skirt and flat-heeled shoes, and, seeing her from a distance, he recognised, with the diminution of her height, a childlike quality not only in her build but in her expression.

She mouthed a word which, with a gesture – shifting the plastic cup from hand to hand – indicated, 'Hot,' and sat beside him once again.

The actors repeated their moves; the voices echoed: feet shuffled. Phyllis, mouthing words, turned her script with a swift, clipping rasp of the paper.

'It's purgatory,' she whispered. 'I'll never learn it.'

Towers, having returned to the table, reapproached the group across the room: he manœuvred a figure beside him, beckoned another, moved a third, called out a line, gestured, and, indicating to one of the actors to imitate his actions, came back to the table.

In the street a lorry thundered past; glass rattled in the doors.

'It's very boring, if you're not involved. All those tapes,' she indicated the floor, 'mark the set. That one over there's a door.'

'Phyl, you must stop talking.' The director avoided looking in Attercliffe's direction, and added, 'We can't concentrate with all this chatter.'

He clapped his hands; the figures returned to their several positions: the girl at the table called out a line.

'Like being back at school.' She returned to her script, murmuring beneath her breath.

Attercliffe leaned forward, his elbows on his knees: it was, he reflected, like watching players rehearse a move, perfecting it by repetition; he regarded the delicately-fingered hand clasping the script beside him and noticed how the paper trembled.

'If you move to your right and allow him to come in front of you.' A whitely-lit face was turned in Attercliffe's direction, the diagonal bandage across one eye, a script held out before it. 'Then, after crossing, move to your left, and you'll find you're in a position to take your cue.'

She whispered, 'This is where they're waiting for the brother, who is in his early twenties, to bring home his fiancée, who has two children as old as he is.' She laughed, watching Attercliffe's expression. 'His father is indisposed towards him, his mother is apprehensive, his three sisters varyingly unsympathetic. I'm up-stairs at the moment, powdering my nose.'

For a while only the murmur of the voices came from across the room, together with the flicking of the pages as Phyllis, with her unpainted nails, stabbed at the lines she'd scored with a pencil.

'It all takes place on a farm.'

'I see.'

'We'll take a break, Meg.' The white-bandaged figure dropped his script, rubbed his hands together, blew into them, called, 'Cold!' and came across, smiling at Phyllis whom, rising, he greeted with a kiss. Turning to Attercliffe, he asked, 'Get anything out of it?'

'Quite a lot.'

'All fresh! All original! All inspiring! As it is,' the eye moved to Phyllis then back to Attercliffe, 'all stale, and familiar, and lacking in spontaneity. Though that,' he added, 'we are looking to Miss Gardner to provide.'

'Too late, dear,' Phyllis said, at which, for the first time, the director laughed.

'Not now we have an audience,' he said.

'A privilege,' she said, 'at this stage, not vouchsafed to many.'

'None at all,' Towers said, 'to be precise. Any publicity,' he went on, 'is welcome.'

'Frank,' Phyllis said, 'is looking for a subject along altogether less traditional lines.'

The single red eye, with its dark iris, examined Attercliffe intently.

'Something more personal.'

'You're not interested in this,' the director inquired, 'for its own

sake?' He gestured round. 'Have you something we can use ourselves? The play,' he added, 'has been done in London and we are
repeating it at something less than secondhand.'

He took Attercliffe's arm and indicated they might go outside.

Breathing deeply – gasping – his stocky figure silhouetted
against the sky, he led the way up a flight of steps; then, once in
the yard, which occupied a derelict graveyard at the side of a
recently-constructed church, he paused, examined a line of cars
parked immediately inside the entrance – tried the handle of one
and looked inside – called, 'Locked, but they broke in the other
day and stole a transistor,' and, gesturing at the town – at its
configuration visible across the street – inquired, 'Is writing for a
newspaper, for instance, a great deal different from composing
dialogue?'

His hands in his pockets, he walked slowly up and down.

'The novel in this country is virtually finished. Not like the
American novel. Here society's too diffuse, lacking in energy.
Drama, on the other hand, is transcendental. It's not restricted by
social convention. You can chance your arm!'

His path had worn a track through the ashes: his shoes were in
holes, his jersey stained, his trousers torn: disconcertingly, he
reminded Attercliffe of Fredericks.

'Phyl is very much taken by you. Sees you as someone who
struck it rich, then found the going tougher later on.' He glanced
across. 'I saw you play.'

Attercliffe didn't answer.

'Years ago.' He gestured, once more, in the direction of the
town. 'I was a young enthusiast in those days. Not for football,
necessarily, but for anything I thought expressive.' His feet rasped
in the ashes once again. 'The discipline required to live in a place
like this is so constricting that even reaction to it acquires a
predictability of its own. I heard about your play.'

He glanced across the street: his one eye examined the passing
traffic, then the buildings opposite, and, finally, the distant spire.

'From Phyl. There must be a great deal that goes on in your
line that no one ever hears about. If I were to offer you a hundred
pounds and invite you to come back in one month's time with a
document which, in your view, amounted to a dramatic text – all
it requires is a list of recurring names with a line of speech beside
each one – would you consider it a challenge?'

Atttercliffe laughed.

'The money isn't mine. It's the theatre's. I have so much at my disposal.' He thrust his hands in his pockets. 'Back in the hall I'll give you a cheque. The contract,' he continued, 'I'll put in the post. So much,' he scrutinised Attercliffe with his reddened eye, 'do I trust to intuition.'

Fredericks said, 'I can't see, Frank, it'll do you any harm.' He picked his nose, observed that this wasn't something that commended him to Booth or Attwood – a small, neatly-featured man, in jeans and a sweater, typing at an adjoining desk – and, drawing out his handkerchief, blew his nose. 'I agree,' he glanced to the window of Holford's Loft, in daylight nothing but a sheet of sooted glass, 'it represents a challenge.'

Booth and Attwood – the former in a variegatedly-patterned sweater, his bald head gleaming in the combination of natural and artificial light – were listening in the hope of discovering what it was Fredericks had to be so cheerful about the better part of one and a half hours before opening-time, only, having blown his nose, Fredericks sneezed, rubbed his face, and concluded, 'Civilisation insists that we shouldn't have to live like rats in a sewer: you can give up this for a start.'

'Now he's getting close to retirement,' Booth said, 'he comes down here and calls the odds as if fifteen years i' The Sump and nought to show for it is all to his bloody credit. O'er my dead body.' He pointed to his jerseyed back.

'O'ppened a hole in the top o' thy 'eard?' Fredericks pocketed his handkerchief, picked up the phone on his desk, dialled for an outside line, dialled again, winked, rubbed his finger at the side of his nose, glanced at Booth, then, less openly, at Attwood, returned his gaze to the window of Holford's Loft, picked up a pencil, announced, 'This is Freddie Fredericks,' and inquired, in response to a voice in his ear, 'Do you know how much it costs me to be in for a workman who never shows up? I hung around all morning.' He turned over a letter, wrote on the back, called, 'I'll hold you to that,' put the phone down and concluded, 'A challenge, Frank. I'd take it up.'

'I thought I'd find you here.' In a pin-striped suit, and looking considerably slimmer than when Attercliffe had last seen him,

Pickersgill gestured across the Buckingham Bar not only to where Fredericks and Booth (Butterworth and Hornchurch, editor and sub-editor) were sitting, but to where the group of men whom he had just left had turned in their seats to gaze in his and Attercliffe's direction. The lunch-time clamour subsided as a name was called on the Tannoy, and he added, 'Let me get you a drink,' looking at Attercliffe's glass and calling, 'Two doubles, Clare,' to the woman behind the bar. 'Seen Sheila lately?'

'At the weekend.'

A heavy face – jowled, with massive brows – was overtopped by a fringe of greying hair which, though combed to one side, enclosed, in its rearward retreat, a bald patch at the crown: the cheeks were shadowed, as were the pouches of flesh beneath each eye.

'Make this my last.' Pickersgill gestured at the glasses as the woman behind the bar held each one up beneath an inverted bottle. 'Lost weight.' He tapped the buttoned front of his jacket. 'Doctor's orders.' He tapped his chest. 'Heart.' For the first time since coming across and clasping Attercliffe's shoulder, he looked him up and down, and added, 'You're looking well. As always.'

He drew the two glasses to him, handed Attercliffe his, dropped money on the counter, said, 'Have one yourself, Clare,' and, turning aside, inquired, 'Say ought daft about coming back home?'

'She did,' Attercliffe said, 'as a matter of fact.'

'Fuss about nought.' Over Booth's back Fredericks's head peered round, then, half-rising, he looked across. 'One of those funny phases she's going through. That's one of her chums o'er yonder. Gavin.' He indicated the group of suited men he had left: the youngest one turned, waved, and remained for a moment half-risen in his chair; finally, prompted by Pickersgill's look, he turned back to the table. 'She's alus hankering after her kiddies. I tell her, she's the worse bloody mother they could have, but she seems to think that's a commendation. You're not after a new car? I can put you in line for a good 'un.'

He swallowed his drink, looked round for somewhere to put his glass, set it on a table, took out a handkerchief, wiped his mouth, unwrapped a cigar, lit it, examined Attercliffe through the smoke, and when Attercliffe himself said, 'I'll bear it in mind,' replied, 'She's with me for life. She knows she's got a house for as long as she wants. I've not let her down in the past, and I never shall. I know what she gave up to come and live wi' me.'

His hair, apart from the fringe, was cut very short: only the greying circuit at the top suggested he was not as old as he looked.

'I don't think it's a passing phase,' Attercliffe said. 'In the past she was very single-minded, and still is.'

'I don't want her to leave,' Pickersgill said. 'I've told her that. The two lads and Lorna are well looked after. And the two lasses when they come across. The au pair we've got at the moment is an absolute cracker. She's ne'er had ought, hasn't Sheila, as you'll know, and as the lads and Lorna'll tell you, but the very best. That's as true of the present,' he took Attercliffe's arm, 'as it will be of the future.'

'She misses the girls,' Attercliffe said.

'She does.' The grip on his arm was released. 'She misses you, in her peculiar fashion. She's probably told you how much she regrets the past, and the misery and anguish she's put you through.'

'She hasn't,' Attercliffe said, 'as a matter of fact.'

'She talks of nought else.' A grey moustache was flexed above a thin-lipped mouth, the corners of which receded – whether to indicate a smile or a grimace, however, it was hard for Attercliffe to tell.

'Though she's worried,' he went on, 'about Veronica.' Perhaps the mention of the name in an unexpected context obviated its significance to such a degree that Pickersgill was, for a moment, unaware who Veronica was.

'She's nought. A bit of fun. Sheila knows Veronica's no more a threat to her than Gavin is to me.' He gestured across the room: only the back of the youthful figure's head and shoulders was visible now, the hair, like Pickersgill's, cut short, but dark, and neatly parted; he gave a feeling not only of youth, but of character, grace, gentility and strength.

'Who is he?' Attercliffe asked.

'I knew his father. Which'll show you how much out of Sheila's way he is. He only talks to her to do me a favour. He's a spare-parts manufacturer. It's a line I should have gone into mesen. A few ups and downs but nought to the tribulations of a dealer. Or being a professional sportsman, come to that. We talk the same language, Frank, and always have.' He replaced his hand on Attercliffe's arm.

73

As for Attercliffe, he was wondering whether, even at this late stage, and despite the (advantageous) disparity between their ages, he might hit Pickersgill in the mouth, on the nose, beneath the jowled but nevertheless still conspicuous jaw, or even in the belly: if ever there were an individual who summed up his willingness to risk spending the rest of his life in a prison cell it must have been this balding, redolently-perfumed, dark-suited figure who stood before him now, his short-fingered, square-shaped hand measuring its grip on his arm.

'It's what I say to Sheila whenever she speculates about what brought us both together. "Frank and me," I tell her, "are two of a kind." ' He flexed the moustache again and a line like a bracket formed a little distance from each corner of his mouth.

'She's more determined,' Attercliffe said, 'than you imagine,' and saw Pickersgill glance away: he was not contemplating the bar but savouring the content of what Attercliffe had said. 'Who is this Veronica?' he asked.

'Tha knows how it is. My age, I can't so much lake around as swan around, wi' more in the eye than I know I can have. She's no more a threat to Sheila than Gavin is to me,' and, reminded that he'd mentioned this already, he added, 'I'd never get wed to Sheila for fear o' spoiling what we have. Maybe it's that that gets her goat.'

Attercliffe saw the youthful figure of Gavin rise from his chair and, laughing at something someone amongst those sitting at the table had said, start in their direction.

He was a slim, slenderly-featured man: from a thickening of the bridge of his nose, and a not dissimilar thickening of his brows, he gave the impression that he might, at one time, have been an amateur or perhaps even a professional boxer.

'Morry told me,' he said, 'I could come across. He's worried that Sheila is taking her hook.' He smiled, as if to set Pickersgill, but not Attercliffe, at his ease.

'You haven't met Gavin, Frank.' Pickersgill clasped the young man's back. 'This is the young man, Frank, I've told you about.'

Gavin said, 'I've heard a lot about you,' seized Attercliffe's hand, sustained his grip, his brown, black-lashed eyes flickering on a smile, and added, 'Sheila talks of no one else. We're both, my wife and I, very fond of her.'

'She's told me a great deal about you,' Attercliffe said. 'And how she's concerned she doesn't in any way upset your wife.'

'Chris's very fond of her,' Gavin said. 'I'm often away with my work,' he added, 'but we've always time for Sheila whenever I'm back.'

'Once the wind's blown out of her sails she'll turn on course.' Pickersgill, having released Attercliffe's arm, placed his hand on Attercliffe's shoulder. 'Gavin's very patient wi' Sheila. There's nothing he and Chris wouldn't do. They idolise the boys.'

'Not to mention Lorna.' Gavin laughed.

'Nay, Lorna's my especial favourite.' Pickersgill flushed.

'It's very good of you,' Attercliffe said, 'to have the welfare of the children so close to your hearts. As far as I can see,' he added, 'you won't have to be preoccupied by them for very much longer.'

'Why's that?' Gavin said.

'Sheila's determined to come back,' he said.

'It's a temporary business,' Pickersgill said. 'She means nought serious by what she says. You have my word on that. If I don't know her moods by now, I never shall.'

His look moved away: this time it was Fredericks who was coming across, his head – grey, close-cropped – raised only as he encountered two figures flanking a third obstructing his path; to the central one he said, 'Not teaching these young 'uns the same old tricks, Morry?'

'Nay, Freddie, no tricks up my sleeve.' Pickersgill laughed, hitching up the sleeves of his jacket to reveal his cuff-linked shirt. 'There ne'er wa' in the past, and I've no need of 'em at present,' clasping Fredericks's shoulder and adding, 'Freddie and me are from the days when a sportsman knew his proper place, and that was some road,' he concluded, 'behind the gaffer's back.'

'Some poor bloody sod to have you behind him,' Fredericks said. 'I wouldn't have Pickersgill behind me for all the tea i' China.' He gazed into Gavin's face.

'This is an old friend of mine, Freddie Fredericks, Gavin,' Pickersgill said. 'This is Gavin Proctor, a man of the future. Where he goes,' he continued, 'others follow.'

'Another front man,' Fredericks said, nodding at Gavin but not shaking his hand.

'Nay, I'm apologising, Freddie,' Pickersgill said. 'It's my fault Frank's been imposed upon. I've wanted, as you know, to intrude as little as I can on his private life. If I didn't think it was important,' he added, 'I wouldn't have bothered him here.'

'And he wouldn't have bothered you here, if he could have bothered you somewhere else,' Fredericks said. 'Discounts with Maurice still show a big profit.'

'Some less than others, Freddie,' Pickersgill said, and added, 'I hear thy's due for retiring.'

Fredericks smiled.

'Bars have ears, tha knows.' Pickersgill gestured to the room. 'When you get to a certain age, like yours and mine, you hear some things more clearly than others.'

'I'm not retiring,' Fredericks said. 'I might be deein', but I'm not retiring.' He laughed. 'There's more punch in one line from Attercliffe and Fredericks than there is in one paragraph from anybody else.' He showed his stained, irregular teeth. 'I wouldn't trust these two an inch. Not that I've met this young 'un afore,' he added. 'But if he's a friend of Maurice's he's no friend of thine,' and, calling, 'I'm off to the bog,' released himself from Pickersgill's hand and continued across the bar to the opposite door.

'Never loses his flavour,' Pickersgill said. 'If bullshit could be sold in bottles he'd have made a bloody fortune.' His dislodged hand returned to Attercliffe's arm. 'Gavin can vouch for everything I've said. Sheila's going through a difficult patch. I know what an intrusion these things can be. My wife's second husband is a case in point. He still comes to me, would you believe it, for my advice. I don't think there's a month gone by that I haven't taken him out to lunch. Mind you, I've sold him three motor-cars in that time.' He leaned back, his head turned to the ceiling, and laughed. Attercliffe watched the Adam's apple convulse inside his collar, and observed the metal lining to several of his teeth at the back. 'It's the children we have to consider. It's their welfare that lies at the heart of it. Keith and Bryan. The two girls. Little Lorna. Sheila's told me the problems you have. And Gavin. He's given me one or two insights. Sheila's a great conversationalist, but can shut up tight the moment she's back inside the house.'

'We've everything to gain,' Gavin said, 'by sticking together. These things are settled better by talking.'

'Instead,' Pickersgill said, 'of going behind each other's backs. I've been meaning to give you a ring for some time. I could see this blowing up a while ago. I just want you to feel assured we'll be doing all we can.' He slapped Attercliffe's arm and added, 'Stay and talk to Gavin.'

He was already halfway across the room before Gavin said, 'He's been a good friend to Chris and me, and a hell of a brick to Sheila.'

'Do you believe all he says?' Attercliffe asked.

'Why shouldn't I?'

'Sheila's account of your relationship isn't as bland as the one you've just described to me.'

'I can hardly pay Morry back,' he said, 'by telling him his wife has asked me to fuck her.'

'She's my wife, as it happens,' Attercliffe said.

'Is this the time to go into technicalities?' he asked.

Long before he had realised he would never have the opportunity to hit Gavin a second time – having hit him the first time as hard as he could – Attercliffe felt a pain in the pit of his stomach, followed by a second at the side of his head, and the interior of the bar, together with its inhabitants, went out of focus. All he recalled of Gavin was Sheila's remark testifying to his thoughtfulness, his sensitivity, and to – he might have known – his capacity to see ahead; from a distance of scarcely less than a foot he scrutinised, on all fours, the toes of Gavin's shoes – both of which were displaced by a hand attached to a cuff-linked arm, and a moment later he was drawn to his feet.

'Are you all right?' The inquiry was made by Gavin himself. To an inquiry from someone behind his back he added, 'He must have slipped,' and, to a further remark, 'He must have had too much to drink,' he replied, 'I should get him outside.'

He caught a glimpse of the genial features of Pippy Booth, followed by the even – surprisingly – more genial features of Attwood, Butterworth and Hornchurch.

'I can't see how he fell. He was as sober as a judge,' Fredericks said, coming into his field of vision. 'Though I might just as easily have said, as sober as an Attercliffe.'

'He's cut his ear,' someone said and he felt a piece of cloth applied to his head, held there for a moment, wiped, then Fredericks said, 'Are you all right?'

A moment later he was standing in the street.

He recognised a shop.

'I'm fine.'

77

'Must have been the floor.'

'It's got a carpet.' He held a handkerchief behind his ear.

'In that case,' Fredericks said, pursuing the subject, 'it must have been the table.'

'Going in for the noble art, Atty?' Booth inquired, passing on the pavement and on his way back, evidently, with Attwood, Butterworth and Hornchurch, to the office.

'How are you, Frank?' Pickersgill, too, inquired, smiling, stooping. 'Hell of a bang.'

'The table, Maurice,' Gavin said, but Attercliffe turned and, with someone he assumed to be Fredericks at his side, followed the group of backward-glancing figures in the direction of the office.

'The day,' Fredericks said, 'goes to the younger man.'

'I was a fool to do anything about it.' Attercliffe drew the handkerchief down. 'I've never felt so old.' He felt the swelling behind his ear.

'It's not so much a question,' Fredericks said, 'of self-recognition, as choosing in which direction to use your resources. Everyone has their problems, Frank. A hostage to fortune. What happens to the professional athlete when all that fulfils him in life is achieved by the time he's thirty? He can't distract himself by behaving like he did at twenty, recapturing a grace that has gone for good.'

They walked for a while in silence.

'Pickersgill's intention, and Gavin's,' Attercliffe said, 'is to return me to my wife. Or, rather,' he continued, 'the other way around.'

Fredericks laughed; even the group ahead, as they passed across the front of All Saints Church and turned down Benton Lane to Norton Square, glanced back – Butterworth, the editor, a tall, stoop-shouldered man with a mop of greyish hair detached in a corkscrew fashion at the back of his neck, calling, 'Are you all right?' – and, although the nodding of his head induced another sensation of dizziness, Attercliffe laughed as well.

'That Gavin is a part of it?' Fredericks quickened his pace.

'Sheila's latest find.'

'Not content with Maurice.'

'Maurice,' he said, 'is not content with her. Neither,' he continued, 'is Gavin.'

'Lets you have her back.'

'Returned to previous owner, used, but good for a few more miles.'

Fredericks laughed, signalled the towered building halfway down the slope on their right, and announced, 'Still, Destiny, you could say, Frank, at this late stage, has come back into your hands.'

8

The interior was dominated by a chandelier suspended from within a glass-panelled dome; curtained boxes rose on either side: below the dome, in the furthest recess, fronting the benches of the gallery, gleamed a curved brass rail.

Up there, high above his head, Attercliffe had caught a glimpse, before the lights went out, of the pneumatically-proportioned figure of Harry Towers.

The theatre was crowded; having, on his arrival, left his unused ticket at the box-office, the seat beside him was still unoccupied when the lights went down but when, after an interval of several seconds, a reciprocal light came up from the stage a half-stooped figure, apologising to those already seated, came along the row, sank beside him, and a voice he recognised said, 'Remember me? I'm Heather.'

Animated to a degree out of all proportion to the vitality of the scene before them – two sisters (one of them Phyllis) discussing a third whose activities were represented by a hammering off-stage – she sighed, leaned back, and added, 'It isn't taken, is it?'

'No,' Attercliffe said, and shook his head.

'Phyl is in a tiz.'

'Why's that?'

'Douglas hasn't turned up.'

'How does she know?' Attercliffe asked.

'Says he can't get off training.'

'Does she mind?'

There was a hiss from behind and, leaning closer, she said, 'Not much!'

He felt the pressure of her arm: a fur-collared texture, when he

glanced sideways, underlay her face and, in the illumination from
the stage, the profile of her head was outlined against the darkness
of the heads behind: the brow receded, the hair was ruffled: a
slender throat subsided beneath a sharply projecting jaw.

Aware of his scrutiny, she smiled; a moment later, she glanced
across, smiled more broadly, and said, 'Are you all right?'

Her hand squeezed his.

'I'm fine.'

The sisters on the stage had been joined by the third: a window,
at the back, looked out to a moor. The sisters squabbled; they
talked about their mother: their father arrived.

'Phyl is good.'

The lights went up at the end of the scene.

'Isn't she?'

She turned in her seat.

'To say she's in a tiz, she seems, in my view, to be better than
ever.'

She acknowledged someone seated behind, then returned her
gaze, first to a close inspection of Attercliffe's face, then of his eyes.

Her cheek-bones were widely spaced, the eyes devoid of
make-up: her hair, flung upwards, was caught by a ribbon.

She smiled.

'Come here often?'

'First visit.'

'Finished your article?'

'Not yet.'

'What's it like?'

Her mouth was broad, her teeth unevenly spaced: she regarded
the effect of her inquiry by re-examining his face, her eyes moving
downwards, returning upwards, smiling.

'Not bad.'

'I heard about your fracas at the Buckingham.'

'How's that?'

'Pickersgill has a mouth as big as his wallet.'

She laughed; the lights went down; the mother returned from
night-school. The family quarrelled.

The father went to bed; two of the daughters followed: the
mother and the youngest daughter remained by the fire. They
talked of the past. The mother retired. Through the darkened
french window, looking out to the moor, the daughter's boyfriend

arrived. An artisan, employed in a factory, he was as nervous of the daughter as he was of the house. The daughter expressed the same irritation with him as she had with her mother – the same passivity she identified in both. The boyfriend left: no sooner had he gone than Phyllis, as the eldest sister, reappeared; she took a drink, lit a cigarette and, having heard something of the conversation between her sister and the boyfriend, initiated a further quarrel. The younger sister, defeated, went to bed and for a moment Phyllis was left alone on the stage.

Heather leant back.

Phyllis, too, leant back, lit another cigarette, drank: a shadow moved in the window. The latch was raised: a figure entered then, as Phyllis stood up and switched on the light, stumbled.

Long-haired, slenderly-featured, roughly-dressed, the figure was embraced by Phyllis, given a drink, and revealed himself to be her reputedly dissolute younger brother.

After expressing his misgivings about coming back, and recalling some of the unhappiness of the past, the brother announced his intention of getting married.

The woman – almost twice his age, an actress, who had been divorced and who had two teenage children – was staying at a local hotel, but the brother intended bringing her up the following day when he had broken the news to his parents.

The sister noticed the shaking of his hands, and inquired about his life away from the woman – he was writing poetry, had worked in hotels, but was presently unemployed.

The scene ended with the two of them starting upstairs.

The lights came up; the curtain descended: Heather smiled.

'Fancy a drink?'

'I think I ought to get you one,' Attercliffe said.

'I'll get you one,' she said, rising. 'Phyl asked me to look after you.'

They moved up the aisle to the bar: Heather laid down the money, retrieved the change and, returning to where Attercliffe had found a space, gave him his glass, glanced round, and added, 'Phyl told me you've been invited to write a play.'

'It's been suggested.'

'She told me,' she said, 'that you'd tried before.'

'Long ago,' he said.

'Perseverance is not your strongest suit.'

'Other things,' he said, 'got in the way.'

'Oh, that.'

'Have you a family?' Attercliffe asked.

'I haven't.' In the babble of voices, and the compression of bodies, he found it difficult to hear her announce, 'Not yet.'

'But you've worked in the theatre,' Attercliffe said.

'Before my marriage. After my divorce I went back to it.' She added, 'I found, in a way, I'd left it too late.'

'You're telling me,' he said, 'it's never too late.'

'There's something extraneous about acting. Don't you think?' Having acknowledged several figures in the bar, she turned, frowned, and added, 'I'd like to base my life on something solid.'

'What work did you do?' he asked.

'I auditioned for Phyl's part. They thought I looked too old.'

'Are you older?' he asked.

'More experienced.' She laughed, glanced about her once again, and added, 'I wouldn't have done as well. I *sounded* older, which is just as bad. Particularly with someone,' she concluded, 'like Harry.'

The figure of the director approached across the bar, the bandaged head held up at an angle, the pneumatically-featured face turned in their direction – turned in another to acknowledge a greeting, a soft, square-fingered hand inserting itself between a pair of shoulders (finding a place on Heather's back, drawing her to him, the bandaged eye laid beside her cheek, withdrawn, the same hand thrust in Attercliffe's direction) – and a narrow, full-lipped mouth declared, 'Good of you to come.'

'I can't say he's enjoying it, but,' Heather said, 'he's doing his best.'

'His best is all I ask for.' Towers laughed, his irregular teeth forced from his mouth as if, Attercliffe reflected, he were about to bite him. 'Heather's not been disillusioning you about her life in the theatre?'

'About my career I have,' she said. 'But not,' she went on, 'about his intentions.'

'Oh, those,' the director said, 'are the ones we shall have to talk about.' He added, 'I'm off backstage. Anything I should say to Phyl?'

'To be more,' Heather said, 'of what she is already.'

'I'll tell her that,' he said. 'More of the same, but better.'

83

He passed to a door across the bar, released it, and disappeared inside.

'Do you fancy another drink?' Attercliffe asked.

'Oh, you can buy me another,' she said, 'next time.'

They returned to their seats.

'I have half-shares in a flower-shop at present,' she said. 'Not enough to live on but, with the occasional work, I get by. Whereas you,' she added, 'are a reporter.'

'That's right.'

'With the legendary Freddie Fredericks.'

'Do you know him?' he asked.

'Who doesn't? He used to be on television when I was young. After that, I'm told, he turned to drink.'

'But not to moralising,' Attercliffe said.

'It can't be as bad as that,' she said. 'I'm not a do-gooder. Nor am I a preacher.'

'Do you have any influence on Phyl?' he asked.

'A lot.'

'What about Dougie?'

'On him especially.' She laughed. 'The hours I've had to listen to descriptions of his matches, whereas all he cares about is being seen with her in public.'

The audience returned to their seats.

The houselights began to go down.

The mother, when the lights went up, was seated at a desk; the two eldest daughters, both teachers, were preparing to leave for work: as the mother added up sums aloud the news was introduced by Phyllis that the son had come back the previous night: a short while later he entered. The son and the mother were reunited: news of the marriage came out; the daughters waited for the encounter with the father.

Heather glanced intermittently from the stage to the faces around her; in the half-darkness Attercliffe saw her smile.

'Are you all right?' Again the inquiry came, followed by the touch of her hand. 'Phyl is up.'

And when, finally, the father came in and had been reintroduced to the son, and Phyllis and her sister had departed, the father, antagonised at finding his alcohol consumed from the previous evening, turned on the son. The news of the marriage came out, the father's rage culminating in a speech in which the ineptitude

84

of his son and his own destitution as a father were contrasted with the belief he still felt in his work.

The lights came up.

'We'll sit here,' Heather said. 'I don't fancy all that crush. You can buy me the drink you owe me later.'

She turned a page of the programme; a photograph of Phyllis was framed by several others: a biography mentioned, in italics, the plays she'd appeared in, the film she'd made. More certainly, however, Attercliffe was impressed by the hand which held the page, and the proximity of the head which was inclined to his own: the fingers were strong, the nails unpainted – one of them broken – the thumb, in its slenderness, slightly curled back.

'What happened to your marriage?' Attercliffe said.

'It broke up.'

'Through what?'

'The pressure of his family that he ought to succeed.'

'As what?'

'They were in the engineering business.'

'Did he marry again?'

'He has two sons.'

'Would you remarry?'

'I value my freedom too highly,' she said.

'That can exist within a marriage, just as it can without,' he said.

'You're a living example.' She laughed.

'Freedom only exists,' he said, 'within limits. It's no good, for instance, saying you're free if you're standing in the middle of a desert.'

Her gaze was directed to the curtain; odd figures, in the aisle, glanced down: one of them called out.

She waved.

'I don't think of this,' she said, 'as a desert. But in the best regulated marriage the odds are stacked against the woman. It's one of the assertions of this play.'

'Have you seen it before?' he asked.

'I haven't.' She smiled. 'It succeeded in London because of its cast. Here,' she gestured round, 'it has to succeed on its merit.'

He examined the curtain himself.

'Would you marry again?' she asked.

'Yes.'

'Not the same woman.'

'Hardly.'

She laughed, leaned back, and examined the chandelier above their heads: it hung from a central chain let into the glass-panelled dome; distorted in each of the panes was a reflection of the scene below, each segment joined at an irregular angle and irradiated by the light from the chandelier itself.

'Perhaps,' she said, 'you're too old to change.'

'I'm only forty-seven.'

'How many children do you have?'

'Five.'

'Boys and girls?'

'Three of the latter, two of the former.'

'Like talking to a soldier in the heat of battle.'

'It is.'

'What about your wife?'

'She's misunderstood as well.'

He watched her laugh.

'You've really come adrift.' She contemplated the dome again, the chandelier, the glittering glass: a patina of reflections was cast across the seats and on to the walls of the theatre, speckles of illumination which flickered across the boxes.

Her hands, disengaged from the programme, were clasped together: the knuckles, in the half-light, glistened.

'I still have an appetite to succeed,' he said.

'At what?'

'Extracting something,' he said, 'from the shambles.'

She said, 'Haven't you, in that sense, done rather well? Better even,' she went on, 'than most? Better even, secretly, than anyone around you?'

A bell sounded at the back.

'I don't see how.'

'Maybe not,' she said, 'but others can.'

Figures crowded the corridor, their heads, in the congestion, bobbing up and down, the doors to the dressing-rooms swinging open. A figure ran past, called, 'I shan't be a minute,' and clattered down a flight of stairs.

Heather, in ascending the stairs, had taken Attercliffe's hand and, with an infrequent, 'Excuse me,' inserted herself amongst the crowd; finally, reaching one of the dressing-room doors, she stepped inside and, releasing Attercliffe's hand, was embraced by Phyllis.

'Marvellous,' Heather said.

'You're not just saying it?' Phyllis inquired.

'I am just saying it,' Heather said. 'It happens to be true,' and added, 'Never say die, but Dougie has arrived.'

The bearded and overcoated figure of Walters, his pugilistically-featured face incongruous in this setting – and to some extent a facsimile, if younger, of Attercliffe's own – appeared inside the dressing-room door.

'I hear she's very good,' he said.

'Very, Douglas,' Heather said.

'I'm sorry,' he said, 'I couldn't see it. I'll come along tomorrow.'

'The night before a match?'

'Maybe next week. It's on for a while.' He thrust his hands into the pockets of his coat and added, 'How long are you going to take to get ready?'

'Give me time to recover, Dougie,' Phyllis said. Turning to the door she added, 'Events like this don't happen all the time,' as the bandaged head of Towers appeared.

'Energy is all that counts,' the director said. 'And more and more as it came to an end.' To Walters, glancing up, he added, 'Didn't see you out in front.'

Walters glanced at Phyllis, said, 'I'll be in the bar for about ten minutes,' examined the single eye of Towers – contemplated it for a full clear second – and disappeared to the stairs outside.

'His charm,' Towers said, 'grows by the hour,' turning to Attercliffe and adding, 'No revelations from you, I take it?'

'Don't bully him,' Heather said. 'Not that he can't,' she added, 'stand up for himself.'

'I'm only anxious to see Phyllis get her just deserts. And not just the ones,' the director said, 'that have gone out through the door.'

A group of figures came inside; another group departed: Heather said, 'We'll see you in the bar.'

A moment later, returning down the stairs, she added, 'It's in the pub. We can have another talk with Dougie.'

The square at the front of the theatre – full of vehicles when Attercliffe had arrived – was now deserted: adjacent to the theatre – and separated from it by a cobbled alley – the corner of the square was brightly lit, the illumination coming from the windows of a public house.

The bar was full to the door; on this occasion Heather walked behind him, her hand in his until, at the bar, two glasses were passed across, the money was given, and they were absorbed into a group of people whom Heather knew and Attercliffe didn't but to whom, individually, he was introduced. Across the bar, Walters was engaged in a conversation in which he appeared to take little if any interest: periodically, raising an arm, he examined a watch.

'Not your cup of tea either?' Heather's face was turned to his. Over her back Walters called, 'If you see her, tell her I've gone,' and adding, 'I don't know how you stick it,' disappeared, through the crowd, to the street outside.

'I don't know who to sympathise with more.' She gestured round. 'Them or us.'

'Do you see us united against a common enemy?' Attercliffe asked.

She laughed. 'I do sense a compatibility between you and Dougie.'

'Dougie has as much respect for me,' Attercliffe said, 'as you might have for a critic.'

'More.' She shook her head. 'He sees you as a light to follow.'

They didn't stay long; no sooner on her appearance had Phyllis been told of Walters's departure – calling, 'That's his look-out'; vanishing across the bar – than Heather suggested that the two of them might leave. To get to the door took several minutes, Towers appearing by Attercliffe's side and declaring, 'There's so much we have to talk about.'

'Another time.'

'I'll hold you to that. Once I get my teeth into a thing I never let go.'

'What's happened to your eye?' Attercliffe asked.

'It helps to give me focus, particularly,' he added, 'in trying times.' Securing Attercliffe's arm as far as the door, he called, 'Don't let Heather subvert you.'

A night wind blew through the leafless trees in the centre of the square; the front of the theatre was dark: chains could be seen securing metal bars inside the glass doors of the foyer.

She put her arm in his.

'Who looks after your children?'

'The eldest two look after themselves. The other three,' Atter-cliffe told her, 'live with my wife.'

'Where does she live?'

'With Pickersgill.'

'He once came to a party.'

'That's right,' he said. 'Phyl told me.'

From the square an alleyway led to the main thoroughfare of the town; a second turning brought them into the side-street and from there to the door of the flats.

'It's still early,' she said. 'Do your children not mind what time you get in?'

'I prefer to get in earlier than later,' Attercliffe said.

'Do you want to come up?'

She took out a key, unlocked the door, waited for him to enter then, the door closing behind them, led the way upstairs.

'You're a circumspect person, Frank, despite your past. I sup-pose, at times, with so many children, it must play a significant part.'

'That,' he said, 'or the lack of it.'

They had reached the flat door; a key was inserted: she led the way in, took off her coat, offered him a drink, disappeared to the kitchen, returned, sat down and, raising her glass, having given him his, said, 'The professor and the flower-girl.'

She wore a brown frock, secured with a belt and trimmed at the neck and the sleeves with lace.

'Phyllis had a triumph.'

'She had.'

'These things come and go.'

'Like flowers.'

'It's the spirit alone,' she said, 'that counts.'

It was a child, as she had suggested, rather than a woman who was facing him across the hearth – aloof, detached – like one of his daughters, looking for an opportunity not so much to criticise, or even comment, let alone condemn, as to indicate to him her youth.

'Good ending to the play.' She smiled.

'It was.'

'When the woman they were all waiting for doesn't turn up.'

'The last scene in particular.'

'The family at breakfast when the youngest daughter's boy-friend walks in and is welcomed like a son, unlike,' she added, 'the departing offspring. Perhaps,' she went on, 'you shouldn't have come up either.'

'It raises the kind of expectations,' Attercliffe said, 'that at my time of life I can't fulfil.'

The tousled hair fell back from her brow; she pushed it up, laughed, put down her glass, and said, 'I've never seen anyone look so frightened. Nor anyone,' she added, 'who looked so sad.'

'If I'm preoccupied elsewhere it affects the attention,' Attercliffe said, 'I'm giving you. And if I'm preoccupied with you,' he added, 'it affects the attention I'm giving to someone else. The idea of limitless freedom, either here or somewhere else, isn't one I understand. Everyone's life is circumscribed.'

'Coming up here,' she said, 'has not been a great success.'

'I'm glad I came,' he said.

'I wouldn't care,' she said, 'to be your daughter.'

'Why not?'

'I'd feel an ominous sense of obligation.'

'My actual daughters,' Attercliffe said, 'feel none at all.'

'In that case,' she said, 'they have more spirit than I have.'

'I don't know,' he said. 'About the same.'

She came with him to the landing when he left, and although she remained there until he'd disappeared, she didn't come to the window when he reached the street and he had the feeling, once the flat door was closed, she had forgotten all about him.

9

A scamper of feet came from the front of the house and a figure
darted over the garden wall and, at a pace much faster than
Attercliffe could run, set off along the pavement.

When Attercliffe unlocked the door a crescendo of music came
from overhead. A light went on in the kitchen.

'Cathy?'

'Who is it?'

Catherine, her hair dishevelled, came out from the kitchen; her
face was flushed, her hands wet: around her waist was fastened an
apron.

'I'm washing up.'

'Who went out just now?'

'Just now?'

'A minute ago.'

The wild-eyed look beneath the dishevelled hair reminded
Attercliffe of his wife – the moment when, gathering her possessions around her, she had announced, in the manner of someone
who had announced it once already, that the time had come for
her to leave.

'That'd be Benjie.'

'Has he stolen something?'

'Why should he have stolen something?'

'He ran off down the road.'

'He heard you arrive.' She turned back to the kitchen.

The tap was running: the washing-up had scarcely begun; he
could hear Elise at the top of the stairs, the banister creak, then her
footsteps as she descended.

He closed the kitchen door and asked, 'Why should he run off?'

'He's frightened.'

'Why should he be frightened?'

'He knows your attitude.'

'I'm not against him,' he said. 'I'm only against his criminal record and the inadvertent effect it'll have on you.'

'We've been through this before.' She stooped to the sink.

'Did you cook him a meal?'

'That's right.'

Her gaze – her back turned to him – was directed, when not at the sink, at her own reflection in the kitchen window.

'What does he know of my attitudes?' Attercliffe asked. 'He hasn't even met me.'

'I've told him,' she said.

'What have you told him?'

'That you're prejudiced.'

'I'd like him to form his own opinion,' Attercliffe said.

'He already has.'

'How?'

'He's seen how we live. He says you're orientated towards money, material possessions, and living a comfortable life.'

'Is that his vocabulary,' he asked, 'or yours?'

'He's not illiterate,' she said.

'Still,' Attercliffe said, 'he's not at school.'

'That's right.'

'Any examination results?'

'Examinations are to do with white conditioning.'

'Jesus.'

'And that's another element,' she said, 'of white propaganda.'

'What is?'

'Christ.'

Turning, she pressed past him, dried her hands, removed her apron, opened the kitchen door, and went upstairs.

'Can't we talk about it?' Attercliffe asked.

'There's nothing to talk about,' she said. 'You don't want him here. You've made your attitude perfectly clear.'

There was a murmur of voices at the head of the stairs.

He went through to the living-room, looked in, came out, took off his overcoat, hung it in the hall, found he had the theatre programme in his pocket, and took it upstairs.

In the tiny back bedroom he placed the programme on the desk, came back out, tapped on Cathy's door, heard her and Elise's voices pause, then, when Elise said, 'Yes?' he opened the door to find Catherine lying on her bed and Elise sitting sideways to her on the only chair.

'Has someone been in my desk?'

'I have.' Catherine raised her head.

'Why?'

'I was showing Benjie round.'

'Why my desk?'

'I wanted,' she lowered her head, 'to show him that we had nothing to hide.'

'Why should he think we had something to hide?'

'Because of prejudice,' she said.

'In my desk?'

'Your desk had nothing to do with it.'

'Then why show him it?'

'I was showing him,' she said, 'some of your cuttings. He's interested,' she continued, 'in football. Though,' she concluded, 'not your kind.'

'Perhaps he wants to be one.'

'Not really.'

'What would he like to be?'

'A pop-star.'

Elise leaned forward, her hands on her knees: music thundered from the door of her room.

'I thought he despised affluence.'

'Not really.'

'Then why despise it here?'

'He despises,' she said, 'our way of life.'

'If he's so sure of his convictions, why did he run off?' he asked.

'He knew you wouldn't like him.'

Elise stood up; she yawned: her mouth opened to a perspective of metal-capped back teeth.

'How did it go?' she asked.

'It went all right,' he said, and added, 'Is his attitude to you as belligerent as it is to me?'

'Not really.' Elise yawned again, her arms outstretched, and added, 'I'm off to bed.'

'Did he come in here?'

'Of course he came in here.' Catherine, too, got up.

'Isn't it possible for us to talk about this situation, without one of us,' he asked her, 'running off?'

Elise, hearing this inquiry, paused in the door.

Catherine said, 'I'm not running off.'

'You keep running away from me,' Attercliffe said, 'whenever I'd like to talk.'

'We've been through this before,' she said. 'You don't like him coming. I do.' She pushed past Elise and went through to her sister's bedroom, closing the door.

'Do you want a cup of tea?' Elise asked.

'No thanks.'

'Why are you so upset?'

'I don't like Cathy's furtiveness, or the furtiveness,' he said, 'of Benjie.'

'It's because of your attitude.' Elise remained on the landing, disinclined – now her sister had gone there – to go to her room.

'If you had a child would you be content to see it go off with a criminal?' Attercliffe asked.

'I might have one,' she said, 'as a matter of fact.'

'You're only seventeen.'

'A woman matures,' she said, 'from the age of thirteen, or even younger, nowadays.'

'Who's the father?'

'I don't know,' she said.

'You mean, there's a choice.'

'There is a choice.' Lightly, glancing round, she ran her hand along the banister.

'Retrospectively,' Attercliffe said, 'there is a choice, or,' he went on, 'there will be?'

'There will be.'

'Are you coming off the pill?'

'Naturally.'

'Have you talked about it to Sheila?'

'It's my concern, not hers.'

'She ought to be informed. Just as you're informing me,' he said. 'Otherwise,' he added, 'she'll think you've done it behind her back.'

She flushed: a white tinge showed at each of her temples.

'How are you to support this child?' he asked.

94

'The state takes care of it,' she said, and added, 'Lots of people my age have a child.'

Her eyes were mascaraed, her lips were reddened, her hair was ruffled up: she had made an effort – she was wearing jeans and a blouse, the front unbuttoned – in order to impress upon Benjie, Attercliffe suspected, that there were more experienced women about the house.

'Does it mean you give up your education?'

'Not necessarily.'

'You'll take a child to college.'

'It's just something,' she said, 'I thought I might do.'

She turned to the room; the door opened: music thundered out, burying what sounded like an inquiry from Cathy.

Two figures in jeans and sweaters and a third, tinier figure in brown overalls and jumper ran up the drive, banged on the door, tried the handle, found it open, and came inside.

From the door of the car Sheila appeared; she carried a hold-all: without glancing at the house she approached the door, opened it, stepped inside, carried the hold-all to the foot of the stairs, set it down, then, having glimpsed Attercliffe at the living-room window, and hearing Lorna demanding to be lifted, came in and said, 'I'll pick them up on Sunday.'

'Right,' Attercliffe said.

'How's your head?'

'It's in pretty good shape.'

'I hear you banged it.'

'I did.'

'A bit juvenile at your age. Brawling in a pub.'

'He was twice my size.'

'Gavin is slighter and slimmer, and half your age.'

'He felt thicker and fatter, and twice as old.'

He had already picked up the overalled and jumpered scrap of a child – thin-armed, thin-faced, dark-eyed, dark-haired – while, from overhead, came the sound of the two boys rushing round the room they shared (Cathy's: she moved into Elise's whenever the boys came back, Lorna sleeping in his 'study'); now, as she poked her finger in his eye and asked, 'Is there anything to eat?' he turned to the door and said, 'I'll see you Sunday.'

'You haven't forgotten our conversation?'

'I haven't.'

'The plans,' she said, 'are under way.'

She kissed Lorna's cheek, said, 'Be a good girl,' called, 'See you Sunday, boys,' and was already out of the door before she added, 'The girls are out, I know. They rang me this morning.'

'Tell you much,' he asked, 'about themselves?'

'It was more my news,' she said, 'I was telling them.'

'About returning.'

'That's right.'

She set off down the drive and, seeing her go, Lorna called, 'Mummy?' but Sheila either didn't hear or chose to ignore her and only when she was behind the wheel and the car door closed did she wave, without looking, and drive away.

Footsteps sounded on the stair as first the fair-haired Keith came down, then Bryan.

'Anything to eat, Dad?'

They went through to the kitchen; they sat at the tiny table, next to the sink, Lorna, now she had had some food provided, sitting on Attercliffe's knee, her arm around his neck, her head buried in his shoulder.

'I thought you were hungry, Lorna,' he said.

'I'm not.'

Her head was shaken.

'Maurice shouted at her,' Bryan said. The smaller of the two boys – lean-featured, dark-eyed, dark-haired – his figure contrasted strangely with that of his more gravely-featured, fair-haired, younger brother.

'What did he shout at her for?'

'She wet the floor.'

'Not again?'

Keith, wearily, glanced at the back of his sister's head.

The tiny figure wriggled closer.

'That's no need to shout,' Attercliffe said.

'He was telling Mum that Gavin beat you up.'

'Who's Gavin?'

'Mummy's friend.' Keith laughed.

His brother flushed.

'He's younger than me,' Attercliffe said.

'And stronger.'

'Only half as strong,' he said.

'It doesn't look it.'

Lorna looked from her brother to her father, then to the bruise behind Attercliffe's ear: she touched it with her finger.

Attercliffe cried out.

She laughed.

'I'm sure he has to shout,' he said, 'to make himself heard.'

'We hardly make a sound,' Keith said.

'How about Lorna?'

Her small, slight arm was flung around his neck; she buried her face once more in his shoulder. 'I never say anything,' she said.

'Can't you beat up Gavin and Maurice?' Bryan asked. As the older brother something of his concern was reflected in his dark-eyed look, his slender features suffused with colour, his cheeks gaunt, his mouth firm-set.

'Why should I beat them up?' Attercliffe eased the weight against his neck and felt the damp of Lorna's tears run down inside his collar.

'Gavin hit you.'

'Only,' Attercliffe said, 'in self-defence. I'm too old for fisti-cuffs,' he added.

'We'll be coming back home, in any case,' Keith said.

'Who says?'

'Mum. She has to sort out the legal side.'

'What legal side?'

'She rings up her solicitor.'

'What about?'

'Coming back here.'

'I want to come back,' Lorna moaned by Attercliffe's ear: her body vibrated.

'You can always come back here,' he said, and added, 'As often as you like.'

'I'd like to come back as well,' Bryan said. 'But there's never any room.'

'At Maurice's,' Keith said, 'we have a bedroom each.'

'I don't like it on my own, Dad,' Lorna said.

'She's always coming into my room,' Bryan said.

'It's super,' his brother said, 'at Maurice's. He lets us drive his car.'

'In the road?'

'In the driveway.'

'If Mum didn't live there would you want to live at Maurice's?' his brother asked.

'I wouldn't mind.' Keith flushed.

'I wouldn't want to.'

'I want to come back home, Dad.' Lorna kicked her legs against Attercliffe's stomach: her shoes dug into his thighs. 'So does Mummy,' she added.

'When Maurice talks to her she cries.' Bryan, after finishing his food, got up from the table.

'I don't want to hear any more about it,' Attercliffe said. 'If Sheila wanted me to know she'd tell me.'

'She asks us things about you,' he said.

'What sort of things?'

'Who rings up. Who you see. How often you go out.'

His brother ate more quickly.

Lorna kicked her feet more briskly.

'She always mopes around Maurice,' Keith announced.

'Who does?'

'Lorna. She hangs around his neck. He's pretty sick of her, I reckon.'

'I don't like him,' Lorna said.

'Why go after him, in that case?' her brother asked.

Lorna bowed her head; her arm tightened around Attercliffe's neck: he drew her head towards him.

'Don't you want your food?'

She moaned.

'She's like that all the time with Mum,' Keith said. 'She's never very happy.'

'I am.' The confirmation came from within Attercliffe's chest, a half-tortured exclamation: she raised her head; her tiny hand picked up a fork and, her body racked by spasms, she began to eat.

The first mouthful was followed by a second: the fork was lowered.

Having finished their food, the boys rushed out, calling, 'Is Janet coming over?' and disappeared, without waiting for an answer, to the drive, their voices echoing between the houses and joined by the shouts of several others from the road itself.

'I'm not very hungry,' Lorna said.

'You don't have to eat it,' Attercliffe said.

'They haven't washed up.'

'That's right.'

'Maurice always makes them.'

'Does he?'

'He won't let them go until they have.'

'It sounds a good idea,' he said.

He took her through to the living-room; they looked at a book: he read a story.

'Are you going out?' she asked.

'This afternoon,' he said.

'Mummy says you never spend any time with us.'

'I have to work at weekends,' Attercliffe said.

'Why don't we stay here in the week, and go and see Mummy at the weekend?'

'It was,' he said, 'your mother's choice.'

She kicked her heels against his legs.

'I don't like Janet coming.'

'Why not?'

'She shouts.'

'I shall come back especially early,' he said. 'As soon as the match is over, and I've phoned in my report.'

'Then you'll have to go out Sunday.'

'Only in the afternoon.'

'Then Mummy comes and picks us up.'

'It's my work,' Attercliffe said. 'We couldn't live without the money.'

'Maurice is always there,' she said.

'Not always.'

'Nearly always.'

Through the window they watched the heads of Keith and Bryan as they dashed to and fro in the road outside: their voices, together with those of several other boys, echoed amongst the houses.

'Don't you want to play out with Audrey?' He mentioned a friend in a neighbouring house.

She shook her head.

'Where's Cathy and Elise?' she asked.

'They're out,' he said, and added, 'Shopping.'

'What are they buying?'

'I've no idea.'

'I don't feel very happy,' she said.

'I want you to be happy,' he said. 'I love you very much.'

'If you love me,' she said, 'why are you never there?'

'I am here, Lorna,' Attercliffe said.

'You're always out at work.'

'Not always.'

'Mostly,' she said, a word, he assumed, she had learnt from her brothers.

'Your mother also loves you, as I'm sure does Maurice, and she, and he, want to spend their time with you as well. When you're older you can come and stay with Elise and Cathy.'

'Mummy could have Elise and Cathy, and me and Keith and Bryan can come and live with you.'

'If that,' he said, 'is what your mother wants.'

'We'll be coming here in any case,' she said.

'It hasn't been decided.'

'Aren't you and Mummy friends?'

'We are.'

'Why are you always quarrelling?'

'We aren't.'

'Maurice says you are.'

'How does he know?'

'He says to Mummy, "You're always quarrelling with me the same way that you quarrelled with your husband."' She added, 'That's you.'

'That's right,' he said. 'It is.'

A car went past; the boys in the road stood back.

'Your mother and I wouldn't like to live together,' Attercliffe added. 'Which doesn't mean,' he went on, 'we don't love you very much.'

'Do you love me as much as Mummy does?'

'Just as much.'

'As much as Maurice does?'

'More.'

'Why more?'

'I'm your father.'

She turned her gaze to the window.

'Why are you my father?'

'Because I married your mother.'

'Audrey's mother and father have always been married.'

'I know.'

'Why aren't you?'

'Your mother and I decided we didn't want to be,' Attercliffe said.

She kicked her legs, glanced at the wall, then returned her gaze to the window: a group of boys came into the garden, retrieved a football, and went out again.

Footsteps thundered down the drive; the back door was opened: the cold tap ran. The door was slammed: footsteps ran back along the drive.

'Bryan and Keith like coming back.'

'They do.'

'I do.'

'That's right.'

'When Mummy comes back, we can all come back for ever.'

She picked a scab on her knee; then, when he distracted her, she picked at a scab on the other.

'How did you fall down?'

'Someone pushed me.'

She got down from his knee and added, 'I'm going to the lavatory.'

She started upstairs; he went back to the kitchen and began to clear up: by the time he'd washed the pots and she hadn't returned he went out to the hall and called, 'Are you all right?' and, getting no answer, still carrying the tea-cloth, went upstairs.

She was sitting on the floor of Catherine's room gazing at a book of drawings.

'Have you been to the toilet?'

'I'm just going.'

She put the book down, got up and, after glancing back at it, and then at him, went out to the landing, opened the bathroom door, climbed up on the toilet, climbed down, came out, went back in, pulled the chain, came out again and said, 'Can I bring Audrey?'

'Sure.'

She ran swiftly down the stairs, across the hall and out of the door: her voice called from the road outside.

Attercliffe went in to his 'study'; removing the drawers from his desk he carried them one by one to his bedroom and placed them by his bed: returning to the back-bedroom he carried the shell of the desk along the landing and, having set it in position beneath the window, reinserted the drawers and for a while gazed down at the group of boys who, no longer playing football, were sitting on the wall, listening to what Bryan and Keith, alternately, had to tell them.

Further along the road Lorna appeared with her diminutive friend and, hand in hand, ran along to the house.

The back door slammed; footsteps thundered up the stairs: a moment later Lorna called, 'What's happened to the desk?'

The tea-towel in his hand, Attercliffe returned along the landing.

'I've moved it to my bedroom.'

'Why?'

'It gives you more room.'

Now the back bedroom was occupied only by a bed and a chest of drawers and a chair.

Audrey, a pigtailed, dark-eyed child, wearing a tartan dress, white stockings and a pair of sandals, was already busy on the floor amidst a collection of Lorna's toys which, before her arrival, Attercliffe had set out for her.

'Can it stay like this for good?'

'It can.'

She clapped her hands, jumped up and down, noticed the effect this had on the floor, and jumped again.

Her friend, springing to her feet, jumped also.

'If you want the house to stay up,' he said, returning downstairs, 'you'd better play quietly.'

A short while later, whistling, he was standing at the kitchen table, peeling potatoes, and preparing the Saturday lunch.

10

'What's new?' Morgan unfastened the lid of his typewriter case, rolled in a sheet of paper, typed out the date, examined his watch, set his stop-watch, licked his lips, pulled down the brim of his trilby hat, glanced to the pitch and, adjusting the binoculars suspended around his neck, announced, 'I saw your piece. Branching out. A new line of country,' he added, 'entirely.'

The box at Garrilston had central heating, a fitted carpet, upholstered chairs and, for those who got there early, individual desks; the roof, however, was characterised by an overhanging cornice which, while directing the eye to the pitch below, threw up a glare from the stand: it was for this reason, perhaps, that Morgan was wearing a pair of dark glasses.

'Dougie must be pleased.'

'That's right.'

'Not to mention,' Morgan removed his glasses and glanced along the row at Davidson-Smith, 'Phyllis.'

'Phyllis must be pleased,' Davidson-Smith responded. 'Also' – he, too, glanced along the row of attentive heads – 'I should think, very, very grateful.'

'Freddie not with you?' Morgan inquired.

'That's right.' Attercliffe got out his notes, placed them on the desk, unscrewed his pen and waited to write.

'"Actress of Our Time",' Davidson-Smith continued.

'I like the "our",' Morgan said. 'Gi's us all a bloody chance.'

Davidson-Smith remarked along the bench, 'I gather Freddie's got cancer.'

'You'd better ask him,' Attercliffe said.

'No need to get bolshie,' Morgan said. 'Theatrical correspondent on the *Northern Post*. We all,' he glanced once more along the row of heads, 'have to bloody well start somewhere.'

Davidson-Smith took out a hip-flask, unscrewed the top, poured out a measure, drank, coughed, screwed the top back on, and announced, 'Colder today than it was last week.'

Attercliffe examined his programme; players ran out on to the pitch: several did exercises, others ran up and down.

A ball was passed, another kicked.

A figure subsided on to the bench beside him, wheezed, and said, 'Ought for me to do this week?'

Fredericks's cheeks were blotched, his eyes red, his short-cropped hair covered in dust: he smelled not only of drink but perspiration.

'You'd better get off home,' Attercliffe said.

'I've just paid off the taxi, Atty.'

'Get another one,' he said.

'Can't.'

'Why not?'

'The bloody bar's still o'ppen.'

Two figures came together at the centre of the pitch: a coin was tossed; the fanfare changed to a pop-tune.

Fredericks's hands shook as he endeavoured to light a cigarette.

'I'll give you a hand,' Attercliffe said.

The cigarette dropped into Fredericks's lap.

Attercliffe added, 'Let's go down and have another.'

'Say when.' Fredericks struggled to his feet.

Someone else stood up: the roar of the crowd intensified; a whistle sounded on the pitch below.

'Do you want a hand?' Davidson-Smith inquired.

'He'll be all right,' Attercliffe said.

'Since when,' Fredericks said, 'have I needed a hand from Wichita-Jones?' He reeled, staggered through the press-box door and, defying any attempt by Attercliffe to hold him – his arms outstretched, his legs flung out – landed at the bottom of the steps outside.

When Attercliffe reached him he was endeavouring to rise, feeling with his hands at the floor: his shoulders hunched, his head stooped, he said, 'I've lost my matches,' and, inconsequentially, as Attercliffe dragged him to his feet, 'My cigarette, an' all.'

'How are you, Freddie? Do you want a lift?' Morgan stooped by Attercliffe's shoulder.

'I dropped my matches,' Fredericks said and, ignoring Morgan, added, 'Did I tell you, wi' nought to lose, I've decided to gi'e up smoking?'

'I'll call an ambulance,' Attercliffe said, and as a roar went up from the crowd and Morgan looked up, dark-glassed, to where his typewriter could be seen on the desk, several feet above his head, he added, 'There might be one waiting. I shan't be a minute.'

The curtains were drawn; no lights showed at the windows: only when he tried to open the back door and found it locked did he hear a stirring in the living-room and a moment later a figure appeared behind the two glazed panels and Sheila's voice inquired, 'Who is it?'

He went round to the front: there, too, Sheila's figure materialised behind the frosted panels.

The bolt was drawn: the door swung back.

'Is anything wrong?' he asked her.

'I've come back home.'

She smiled.

'Where are the children?'

'The boys are in bed. So is Lorna. Cathy and Elise are out.'

Having switched on the light in the hall, she switched it off.

When he followed her into the living-room she was yawning and stretching, the light on.

On the settee, the shape of her body was outlined in the cushions.

'You'll have to leave,' he said.

'I've every right to come back,' she said.

'The law,' Attercliffe said, 'is on my side.'

'I'm sorry, Frank,' she said. 'You'll have to lump it. I've come back now and I mean to stay. All my things,' she added, 'are in the bedroom.'

'In that case,' he said, 'they'll have to come out.'

'No doubt,' she said, 'being a man, you can put them in the street. I shall only shout and scream.' She smiled, touched her hair, and added, 'I can't see that it will do the children a lot of good. Particularly Lorna.'

Attercliffe sat down.

'You left of your own free will,' he said.

'Our relationship,' she said, 'had broken down.'

'You made no mention of it,' he said, 'until the night you left.' He added, 'You made a new life. A better life. "Infinitely better". You wrote it, I remember, at the top of the page.'

'Do you still have the letter?'

'I've given it to my lawyer,' he said.

'Do you want a cup of tea or coffee?'

'I don't want anything,' Attercliffe said.

He went upstairs to look at the room. Two suitcases were standing on the floor: two further suitcases were lying on the bed, unpacked.

He went through to the boys' room; they were both asleep. In Lorna's room a night–light burned: he removed her thumb from her mouth and turned off the light.

'I've made myself some tea. Are you sure you wouldn't like some?' she said when he went back down.

'I'll pack your things,' Attercliffe said. 'Ring up Maurice and tell him you're coming.'

'I'm not going back,' she said. 'I've made that clear not only to Maurice but to Gavin. I've also made it clear,' she added, 'to the children. They know,' she concluded, 'that I'm back for good.'

He returned upstairs; he had already repacked one case and had started on the second when he heard her bring the telephone into the hall.

'Is that the police?' she asked, and added, her voice directed to the stairs, 'I wonder if someone could come and help me. I've no one here except my very young children. My husband has attacked me.' She gave a maundering cry. A moment later, more soberly, she gave her name and address.

He completed the packing of her clothes and took two of the suitcases down to the hall. He returned upstairs and, lifting the two remaining suitcases, was halfway down the stairs when – her hair dishevelled, her blouse torn – she came out of the living-room and started to scream.

Her screaming reverberated inside the narrow hall. Attercliffe put the suitcases down at the foot of the stairs and Sheila, uncertain of his intentions, opened the front door and stepped out to the drive.

Attercliffe closed the door and locked it.

Her screams intensified; doors opened; a voice called out.

Amidst her screams came the cry, 'Don't hurt me,' then, more specifically, 'Don't beat me! Don't!'

The glass in the living-room window broke: fragments fell behind the curtain.

He went out to the hall, picked up the phone and, with her screaming through the broken glass, called the doctor. A muffled voice answered the other end; he held the telephone in the direction of the window: the doctor, after suggesting he should call an ambulance, inquired, 'Her usual, would you say, or something worse?'

'Worse,' Attercliffe said. 'She's off her head.'

'I'll call the ambulance myself,' the doctor said. 'I'll be there inside ten minutes.'

Glass broke in the kitchen.

He unlocked the front door and went out to the garden.

Several people had collected in the drive; only as he drew nearer did he recognise a man in a dressing-gown and slippers and a woman, also in a dressing-gown, from a house across the road.

'Perhaps you'd like to help?' he asked the man.

He led the way down the drive, past the car, and found Sheila, her shoulders hunched, her fists clenched, screaming on the lawn at the back of the house.

'I've called the doctor,' Attercliffe said, and added, 'This is a neighbour from across the road.'

Lights had gone on in the surrounding houses.

'He attacked me,' Sheila said.

'The doctor,' Attercliffe said, 'can examine your wounds, and decide,' he went on, 'if they're self-inflicted.'

She looked up at the man, and might have collapsed, only, moving forward – recognising her intention – the man took her arm and then her waist: he turned her to the house.

'If you can take her to yours,' Attercliffe said. 'I'm not having her back in mine. Or, conversely,' he added, 'you can leave her in the road.'

She was still screaming, some time later, when the doctor's car drew up: Attercliffe, by that time, had relocked the front door and gone upstairs.

The doorbell rang; when he went down a policeman was

standing on the step: from across the road the screaming of Sheila continued.

A moment later it stopped.

'Come in,' Attercliffe said and, having secured the door, showed the policeman into the living-room.

'Your wife reported an assault,' he said.

'I haven't touched her,' Attercliffe said. 'For the past two and a half years she's been living with another man. I found her here when I came home this evening and asked her to leave. She threatened, if I insisted, she would create a scene, the effects of which,' he indicated the broken glass beneath the curtain, 'you can see around you. Apart from that,' he concluded, 'there are three children asleep upstairs.'

'Mrs Attercliffe is your wife?' the policeman asked.

'We've been separated,' Attercliffe said, 'for over two years. I don't want her back.'

'She'll have to go somewhere.' Perhaps not much older than Elise, the policeman glanced around the room: the rim of his helmet was imprinted across his brow, his fair hair ruffled, his blue eyes alert.

'I'll give you the address you can take her to,' Attercliffe said. He went upstairs, tore a sheet out of his notebook, wrote Maurice's name and address on it, and went back down.

The policeman, having drawn back the curtain, was standing by the window.

'I called the doctor earlier. Otherwise,' he gave him the sheet of paper, 'that's where she lives.'

He accompanied the policeman back to the door.

'I'll leave her cases outside,' he added.

'Our policy,' the policeman said, 'if it's a domestic quarrel, is not to intervene.'

'It's a public quarrel,' Attercliffe said and, having opened the door, took out the first of Sheila's cases.

He was taking out the last when the screaming started again.

'She says you've assaulted her,' the policeman said.

'I'm telling you,' Attercliffe said, 'I haven't.'

The ringing of an ambulance bell came from the end of the road.

'And this is the address?'

'That's right.'

'I'll be back to you in a minute.'

Some time later the doctor came across; grey-haired, moustached, dishevelled, he said, 'I've sent her off to hospital to quieten her down. You haven't got a sup of ought, then, have you?'

He came into the kitchen, red-cheeked, dark-eyed, took the glass Attercliffe offered him, and returned to the living-room where, drawing back the curtain, he surveyed the damage. 'Not like the old days,' he announced. 'Now nobody knows whether they're coming or going. I ought to warn you. She'll kill herse'n if she's left like this. You'll have to have her back, tha knows.'

'No thanks.'

'She's not equipped for this liberation.'

'I think she is,' Attercliffe said. 'There's more in Sheila than you imagine. It's because she is that I insist she shouldn't come back. She's only relapsing into what she was. Out there,' he added, 'she stands a better chance.'

'If you can't better 'em you've to butter 'em,' the doctor said. 'It's t'on'y thing they understand.'

'I'll sell the house,' Attercliffe said, 'and give her half.'

A door was closed in the road outside; a moment later the doorbell rang. When the policeman came in the doctor said, 'There's no question of assault, officer. No signs of marks or bruises,' and, calling, 'Good night,' went out to his car.

A little later, after Attercliffe had outlined, in detail, the events of the evening, footsteps sounded on the stairs and across the hall, and the living-room door was opened. Bryan came in: his eyes half-closed, he gazed from Attercliffe to the policeman and back again.

'I came for a drink.'

'I'll come up,' Attercliffe said, 'and tuck you in bed.'

With one more look at the policeman Bryan went: a moment later, coming back in, he said, 'The window's broken in the kitchen.'

'We'll get it mended on Monday,' Attercliffe said.

He went back out; the tap was run: a moment later the sound of his feet came from the stairs. His bedroom door was closed.

'I'll let you know if we take these inquiries any further,' the policeman said. 'It's largely up to Mrs Attercliffe. We'll be in touch.'

The sound of his car engine, a short while later, faded in the road.

When Attercliffe went upstairs, Bryan was asleep; only as he resecured his blankets did the boy raise his head, and ask, 'Have we had a burglar?'

'An accident.'

'Mummy came back.'

'I know.'

Almost instantly, his blankets rearranged, he fell asleep.

'They're doing tests,' Fredericks said. 'The nurses,' he went on, 'are bloody murder.'

He lay back against the pillows, his sheet and blankets and cover rumpled.

His chin was unshaven, his eyes glazed.

'Now they've got me in I'm afeared they won't let me go again.'

Attercliffe said, 'They sound pleased with you.' He indicated the nurse who, having shown him in, was busying herself at a desk in the adjoining alcove of the open-fronted ward.

'They're pleased with ought in here,' Fredericks said. 'Particularly if you're deein'.'

'Sheila's in here as well,' he said. 'She's in the psychiatric wing.'

Fredericks pulled himself a little higher, revealing, beneath his pyjama jacket, the pale expanse of his paunch. 'What's Maurice got to say?'

'I haven't got hold of him yet.'

'What about Gavin?'

'Nor him either.'

'What about the children?'

'I'm bringing them up this evening.'

Fredericks rubbed his head; his cheeks were flushed, his lips dry: intermittently he flicked out his tongue and wet them.

On a cupboard, beside the bed, lay a copy of the paper.

'I saw thy report.'

'That's right.'

'Venturing out i'to summat else has given you a fresh perspective.' The half-glazed expression of the eyes was replaced by something brighter: he drew himself upright and, as he leant forward, Attercliffe reset his pillow.

'What are these tests for?' he asked.

'A formality.' He waved his hand. 'Suggest I should gi'e o'er smoking, get off the bottle, and walk fifteen mile a day. Damn it all.' He coughed; phlegm rattled in his throat: he drew his hand across his mouth, looked round, and added, 'I fell down a flight of steps. Any man my age could do the same.'

Occupying one corner of the fourth floor of the hospital block, the windows of the ward looked out across the town, or, at least, across that portion of the town that could be glimpsed in a northerly direction: fading in the evening light lay the line of the valley slope.

The brightness in the ward intensified, irradiating the whiteness of the paintwork, the sheets, even the pallor of Fredericks's face: a book, its spine uppermost, lay open on the bed.

'What are you reading?' Attercliffe asked.

'Nought.' He tapped it with his hand, 'Plays. Done anything in that line lately? Don't gi'e up because I'm no longer theer.' Aimlessly, he added, 'Is she likely to be in for long?'

'She came to the house,' Attercliffe said. 'When I asked her to leave she called the police, broke the windows, and made me,' he concluded, 'a local pariah.'

Fredericks, after gazing past him to the nurse at the desk, closed his eyes, and said, 'Thy misjudgment of women is something which, even in my old age, I shall never understand.'

Later, when Attercliffe left, he went up to the psychiatric wing: he didn't go into the ward, although, from the door, he could see the corner of Sheila's bed.

'I shouldn't advise you to see her,' the nurse on duty said. 'Your daughters came this evening and cheered her up no end. She says her two sons are coming shortly. Maybe next week,' she added, 'would give her a better chance.'

At home, when he arrived, a group of people whom Attercliffe had never seen before - jeaned, booted, ringleted, beaded - was assembled in the living-room: music vibrated from the open door; on the sideboard stood the twin speakers of Elise's record-player, taken from her bedroom. The air was full of smoke. For a while, amidst the shouts and the bursts of laughter, his arrival went unnoticed.

'You have a visitor,' a figure finally announced, and Catherine, jeaned and sweatered, her hair in pigtails, appeared from behind the door and said, 'Mum all right?'

'I haven't seen her,' Attercliffe said.

'We went this evening.' She indicated Elise, bloused and jeaned, sitting cross-legged on the floor by the fire.

'Where's Lorna?'

'Upstairs.'

'And the boys?'

'They're out.'

'Where?'

'Dunno.' Already, turning away, she added, 'Playing.'

He closed the living-room door; the kitchen was occupied on all its flat surfaces by used utensils.

He went upstairs; Lorna, asleep but dressed, was lying on her bed.

He stroked her head; she woke, looked up, and when Attercliffe said, 'Shall you get into your night things?' she stood, raised her arms, and allowed him to undress her.

'I don't like all that banging,' she said.

'I'll go down and turn it off,' he said.

'I'm hungry,' she said.

'I'll bring you something up.'

'In bed?' she said.

'The two of us together.'

She went to the bathroom, came back, and said, 'There's someone there.'

When he went out to the landing a youth, buttoning his flies, emerged from the bathroom; after glancing into Elise's and Catherine's bedroom, he clattered down the stairs.

Water was splashed about the bathroom floor; a yellowish liquid occupied the basin.

He wiped the floor, allowed Lorna in, took her back to bed, went back to the bathroom, washed out the basin, went downstairs, opened the living-room door, took the gramophone needle off the record, and said, 'I want you all to leave.'

'All of us?' Catherine said.

'I'd prefer you and Elise,' he said, 'to stay.'

'If my friends can't stay,' Catherine said, 'neither can I.'

'They can come back,' Attercliffe said, 'another time.'

'Let's get out of here,' his daughter said. 'I can't stand this place another minute.'

The figures cascaded across the hall; the front door banged. Only Elise was left behind.

'I'd prefer you,' Attercliffe said, 'to clear up.'

He went out to the kitchen.

He heard her, a moment later, straightening the chairs; when she came through to the kitchen she said, 'I thought it was pretty poor.'

'That's right.'

'Catherine will never forgive you.'

'There are a lot of things she will never forgive me,' Attercliffe said. 'This is only one of them.'

'Turning her out.'

'This is my home,' Attercliffe said. 'My home,' he went on, 'as well as hers.'

'Some home,' she said.

'It's not through want of trying,' he said. 'There are five other people living here, apart from Cathy.'

'I don't mind them coming,' she said.

'So it seems.'

She looked round at the crockery and said, 'That's Cathy's mess. She cooked them a meal.'

'Is this the stuff they've been smoking?'

'It could be.'

He indicated the residue in one of the saucers.

'It's only hash.'

'This is a home, not a dope den,' Attercliffe said.

'Why have alcohol?' she said.

'Alcohol,' he said, 'is taken in moderation. Nor does it stone people in front of Lorna.'

'It's no different,' she said, 'from everything else.'

'If you'd help to clear up the mess,' Attercliffe said, 'I'd deem it a very great favour.'

He took the tray upstairs; Lorna, a doll propped beside her, smoothed out the sheet, looked at the food, and said, 'Only cornflakes?'

'What else would you like?' he asked her.

'I thought you were cooking something,' she said, yet nevertheless took the spoon and began to eat. 'Have those people gone?'

'That's right.'

'Do I have to go to sleep?'

'As soon as you've eaten,' he said, 'you ought to try.'

The large round eyes examined the wall, the back of the door and, finally, the ceiling.

'Is Mummy better?'

'A lot,' he said.

'Did they say anything about the window?'

'There'll be someone coming to mend it tomorrow,' he said.

She released the spoon and gazed before her; having sat on the bed he took her hand. 'I don't like all those people coming.'

'They won't be coming again,' Attercliffe said.

'Cathy says they will.'

'They won't.'

'Can I see Mummy?'

'Later,' Attercliffe said.

'I don't like sleeping on my own,' she said.

'Why not?'

'I don't like it.'

'Would you like to sleep with Elise?' he asked. 'I'll move you into Cathy's bed.'

'Where will Cathy go?'

'If she comes back,' he said, 'she can sleep in here.'

Her head sank lower, her chin tucked in against her chest: her tiny hands were knotted.

From downstairs came the sound of Elise stacking pots: the back door opened and Bryan's voice was followed by Keith's. The stacking of crockery recommenced.

'I don't want to sleep with Elise,' she said.

'In that case,' he said, 'you can sleep with Cathy.'

'Can't I sleep in your room?'

'We've been through that before,' he said.

Her head sank lower; he reached across and disengaged the tray from the bed: cornflakes were scattered across the cover.

Below, the telephone rang: feet scampered out to the hall; a moment later Bryan called, 'It's for you, Dad,' followed by a pause. 'It's Maurice.'

He went through to the bedroom, picked up the extension and, after Maurice had inquired, 'How is she?' answered, 'Better than she was.'

'Give her my regards.'

'Go in,' Attercliffe said, 'and tell her yourself.'

'I would. Only,' he said, 'I've learnt my lesson. You know what Sheila says. "Frank is an angel compared to you." She said the same to Gavin.'

'To me, too,' Attercliffe said, 'in reference to you.'

'She reads these articles about liberation and it turns out her only idea of freedom is to find the biggest cunt of the opposite sex and measure her liberation by his example.'

'I thought you wanted her back.'

'Betty wouldn't wash it.'

'Who's Betty?'

'Didn't Sheila tell you?'

Attercliffe shook his head, said, 'No,' and added, 'She didn't.'

'She's an attractive lady, recently widowed, with whom I have a very real and moving relationship at present.'

'More real than the one you had with Sheila?'

'That never got off the ground,' he said.

'After two and a half years?'

'People can be very peculiar, Frank. Sheila,' he went on, 'is a case in point. She's clearly much better off with you. Gavin feels the same. He says she's basically a one-man woman.'

'I don't want her back,' Attercliffe said. 'It's why,' he concluded, 'she's where she is at present.'

'She certainly can't come back here,' he said. 'Not only wouldn't it do her any good, but I don't think, legally, I'd allow it.'

'Why not?'

'She left,' he replied, 'of her own free will.'

The sound of a record came from below: its beat reverberated through the floor, across the wall, and shook the lamp suspended from the ceiling.

'If there's anything I can do,' Maurice added, 'ask. Short,' he went on, 'of what we mentioned.'

'My bed's wet,' Lorna said as he came out on the landing.

'What with?' Attercliffe said.

'Cornflakes.'

'I'll find a clean sheet,' he said. 'Short of that,' he added, 'you can go to sleep in Elise's room.'

'I'll stay in here,' she said, starting down the stairs.

The beat of the music intensified: her face lit up as she descended.

★

They were dancing together when Attercliffe reached the living-room; they looked up, laughing, as he stepped inside and, to their amazement – holding Lorna at arm's length – began to dance himself.

II

A haze covered the hospital forecourt and amplified the light from the lower windows: in getting out of the car, the boys stepped into a puddle.

They took Attercliffe's handkerchief, sponged down their jeans and, tip-toeing between the puddles, approached the lighted porch.

A lift took them up to the seventh floor; they walked along a corridor to a double door, pushed it open and, with several other visitors, passed amongst the beds, arranged in cubicles in groups of four.

Sheila, her hair drawn back beneath a ribbon, her face bright with make-up, was sitting up in bed.

'Keith.' She clapped her hands. 'And Bryan!' Embracing each of the boys in turn, she looked into the bags they'd brought: beside the bed itself stood a vase of flowers, a box of tissues and a bowl of fruit. 'I hope you're both behaving yourselves.'

The three other beds in the alcove were occupied by one younger and two older women; the latter were receiving visitors: an aged man, stoop-shouldered, sat beside each one.

The younger woman was knitting.

'How's Lorna?'

'She's very well.' Bryan pushed back his hair after Sheila had disturbed it.

'I miss her so much.'

'She misses you.' Keith allowed himself to be embraced, hanging in Sheila's arms while she tapped at his back, her eyes closed.

'You must tell her I miss her.'

'We do.'

'When I feel better you can bring her up.'

'She'd like to come,' Attercliffe said.

The clicking of the needles stopped; a page was turned on a knitting pattern: the woman counted numbers beneath her breath.

'I miss her so much,' Sheila said again. 'Whereas you boys, and the girls, can look after yourselves. You don't need me,' she added, 'at all.'

'Dad does a lot, Mum,' Keith responded.

'He's always washing up and cooking,' Bryan said.

'I'm sure you all do your share,' Sheila said.

The clicking of the needles recommenced.

She took Bryan's and then Keith's hand, tapping each in turn, and, indicating the bowl of fruit, she announced, 'You can have one if you like.'

The offer was declined.

'We must have a big party when I come out.'

'When are you coming out?' Keith asked.

'Oh, very soon. I feel so much better,' she said, 'already. And to hear,' she continued, 'you're managing so well.'

It was to Bryan that she turned, straightening his collar, retaining his hand, adjusting the front of his jacket, brushing back his hair.

'I'm okay,' he said, and backed away.

'Have a look round.' She indicated the ward. 'The nurses,' she went on, 'are very nice. So patient,' she added, 'and understanding.'

She lay back in the bed; the boys wandered off: Attercliffe, a moment later, could hear their feet stamp along the floor of the corridor outside.

'This is my husband, Wendy,' Sheila said.

The woman opposite smiled.

'Wendy's husband isn't available this evening,' Sheila added.

Returning to her knitting, the woman smiled again.

'Is there anything you need?' Attercliffe asked. 'Anything I can get you?'

'Peace of mind.' She examined a thread in the cover of the bed. 'It's not a lot to ask. It's not a great deal,' she went on, 'after all I've been through.'

'Maurice rang,' Attercliffe said. 'He sends you his regards.'

Leaning back, she gazed at the ceiling.

He added, 'So does Gavin.'

'The doctor says,' she said, 'I haven't to get upset. I want no further contact with either of those men.'

She smiled across the cubicle at one of the two older women, whose hand had been enclosed in both those of the stoop-shouldered man sitting beside her bed.

'Freddie is in here as well,' Attercliffe said.

'Is he?'

'Three floors down.'

'Anything wrong?'

'He's dying.'

'What of?'

'Cancer.'

She bit her lip, looked away, raised her head, and said, 'He's lucky.'

'You've everything to live for,' Attercliffe said and noticed that, rather than raising her voice, she'd lowered it.

'I've nothing to live for.'

'You have five children.'

'They don't need an additional burden,' she said. 'I was born before my time.'

From a distant cubicle came the sound of someone crying and the words, repeated like a chant, 'I can't! I can't!'

'I may be transferred from here,' she added. 'Therapeutic treatment goes on elsewhere.'

'Do they say when?' Attercliffe asked.

'Getting ready to throw me out again?' she said.

'It's something we'll have to discuss,' he said.

'Gavin and Maurice were good at discussing. They'll discuss anything,' she said, 'for hours.' She added, 'It's a man's world. Women's rights are another illusion.'

The young woman on the bed opposite looked up; to Attercliffe's surprise he saw she was crying: the tears, suspended from her chin, dropped on to her knitting. She wiped her wrist across her cheek, rolled up her wool and, getting up, crossed the alcove and said to Sheila, 'I haven't had a good cry for years.'

She returned to her bed, took out a handkerchief, blew her nose, turned and, crossing the cubicle, disappeared to the outer door.

'She's upset because there's no one to see her.'

'I thought she had a husband.'

'He never comes. Guilt is the only thing that brings them.' She gestured to the women in the other beds.

'You shouldn't let this bitterness get a grip of you,' he said.

'I shan't,' she said. 'Once I get home, everything,' she added, 'is going to be different.'

'That's something we'll have to discuss,' he said again.

'Discuss,' she said. 'We're back to that,' and added, 'It's all very well for you, offering advice to a woman. One, I might add, that you helped to destroy.'

'I did nothing of the kind,' he said.

'A woman is a victim in these situations. She is conditioned into submission, and when that submission ends in her destruction those who are responsible have to be called to account. The doctor here has mentioned that. "Your husband, Mrs Attercliffe," she told me, "is as much a part of this as you are."'

'Perhaps I could have a talk with her,' Attercliffe said.

'When I told her of the way I've been treated it was all I could do to restrain her from taking out a prosecution. She said, "A woman in this world, Mrs Attercliffe, doesn't stand a chance. We are all victims, and must stand together."'

The two male visitors raised their heads; tired faces gazed across the ward in Attercliffe's direction.

He could hear the footsteps of the boys coming back; a moment later they appeared at the cubicle entrance.

'Can we have some money for the shop?' they asked and, after Sheila had revealed, for their benefit, a sudden tear, he handed them the money and they scampered off.

'None of this is true,' he said.

'Isn't it?'

'It's propaganda.'

'Propaganda to you,' she said. 'Reality to me.'

'Why don't you concentrate on the practicalities?' Attercliffe asked.

She buried her face in a tissue taken from the box beside the bed. 'Such as?'

'The impracticality of you and me living in the same house. We'll have to sell it.'

She subsided into the pillow, turned on her side, and drew the covers about her.

'I've no intention of thinking of anything,' she said. 'Except myself. Which is all you've thought about,' she went on, 'all the years I've known you.'

'There isn't much time for self-absorption with a wife and five children to support,' Attercliffe said.

'The traditional patriarchal attitude,' she replied, her mouth half-turned to the pillow.

'Which doesn't exclude a matriarch,' Attercliffe said.

'Matriarch. Patriarch.' She laughed. 'Another sop. Like knitting, and looking after your children.'

The woman from the bed opposite returned.

Attercliffe got up and stretched his legs.

'The doctor suggested,' she added, 'I shouldn't even speak to you.'

'That's what you get,' he said to the three other women and the two other men, 'for doing her a favour.'

'Favours!' Sheila said.

She got up from the bed and would have picked up the vase of flowers or the bowl of fruit, only a figure in white appeared at Attercliffe's shoulder and a hand was laid on Sheila's arm and as the young woman across the cubicle, having sat down on her bed to recommence her knitting, began to laugh, and the two men stood up by the other beds, the white-gowned figure said, 'It may be better, Mr Attercliffe, if you leave,' while Sheila cried, '*I'll kill him!*'

From the bed opposite the laughter ceased and calls of inquiry came from the ward outside.

'It's a healthier response than all that other crap,' Attercliffe told the nurse who, drawing Sheila back, declared, 'Into bed, Mrs Attercliffe. You've been told about your temper,' and, finally, to Attercliffe, 'I really think you ought to leave.'

Nevertheless, she allowed him to take Sheila's other arm and, between them, they guided her back to the bed: she sat, lifted her legs, allowed her dressing-gown to be drawn around her and, the covers having been raised, she slid herself inside. Gazing at the nurse, she announced, 'Thank you,' and, a short while after, when the boys came in, she called, gaily, 'Good night, boys. I'm off to sleep,' scarcely raising her cheek, her eyes closed, as each stooped down to kiss her.

★

121

'Why will it do us good?' Bryan asked.

'Because,' Attercliffe said, 'it'll do Mr Fredericks good,' only, when they got out of the lift at the appropriate floor and saw the signs of discomposure in most of the faces in most of the beds in most of the alcoves on either side, he added, 'Apart from one or two players, there's scarcely anyone he sees.'

Fredericks had been moved from his previous alcove to a smaller one further along the ward; his colour, from its more traditional blend of red and white with bluish tinges, had faded to a uniform yellow. His eyes were shadowed, his cheeks drawn in.

'These thy young 'uns? O'd enough soon to look after thee,' he said.

'They were against coming in to see you,' Attercliffe said.

'That's the spirit,' Fredericks said to each of the boys. 'Do what thy's told, and not what thy wants. It goes against conventional opinion nowadays, but it's t'on'y advice thy should have.'

The boys drew up chairs to sit by the bed. Raising his head, Fredericks added, 'You haven't brought me a snifter?'

'I haven't,' Attercliffe said.

'Been to see your wife?'

'I have.'

'Better?'

'By the time we left.'

'This place'll do wonders,' he said. 'It's done wonders for me,' he added to the boys, 'already.'

'She's being moved to another hospital,' Attercliffe said.

'Be seeing less of you, in that case,' Fredericks said.

'I doubt it.'

'On the way theer, is it, or on the way back?' A disturbance took place inside his chest: he wheezed, coughed, and added, 'They've got me buttoned down.'

He indicated a harness which, restricting his movements, was attached to a framework at the head of the bed.

'I've had that many things pushed up, stuck in, pulled out, I've near nought left to come out inside.' He winked at the boys, adjusted the front of his pyjama jacket, and added, 'See thy does what thy faither says. Thy'll never get another chance.' He winked again.

*

122

'Is he going to die?' Keith asked when they were outside, and when Attercliffe decided to tell them, 'Yes,' they got into the car without adding anything; only when they were halfway home did Bryan ask, 'Will we go mad as well?'

'Why?'

'Our mother's gone mad already.'

'Your mother's only tired,' he said. 'Tiredness,' he continued, 'takes many forms. Mr Fredericks's is one way,' he concluded, 'your mother's is another.'

'Why do you call him Mr Fredericks?' Keith asked.

'Because he is Mr Fredericks to you,' he said.

Long before they had left, unable to concentrate on anything for very long, Fredericks, suddenly, had said, 'What do you think to pain?' and, without waiting for an answer, had added, 'It has to have a purpose. I never thought it had to have before, but now I'm beginning to wonder,' and, moments later, he had begun to hum a tune, lightly, his gaze directed beyond a glass partition to the ward from where a voice had called, finally, 'Singing again, then, Freddie?'

Bryan said, 'I don't think he knew we were there.'

'He asked about Sheila,' Attercliffe said.

'I think, after a while, he forgot who we were.'

Only when they were leaving had Fredericks looked across and, as he shook Attercliffe's hand, glanced down and said, 'If there isn't a reason, it all comes down to nothing-othing-o,' and, grasping Attercliffe's hand more tightly, concluded, 'Here's to the old times, Frank.'

'You didn't cry when we left Mummy,' Keith said.

'No,' he said.

'She doesn't mean as much.'

'She doesn't in some ways, Keith,' he said.

'How can you love someone one year,' Bryan said, 'and not the next?' He sat beside Attercliffe in the front of the car, Keith by himself in the seat behind.

'It only happens between the sexes,' Attercliffe said. 'In a family,' he added, 'it never quite subsides.'

'It has with Mummy.'

'Yes,' he said. 'It has with her.'

Only as they turned into the lane and approached the house did Keith remark, 'I'm glad we went. I didn't want to when we first set off. But,' he went on, from the seat behind, 'I shouldn't like to go again.'

'Why not?'

'Somehow I don't feel,' he said, 'we shall have to.'

The glare from the television was visible from the road but, a moment after the door was opened, the set was switched off, followed, an instant later, by Lorna's complaint, 'Why not?' then the living-room door opened and Elise came out and said, 'Would you like some tea?'

She brought it in on a tray; Lorna sat with her legs kicking against the settee: the boys each took a piece of cake and went to their room. Finally, taking a piece, Lorna sat on Attercliffe's lap, kicked his shins, tucked her head against his chest then, jumping down as she heard a record being played upstairs, banged up to the landing.

'How's Mum?'

'Argumentative.'

Cathy sat in a chair by the window; after her departure with her friends from the house, she had returned, without speaking, a short while later and, since then, scarcely a word had passed between them.

'Argumentative about what?' she asked.

'Her usual obsessions,' Attercliffe said.

'Obsessions to you,' she said, 'are realities to other people.'

'That's very much what she said,' Attercliffe said.

'She's had a hard life.'

'She has.' To Elise, he added, 'I appreciate the tea.'

'Appreciate,' Catherine said, 'like everything else.'

'How else should I describe it?' Attercliffe asked.

'Mum is in that hospital,' she gestured with her arm in the direction of the town, 'because of you.'

Attercliffe said, 'I don't see why.'

'Your whole life is based on prejudice,' she said. 'And prejudice,' she added, 'is depicted blind.'

'I thought,' Attercliffe said, 'that that was love.'

'Life,' she said, getting up from her chair and standing by the unlit fire, 'has moved on since the time when you were living it. It's gone a long way. The attitudes you have are no longer relevant. They denigrate,' she went on, 'everything of value.'

'Like what?'

'Like when I bring my friends home.'

'I don't want this place turned into a dope-den,' Attercliffe said.

Tossing back her head, her hands on her hips, she laughed. 'Like drinking alcohol.'

'I want Lorna, and the boys, to stand a chance.'

'Of what?'

'Of growing up without apeing their sisters.'

'It's better they follow their sisters' example than they follow yours,' she said. 'Just look at the place they live in, with windows broken, with never a meal,' she continued, 'ready on time.'

'I'm here as often as I can get,' Attercliffe said.

'This place is a shambles. And all the while,' she glanced at Elise, 'he's setting an example we ought to follow.'

'There are other values which operate in here, apart from mine,' Attercliffe said.

'There are,' she said, 'And those are mine. And Elise's. But not Sheila's. She's still caught,' she added, 'by the old mystique of male domination and female submission. Look around you. All your values are irrelevant, Dad. They represent everything that's finished. Whether it's running people out of your home, or driving our mother mad.'

'She isn't mad.'

'She's the next best thing.'

'The only illness she's ever had is listening to half-baked ticks like you.'

'Who's half-baked?'

'You are.'

Elise clapped her hands and began to stack the tray, collecting the cups and saucers.

'We're like orphans,' Catherine said. 'We can't have a mother and we don't have a father.'

'You've never once asked how Sheila is,' he said.

'I don't have to ask,' she said. 'I know. She'll go to that place, or one just like it, and in a few weeks' time she'll come back out in much the same shape as she was when she first went in. They'll make her more,' she went on, 'of what she was before.'

Elise went out; crockery rattled in the kitchen: voices went past on the pavement outside.

'Your attitudes to everything are no longer relevant. Your

125

attitudes to Benjie, your attitudes to my friends, your attitudes to me. You're a man,' she continued, 'who has outlived his time. None of the teachers, some of whom are older than you, at school, has any of your attitudes. They don't believe in crime and punishment. They believe in sympathy and understanding. They believe,' she concluded, 'in being free.'

'To me,' Attercliffe said, 'they look like people who've compromised with everything because they haven't the strength to do anything about it.'

'They're not like that at all,' she said. 'Those that are good reflect society and don't oppose it. They go out and meet it and don't strike back. They try to understand and not criticise. They offer sympathy instead of rebuke.'

The house, apart from the music from upstairs, was silent: Catherine dug her toe at the carpet. 'If it wasn't that your attitudes were so destructive, you could even describe them as comic, Dad.'

'You have such a clear-cut view of everything,' Attercliffe said.

'I don't have a clear-cut view at all,' she said. 'I expect to learn a great deal more, but not from people who have shut up shop.'

The room – not unlike the cubicle at the hospital, he reflected – had taken on the configuration of a prison cell. At the hospital, he recalled, there'd been bars on the windows: here there were the vertical folds of the curtains. 'There is no escape,' these folds announced; 'there is no escape,' beat the tattoo of noise above his head; 'there is no escape,' suggested the silence from the kitchen; 'there is no escape,' declared the estate of detached 'executive' dwellings; 'there is no escape' (his wife had told him): 'there is no escape' – he had had it, finally, on the authority of a dying friend.

12

'I inveigled you into getting me in.' Fredericks smiled. 'I wa' too
bloody freetened to do it mesen. I got drunk, made a scene, and
had you do it for me. A back-door job, and I wish to God I'd
cho'ssen a front 'un.'

His eyes moved from side to side; shadows ran from the corners
of his mouth and across each cheek: the backs of his hands had a
scoured look, the skin scaling along the fingers.

'They've taken me bowel out.' He drew back the bedclothes
and revealed a system of tubes running to a plastic receptacle on
the floor beneath the bed. 'If tha knows of any tablets I can take
I'd be very grateful. The fact is,' he pulled up the covers, 'none of
it is worth all this.'

Fredericks leaned forward and cried, so that Attercliffe, in holding him, could feel the harness on his back, and the pressure of the
tubing, and in that instant it was as if he were holding Keith or
Bryan, or Catherine or Elise, or even Lorna.

'I'm frightened.'

'There's no need to be,' he said.

'Think nought of this. It's not me, but only summat, tha knows,
I left behind.'

'Now I'm in here,' Sheila said, 'everything at home, I suppose, is
going well.'

'Not exactly,' Attercliffe said.

'Who's this girlfriend you're supposed to have?'

'She's already engaged.'

'That won't stop anyone from doing what they want,' she said.

127

They were walking in the grounds of Beaucliffe Hall: a chapel at one end of its Victorian façade balanced a conservatory at the other; from behind its glassed-in walls patients gazed out at the uncut grass and overgrown flowerbeds between which, along a meandering footpath, he and Sheila were walking.

'You were always very popular, Frank.'

'Not always, Sheila,' Attercliffe said.

'I've been let down,' she said, 'by everyone.'

'The children come and see you.'

'Do they?'

'They see it,' he declared, 'as an achievement. To have,' he went on, 'a mother who's mad.'

Bare-headed, her coat pulled up beneath her chin, her gloved hands fisted at her sides, she rapped her heels into the ash of the path and looked across the fenceless walls at the traffic passing in the road outside.

'I don't see anything to be proud about,' she said.

'Catherine admires you a great deal,' he said. 'There's scarcely a moment, when I'm in the house, that she isn't lecturing me about your example.'

'What example?'

'Only a real person could have reacted like you did. All the unreal people, like me, do nothing.'

Sheila smiled at a gardener who, straightening from digging up weeds in one of the flowerbeds, nodded, and smiled back at her in turn.

'How's your friend,' she said, 'who's dying?'

'He had his bowel removed,' he said.

Her stride lengthened; she stooped, watched the flicking of the ash from the toes of her shoes, and asked, 'How does he manage without one?'

'He has a container.'

'How awful.'

'He's talking of coming out. In one or two weeks,' he added, 'they hope to have him walking.'

Having crossed in front of the building, they approached the chapel with its metal-studded door.

'A God who gives you free will in order to have you suffer like this, to my mind, doesn't make sense,' she said.

She kicked her toes against the ash, first one toe, then the other.

'What about love?' Attercliffe asked.

'Don't talk to me about love,' she said. 'Talk to me about a gratuitous impulse. Talk to me about egotism. Talk to me about *fantasy*.'

'If there's such a thing as a gratuitous impulse,' Attercliffe said, 'there's such a thing as love.'

'Don't you understand?' She pointed to the chapel door from which, as they approached, two figures emerged: both women, one nodding, the other smiling, they passed on either side of Attercliffe and Sheila. 'Love,' she announced, 'is a get-out.'

'I'd have thought,' Attercliffe said, 'it puts us deeper in.'

'Oh, does it?' She started back, past the door of the chapel, towards the central door of the building. 'I never realised until I came here and listened to a vicar talking that all religions are based on despair. The world becomes unbearable and we start inventing another. On the one hand it doesn't matter what we do, on the other we feel pain and out of that grows the necessity to make ourselves as comfortable as we can. That comfort comes,' she went on, 'from gratifying ourselves by doing good, by being charitable, by having children, by taking an optimistic view of things. It's all,' she concluded, 'a gratuitous urge.'

The hallway of the building, as they entered, echoed to their feet for, unlike the corridors and wards, it was lined by flagstones: an interior of plastic chairs and tables was overlooked, on one side, by a counter at which, throughout the day, it was possible to buy items of food. A white-overalled figure stood here serving tea and coffee.

They sat at a table; Sheila stirred a plastic spoon inside a plastic beaker: the handle came out bent: she set the spoon by her plastic plate and ate a paper-thin sandwich.

'Every generous act,' she said, chewing, 'is part of the same egotistical urge.'

Picking up the plastic spoon, she bent it until, with a snap, it came apart.

'I felt it at the beginning. It really is a case of the Emperor's clothes. At first you're accused of paranoia, then certain things occur and you see how everything is pointless.' She laughed. 'Even if you are "saved", what's the purpose? "I am saved!"'

Although there were only two other people in the room – the two women from the chapel – one of them threw up her arms and called, in a strange falsetto, 'Alleluia!' and smiled in their direction.

'She believes you.'

'I don't see the point,' she said, 'in going on.'

'When you get out of here you'll feel differently,' he said.

'I can easily get out of here,' she said. 'I haven't been certified,' she added.

'Are you going to kill yourself after you come out or before you leave?' Attercliffe asked.

'You don't believe a word of it.'

'All this is a smoke-screen,' Attercliffe said, 'in preparation for your coming home.'

She shook her head; having raised her cup she drank her tea. 'It's one thing you've never understood.' She put the cup down. 'I've reached the point of no return.'

'Did you talk like this to Maurice?'

'Never.'

'How about Gavin?'

'I tried to make it seem it mattered.'

'They weren't convinced?'

'It was me who wasn't convinced. No matter how hard I tried, in the end I knew each one of them, like you, was only out for himself.'

The cafeteria was filling up.

'End of recreation time.' She picked up her gloves, got up, and led the way to the stairs which led, in turn, to her ward.

'I've been asked to see your doctor,' Attercliffe said.

'She never mentioned it.'

'It's a prelude,' he said, 'to your coming out.'

'I can come out of here,' she said, 'whenever I like,' but when they reached the first-floor landing and, at the far end, they could see the sitting-room alcove with its wooden-armed chairs turned towards a television screen, she began to cry.

'You don't have to stay,' Attercliffe said.

She said, 'Of course I have. To live in this society I need all the help they can give me.'

The corners of her mouth were wet; a dampness ran down on to the collar of her dress.

'Women are encouraged to strike out for themselves, and all they strike out for is something that men have prescribed for them already.' And when, a moment later, Attercliffe endeavoured to take her arm, she suddenly cried out, 'Don't *touch* me!'

'You've received the letter,' Butterworth said. 'I was hoping that you had.'

'It's the first I've heard of it,' Attercliffe said.

'Discussions have been going on for months.' He stroked his square moustache, first one way then the other. 'Decisions have to be made,' he added.

'What about Freddie?' Attercliffe asked.

'Freddie doesn't come into it.'

'He's talking of living,' he said, 'and coming back here in ten or twelve weeks.'

Leaning to his desk – a square, broad-shouldered man, with absurdly long grey hair – in shirt-sleeves, a worsted jacket draped on the back of his chair (the offices of the paper were grossly over-heated), Butterworth announced, 'The redundancy pay alone is worth it. Not to mention the prospect of another job.' He added, 'Use us as a reference. I'll write you a good 'un, you can be sure of that. Your recent work has taken a lift. I'll be sorry to lose you.'

He took a pipe from a rack on his desk, tapped its bowl against the flat of his hand and, reaching behind him to the pocket of his jacket, took out a pouch of tobacco and a box of matches.

'Thy's alus had this problem. As a professional athlete obliged in early maturity to find a new profession. There's also,' he continued, 'the problem of class. Professional rugby is a bloody long way, tha knows, from writing on entertainment. I know. I was a rugby union man myself.'

Butterworth's office looked out on to Norton Square: cars were parked around the central gardens, characterised not by trees but by a tarmacked playing-area given over to children.

Booth, his head gleaming in the light, passed across it and, stooping, got into a recently purchased car.

'You're a loner. Which is why you and Freddie got on so well.' He pressed his finger into the bowl of the pipe, depressed the mound of tobacco, and added, 'He taught you a lot. Stand you in good stead.'

'There's hardly an opportunity, at my age,' Attercliffe said, 'to find another job.'

'You mustn't give up,' Butterworth said. He added, 'We'll help you all we can.'

'How?'

'I have connections.'

'Where?'

'All over.' He struck a match. 'Didn't Freddie tell you it was coming?'

'Perhaps he was hoping I'd take over,' Attercliffe said.

Butterworth produced a cloud of smoke, puffed, produced another, took out the pipe, and said, 'We've to take account of rising costs. If this paper doesn't do summat drastic I'll be out of a job mesen.' He returned the pipe to his mouth. 'There was one notion, at one time, you might take o'er a pub.'

Attercliffe allowed his gaze to rise, above the square moustache, to the pugnacious-looking nose, then to the eyes – dark-brown, yellow-flecked and bushy-browed – then to the absurd avalanche, parted to one side, of greying hair.

'You could retire for a month or two on this.' He tapped the redundancy notice, still folded, with his finger. 'Rather than one door closing, another opens. There's still life, tha knows, o'er fifty.' He showed his teeth. 'Circumstances will not always remain,' he added, 'as they are at present.'

'They might get worse.'

'That's the spirit,' he said. 'Take the gloomiest view and the good news alus turns out better.'

He banged the desk with his hand.

'I'll pass on your complaints,' he added. 'I've already made my own views known. I hate to lose a good 'un. There are quite a few I shall have to say goodbye to at the end of this month.' He laughed. 'I may be saying goodbye to mesen in the not too distant future. Nobody's job is assured.'

Attercliffe got up, debated whether he might shake Butterworth's hand, and turned to the door. Butterworth pushed back his chair, got up and, extending his hand, called, 'We'll see you around in the next few weeks.'

Attercliffe glanced down, looked up and, having taken Butterworth's hand, said, 'If you don't do something with this you'll be likely to lose it,' and, having shaken it once, went out: the clattering of typewriters from the general office, together with the closing of the door behind, obviated any response that Butterworth might have made.

13

'What I don't understand,' Doctor Morrison said, 'is your need to antagonise your wife whenever you come.'

'I don't,' Attercliffe said.

It might, to some extent, have been a repeat of his interview with Butterworth: the attitude behind the desk, he reflected, was very much the same.

'You appear to be without any sympathy for her whatsoever.'

Beneath Dr Morrison's glasses her eyelids were tinted green, and marked with a line around the lashes: grey-green eyes gazed out like specks of light at the end of a tunnel. She smiled; lavender-tinted lips (a fashion popular with Elise) encapsulated a line of lavender-tinted teeth: her unbuttoned overall – revealing a buttoned blouse beneath – rasped against the desk: not only did she not look a great deal older than his eldest daughter, but she was having trouble with spots on either cheek, the upper contour of each of which was under-edged by a smear of rouge.

'A revolution,' she added, 'has taken place.'

'Recently?' Attercliffe asked.

'Quite recently,' she said.

Sheila's file was open on her desk; apart from an inconsequential drawing of a bird in flight attached to the wall, the room was devoid of decoration: filing-cabinets occupied all the available space not taken up by the desk, a visitor's chair and the window.

'Your wife's situation,' she went on, 'has changed. The transition, for a woman of her generation, has been difficult to make. For your daughters no such transition has had to take place. They have no need of the adaptative techniques necessary for, but not peculiar to, your wife.' She tapped on the file with a pen. 'Mrs

Attercliffe's independence can only be achieved by a great deal of assertiveness on her part. It's an act of courage, like plunging into the sea merely on the insistence of her instructor that once she is in she will know how to swim.'

'It doesn't seem to have done her,' Attercliffe said, 'a lot of good.'

'I realise a great deal of your attitude is merely obtuse.' The grey-green eyes ignited. 'It's the kind of obtuseness,' she went on, 'which, while antagonising your wife, merely impedes my trying to help her. I can do it,' she continued, 'with or without your co-operation, though naturally I'd prefer to take you with me.'

'She has had all the help I can give her,' Attercliffe said.

'Her problems are different from yours.' She raised her hand to her glasses, smiled, and added, 'In certain areas there is a recognition of this, in other areas not. Her principal concern,' she smiled again, 'is where she is going to live.'

Attercliffe leaned back. Sliding the pen between her thumb and finger, Doctor Morrison tapped at the file.

'Part of her strategy in going mad is to put herself into such a position that the offer of our home,' Attercliffe said, 'is the only solution.'

'She's been happy there in the past.'

'She won't be in the future.'

'The symptoms that you describe have a cause,' she said. 'She has sacrificed whatever opportunities she may have had in order to fulfil the traditional role of a mother. She is, in short, dependent on you. She needs a home. And specifically the home that you and she have created together.'

'She left it.'

'She wants to come back.'

'The house,' Attercliffe said, 'is all I've got.'

'What about the children?'

'All I care about,' he said, 'is the children.'

She dropped the pen on the folder. 'However motivated you say she is, these motives represent a legitimate need.' She took off her glasses, smiled, pressed her forefinger and her thumb against the corners of her eyes, blinked, replaced her glasses and said, 'One way of alleviating that condition is to provide her with a home in which she can live with her children.'

'She turned it down. It's why,' he went on, 'she threw this fit and got you to persuade me to let her have it.'

'All I'm proposing,' she said, 'is that your wife and children should live together.'

'What you're offering me,' Attercliffe said, 'is exclusion from my home.'

'All we've decided,' she said, 'is that you and your wife should live apart. The material advantages of this arrangement are entirely in your favour.'

Attercliffe stood up.

'Think about what I've said. Your wife, after all, has little left to lose.'

'You'll have to reconcile her,' Attercliffe said, 'to living in a smaller house, and with only those children who choose to live with her.' He added, 'She may have to go out to work as well. I've lost my job and the redundancy I've been paid will not be enough to keep either of us.'

'Perhaps when Mrs Attercliffe hears about your job,' she said, 'it will add a different complexion.'

'She'll be out of here in a flash.'

She smiled. 'I'd like to think,' she said, 'we both have the welfare of your wife at heart.'

Over his shoulder, from the door, she called, 'I'll see Mrs Harrison next.'

A gaunt, grey-haired, dark-eyed woman looked up from the row of chairs in the corridor outside.

The voice behind him called again.

The door closed.

The sound of voices, speaking simultaneously, came from behind the frosted glass.

'This is Benjie,' Catherine said.

Wearing a hat of variegatedly knitted wool, the jeaned and denim-jacketed youth stood up: his features were sharply defined, the forehead low, the mouth protuberant, the nose snubended.

'This is my father,' Catherine announced.

'Hello, Benjie.' Attercliffe shook his hand. 'We've almost met before.'

A second figure, too, stood up; over six feet tall, its hair close-cropped around a black and neatly-featured face, it too leaned across and shook Attercliffe's hand.

'This is Tiny,' Catherine added.

'Do you have another name?' Attercliffe asked.

'Steve.' The jeaned, dark-shirted, six-foot figure looked from Attercliffe to Catherine then back again.

'Make yourself at home,' Attercliffe said, and added, 'Have you had a cup of tea?'

Elise, sitting on the floor by the hearth, indicated a tray on the sideboard: music, as he had entered the house, had been turned down, and had been turned down further as he had entered the room itself, followed, the moment after he had come in, by the sound of Elise's laughter.

From overhead came the sounds of the boys and, amidst their voices, the plaintive call of Lorna.

Catherine announced, 'We were having a cup before Benjie and Tiny left. I cooked them a meal. We've washed up the pots in the kitchen.'

'Do you know this part well?' Attercliffe asked.

Benjie shook his head.

Tiny folded his muscled arms: his massive hands were fisted.

'No,' Benjie said. 'I've been up once or twice with Cathy.'

'Do you work in town, Steve?' Attercliffe asked.

Tiny shook his head, glancing across, then down.

'Have you thought of playing football?'

'All these questions!' Catherine said. 'It's not an interrogation, Dad.'

The two black figures laughed.

'It's a good way to earn a living,' Attercliffe said.

'And a good way, an' all, of getting hurt.' Tiny laughed, lightly, at Catherine, and Benjie laughed as well.

The two girls joined in.

'The pay in my day,' Attercliffe said, 'was less than it is at present. As for getting hurt, it's better than doing nothing.'

They laughed again: Elise drew up her knees, resting her chin against them, her mouth ajar.

'There's also the pleasure of playing,' Attercliffe said.

'I don't mind kicking a football around.' Tiny folded his hands behind his head. 'Doing it because I have to,' he gazed at the ceiling, 'is a different matter entirely.'

Benjie laughed – a high-pitched, gurgling sound, prolonged, and taken up by the figure beside him, then by Catherine and, finally, her gaze still fixed on the figures before her, by Elise.

'Mum any better?' Elise finally inquired.

'I didn't see her this time,' Attercliffe said.

'Cathy and I,' she said, 'go up tomorrow.'

'I'll give you some things to take,' he said.

'We ought to be going.' Benjie turned to the door.

'Don't go on my account,' Attercliffe said. 'I'll make some more tea,' and, picking up the tray, went through to the kitchen.

'Don't go yet,' and, 'You don't have to go,' had come, alternately, from Elise and Catherine, followed by a murmur as Attercliffe had closed the living-room door then, more clearly, 'Just because he's back,' followed, as he had entered the kitchen, by a high-pitched laugh.

He put on the kettle and went upstairs; the boys, a number of toys around them, were playing in their room: Lorna, lying on her eldest brother's bed, raised her arms to be lifted.

'Have they gone?' Keith said. Both he and Bryan were playing on the floor. 'They've been here hours,' he added.

'Not that long,' Bryan said.

Attercliffe picked his daughter up, sat down, and said, 'Go downstairs, if you want to.'

'I don't like them,' Keith said.

'Why not?'

'I don't.'

'There has to be a reason.'

'They're both criminals,' Bryan said. 'One of them's on trial.'

'You're innocent until proved guilty,' Attercliffe said.

'That's not what Cathy and Elise have said.'

From downstairs came the slamming of the door: a moment later, humming, Elise ran up to her room.

The door closed.

Lorna pressed her head against Attercliffe's cheek; taking her with him he returned downstairs.

The living-room was empty; in the kitchen the kettle steamed: no sooner had he prepared tea than the boys appeared, sat at the kitchen table, and started to eat.

'We can go and watch telly,' Keith said and, taking their food, they both departed.

Releasing herself from Attercliffe's knee, Lorna slipped down, ran to the door and joined them.

'Shut it,' came the cry from the living-room and, a moment later, the door was slammed.

He had scarcely tidied the kitchen than the back door opened and, red-cheeked from running, Catherine came in.

Slamming it behind her, the glass rattling in the panes, she said, 'Anything left?'

'I thought you'd eaten?'

'Ages ago.'

'Benjie and Tiny didn't have to leave,' he said.

'They only stayed out of politeness,' she said.

'Why?'

'I said you'd be coming back.' She looked in a cupboard, got out a tin of food, opened it, poured it into a pan, set it on the stove and, going to the bread bowl, got out a loaf of bread.

'Have you washed your hands?'

'Do I have to?' She ran her hands beneath the tap, dried them, then buttered the bread.

'How about a plate?' he asked.

'This is *purgatory*!' She slammed open a cupboard, got out a plate, slammed it down, picked up the bread, dropped it on to the plate, turned to the stove, stirred the food, and added, 'You made them feel at home.'

'That's good,' Attercliffe said.

'All those questions.'

'I invited them to stay. I offered them tea. I showed I was interested in what they did.'

'Tiny was impressed.'

'Why's that?'

'He doesn't meet many typical whites. When he does,' she added, 'unlike you, they invariably cover it up.'

'If he'd been white he wouldn't have had such a neurotic reaction,' Attercliffe said.

'If he'd been white,' she said, 'he wouldn't be where he is at present.'

'Does he live on the dole?' he asked.

'He might.'

She stirred the pan, looked round for a plate, went to the cupboard, got out a bowl, picked up the pan and poured the food out.

Steam rose in the kitchen: she dropped the pan in the sink.

'Why tell the boys he's a criminal?'

'He is.'

'How do you know?'

She bit the bread, pulled open a drawer, took out a spoon, closed the drawer, stirred the food, releasing a fresh cloud of steam, then, still chewing, raised a spoonful, blew across it, blew again, then sipped it.

'Elise told me.'

'How does she know?'

'He came to her college one afternoon and asked her to hide a gun and say he'd been with her all that morning.'

'Jesus.'

'You keep invoking him,' his daughter said, 'but it never seems to do much good.'

She blew on the spoon again, sipped, took a bite of bread, then, getting up, opened the fridge door, took out a bottle of milk, poured some of its contents into a glass and, returning to the table, sat, sipped, gasped, chewed and swallowed:

'Benjie, you'll be glad to hear, is in the clear.'

'He won't be going to prison?'

'They all got off.'

'How?' Attercliffe sat down.

'When the man they attacked was asked if he recognised any of the ones who attacked him he said, "All these blacks look alike to me."'

'How do you know?'

'I was in court.'

'You never told me.'

'I don't have to tell you everything, Dad.'

'Was that enough to get him off?'

'He was the only witness. Earlier he'd said he'd recognise all of them again, but at the parade he picked out all the wrong ones.'

She swallowed her food more quickly.

'What about their statements?'

'Benjie and his brother said they were intimidated by the police and made them under duress.'

'Benjie told you he did it.'

'You don't know how black people have to live,' she said. 'They only survive,' she added, 'by using the means that are used against them.'

'His brother stabbed a man,' Attercliffe said. 'Eight of them,' he added, 'tried to kick his head in.'

'He provoked them.'

She drank from her spoon again, slurped, sipped, blew, swallowed.

'I don't understand your preoccupation with these people,' Attercliffe said.

'Why not?'

'Coming from a home like this.'

'This isn't a home,' she said. 'It's an anachronism. What you don't understand,' she went on, 'is the persecution they have to endure, moral, spiritual, physical and economic. It's a war. No one wants to accept it as such, least of all the liberals. But it's a war of survival. *Their* survival. The whites,' she concluded, 'look after themselves.'

'Did the police intimidate them?' Attercliffe asked.

'They intimidate them by being what they are,' she said. 'If the world were a better place they wouldn't have to defend themselves. They'd live like you and me.'

'You're like your mother,' Attercliffe said. 'Right becomes wrong, reason unreason.'

She clattered the spoon in the bowl, rinsed the bowl beneath the tap, turned it upside down beside the sink, wiped her mouth on the sleeve of her jacket and said, 'Do you know what's written up outside the Fosters' house? "Any blacks here next week and this house will be burned to the ground." At night they have messages pushed under the door and regularly people knock at the window. Mrs Foster has to have medical treatment and her daughters are frightened to go out at night.'

'The police aren't superhuman,' Attercliffe said. 'They can only keep order in a society that wants it.'

'Benjie's parents want it.'

'They don't seem to have succeeded,' Attercliffe said, 'where Benjie and his brother are concerned. Not to mention Tiny.'

'Tiny was kicked out of his home by his parents.'

'Why?'

'His stepfather thought he'd become a criminal.'

'He had.'

'That's right.'

'Can you keep your voices down?' came Elise's voice from the stairs. 'It comes right through the ceiling.'

'To accommodate one injustice,' Attercliffe said, lowering his voice, 'you turn the whole of justice upside down.'

'It's a revolution,' Catherine said. 'No one wants to admit it. They prefer to pretend it isn't there, and scream like you when it's pointed out. Benjie and his brother, and Tiny, are people I respect. What legality has a law which accepts as uncontrollable the illegalities that are thrust on them? The whole of it,' she turned to the door, 'is an injustice in itself.'

All Attercliffe was aware of, apart from the music drumming through the adjoining wall – and a reciprocal drumming coming through the ceiling above his head – was the back of his daughter's skirt, her stockinged calves, her jerseyed shoulders, arms and waist – her hair suspended loosely down her back – as, uncertain which direction she might take, she turned to the living-room and, opening the door, inquired, 'What's on?'

The door banged to behind her.

He went upstairs; when he knocked on Elise's door and pushed it open he found her standing stripped to the waist and, stepping back, called, 'Could I come in?' to which a muffled voice replied, 'For Christ's sake, Dad, I'm only dressing.'

A jersey was being pulled over her head and the torso which, moments before, had been turned to a mirror was turned to the door.

'Did you know Tiny was a criminal?' he asked.

She laughed, picked up a raffia basket from her bed, took out a lipstick and, turning back to the mirror, began to paint her mouth.

'Are you going out?'

'I don't think so.' She tightened her lips, her brows puckered, then, her head drawn back, she examined the effect from a greater distance.

'He asked you to look after a gun.'

'Oh, that.' She ran her finger along her lower lip, stooping, peering at the mirror, then leaning back. 'Only for a morning.'

She glanced up.

'He only asked me to hide it.'

'If he'd killed someone with it, you'd be an accessory,' Attercliffe told her, 'after the fact.'

'What fact?' She returned her gaze to the mirror.

'Of murder.'

She laughed, examining the effect in the mirror then, turning to the bed, she picked up a tissue, wiped her lips, picked up a second tissue, wiped them more thoroughly, ran her tongue across them, wiped them again then, stooping to her raffia basket, took out a second lipstick, unscrewed the top, and applied to her lips the colour which, earlier that day, had characterised those of Doctor Morrison.

She said, 'Tiny wouldn't murder anyone.'

'Benjie,' Attercliffe said, 'had a damn good try.'

'That's his brother.' She moistened her lips with the tip of her tongue. 'He was innocent, in any case,' she added.

'He said he'd done it,' Attercliffe said.

Elise stooped, retouched her lips then, leaning back, inclined her head first to one side then the other. She examined her mouth through narrowed, mascaraed, eye-shadowed eyes. 'If he's innocent he can't be guilty.'

'Were you questioned about the gun?' he asked.

'He came in the afternoon and picked it up.'

'Doesn't any of this concern you?' Attercliffe said.

'Why should it?'

'That you're involved with people who thieve for a living.'

'If they lived in a society that wasn't racialist and didn't try all the time to cover it up they wouldn't have to be like they are,' she said.

'Not all of them are like that,' he said.

'The best of them are. The ones,' she said, 'who have any spirit.' As the record on the turntable came to an end she switched it off. 'I don't know why you go on about it, Dad. You'll end up like Mum. When you talk to Benjie and Tiny in the way you do, all you do is make them laugh. Pretending like the rest that what they do is wrong, yet condoning the world that compels them to do it.'

She replaced the cap on the lipstick.

'It's horrible sharing your room,' she added.

'When you leave home,' he said, 'you can do what you like.'

'I can't wait for it,' she said.

'I'll be losing my job,' he said, 'in a month.'

'What for?'

'Redundancy.'

'What will you do for a job?'

'Join Benjie's gang.'

'Wrong colour.'

'I could, following your logic, start one of my own.'

'I don't see you as a criminal, Dad.'

'Don't you care about how I feel?' He sat on the edge of Catherine's bed. 'I don't mean as your father, but as someone who is trying to do certain things with his life.'

Moving to the door she announced, 'All these values are only values to people who can afford them. It isn't that we don't love one another, but,' she went on, 'love, as Mum is finding out, means the opposite of what was intended.'

Her footsteps stamped from the stairs; the living-room door was opened; a crescendo of music intensified then faded.

14

Standing in a row, the sea lapping against their ankles, they gazed out at the brightly-illuminated bay: the sun was suspended to their right, above a projecting headland.

'It's cold.' The boys paddled out while the girls, distracted, wandered along the water's edge: only Lorna remained, holding Sheila's hand, periodically running back as the waves lapped higher – venturing out again, taking her mother's hand, distracting Sheila with her screams and shouts.

The boys were kicking a football; the girls wandered towards the headland, picking up shells, Catherine holding up her skirt, Elise paddling in her rolled-up jeans.

Sheila's gaze was fixed on the expanse of sea directly ahead; to their left a boat manoeuvred in the harbour, its funnel visible above the roofs of the offices and the fish warehouse that lined the harbour wall. Beyond the harbour, lit by the morning sun, loomed an overhanging cliff at the crest of which stood the sharply-ascending walls of a castle and, on the highest prominence of the overhanging cliff, the square-shaped shell of the keep.

The beach was deserted, the road beyond devoid of traffic; apart from the figure of a man and a dog, Catherine and Elise were the only people in sight.

Sheila turned and, her skirt held absently before her, splashed back to the sand: Keith ran off as the football bounced along the beach in the direction of the harbour.

Lorna, picking up a spade, began to dig.

'It's too cold to sit,' Sheila said when they reached the blanket which they'd set out on the sand. 'It's madness to have come on a day like this.' She gestured to where the girls, in the distance, against the sun, had been joined by the man with the dog. 'We're the only people here.'

'Come and have a game of football,' Attercliffe said.

They put down two coats and shot the ball in, first at Keith, then at Bryan and, finally, at Attercliffe himself; Sheila, after scraping out a hole with Lorna, eventually got up, kicked at the ball, ran after it, attempted to dribble it, then to intercept it, then shot at the goal as the ball was passed to her first by Keith and then by Bryan: breathless, she ran to and fro, her cheeks flushed, laughing.

'You go in goal, Mum,' Bryan said, and shot the ball at her.

Attercliffe ran off to fetch it; he kicked the ball high: it passed over Sheila's head. Lorna, shielding her eyes, watched its progress, her face, as she turned in Attercliffe's direction, a distant speck yet showing in a smile.

Sheila, too, was looking up, 'Did you see how high it went?', then laughed as the ball bounced along the water's edge, Keith darting off, flat-footed, sending up splashes as he ran through the pools. 'Don't get wet,' she called and added, turning, 'Just like you to start showing off.'

The ball coiled back across the sand, kicked by one of the girls returning – Catherine, running in her skirt, kicking at the ball again, missing, turning, lashing with her foot in a spray of water, the ball coiling off, once more, at an angle, the boys groaning, and calling, 'Throw it! Don't kick it!' while, laughing, she lashed at it again.

The ball rose, fell, was kicked on by Bryan, was caught by Sheila and, tossing it in the air, she kicked at it herself, missed, fell down, her head bowed, and as the boys called, 'Mum! Oh, kick it!' she rose and, round-shouldered, kicked at it again.

It flew off at an angle.

'Kick it straight.' (Keith.)

'I can't.' (Sheila.)

'You kick it too quickly.' (Bryan.)

'I kick it the best I can.'

'Just like a woman.' (Keith.)

'What's matter' (Sheila), 'with being a woman?'

Her bare feet flapped against the sand.

'This is ridiculous,' Catherine said. In her jersey, clutched to her, she held a collection of shells. 'It only puts Mum back in the state she was before.'

'I don't want a lecture,' Attercliffe said.

'The forecast is for rain.' She indicated clouds above the headland – below which Elise could be seen as a dot, still walking, her back to them, along the water's edge. 'Nobody believes in this any more. It's weird. You're insisting on a structure that no longer exists.'

The shells rattled in her jersey.

'It's better than her staying at home on her one day out from hospital.'

'Why didn't you go off on your own? I despise the blackmail involved in getting us to come.'

'Sheila knows,' Attercliffe said, 'you're doing it for her.'

'Precisely,' Catherine said.

'In which case,' he went on, 'to hell with all your theories.'

'Doesn't Oscar Wilde say something about betraying with a kiss?'

'Oscar Wilde,' he said, 'didn't have five children.'

'Nor did Christ, but,' she said, 'it didn't devalue his judgment.'

'It did in my book,' Attercliffe said. 'He'd never have been a saviour with a family to support.'

'The family,' Catherine said, 'is a reversion to a time when conformity was all that mattered. Individuals now can be what they like, without the compromise of this.'

She gestured to her mother, as she moved away, the shells rattling in her jersey, and perhaps it was this gesture alone that – once the ball had been kicked and she had been replaced in the goal by Keith – prompted Sheila to come across and ask, 'What was that about?'

'Families,' Attercliffe said, 'are a vestige of the past.'

By Lorna's hole Catherine disgorged her shells and her sister, kneeling, picked them up, dropping one suddenly as Catherine laughed and called, 'Honestly, it wouldn't bite!'

'I'm glad we came,' Sheila said. 'Though even then,' she went on, 'Catherine could be right. It isn't very real. More an insistence on your part,' she concluded, 'than anybody else's.'

'I can't believe,' Attercliffe said, 'that I'm alone. I still believe,' he went on, 'that a part of this still matters.'

'And for that,' she said, 'we ought to live together?'

'Because of that,' he said, 'we can't.'

Far off, Elise was waving; her shouts echoed along the beach: the man with the dog had disappeared.

Sheila dug her toe at the sand. 'You don't have to sell the house,' she said. 'With your money from the paper you could live somewhere else for a year before you get another job.'

'We're selling the house,' Attercliffe said, 'splitting the proceeds, and sharing,' he went on, 'the lives of the children.'

'The family,' she said, 'is all I want. I won't ask you,' she added, 'for anything else.'

Attercliffe said, 'I'm offering to share everything we have.'

'You've always got the chance of going on to something else,' she replied.

'I've brought us out here,' he said, 'not to argue, but to spend some time together.'

'The girls resent it.' She indicated where Catherine had joined the boys and, standing in the goal, was – ineffectually – trying to stop them shooting in.

'I need a home for the children,' he said. 'You need a home for them as well. I'm not asking you to have anything less than what I'm hoping to have myself.'

'They don't want to live with you,' she said.

'How do you know?'

'I've asked them.' She added, 'It's only your insistence that keeps us all together. You have to let go,' she concluded, 'of what you never had.'

'It's me,' Attercliffe said, 'who's provided a home for the past two and a half years while you went off and did what you wanted. It's the home,' he continued, 'that you've come back to.'

'The material side of my life is over,' she said. 'Whereas you have the opportunity to start your life again.'

'Start again,' he said, 'at forty-seven?'

'Society is geared,' she said, 'to the requirements of a man. Not to the requirements of a woman.'

'Are you two arguing?' Catherine picked up the ball from behind the goal. 'I thought we'd come out to enjoy ourselves.'

'We have,' Attercliffe said and – picking up the ball as she kicked it towards him – called, '10p to anyone who can catch me,' and set off running across the sand.

*

147

In the car, going back, Lorna fell asleep, lying in Sheila's lap, Catherine squeezed between her and Attercliffe in the front, the boys and Elise silent in the back. It was growing dark by the time they reached the house. They had a meal; Attercliffe lit a fire.

Later, at the door to the hospital, Catherine had embraced her mother then waited in the car while Attercliffe took Sheila up to her ward. But for the cacophony from the television sets, the place was silent: she began to cry, turning from Attercliffe when he took her arm. 'It doesn't seem right. The only freedom a woman has is the freedom to end up like this.'

He took her back to her bed; she opened a locker, put in the parcel that they'd brought, nodded to a nurse who passed at the door, and sat on her bed, her feet by her slippers.

'If it wasn't for men I wouldn't be in here,' she said. 'Men have done this to me. Not deliberately. But by being what they are.'

'I don't want to leave you angry,' Attercliffe said.

But for one other person, already in bed, and asleep, the ward was empty: only the noise of the television came from the adjoining room.

'I've enjoyed today,' she said, 'but,' she gestured round, 'it's coming back to this that's spoilt it.'

It was the slippers, Attercliffe suspected, that distressed her most: she pushed them first to one side, then the other.

'I was wrong to go off in the first place.'

'I'm glad you went,' he said.

'It's not what you said at the time.'

'I had other things on my mind. My own feelings,' he said, 'as well as the children's.'

She said nothing for a while; the counterpane covering her bed was ruffled by her sitting down: she smoothed it with her hand.

'I enjoyed today,' she said again. 'I'm glad we went. That all of us went.'

The nurse came in at the door: she carried a plastic container and, on a tray, a beaker of water.

'Had a good day, Mrs Attercliffe?' she said, and added, without waiting for an answer, 'Evening rations, dear.'

Sheila took the pill, swallowed it, sipped the water, and the nurse passed on to the occupied bed, roused the figure lying there who, moaning, dragged herself on to her elbow, took a pill, followed it with a drink and, still moaning, lay back again.

148

'Supper's over,' the nurse called as she walked over to the door. 'You should have come in sooner. Visitors out, as well, by now.'

In the car, as they drove out of the gates, Catherine said, 'You have no choice but to give her the house. It's the least,' she added, 'you can do for her.'

'I don't see why,' Attercliffe said.

'Since Maurice threw her over, then Gavin, her attempt to intimidate you was her last chance to salvage something out of the ruin.'

'According to you,' he said, 'she's about to succeed.'

'It's only right,' she said. 'In addition to which, she ought to have the children. It's the only chance she's got, living the life that she had before. The only consolation,' she concluded, 'is that her daughters will have learnt her lesson.'

'I have more hopes of her,' Attercliffe said. 'There's more in Sheila than meets the eye. Difficult to get out but, despite her children's and her own misgivings, it's in there all the same.'

They drove through the darkened town and out through the suburbs to Walton Lane; gazing out, solemnly, through the windscreen, it might, Attercliffe reflected, have been a facsimile of Sheila sitting beside him, and when he said, as they approached the house, 'You've always supported the opposite view, independence, rights and self-assertion,' she replied, 'Mum's too old to go on fighting. She'll only be crushed all over again.'

'You might wash your hands of Sheila, I haven't,' Attercliffe said, and, when the car stopped, and he turned off the lights, she answered, 'You're a very odd man,' and added, 'You go on fighting for values that don't exist. And in a way,' she went on, 'that isn't true of anyone else I know.' She gestured to the house. 'Everything you've built has been destroyed, your marriage, your family, your job, your friendships – even, considering your age, your prospects – yet you go on pursuing values that have been discarded for over a generation. If you lived in America you'd be a joke, an irrelevance, once the novelty of what you're doing had been exploited. Fidelity, trust, honour: I can't make you out. You're trying to light a fire when no one wants it. They have central heating and electric cookers and the boy-scout morality you're insisting on passed out with the horse and cart.'

She got out of the car and slammed the door: he could hear her stamping up the stairs as he came into the kitchen and Elise, looking up from the sink where – surprisingly – she was washing up, inquired, 'Had a good evening? I told you she shouldn't have gone,' and hummed a tune which was playing on the radio propped on the draining-board beside her.

'I walked a good three steps today. I reckon tomorrow I'll manage a dozen. A week from now I'll be out of here.'

Fredericks raised his head to indicate the confines of this, the fourth ward in which Attercliffe had visited him.

'You can see I'm getting better. They're moving me round like a yo-yo.'

'Do you do your walking in here?' Attercliffe asked for, with the several screens around the bed, and between Fredericks's bed and the others, there appeared to be no space to move at all: the chair he was sitting in had been placed at the foot of the bed and he was facing Fredericks along the length of it.

'They lift me out of here and set me in a metal apparatus and let me loose like a clockwork mouse. "See how far you can run," they tell me. I'll give them their due. They've got more faith in me at present than the nurses have.'

He addressed this last remark to a uniformed figure passing by his bed; the woman smiled, tucked in his cover, and said, 'Swanking again, Mr Fredericks.'

'I'll swank you when I get out of this bed.' Fredericks endeavoured to rise then, having thrust down his hands, subsided.

'Your girlfriend,' the woman said, 'will be very jealous.'

'Jealous,' he said as the woman passed on. 'The one they've foisted on me can't be a day over seventy-five. It's these young 'uns,' he went on, 'they go for.' He indicated three considerably older figures in the adjoining beds: one was asleep, one reading, and one was attached to a machine from which, periodically, he detached a transparent plastic mask.

Attercliffe realised, for the first time, that all the patients in this ward were dying.

Fredericks's face was yellow, his eyes glazed, his movements slow; periodically, his hand reconnoitred the bed, fingered a fold of the cover, a book, a box of tissues, a sheet of paper, paused, passed on, then paused again.

'I've heard about your job. Pippy Booth came in and told me. You'll be better off wi'out it.'

'Financially, or otherwise?' Attercliffe asked.

'On all counts.' He laughed, the sound rumbling in his throat. 'There's nought like being in a rut. And nought like being at an age when you can still do summat about it. You ought to be grateful, say good riddance, shake Butterworth's hand, and bless the good fortune that's enabled you to start again.' His eyes, glazed, took in the blankness of the screens. 'Butterworth told me. Not so much you'd be going but that you and a lot of others might.' He gestured round. 'Do summat meaningful with the time you've left. Thy's been offered a reprieve. Summat,' he went on, 'I never had. When you see what lies at the end of the line every second that you've got takes on a different meaning. The most valuable thing a man can have is to have something in his life that transcends his limitations. I mean to look into that myself,' he concluded, 'the moment I get out.'

The dolorous inhalations of the man with the mask punctuated the silence of the room; all they could hear, apart from that, was the cacophony of the television in the adjoining room, an area – like the one adjoining Sheila's ward – given over to the set and a rank of upholstered, wooden-armed chairs.

'How's Sheila?'

'Recovering.'

'Got her own way?'

'I have great hopes of her,' Attercliffe said. 'Just as I have,' he continued, 'of you.'

'I can tek care of myself,' Fredericks said. 'In here especially. Don't look behind. Start afresh. I can't tell you the relief it gives me to feel I've turned a corner.'

'Why did you never mention I might be fired?'

'That's why I suggested an interview with Phyllis. Not a solution in itself, but an indication,' he concluded, 'of something different.'

'It's certainly proved to be that.'

'That way, in my view, lies your future. More than it does for me in here.'

'It's not something tangible I'm looking for,' Attercliffe said. 'Sheila wants to go back to a past she feels she can cope with. I'm still hoping,' he went on, 'to bring her into the present.'

He told Fredericks this in order to distract him from the rasping of the man with the mask behind his back, and to distract him, too, from the irrefutable evidence of the swing-doors, the black-and-white tiled floor, the blank, round-cornered walls, the screens, the other beds.

'Phyllis, and what she represents, has put you,' Fredericks said, 'on the proper lines, a reminder, perhaps that the way you've seen things in the past is not the way you should see them in the future.'

His head sank back, its momentum as he made this assertion accompanied by a spurt of saliva and a watering of his eyes.

'I'll see you tomorrow,' Attercliffe said.

'That's right.' He added, 'You might, if you like, look in at the flat.'

'I've been there once,' he said, 'already.'

'Did you turn off the gas?'

'I did.'

'How about the electric?'

'I switched it off at the mains.'

'I never liked living there. Looking out at that bloody church. Religion's based on despair, tha knows. Listen to the music, never mind the words.'

He closed his eyes.

Attercliffe took his hand.

'Don't forget,' Fredericks said, 'what I've told you. This is a door opening, and good riddance to the one that shuts behind.'

15

'The will,' Norton said, 'leaves everything to you. Including,' he went on, 'the lease of the flat. It has,' he continued, 'another twelve years to run. Read it if you like. It's addressed to you.'

He handed him the sheet of paper, folded down the middle.

'You might tell my legatee,' Attercliffe read, 'that I've decided to sign him on to my team. It's not a large team, and doesn't put up a great deal of collateral (seven or eight thousand, or thereabouts), but it is, I can assure him, very select. Moralising has always been my strongest suit and I hope he will excuse this lifelong indulgence and take the dough in the spirit in which it is given. Tell him to keep alert, stay fit and, when he comes off the field, I shall want to know the score.'

'He was in a great deal of pain,' the solicitor said.

Looking no older than Elise, or, on second thoughts, Attercliffe reflected, scarcely older than Catherine, long-haired – more so than either of his daughters – wearing a dark suit, a long-winged collar, a tie with a knot as large as his hand, he leaned across the desk to take back the sheet of paper and announced, 'He talked all the time of living.'

'What about his relatives?' Attercliffe asked.

'A nephew.'

'Shouldn't he,' Attercliffe said, 'be taken into account?'

'It's mentioned in the second paragraph. Mr Fredericks paid him a substantial sum of money some years ago in lieu of what he would leave him.'

'If he decided to contest it,' Attercliffe said, 'I'd not oppose it.'

The solicitor smiled. 'The nephew has been made provision for. He won't protest. Mr Fredericks,' he went on, 'took care of that.'

Attercliffe got up, glanced across to the window and the activity of the street outside – only a short distance from the paper's office – and, as the solicitor extended his hand, shook it, turned to the door and asked, 'What about the furnishings?'

'All yours.' He added, 'I understand there are lots of papers. Juvenilia, he described them, but he's left them to your care.'

'It'll take some time,' Attercliffe said, 'to sort them out.'

'Do with them, Mr Attercliffe, what you like. The flat, its contents, and the residue of Mr Fredericks's estate are yours.' Adding, 'If there are any problems you'll let me know,' he closed the door behind him.

> Sunset and opening-time
> And one clear call for me:
> May I not be intemperate
> At the Buckingham Brasserie.

Going further back in the notebook he read, 'I don't think anyone knows I have a brother. Perhaps my mother and father were mad ever to have come together, she intransigent, self-contained, self-reliant, self-composed, he ebullient, contentious, fractious; she censorious, he licentious; she educated, he scarcely at all. My brother's resentment of his mother for having produced a second son grew, over the years, into a resentment of me – to the extent of his imitating everything his younger brother did. He even, for a while, got a job on a paper (albeit on the strength of my reputation). In his later years he involved himself in the writing of a book which – worthless except as a symptom of his delusion – took up his life entirely, and for the writing of which, surreptitiously, he sacrificed the welfare of everyone around him. He died – I scarcely need to add – as nutty as the day we met.'

A letter from a solicitor announced the intention of Fredericks's nephew to contest the will: it was followed by a letter from the nephew himself proposing that he and Attercliffe might meet and suggesting as a suitable rendezvous the Brasserie Bar at the Buckingham Hotel. At the appointed time the nephew walked in – balding, bearded, stocky; dark-eyed, red-cheeked, protuberantly-nosed, thick-lipped (in age perhaps ten to fifteen years younger than Attercliffe himself) – and, having sat down and accepted a drink, announced, 'So this is where it all went on. I heard a lot of it from Freddie.'

Overcoated, dark-suited, his beard thrust down over a tightly-knitted scarf, he reminded Attercliffe of what Fredericks might have looked like before his disillusionment with television had been announced, three to four years before he'd met him.

'I realise,' the nephew said, 'this is unofficial, but I wanted you to know there's nothing personal in my contesting the will. The family,' he went on, 'isn't – to me – something you can put down in black and white.' A small, square fist was thumped against his chest. 'It's a question of blood, and the mystery of where you come from.' He sipped from his drink, sitting sideways to the table, his legs thrust out.

'Freddie never mentioned he had a brother,' Attercliffe said.

'My father made a mess of his life. He was eaten up with jealousy and tried to contain it by imitating everything my uncle did. It's a familiar pattern, envy of a more gifted younger brother, but it was odd to see the way it finally consumed my father's life. He tried to become a reporter himself, and spent his last years preoccupied entirely by writing a book which no one in their right minds would have wanted to read – assuming, that is, he'd got it published.'

'I'm surprised,' Attercliffe said, 'you'd want to revive the past.'

'I want to reclaim it,' the nephew said. 'When everything's said and done, he was my uncle. I have two sons. It's for their sake that I'm contesting the will. They never knew their great-uncle, though I've told them about him from time to time. If there is an inheritance, they ought to have it.'

He finished his drink and, raising his arm, he ordered another, paying for Attercliffe's when the barman came across, laying the money out from his overcoat pocket, counting the coins, taking one back, then replacing it with another – a tip calculated, in a manner reminiscent of Fredericks himself, with a slow movement of his lips.

'It comes down to this, Mr Attercliffe. Legally, although you have a case, morally, I've a better one. He was my uncle, and he was my father's only brother. Blood, as they say, is thicker than water.' He sipped from his glass. 'It'll cause a lot of bad feeling,' he went on, 'which I don't mind. I'm doing this, as I say, for my sons. My father sacrificed me in pursuing his fantasy of being a writer. I have a right to some recompense for the family squabble. I mean,' he continued, 'you could say my life was screwed up in the past by my father's preoccupation with rivalling his younger brother and, now they're both dead, I am morally entitled to whatever recompense there happens to be going.'

'I've no intention,' Attercliffe said, 'of disputing Freddie's will.'

'You haven't?'

'None at all.'

'He wrote it,' the nephew said, 'when he was mentally disturbed.'

'I don't think so.'

'It was shortly before he died.'

'Did you see him before he died?'

'I didn't hear about it until after the funeral.'

'I understood he made provision for you before he knew he was dying.'

'That's the point,' the nephew said. 'If he'd known he was dying he might have arranged it another way.'

'I think the legality of the will,' Attercliffe said, 'is beyond dispute. It's not my reason for not contesting it.'

The nephew sipped from his drink again, glanced up, and inquired, 'You'll be putting that in writing?'

'You can have the whole of the estate,' Attercliffe said.

'That's very handsome of you.' He extended his hand. 'I know Freddie,' he went on, 'would appreciate this gesture. Not wanting to cut you out but, at the same time, knowing what you were, how you might react to your knowing he had an obligation.' He added, 'I can't tell you what a relief it is. I've been made redundant a month ago and, as far as I can see, I shan't find another job.'

'I know the feeling.' Attercliffe got up from the table.

'Shake hands on it?' he asked.

He stood up as well, shook Attercliffe's hand and, as he turned to the door, added, 'If there's ought of his possessions you'd like, I don't mind you taking summat.'

'He's appointed me his literary executor,' Attercliffe said. 'If there's anything in his papers of financial value I'll let you have it at the appropriate time.'

'That's very fair of you,' he said. 'I've heard,' he went on, 'you're a very fair man. You were a player, weren't you, at one time yourself?'

'That's right.'

'I've never watched the game, but I've heard about it,' he added, 'from Freddie.'

At the door, when Attercliffe left, the nephew turned back inside the bar and, some time later, when Attercliffe drove past, he saw him coming out with a woman, arm in arm, the two of them laughing, his flushed face thrust down to kiss her cheek.

'The man hasn't a leg to stand on,' Norton said. 'His solicitor's letter will tell you that. All he's doing,' he bridged his hands beneath his chin, his elbows resting on the desk before him, 'is exploiting your regard for his uncle. I can't possibly advise you not to contest it and, frankly, if you don't, you'll have to write me a disclaimer saying it's against my advice.' He added, 'I couldn't sleep a wink without.'

As bemused by Attercliffe's reaction as he had been by Fredericks's nephew's solicitor's letter, the contents of which, leaning forward, he began to re-read, he announced, 'His father was a sponger. It's in the accounts. I've had to go through them. The brother did well out of Mr Fredericks, and the nephew, apparently, is going to do better. With your collusion. It's not what Mr Fredericks intended and any court of law will say the same.'

'His only claim,' Attercliffe said, 'is because of the family.'

'If he'd wanted there to be a provision for them he would have said so.'

'He made a mistake,' Attercliffe said.

'How?'

'His duty to his family was one thing. His loyalty to me,' Attercliffe said, 'was another.'

Norton came with him to the door; in a manner reminiscent of Fredericks's nephew, he laid his hand on Attercliffe's shoulder, and declared, 'I never saw you play, but I doubt even in those days that you'd pass the ball to the opposition.'

'The rules of this game,' Attercliffe said, 'are different.'

The flat Attercliffe had found was not much larger than a cupboard. In the main room he arranged his bed, a desk and two easy

157

chairs; two single beds occupied the second room and, in the tiniest, he set a divan.

When the two boys and Lorna came to stay, the first weekend of his occupation, they scarcely spoke; the two girls, having come to see the flat, departed in the evening, Lorna taking her place on the tiny divan and the two boys occupying the single beds. Although they had gone out to the pictures after the girls had left, when, finally, they returned to the tiny kitchen, which adjoined the even tinier bathroom, Lorna, weeping, asked to go home.

Having nursed her to sleep Attercliffe came out to find the two boys sitting by his bed examining the walled-up fireplace.

'There's Mum,' Bryan said, 'with our bedroom empty,' for Sheila, the week previously, had returned from the hospital, and radiant with health, was now in occupation of the house. 'Couldn't you sleep downstairs?' he asked.

'Where?'

'In the living-room.'

'It's hardly a living-room if it's a bedroom as well,' Attercliffe said.

'This is a bedroom as well,' Keith said.

He was very close to tears; the foreignness of the flat - converted from a semi-detached house, the ground-floor of which was occupied by a family of seven - together with the bleakness of the district (on the outskirts of the town) would, Attercliffe imagined, have oppressed anyone who had come from their own detached, 'executive' dwelling, not to mention Pickersgill's six-bedroomed, neo-Elizabethan mansion: the division of the family into its component parts had never, even in recent times, looked as irreversible as this.

'It's not one you have to share every day,' he said.

'How often,' Bryan asked, 'will we have to come?'

'You don't have to come at all,' Attercliffe said. As they scrutinised the brown tiles surrounding the fireplace, and the magenta-coloured walls with their rectilinear pattern of cabbage-shaped roses, he added, 'There's no compulsion about it, Bryan.'

'I don't like seeing you here,' Keith said.

'Why not?'

'I don't like seeing you living like this. It doesn't seem fair. It makes us feel,' he went on, 'we've thrown you out.'

'Your mother's doctor recommends her living at home,' Attercliffe said.

'You've done nothing wrong.'

He covered his eyes, stooped, leaned forward, and cried.

'Look here, Keith,' Attercliffe said. 'This isn't the way to go about it. When I've looked round,' he went on, 'we'll find a better place than this.'

'I want you to come home.'

'I can't come home,' Attercliffe said.

'I want you to.'

He buried his face in his hands.

'We've been through rougher times than this,' he said. 'Things, after this, can only get better.'

'Or,' Keith said, 'go on as they are.'

'Will you get a television?' Bryan asked.

'I suppose I shall.' He indicated the floor. 'In any case, we can hear most of it up here,' he added.

'If you're out at a match on Saturday and Sunday we don't want to be stuck in here by ourselves.'

'After next week I'll be on the dole,' he said. 'The house will be on the market, and we'll all,' he continued, 'be looking for somewhere else to live.'

'Mum says she'll never leave.' Keith blew his nose. He added, 'She went berserk when she heard about the will.'

'What will?'

'Mr Fredericks's.'

'Who told her about it?'

'She opened one of your letters.' Taking a folded envelope from one of his pockets, he added, 'I've got it here.'

The letter – from Attercliffe's solicitor – was accompanied by a copy of a letter from Fredericks's nephew's solicitor acknowledging the disclaiming of the will.

'She says you must be mad.'

'So do all slaves,' Attercliffe said, 'when they consider a free man's actions.'

'I don't see much freedom here,' Bryan said. 'This place is like a prison.'

It was with this thought that they went to bed; he could hear their voices murmuring in the other room and, after a while, Bryan came back in.

'We can't get to sleep for the television noise,' he said.

Attercliffe said, 'You get to sleep with the same noise at home.'

'It's louder here.'

'You'll soon get used to it,' he said.

Yet when Keith came in a little later to make the same complaint, Attercliffe put on his dressing-gown and went downstairs.

A partition divided the entrance hall in half; after ringing the outside bell the door to the flat was opened by a man wearing a raincoat over a pair of pyjamas: small, balding, with a fringe of greying hair, he gazed out with the air of someone disturbed in the midst of a meal.

'The children,' Attercliffe said, 'are finding it hard to sleep.'

'That's their look-out,' the man replied.

'The cause,' Attercliffe said, 'is the excessive noise from your television.'

'We've always played it like this,' the man announced.

'I wonder if you could turn it down?' Attercliffe inquired.

The door was closed.

Attercliffe went back upstairs.

'Has he turned it down?' Keith leant from his secondhand bed, his head to the floor; Bryan, his head wrapped in blankets, didn't stir.

The sound, after diminishing, returned to its previous level.

'You can sleep in my bed,' Attercliffe said.

'That's all right,' Keith said. 'I'll get used to it in the end.'

Voices shouted in the room below.

A fresh crescendo came from the television.

Attercliffe glanced in Lorna's room: the light, gleaming into the alcove, showed her curled up, almost in a ball, beneath the secondhand covers.

He returned to the boys' room, put out the light, and went back to his own.

The sound, as the night quietened, reverberated more loudly from the flat below; the occasional altercation of voices continued, a man's, a woman's, perhaps a second man's, then a child's.

When a little later, Attercliffe's room door opened and Keith came in, Attercliffe got out of bed and said, 'I'll go back down,' pausing, however, for the television suddenly, below, had been turned off: there was still another hour until closedown.

'I suppose,' Keith said, 'when you were younger, you'd have beaten him up.'

'That would have been my first response,' Attercliffe said. 'Nowadays it's all I can do to remember.'

'After Gavin beat you up.'

'He didn't beat me up exactly.'

'Maurice said he did.' He sat on the edge of Attercliffe's bed. 'In any case,' he went on, 'when you get too old you have to resort to other things.'

'Such as?'

'Lawyers.'

'The law,' Attercliffe said, 'is a world unto itself. It exists apart from reality. I shall never get tangled in that.'

'Have you seen those people,' Keith said, 'with earphones in the street?'

'Better than playing it aloud,' Attercliffe said.

His son's youthful figure was coiled up on the bed, his arm thrust out, supporting his weight. 'Other people's noise,' Attercliffe added, 'is always worse. We seldom, if ever, notice our own.'

'What are you going to do?' Keith blinked in the yellow light.

'What about?' Attercliffe asked.

'Your life,' he said, and added, 'It's almost over.'

'There are all sorts of things I could turn to,' Attercliffe said.

'Mum says you'll never get another job.'

'Hopefully,' he said, 'or in despair?'

'She's mad about the will. She says you've done it on purpose. She got into such a fit that Cathy rang the doctor. She told *her* you'd done it so we can't stay on in the house. "To spite me," she said. "He's thrown it away on purpose." There was quite a racket.'

'Like here.'

'Or worse.'

His fair hair glistened in the light, his features reminiscent of Sheila's, without their look – their maniacal look, Attercliffe reflected – of energised introspection.

'If you can't get a job on a paper, what else are you trained to do?' he asked.

'I could take over a football team.'

'Since you haven't before, they'd hardly let you now.'

'Go into television.'

'You've always despised it.'

'How about the radio?'

'Seriously,' he said.

'Are you worried?'

'I wonder, before I go into the sixth form, if I ought to give up school.'

'Do you want to give it up?' he asked.

'I'd be unemployed.'

'In that case you'd better stay on,' Attercliffe said.

'Mum says your money from the paper will only last another year. She's talking,' he went on, 'of getting a job.'

'She'll have to.'

'Though she isn't trained for anything either.'

'I shouldn't let it worry you, Keith,' Attercliffe said, and added, 'I'll keep us all together, even if,' he concluded, 'we have to be split in half.'

Keith laughed, got off the bed and, calling 'Good night,' went back to his room.

At some hour in the morning Lorna came in; she stood by Attercliffe's bed, a thin, wraith-like figure in her nightgown, while he, wakened by the opening of the door, watched her in the light switched on from the landing.

'Dad?'

'Anything the matter?'

'I can't find the toilet.'

'I'll show you.'

He got out of bed, took her hand, and led her to the door which, in a narrow passage, adjoined the kitchen.

'You can come in if you like,' she said.

'You can manage on your own, I'm sure,' he said.

'I'd like you to,' she told him.

Climbing on to the seat her gaze remained fixed on his figure in the door: her eyes, dark with sleep, followed his expression, and still followed him when, having pulled the chain, she returned with him to the bedroom.

'Shall I have a drink?'

'I'd wait till the morning,' Attercliffe said.

'I didn't know where I was.'

'Safe and sound.' He picked her up.

'Can you put me into bed?'

162

He carried her to the cupboard–like space and placed her under the covers.

'You'll leave the door open? It was closed before,' she said.

'That,' he said, tucking her in, 'was because I thought the noise might wake you.'

'I don't mind the noise,' she said.

He caressed her head until she fell asleep and then, leaving the door ajar, returned to his room.

Within seconds – or so it seemed – he was fast asleep himself.

16

It was the sound of the typewriter that brought Mr Wilkins up; he knocked on the door not with his hand but a spanner (denting the paintwork, Attercliffe noticed, when he drew the door back), and said, 'That tapping is bringing down the plaster.'

'I'll put something under the typewriter,' Attercliffe said.

'I hear you're on the *Post*.'

'Was,' Attercliffe said.

'Me an' all,' he said. 'I'm poking around wi' nought to do.'

In shirt-sleeves, unbuttoned, and wearing a pair of crumpled trousers, his bare feet thrust into a pair of tartan slippers, he looked past Attercliffe into the room.

'B'in trying to mend the plumbing.' He indicated the spanner. 'The wife goes out to work and leaves me wi' the kiddies.'

'Come in and have some tea,' Attercliffe said.

'Nay,' he ducked his balding head, 'I thought you'd never ask.'

He coughed, cleared his throat, rubbed his slippers on the doormat and, fastening one shirt-sleeve and then the other, came inside.

'After another job?'

'I'm not,' Attercliffe said.

'Same here,' he said. 'I've given up trying.'

'How many children have you got?' Attercliffe asked.

'Five,' he said. 'Three mine. Two my daughter's.'

'Is she married?' he asked.

'Not yet,' he said. 'She keeps on trying.'

He made Mr Wilkins a cup of tea; a small man, he sat on the edge of an easy chair while Attercliffe sat back in the other.

'Weren't you a footballer?'

'Some time ago,' Attercliffe said.

'I used to go to the City.' He tapped his slippered feet at the carpet. 'Those were the days when it was still a sport. Nowadays it's all drugs and money.' He set his tea on the arm of the chair, tapped each foot again, in turn, rubbed his hand across his head, and added, 'I've been on the Council list for over five years and we're still in this hole, paying rent. I could have bought this place twice o'er. I never had enough salary to afford a mortgage. I've had five years in the poverty trap. I reckon I'll dee of hunger.'

'Do you want a biscuit?' Attercliffe asked.

'I wouldn't mind.'

Attercliffe brought a packet out: his visitor took two and ate them together.

'Fallen on hard times,' he said.

'Not really.'

'If you're not on hard times you wouldn't end up,' he said, 'in a place like this. I know the face of a man,' he went on, 'who's on the way down. I've looked at my own for long enough.'

'What job did you have?' Attercliffe asked.

'The Post Office.' He sipped the tea, chewed the last of the biscuits, picked the crumbs from his shirt, between thumb and finger, popping each one into a mouth from which several teeth were missing, and added, 'I was in the telephone department. I had a van. Off on your own. I wa're often finished by ten, and back i' bed by eleven.'

'How's that?'

'Unions,' he said and, discovering another crumb, popped it into his mouth. 'But for the union I'd still be in a job.' He crossed his ankles: pale, thickly-veined skin was revealed between the bottom of his trousers and the top of his slippers. 'Some days I'd nip to the races. Most of the time,' he added, 'I went fishing.'

'In your van.'

'I had to take the van.' He laughed. 'They weren't keen on you coming back afore five, even though you had only enough work, when you set off in the morning, to last, at the most, for two or three hours. Sometimes,' he added, 'I'd pick up the wife. We've been all over this county. One or two nice spots round here, particularly,' he continued, 'when everybody's working.'

He laughed, the spanner laid beside his feet.

'Do you realise,' he went on, 'that this is the most unionised

165

nation in the industrialised world, and that not only are we the most unionised but we're the most *politicised* unionised nation in the industrialised world and that, despite that, the working classes are worse off for pay and living conditions than in any other industrialised country? I'm out of a job because I had no work to do, and the reason I had no work to do was that the unions said there had to be two men for my job, and four men for another, when one man could have done both in half an hour. I wa' made redundant because the cost of doing the job wa' so high that it wa' hardly worth ought to anybody for me to do it. Leadswingers United wa' the team I laked for, managed by the unions, owned by the unions, *ruined* by the unions.'

He finished his tea, searched for more crumbs on the front of his shirt, found one, popped it into his mouth, and added, 'The unions look after their own interests. In any controversy they take the short-term view: keep the men on, up the wages. Both things are a guarantee that in the long run there'll be no more jobs to go to. The first priority for any union, if it's genuinely interested in the welfare of the people it represents, is the productivity of the organisation its members work for. Other than that it's organising a public charity. Any union official worth his salt has got to look at a country in which union representation is higher than in any other comparable industrialised state, where union representation is more *politicised* than in any other comparable industrialised state, and he's got to explain to himself why, when this is so, the living conditions of the people he represents are amongst the lowest of all the industrialised nations. I'm talking about the technologically-industrialised nations, not the ones that exploit their labour by paying bloody nought.'

He rubbed his feet at the carpet.

'The working classes of this country would never look back again if, tomorrow morning, the unions went out of business. I'm an example of unionised labour. I've been out of work for eighteen months and, as far as I can see, I'll never get a job again. I'm only your age,' he concluded. 'Forty-five.'

'I'm forty-seven,' Attercliffe said.

'You look much younger. I've had o'er a year wi' nought to do. It ages you,' he continued, 'quicker than ought. The wife, for instance, works in a shop. My daughter works in another. I have the dole, and we pay rent through the nose, supplemented by the

166

council. In two or three months we'll be out on the street.'

'I'd have thought,' Attercliffe said, 'you'd have had a council flat.'

'The one they offered us wasn't fit to live in. The official who showed us round said, "This place isn't fit for human habitation, Mr Wilkins." Fourteen floors up. Lifts broken, as often as not. The slob society.' He gestured round. 'Give it a year,' he went on, 'you'll see what it's like. No more tapping in here. You'll be too despondent to do any work. Thirty years of active life and bugger all to do.'

'I can't see,' Attercliffe said, 'how the unions are to blame.'

'Inhibition of management. Reduced investment. Low prod-uctivity. Over-manning. They're all the consequence of unions acting upon the right of veto. If I've had nought else to do these last few months at least I've had the time to study why it happened. Remove the unions and this country could become the most productive land on earth. For the working classes. Those are the ones I have an interest in. Harness incentive, with no union restric-tions, productivity leaps, profits rise, employment goes up, and the sky's the limit.'

'Do you want another biscuit?' Attercliffe asked.

His visitor took two again, placing one on top of the other. 'What's it like being down with the scrubbers? Scrubbers United, tha knows, round here.'

'I haven't had much time to think,' Attercliffe said.

'You're separated from your wife, I gather.'

'I'm getting divorced,' he said.

'First sensible thing you've done since you last kicked a football. If I had my head screwed on I'd do the same. Persuaded by the wife to move in here. You take more money than you've ever had afore, think you'll get another job, and start to spend. The slave mentality.' He tapped his head. 'They knock the fetters off and the first thing you do is run o'er a cliff.'

He got up, went over to the typewriter, set on a table beneath the window, looked out to the back of the house – old, domestic gardens gone to ruin – and said, 'What're you writing?'

'A play.'

'For the telly?'

'The theatre.'

'Get it on the box. Write a series. I wa' reading in the paper how much a man gets for writing a load of crap that comes out once a week and which I could've written myself if I'd had the inclination.'

'Why don't you?' Attercliffe asked.

'You'll see.' He tapped his head. 'Gi'e it one or two months. After that *the penny drops*.'

When his visitor had gone Attercliffe sat for a while, the type-writer before him, gazing out at the garden; from below came the tapping of the spanner against a communal part of the plumbing.

He began his typing again.

'There's nothing I like so much as being alone,' he read. 'Being on your own is the one thing in life I value the most. There are so few chances nowadays for enjoying the privilege – for a privilege I count it – while those who are merely lonely see being alone as something to avoid.'

'It doesn't sound,' Attercliffe said, 'like your cup of tea.'

'Being alone?' she asked.

'Enjoying the privilege.' He turned the page. 'I've never seen you alone,' he added.

Catherine wore her uniform, a grey skirt and purple jumper, having called in at the flat on her way home from school. It was a habit she had fallen into over the previous two weeks and on this, her third visit, she had brought one of her essays with her for Attercliffe to 'go through'.

'Write an essay on solitude is what she said, and solitude is what I've given her.' She lay back on the bed. 'What a crumby hole. How long are you staying?'

'Curiously,' Attercliffe said, 'I'm beginning to like it. I've never had so much time to be alone. I could write this essay for you.'

'I've often been alone,' she said.

'When?'

'You don't know everything about me.'

'It's true.' He added, 'What with all the noise. Your school. Benjie. My work. Your mother.'

Her lower lip was puckered.

'You've never taken much interest in how I really feel. Only,' she said, 'in how you think I ought to.'

'The two might be complementary,' Attercliffe said.

'I've never really felt a child,' she said. 'I've always felt grown-

168

up. Young people,' she went on, 'are more mature than older people give them credit for.'

'In that case,' he said, 'how do you explain your relationship with Benjie?'

Having thrust out her legs along the bed she waved each foot, in turn, from side to side. 'Why,' she said, 'did you marry Mum?'

'Because I loved her,' Attercliffe said.

'Where did you meet her?'

'At a dance. The celebration of the centenary of the paper. I was, in those days, looking for a job.'

'What did you like about her?' his daughter asked.

'I felt there was an anarchic woman,' Attercliffe said, 'waiting to be let out.'

She laughed, gestured round, and said, 'It's a terrible hole to end up in.'

'It's only a billet,' Attercliffe said.

'Tomorrow you move.' She rested her head on her knees. 'Mum doesn't know what she wants.'

'The first thing she wanted was to get herself a home. The second was to get me out of it. Her final stratagem,' he went on, 'is to get you on her side.'

'We don't take sides. We see you,' she said, 'as separate people.'

'Marriage,' Attercliffe said, 'was the making of your mother. She was quite something at that dance.'

'Sleeping Beauty.'

'Exactly.'

'You're spending too much time on your own,' she said. 'And with that awful Mr Wilkins.'

'You haven't told me,' Attercliffe said, 'what it is you see in Benjie.'

'Life. Magic. Effervescence. His mother's different from anyone I know. She never hides her feelings. She says anything that comes into her head and the only effect it has on me is to make me feel alive in a way I don't feel with any other person.'

'It's no use running after spontaneity,' Attercliffe said, 'if your own gifts lead you on to something else.'

'The disillusionment of Mum coming back has left you stranded, Dad.' She got up from the bed.

The essay lay on the floor by Attercliffe's feet; she returned it to her school-bag, went to the door, came back, searching for her shoes, and added, 'It's like playing matches in front of a crowd. Something Benjie and his mother would never do. A self-conscious spectacle performed to certain rules. The spontaneity has been sifted out. It's so prescribed.'

She found her shoes and put them on.

'You only insist on what you want. You're too dogmatic. In addition to which,' she said, 'you're on the other side.'

'What other side?'

'The whole of society is based on a handful of people who exercise their power while the rest,' she went on, 'have to work like slaves.'

'You talk of Benjie without looking where you might be leading him,' Attercliffe said.

'You led Mummy to freedom. According to you.'

'By the time I met your mother I'd had every limb in my body broken. I was a veteran. Whatever Benjie is, he is also, objectively, a thief. What you're converting him into in your imagination isn't necessarily something better but an endorsement of the way he is.'

Having put on her shoes she picked up her bag.

Attercliffe asked, 'Are you going because we've quarrelled, or because you haven't any more time?'

'I'm going,' she said, 'because I have to.'

'Will you come at the weekend?'

'If I have the time.'

He followed her out to the landing and, though he went downstairs, she was already out of the front door by the time he reached the hall.

'Why do you always have to go on at her?' Sheila said.

'It's more,' Attercliffe said, 'the other way around.'

She tapped out a cigarette in an ashtray; a new habit, and one, curiously, not discouraged by her doctor: 'Only two a day. It brings me, I can assure you, a lot of relief.'

Leaning back to cross her legs and, at the same time, to puff out a cloud of smoke, she said, 'You never consider that anything she may feel or think has any validity whatsoever.'

'I can't understand your complacency where Benjie is concerned,' he said. 'Many of the things she has are stolen. To the extent that she's accepted them as gifts she's an accessory after the fact.'

'You've no proof of that.'

'She told me.'

'That's still no proof.' She closed her eyes: the cigarette trembled in her hand. 'You're not going to dissuade her from what she's doing by hammering at her morning and night, running down blacks, running down Moslems, running down anyone who doesn't fit in with your particular plans.'

'I don't hammer at her morning and night, and I don't run down Benjie because of his colour. Nor do I run him down because of his parents' religion. If I do run him down it's because he's a thief.'

Crossing her legs, and puffing once more at the cigarette, she said, 'It's because he is what he is that he does what he does.'

'What if he ends up in prison?'

'He's been to Borstal once already.'

She got up from her chair, crossed the room, gazed out through the window and said, 'Do you want a cup of coffee?'

'No thanks,' he said.

'She has to work through these things herself. I have more faith in her than you have.'

'Cathy,' Attercliffe said, 'is still a child. Despite her intellectual achievements, she's not much more than an infant.'

Framed by the window, she couched one elbow in the palm of her hand, the cigarette smoking by her ear. In much the same manner he'd pictured her over the previous two and a half years standing at one of the ground-floor windows of Maurice Pickersgill's mansion, gazing out at the gardens, and had thought then as he was thinking now: 'She's stepped from the frying-pan into the fire.' Getting up, he said, 'It might be better if you take her side. What I represent is crystal clear and, if she feels animosity to me, there's always you she can turn to.'

'Are you going?'

'I'm waiting for a man to come.'

'Here?'

'It's the house he's coming to look at.'

Her elbow propped in her hand, the instep of one foot turned over, her weight on her other leg – her clothes neat, her hair freshly-styled, her face carefully if not austerely made-up (lipstick, rouge, mascara) – she smiled.

'Who is he?'

'A house agent.'

The cigarette was lowered.

'I won't let him in.'

'You didn't let him in before,' Attercliffe said. 'Which is why I've had to come over.'

'I never heard him.'

'He rang the bell.'

'I didn't hear it.'

'He saw you moving about.'

She stubbed the cigarette out.

'You have no right to sell it.'

'It is my house.'

'It's also my home.'

'It was also mine.'

'I have more rights to it than you have.'

'You have equal rights,' Attercliffe said. 'The fact is, we can't afford to keep it.'

'Doctor Morrison said you'd behave like this. She told me you'd try to exact your revenge. She told me I'd have to be resolute. That woman,' she went on, 'is a god-send.'

'We'll have to sell the house. You'll have half the proceeds,' Attercliffe said, 'plus what I can provide to keep the children.'

'This is your way of getting back.' She paced to the door and back again.

'I'll help you all I can,' he said.

'I have more right to the house than you have.'

'I don't see why.'

'I'm telling you, Frank, this is all I have. This is the only thing that keeps me together. I have nothing else to fall back on.'

'You've got the children. You've even got me as a moral support.'

'Moral!' She added, 'It's not fair. It's always you who dictates the terms.' She turned to the window. 'I knew you'd get your own back.'

'If I were Maurice,' he said, 'I wouldn't have minded.'

'I've been waiting all along for that.'

She turned back to the room.

'For you to bring up Maurice.'

'It's someone,' Attercliffe said, 'with whom you've spent the better part of the past three years.' He added, 'It's only natural he

172

should be, not only a part of your life, but also of mine.'

'Pathetic!' She turned aside, walked past him and, after hesitating in the hall, went out to the kitchen.

When he followed her she was stacking pots in a cupboard.

'You let him walk right over you.'

'It was you who did the walking,' Attercliffe said.

'Pathetic!' She glanced at a cup, ran her finger around the rim, then set it down. 'If I were a man I'd have killed him.'

'If I'd have murdered him,' Attercliffe said, 'I might have got off with six or seven years, on the grounds of justifiable homicide, but I would,' he continued, 'still be in prison. Not only would you have had to move from the house but I wouldn't have had any severance pay.'

'Like you,' she said, 'to see everything before, during and after in terms of cash.'

'I see part of it in terms of cash since I have no alternative,' Attercliffe said.

'My whole life is determined not by what I choose but by what other people,' Sheila said, 'choose for me.'

'I'm tied down by this as much as you are. It wouldn't be my choice,' he said, 'to live in a slum. Nor,' he added, 'do we have to.'

'We can go on as we are,' she said. 'I live here with the children. You,' she went on, 'can live in a room.'

'How can I live with the children?' Attercliffe asked.

'You live in a room which costs very little and come here, say, on Saturday night, or, if you like, on Sunday, and I sleep there. It's the perfect solution to all our problems.' She added, 'You're punishing me because of Maurice. And punishing the children, too. They don't want to move. All their friends live here. It isn't fair.'

'Away from here,' Attercliffe said, 'things will fall into place in a way in which, at present, you can't imagine.'

'You haven't changed a bit,' she said. 'You're exactly like you were before. Cathy feels the same. People like me don't stand a chance.'

There was a knock on the door: it was followed, a moment later, by the ringing of the bell.

'There he is now,' Attercliffe said. 'I shan't be a minute.'

She remained standing by the kitchen table and was still standing there when, a few moments later, Attercliffe returned with a dark-suited, youthful-looking figure who, a brief-case under his arm, shook Sheila's hand, and asked, 'Do you mind if I look around? It shouldn't take a minute.'

'I don't mind at all,' she said.

Having declined a cup of coffee, he returned to the hall, glanced in the cupboards, stepped through to the living-room, then started upstairs.

The floorboards creaked above their heads.

'Strange his name being Morrison,' Attercliffe said.

'Is it?'

'Must be an omen.'

'I don't see why.'

'Your doctor having a positive influence on your life, perhaps he'll have the same on mine.'

His feet came down.

'Would you like a cup of coffee now?' Sheila asked when he came back in the kitchen.

'I wouldn't mind, Mrs Attercliffe,' he said.

He sat at the kitchen table.

'We can go through to the living-room,' Sheila said.

'It's perfectly all right,' he said, 'in here,' and, opening his brief-case, added, 'Mrs Attercliffe,' once again.

He took out a paper.

'The market, of course, at the moment, with this type of house is very depressed.'

'Why this type especially?' Attercliffe asked.

'The ones most hit in the private sector are the lower to middle management. You'd be amazed how many houses of this description are coming on to the market. I shouldn't count,' he added, 'on a very quick sale.'

'We'll lower the price,' Attercliffe said.

'I shouldn't advise it.' He glanced at Sheila who smiled. 'It's unusual to have someone who is asking us to lower it.' He laughed, nodded his head, and added, 'Instant is fine with me, Mrs Attercliffe,' as Sheila, still smiling, held up a jar.

They sat at the table discussing the prospects and, after the agent had named a price, considering how much they might lower it.

'You have to think of a time-span,' he said, 'of something like a year. If the market doesn't pick up,' he added, 'it could be even longer.'

174

'It may, in that case,' Sheila said, 'be more economical not to sell it.'

'It works both ways, Mrs Attercliffe,' the agent said. 'If,' he went on, 'you're buying another. Prices,' he continued, 'have never been as advantageous to the purchaser as they are at present and, after all,' he gestured round, 'we mustn't take too gloomy a view.'

'Still, we might have to think of a year,' she said. 'Or longer.' She smiled at the agent again. 'It's all the capital we have. I wouldn't want to throw away my share.' She added, 'Whether my husband would wish to throw away his share or not.'

'Oh, we'll set a fair price,' the agent said, and added, 'I'll take my measurements now, if I may,' finishing his coffee, 'then do my sums and come up, I hope, with an appropriate answer.'

After he had gone Sheila went upstairs: she returned with her make-up freshly done. She smiled, tidied the kitchen, then, fetching her coat from the cupboard in the hall, called, 'You can give me a lift into town, if you like.'

'I'm going the other way,' Attercliffe said.

'It doesn't matter,' she said. 'I can catch a bus.'

He dropped her off at the end of the lane and, as she got out, she added, 'We could still be here this time next year.'

'I doubt it,' Attercliffe said.

'I don't see why.'

'We'll lower the price till we sell it.'

'I won't lower mine.'

'In that case,' he said, 'I'll lower mine.'

He watched her frown before, turning, she smiled again.

'See you soon,' she added.

He drove off in the opposite direction: a circuitous route brought him back into town – in time to see Sheila descending from a neighbour's car outside the Buckingham Hotel: she glanced at her reflection in the window of a shop, then, her shoulders straight, her head erect, walked briskly through the doors of the Brasserie Bar which flapped to for several seconds behind her.

17

'What I don't understand,' Attercliffe said, 'is why the exercise books are never marked.'

'They're marked at regular intervals,' the teacher said.

'Keith's hasn't been marked for over two months.'

The teacher – in appearance, not much older than Keith himself – opened his file: he ran a bitten-down finger along a row of inked-in figures.

'Every two weeks, according to my records.'

The hall was crowded; queues of parents stood at the tiny desks: to the lid of each was attached a teacher's name. 'Mr F.N. Perkins', in a decorous red script, was fastened to the lid of the one on the opposite side of which Attercliffe was sitting: long-haired, pale-featured, acne-cheeked, leather-jacketed, Perkins consulted his figures again.

'When it is corrected,' Attercliffe said, 'more mistakes are left uncorrected than the ones you've underlined.'

'I'll look into it,' the teacher said.

'The appearance, too, of his work is scruffy. Nowhere in the book is there any comment either on his spelling, the lay-out of his work or the tattiness of its presentation. Large parts of it are illegible, most of what you can read is misspelt, and a lot of it is poorly constructed.'

'You'll have to allow me,' Perkins said, 'to judge his work.' He glanced at the parents waiting in the queue behind Attercliffe's back.

'I've left you,' Attercliffe said, 'to make judgments for the best part of a year. I'm capable of coming to my own conclusions.'

'If you wish to make a complaint it may be better,' Perkins said, 'to put it in writing.'

'I've come to the parents' meeting instead.' He indicated the crowded hall at the far end of which, on a curtained stage, the headmaster was talking to a group of parents. 'I'd prefer to hear the excuse first hand.'

'I've made my remarks on Keith's work. If,' Perkins said, 'you're not prepared to accept them I'd take it up with someone else. I'm doing,' he concluded, 'the best I can.'

'Why isn't he set any homework?'

'He is set homework.'

'When do you mark it?'

'It's marked in class.'

'His book hasn't been marked for the past two months.'

'I give out the answers: they mark it themselves.'

'Of this homework,' Attercliffe said, 'which isn't set.'

'If you've any complaints,' he said, 'you know where to take them.'

'Before I do,' Attercliffe said, 'perhaps you could tell me which work you set in his book to be done at home.'

'I ask them to complete their classwork,' he said.

'He completes it,' he said, 'in every lesson.'

'He does his homework, in that case, in class.'

'The point of the homework is to do it unsupervised,' Attercliffe said, 'so that you're able to judge objectively how well he's doing in class. It sounds to me that what you call homework is what any average child can accommodate in any normal lesson.'

'This is a democratic country,' he said. 'Everyone has their chance. That applies,' he went on, 'to those least able to benefit from a formal education as well as to those who can accommodate it with a little less effort.'

'You're pacing your teaching to the slowest rate of learning?' Attercliffe asked.

'The homework I set is the completion of the work they start in class.' He closed his file.

'You won't set homework?' Attercliffe asked.

'His classwork is sufficient,' the teacher said.

'You haven't even looked at it for the past two months.'

'If you've any complaints, Mr Attercliffe, you know where to make them.'

Attercliffe got up, consulted the sheet of subject-teachers and the cyclostyled map picked up on his arrival, and moved over to a queue at a neighbouring desk.

The murmur of voices echoed within the tall-roofed hall – an interior braced by metal girders and looking out, through glass-panelled walls, to a tarmacked playground on one side and a playing-field on the other.

Beyond stretched the houses of the town and, in the furthest distance, the spire of All Saints Church, the Town Hall tower, and the County Hall dome; darkness was setting in and reflections of the desks and the queues and the seated figures were mirrored in the windows on either side.

The queue moved up; the headmaster, after surveying the hall below, came down from the stage: he took out a pipe, filled it, struck a match, talked to a group of parents, first on one side, then on the other, then, smiling, moved off to a door at the rear.

Attercliffe left his place in the queue and approached the stocky, square-shaped figure – tweed-jacketed, twill-trousered – and, after introducing himself, inquired, 'Why do you not set home-work?'

'Generally, or specifically?' The headmaster didn't look up.

'Both.'

He took out the pipe, examined his and Attercliffe's reflections in the adjacent window – figures moving to the evening institute outside – and, turning, said, 'Keith and Bryan are doing well.'

'As a matter of fact,' Attercliffe said, 'they're doing badly.'

'If you gave me a pound,' the headmaster said, 'for every parent who thought his child wasn't doing as well as he should I'd most likely have a chauffeur waiting out there.'

He laughed.

'Bring it up at the parent-teachers' meeting. It's impossible for one parent to judge from one example the situation that prevails throughout a school.'

He walked on, greeted another figure coming in at the door, directed it to the table in the foyer with its annual reports, its map of the hall and its list of teachers and, followed by a cloud of smoke, disappeared through the door at the rear.

'We've become,' Wilkins said, 'a nation of spongers. If there's one thing that being unemployed has done for me, it's enabled me to see the situation as it really is. I couldn't do that before,' he added. 'I was too much embroiled in the to-ing and fro-ing. Too much, in short, caught up in the racket.'

A mug of tea in his hand, the crumbs from his biscuit dropped across his chest, his legs crossed, his thickly-veined ankles bared, smacking his lips, he listened to Attercliffe's response of, 'The world has changed since the days of unorganised labour,' and declared, 'It hasn't changed a bit. All that's changed,' he took a final drink from his mug, 'is that human initiative has been devalued.'

Attercliffe turned back to the typewriter and tapped the keys.

'Have you seen the streets round here?' Wilkins went on. 'The energy expended by one roadsweeper sweeping the road outside is obscured entirely by his effort in deciding which bits of rubbish he ought to leave and which he ought to pick up. People like me would willingly do a spot of useful work, yet we're not allowed to because it'll be doing the roadsweeper out of a job! Multiply that ten thousand times and you've got this country in a nutshell: subsidised inadequacy, incompetence, inefficiency and scrounging.'

He got up from his chair, set his mug on the table by the bed, straightened the cover, and went to the door: having opened it, however, he came back in, picked up the mug once more and went to the kitchen.

The sound of the tap running came from the open door, accompanied by the rattling of crockery in the sink.

A moment later, standing in the door – a tea-towel in his hand, his hand inside a mug – he declared, 'I admire you for not taking your misfortune lying down. Here you are, with a family to support – even larger than mine, considering,' he went on, 'your overheads – and, instead of accepting your fate, you sit here each morning and afternoon and night, writing your way out of a mess which has crucified many a man before, is crucifying many a man at present, and will crucify many more in the future, and refusing to take a hand-out from anyone.'

Attercliffe looked up from his typing and announced, 'I shall have to get on. I haven't much time.'

'I wish I had your gift of self-expression. There's so much I'd like to say. There's so much I've seen in the past few months, the past year and a half, to be precise.'

179

The sound of a baby crying came from the flat downstairs; he returned to the kitchen and brought back another mug.

'Once you find yourself in a society where everyone expects something to be done about anything that goes wrong on the assumption that it's not really his or her responsibility, the apathy that that induces even undermines those who have a job. Like my wife and daughter: without their money we couldn't live, yet they were only taken on because they were women, and yet neither one of them complains or feels the least inclined to do anything about it.'

'They could join a union.'

Wilkins dried the mug, fisting his hand in the cloth.

'If my wife and daughter joined a union it would only make them more of what they are already. The union creates this mess in the first place by creating the wage demand which reduces profitability, which reduces investment, which reduces jobs, which brings us exactly to where we are at present. The unions create unemployment and, in this country, have created it on a scale greater than in any other industrialised nation.' He came further into the room. 'Do you think it's because the Japanese have got two heads, four arms and six legs that they work, man for man, two and a half times more efficiently than we do? The only difference between this country and the rest of the techno- logically industrialised world – lower productivity, lower wealth and lower living-conditions for the working classes apart – is that this country is unionised more completely than any other.'

He fractured the mug: he held one piece and the cloth in one hand and the remaining piece in the other. Indicating the type- writer, he concluded, 'A message to the nation from one who knows.'

A little later he came back, the baby in his arms, and, a feeding-bottle in his hand, added, 'If this doesn't change,' indicat- ing the baby, 'and I'm left like this for another year, I might run for the local council. I'll have more time than anybody else. I'll have had the opportunity to examine the world as it really is, and I'll have learnt from my elocution and my correspondence courses how to put myself across.'

He sat down in the chair in which, earlier, he had drunk his tea; the baby, suckling at its bottle, murmured.

'My grandchild.' He went on, 'Its father is out of work and

sends my daughter one pound 50p a week. She and her mother, however, steal enough to keep us going. The staff at each of their shops have a corporate thieving system which allows them a certain amount each week. It's taken into account by the owners: so much to shop-lifters, so much to faulty packaging, so much to the staff. It's the world we live in.' He removed the teat from the baby's mouth. The child burped; its head fell sideways: after a moment it puckered up its mouth and cried. He reinserted the teat in the blistered mouth. 'With what we steal, their wages, family allowance, a rent and rate rebate, my redundancy and unemployment pay, together with the contribution from my unofficial son-in-law, we get along quite nicely. Not enough to make a killing, nor to go on holiday, nor to run a car, and we might have to move out of here, as I've said, and take a derelict council flat, but,' he concluded, 'taking it all in all, when it comes down to it, looking at it from both sides of the fence, in the long term, it's not a bad old ticket.'

He watched Attercliffe type for several seconds, adjusted the baby's bottle, rearranged its head against his arm, stroked its bulbous leg, the thigh protuberantly expanded from the elasticated edge of the plastic nappy cover, and, gazing to the window, whistled.

'More peaceful up here than it is down there.' His bald head glistened. 'No one above you. No noise. You can't get a work-man nowadays to do a job without his putting down a radio. Ask him to turn it off and it's as if you're denying him his freedom.' He laughed, removed the teat from the baby's mouth and watched it as, its eyes closed, it writhed against his arm. 'A book I've been reading explains the difference between men and women. It explains,' he went on, 'why women don't do any of the things that they complain that only men are allowed to do. When this 'un,' he indicated the baby in his arms, 'was in the womb it was subjected to certain chemicals secreted by my daughter. Because it was a girl, it was subjected to one kind of chemical but if it had been a boy it would have been subjected to another. It's the chemical structure of the brain that makes a boy behave one way and a girl another. This same chemical structure is the basis of masculine assertiveness. With a girl it has the opposite effect and even though they might be like my daughter, who's an absolute cow, it's not the kind of assertiveness that creates new religions, great paintings or new technologies. It's a resigned aggression which accommodates the world as it is rather than instinctively seeking to change it.'

He raised the baby to his shoulder, winded it, lowered it and, wiping milk from the corner of its mouth, added, 'All these women trying to do what men do are not only wasting their time but forfeiting their intrinsic nature, distorting and perverting it for good.'

The baby slept, its head propped on his arm.

'I should have changed its nappy,' Wilkins said. 'I'll have to leave it now. I don't want to wake it again.'

He stood, adjusted the baby against his arm and, the bottle in his hand, tip-toed to the door. 'All this,' he went on, 'is the latest fashion. When women have given up capering around like men and are reconciled to a world of male assertiveness, they'll go back to what they were before. All this upsurge,' he continued, 'will have been for nothing.'

A moment later, from the hall, came the sound of his door.

The house grew silent.

Attercliffe typed; the table shook: from below came the squealing of a set of pram wheels as, having perhaps disturbed the baby, his neighbour Wilkins pushed it to and fro.

'It's a friend of your Cathy's,' the voice announced.

'What friend?' Bleary-eyed, Attercliffe gazed at the open door of the Wilkinses' flat from within which came the sound of a baby crying.

'Benjie,' the voice declared.

'What time is it?' he asked as a light went on behind the Wilkinses' door.

It had been the Wilkinses' daughter, a wire-haired figure in a raincoat, who had come upstairs and called, 'Telephone!'

Her white, dark-caverned, still rouged and made-up face glanced out before the flat door closed.

'About three o'clock.'

'Anything the matter?'

Benjie was not alone; there was the sound of a scuffle, perhaps of the receiver being dropped, then the voice announced, 'She's been arrested.'

'What for?' he asked.

'I dunno,' the voice continued.

'Where is she?'

'In the nick.'

'When did it happen?'

'An hour ago.'

'How do you know it's happened?'

'I saw her.' Benjie's voice was lowered as he spoke to someone else, the receiver covered at the other end, then he announced, 'She was stopped by a copper.'

'Have you been to the station yourself?'

'I have to go,' he said, and added, 'I haven't got any more money.'

The phone was put down the other end.

'Anything up?' Wilkins said, appearing at the flat door, only his head and his shoulders protruding.

'I have to go out,' Attercliffe said.

'We heard the phone ringing and had to answer it in case it woke the kiddies.'

'Will you shut that flaming door?' came a shout behind his back.

Wilkins asked, 'If there's anything I can do to help?'

'No thanks,' Attercliffe said.

'Otherwise,' he said, opening the door a little further, 'I'll see you in the morning.'

The door was closed; Attercliffe went upstairs, got dressed and, with the baby still crying, came back down.

The street was deserted; a light went back on in the Wilkinses' flat as he started the engine: the bonnet of the car was covered in frost.

Off the city centre he turned from a narrow sidestreet into the yard of the station, an ancient, stone-built edifice with a recent concrete structure behind.

A flight of stone steps took him into a glass-doored foyer: behind a counter stood a desk: a table, beyond the desk, was littered with files, folders, papers and miscellaneous boxes.

Behind a partition voices were raised: laughter broke out.

He pressed a bell on the counter.

The laughter faded to be replaced first by one voice then by several: he heard odd words: 'Inspector', 'safe', 'car', 'office', finally, 'advice'.

He pressed the bell again.

A head appeared around the partition.

'Yes?'

'I've come about my daughter,' Attercliffe said.

The head disappeared.

Doors banged.

Laughter behind the screen was followed by laughter from a greater distance.

A figure emerged from behind the partition, buttoning a jacket and, without glancing in Attercliffe's direction, picked up a paper, examined it, put it down, and called, 'Did you leave the lost property file in here?'

'With Harry,' came a voice from behind the partition and the uniformed figure – slight, tousle-haired, and not looking a great deal older than Keith – finally glanced at Attercliffe and said, 'I shan't be a minute.'

There was a further exchange of voices behind the partition; a door banged; the words, 'legally' and 'offence' were followed by the stamping of a foot.

'Yes?' The tousle-haired figure – a faint growth of beard around its jaw (lean, sallow-cheeked) – looked up.

Pale eyes gazed out from beneath blond lashes.

'I've come to see about my daughter,' Attercliffe said. 'She was brought in,' he announced, 'a little while ago. I was told she'd been arrested.'

'Has she got a name?'

'Attercliffe.'

Without removing his gaze from Attercliffe's face, he inquired, 'Do you know what time she came in?'

'An hour ago.'

'I'll try and find out.'

He disappeared behind the partition.

A further uniformed figure came in, crossed to the desk, removed a sheet of paper, examined a file, sat down, took out a pen, wrote, got up, glanced at Attercliffe, and went back behind the partition.

The first figure reappeared.

'The constable who brought her in will see you,' he said. 'Are you her father?'

'That's right.'

184

'He won't be long.'

A telephone rang; the policeman picked it up, announced, 'City Station,' listened, inquired, 'Where did you say this happened?', listened once again and, glancing up, called, 'Sit down,' indicating a bench behind Attercliffe's back.

The door from the foyer opened; two girls, one wearing a skirt, the other jeans, came in, followed by two men. Behind them came two uniformed figures. A lid was raised in the counter: the girls, both made-up, and the two men, both in dark suits, one dishevelled, one neat, preceded by one of the policemen and followed by the other, passed beyond the partition. A door closed; another opened. Footsteps echoed along a corridor.

Behind the counter the policeman sat down at the table, repeated an address, then a number, said, 'Someone will be along,' and put the telephone down. He returned behind the partition, said, 'It's Mrs Kennedy, if Don's got a minute,' came back and, retaking his seat at the table, opened a ledger and wrote.

A dark-haired, dark-moustached, acned, uniformed figure appeared from behind the partition, glanced across the counter, said, 'This the girl's father?' and, as Attercliffe got up, raised the lid, ducked underneath, and – unshaven, gaunt-eyed, his chin sprinkled with suppurating spots – announced, 'Your daughter's in serious trouble, man.'

He had a Scottish accent; across his forehead a red line from the imprint of his helmet exaggerated the whiteness of his face.

'I'd like to see her,' Attercliffe said.

The dark eyes, the corners of which were lined with mucus, peered out from beneath a pair of brows the hairs of which were flecked with dandruff. 'I'll do all the seeing,' he said. 'She was creating,' he went on, 'a public disturbance.'

'Doing what?' Attercliffe asked.

'Breaking bottles. It's people like your daughter who cause more trouble than they're worth.' He added, 'There are problems we have to deal with affecting people's lives and we're held up continually by people like your daughter who have nothing better to do than waste our time.'

'If you'd let me talk to her,' Attercliffe said, 'I'm sure,' he went on, 'I could straighten her out.'

'The straightening out you ought to have done should have been done ten years ago or even,' he went on, 'before you were married. Between you and me, I'd say you'd made a mess o' yon lassie. As it is, she's responsible for bringing two policemen in from the beat, clamming up a cell, and commissioning hours of filling in forms and taking statements because you couldn'a gi'e her a good lathering when she needed it.'

Moving a step forward Attercliffe inquired, 'Have you any children of your own?'

'If I had one like your daughter I'd think I'd done the community a very poor service. I'm in two minds to charge her.'

'You ought to,' Attercliffe said. 'It'll do her good.'

The policeman glanced away.

'I'll go back and see what the Inspector says. It won't do her career much good, if she's appearing in court on a charge like this.'

'It'll screw up her life,' Attercliffe said.

The dark eyes gleamed. 'People like her are more trouble than a villain. With a villain you're picking up somebody who, as likely as not, doesn't know any better. With her it's privilege gone to rot. There's more time wasted on people like your daughter than any other kind I know.'

He returned to the counter, raised the lid, ducked underneath, lowered it behind him, and disappeared beyond the partition.

When, some time later, Catherine appeared, she was accompanied by a tall, grey-haired, grey-moustached figure who, raising the lid for her, declared, 'Once more in here, it's out of my hands. You'll remember what I've told you.'

Looking cold, wearing plimsolls, jeans and a sweater, Catherine nodded, paused to receive another reprimand, which didn't come, and ducked beneath the counter.

'I've told her the score. I'm sure she understands. Once more in here,' the grey-haired figure said, 'and it's whatever the magistrate sees fit.'

Lowering the counter, he turned, and disappeared behind the partition.

Outside, pale-faced, wide-eyed, gaunt-cheeked, Catherine waited by the car, shivering, while Attercliffe unlocked the door; after getting in she sat, abstracted, gazing out through the windscreen: as he got in behind the wheel she said, 'I'll never do that again.'

'That's all right,' he said.

'That's all I have to say.'

'That's all right,' he said again and started the engine.

She shivered, her hands between her knees.

'Do you want a coat?' he asked.

'It's more my nerves than cold. I'll soon get warm,' she said.

They drove in silence through the town; as he turned down the hill to the river, she said, 'How did you know where I was?'

'Benjie rang.'

'I must have given him your number when you first moved in,' she said, 'and we came to stay for a weekend.'

Attercliffe said, 'What were you doing for the police to pick you up?'

'Fooling around.'

'He told me breaking bottles.'

'Oh, him,' she said. 'He was awful.'

'Did he ask you for Benjie's name?'

'No,' she said. 'Which is just as well. He's still on probation.'

They passed a police car, the only other vehicle on the road. She shivered, folded her arms, and gazed abstractedly at the alternating pools of light ahead.

'They'd caught two prostitutes who'd been picked up by two men in a car which, when the police stopped them, was found to have been stolen. The women were complaining they'd been wrongfully arrested.' She added, 'They'd also caught a gang of robbers. One of them was in the next cell and kept asking for a glass of water. Apparently, they'd raided the Waterworks Office and tried to open a safe. When they found they couldn't one of them said he knew someone who could, so they all went off and fetched him. While they were away the police arrived and were just complaining amongst themselves they'd arrived too late when the gang came back. The argument was whether they could be arrested for breaking in when there hadn't been any witnesses.'

She bowed her head, remained in this position for several seconds, then straightened: she laughed, shivered again, then, as Walton Lane came into view, fell silent.

In the house, upstairs, a light went on as the car pulled into the drive.

A further light appeared in the hall and Catherine, tapping on the kitchen door, called, 'Mum? Are you there? It's me.'

The dressing-gowned figure of Sheila was silhouetted the other side.

A bolt was drawn: the door swung back.

Pale-faced, harrow-eyed, Sheila gazed out. 'Is anything the matter?'

'Nothing,' Catherine said. She stepped inside, went to the kettle, filled it with water, and switched it on.

Closing the back door, Attercliffe said, 'I had a call from Benjie telling me Cathy had been picked up by the police and taken to the City Station.'

'What for?'

'Fooling around.'

Catherine sat down; she watched the kettle: Sheila, her back to a cupboard, stood by the door, uncertain whether she might reopen it and invite Attercliffe to leave.

'What sort of fooling around?'

'Breaking bottles.'

'Why?'

Catherine bowed her head, got up, and started to pace the kitchen in her plimsolled feet: the top of one shoe was worn in a hole through which, spreadeagled, Attercliffe could see her toes.

'It seemed the sort of thing I ought to do.'

'Breaking bottles?'

Over a nightdress Sheila was wearing a dressing-gown, unfastened, the collar folded back to her freckled chest.

'Throwing bricks.' Catherine's gaze was directed to the floor. 'We were having fun. I realise,' she continued, glancing up, 'it looks ridiculous. I'm sorry.'

'It doesn't bother me, Cathy,' Attercliffe said, 'except to the extent that it bothers you.'

'You didn't stand up to that policeman very well,' she said.

'I thought flattery would be more productive than abuse,' he said.

'It certainly succeeded this time,' she said, and added, 'When I said I'd never do it again I meant it. If I ever have to go inside,' she concluded, 'it'll be for something that's really worth while.' Putting a teabag into a mug she poured water from the kettle over it. 'Do you want one, Dad?' she asked.

'I wouldn't mind,' he said.

'Did they put you in a cell?' Sheila asked.

'Two. They had to move me from the first.' She got another mug, put in a teabag, and poured in water.

'Do you want one?' she asked Sheila, who shook her head.

'No thank you,' she said, and looked to the kitchen window. 'I heard the car and saw the lights. I couldn't think what had happened.'

'Didn't you know she was out?' Attercliffe asked.

'I haven't been sleeping well,' Sheila said. 'I lose track of when they come in. This place is like a hotel, with hardly a moment's rest.'

Her knees turned in to one another, pigeon-toed, her elbows at her sides, her hands clenched around the mug, which steamed, and to which, repeatedly, she dipped her head, Catherine sipped, swallowed, then sipped again.

'It's over now,' Attercliffe said.

'Over for you,' Sheila said. 'For me it's just beginning.' She turned to Catherine to ask, 'What will your school say when you appear in court?'

'I'm not appearing in court,' she said. 'Dad got me off. Soft-soaping that policeman.'

'It's a nightmare,' Sheila said.

She sat, her arms held to her.

'What a mess,' she continued. 'What a failure I've turned into.'

'I go my own way,' Catherine said, and added, 'I'm going up to bed.'

'Aren't you going to thank your father?' Sheila asked.

'I've thanked him once already.'

'I see.'

'I'll thank him again, if that's what you want.' To Attercliffe she added, 'It was good of you to come and fetch me.'

She stooped, kissed Sheila's cheek, turned to the door, called, 'Good night,' and, stamping her feet, ran upstairs.

'It's our fault,' Sheila said.

'That's right.'

'And the company she keeps.' She felt in her dressing-gown pocket. 'She doesn't see that boy again.'

'You've always defended him,' Attercliffe said.

She took out a handkerchief. 'He's dragged her down to his level.' She blew her nose.

'Or she,' he responded, 'is raising him to hers.'

'It's not what you've said before.'

'I'm trying to keep,' he said, 'an open mind.'

'To think of her,' she said, 'in a prison cell.'

'She isn't in a prison cell,' he said.

She asked, 'Don't you *care* about your daughter?'

'Whatever values she has, she's acquired them,' he said, 'from living with us. When we've sold the house and bought two establishments she can come and live with me,' he added.

'I'm not selling this house,' she said. 'It's all I've got. I'm not living in anything smaller.'

'We can discuss that,' he said, 'another time.'

'It's what I've decided,' she said. 'I'm staying here.'

She didn't come to the door when he left; when he called good night all he heard, after an interval, was the sliding of the bolt and the turning of the key – followed, after a further interval, by the switching off of the light.

18

'Some homes,' Miss Harrington, the Deputy Headmistress announced, 'are not equipped for the children living there to do homework in the evenings. I know of one such house where each room is occupied by sixteen people. How can we set homework and expect it to be done by a child,' she concluded, 'living in those conditions?'

The library of the school with its racks of books and magazines and its rows of tables, several of which had been pushed to one side, accommodated an audience of thirty or forty people: their attention was focused on the figure of Miss Harrington herself and Mr Mainwaring, the Headmaster, seated behind a desk at one end.

A plain-featured woman in her early thirties, Miss Harrington was wearing calf-length boots and, above a knee-length corduroy skirt, a blouse to the breast pocket of which was clipped a row of pens.

Mr Mainwaring smoked a pipe which, at the beginning of the Deputy Headmistress's introduction, he had slowly filled and which, as she drew to the close of her speech, he finally lit.

'Why should the least able of our children,' Miss Harrington continued, 'be penalised? Homework,' she added, 'would benefit only those who are already catered for, and those who are not so fortunate would be the only ones to suffer. The principle behind this school is that the opportunities we provide should be distributed without favour to all our children. A capacity to exercise one's faculties, after all, may be experienced in any one of a variety of ways. Education,' she concluded, 'is a two-way business.' She smiled. 'If there are any questions,' she drew her skirt behind her,

'Mr Mainwaring and I will be glad to answer them.' She sat.

A man stood up.

He said, 'I'd like to endorse what the speaker has said. It's why we send our children here. In a society where privilege can still be purchased – and it is a privilege,' he turned to address the room, 'to buy an education, since it isn't a *right* for those who can't afford it – this school sets an example which the rest,' he went on, 'could do well to follow. The divisions that exist out there,' he gestured to the windows set high on one side of the room above the bookshelves, 'are not reflected inside this building and,' he raised his arm to indicate the opposite wall which adjoined the main structure of the school itself, 'if, at this early stage in their lives, we can instil in our children the values which the world out there denies, then there's a real chance, when they leave, that the world out there may be changed to accommodate their enlightened aspirations.'

Several people applauded; Miss Harrington got to her feet.

'Although,' she said, 'it isn't a question, I couldn't agree with you more. Which brings me to an additional point, the value which this school attaches to the co-operation of its parents. Without that,' she sat, 'we couldn't succeed to the degree we do at present.'

'What I'm worried about,' a woman's voice called out, 'is that they never seem to learn anything.'

'Who doesn't?' another voice inquired.

'In the Maths lesson my children say they spend most of their time making paper darts.'

Mr Mainwaring, smiling, got to his feet.

'If I've learnt one thing as a headmaster,' he said, 'it's that you can never generalise from one specific example. Dart-making was the fashion, one or two months ago.' His smile was extended to the room in general. 'Now it's moved on to other things. Why,' he continued, 'I used to fire pellets in Maths myself,' and, sitting down to a burst of laughter, concluded, 'And I wasn't so bad at it, I can tell you.'

'They never learn anything,' the same voice continued.

'Oh, shut up,' said a voice from the opposite end of the room.

Miss Harrington got up.

She asked, 'Were there any specific questions?'

'My daughter,' a voice announced, 'has been put down for four

'O' Levels and she needs a minimum of five to get into a sixth form.'

'Anyone can get into a sixth form.' Miss Harrington straightened her skirt behind.

'To go to university out of the sixth form she'll need,' the same voice went on, 'a minimum of five.'

'We can take up your daughter's situation later,' Miss Harrington replied. 'Though the point I would like to make is that an individual's qualities cannot be itemised on a sheet of paper, nor by the marks they receive in a particular exam. One day, arbitrarily chosen, in any one year, must not be seen to be the deciding factor in determining the success of any one child's education.'

'Hear, hear,' said a voice followed, at the front of the audience, by the nodding of several heads.

'I'd like to ask,' Attercliffe got to his feet, 'why, since our children, later in life, will be competing for jobs and university places with children from schools where homework is an established part of the curriculum, the school is so complacent about the setting of homework.'

The Headmaster got up as Miss Harrington sat down.

'I thought we'd answered that question,' he said. 'Our view is that the setting of homework, outside the individual teacher's discretion, is discriminatory.'

'Can't the school set a room aside for children who have difficulty doing the work at home?' he asked.

'That too is discriminatory.' The Headmaster held his pipe in his hand, smiled, and waved it in the direction of the adjoining wall. 'If, for instance, we do as Mr Attercliffe suggests, what will be the attitude of some of our children to those who are stigmatised by disadvantageous home conditions, and are obliged to do their work in there? What will be the attitude of the children themselves when they, staying behind, watch their more fortunate colleagues leaving for homes where this privilege is accepted as a matter of course?'

'That's up to the school,' Attercliffe said, 'to enlighten its pupils to the significance of these arrangements, in the way that, bearing in mind the divergencies of culture present here, and the need for mutual recognition, Miss Harrington has already outlined.'

'It's our school's ambition to be a happy and not a divided school.' Turning to the room, the Headmaster added, 'I recall an incident that happened only the other day when I went to the school toilets to observe the degree of illicit smoking and to issue the appropriate reprimand. Three boys were talking behind a partition. "Everyone," I overheard one of them say, "in Walton Middle School Mixed may not be clever, but everybody's happy." '

A burst of applause, starting at the back and moving to the front of the audience, continued for several seconds.

The Headmaster and Attercliffe sat down.

'Homework,' from a seated position Miss Harrington drew her skirt across her knee, 'is the one element that most parents are concerned about, because it's the part of their children's education that they can see for themselves. On the other hand, apart from egalitarian considerations, which are fundamental to the argument, I'd like to make it plain that the school does not consider the setting of homework as an essential ingredient of the education we provide.'

'My children never learn anything,' came the moaning voice again.

'Neither do mine.' A man stood up; he was short and stocky, with greying – almost whitish – close-cropped hair: his ears were large and red, and so, at the present, was his nose – more than red, Attercliffe reflected – crimson. 'They never learn anything because they can never hear the teacher. And they can never hear the teacher because all the other kids are mucking about. They set off each morning keen to learn, and come home in the evening,' he went on, 'totally disillusioned. And not only disillusioned,' he continued, 'but apathetic. Like all the kids round here.'

'Our children are not apathetic.' Mr Mainwaring glanced at Miss Harrington to decide which of them should answer.

'Hear, hear,' came a voice at the back, followed by a burst of applause.

'I'm afraid, as Mr Mainwaring says, to generalise from one example, and that probably an exception, is always a mistake,' Miss Harrington said.

'Why can't they keep discipline?' the man inquired.

'They do keep discipline,' Miss Harrington said. She crossed her legs: one booted toecap swayed above the other.

'I came up here the other day and walked past the classroom.' The man gestured to the wall of the library adjacent to the school.

'I couldn't hear myself speak. All I could hear was someone shouting, "Silence!" and that wasn't the loudest noise going on. And not only in one classroom,' he went on, 'but several.'

'Anyone who has any experience of teaching,' Miss Harrington said, 'and hasn't heard the circumstances you've described from time to time, must be a very unusual person. We like,' she drew down her skirt, 'to keep a liberal atmosphere inside the building, one in which the children do not get to feel that education is being inflicted upon them, and one in which, too, they feel their own contribution plays a vital and a welcome part.'

'If half of what I hear goes on,' the man continued, 'went on when I was at school, those responsible would get a lathering. We learnt in those days. There was no screaming out in front of a class. If anyone misbehaved they knew where they stood, and if anyone was responsible for stopping the rest of the children working he was, within minutes, standing outside the door of the Headmaster's office.'

Mr Mainwaring puffed out a cloud of smoke, smiled, removed his pipe from his mouth, and announced, 'I don't believe in corporal punishment. It belongs to the past. We have other methods of dealing with recalcitrant children.'

'Like letting them off,' the man replied. 'Why, half the kids in this school are delinquent. They get the biggest beatings of their lives if they misbehave at home, whereas here they're allowed to muck up our children's lives and we're supposed to sit in here and do nothing about it.'

A distant car could be heard outside and, from a closer distance, the sound of a baby crying.

'We're supposed to listen to all this guff while our children are dragged down to a level which my parents never even knew about, and they, I might tell you, were illiterate. My father started down a coalmine at the age of eleven and my mother in a mill at twelve. But they had more dignity and self-respect, and more discipline, than all these yobs who are not only messing up their own lives but messing up our children's. It's a crime. It's not what I, for one, fought for in the Second World War, nor what my brother died for in Burma, nor what other relatives of mine died for at Dunkirk. They didn't sacrifice their lives for us to give up our civilisation, our values and traditions, particularly the tradition of self-discipline and service, for a bunch of blacks and Asiatics. If they want to foul up their own education let them go back to where they came from. Why should we ruin one good thing, and one good country, because we haven't the courage of our own forefathers, who gave their lives to make this a better land?'

Still a baby cried, perhaps from a corridor outside and, after a moment, a woman tiptoed out.

Feet paced up and down: the crying stopped.

'I'm sure the questioner is entitled to his opinion.' The Head-master tapped out his pipe on the heel of his shoe.

'I am entitled. You,' the man continued, 'did no fighting in the war. I did. I've earned my opinion. I've fought for my values, and I'm not going to see you, and people like you, at no expense to themselves, foul them up.'

The redness spread from his ears to his temples; it deepened to purple: it infused his cheeks.

'You have, after all,' the Headmaster said, 'a choice of schools.'

'You mean a native of this country, who has fought for it, and whose relatives have given their lives for it, has to take his children away if he wants them to have a decent education, while all the blacks and orientals who owe nothing to this country and see it only as something to exploit can stay and foul up the place as much and as often as they like? If these cretins here think that's what their children want it's not something I go along with. In ten years' time they'll look at their children, find them out of work, because their qualifications are indistinguishable from the coloureds and the blacks they were taught with, and begin to wonder whatever happened. I'm not staying around to see it. I'm taking my children away from Walton Middle School Mixed right now. I only came this evening to see what sort of excuses you'd come up with and everything I've heard in here, from parents who don't know how to complain, to teachers who've given in to being amateur sociologists – a cop-out, to me, if ever there was one – has only confirmed what I've already suspected from the bits I've seen walking round this school and the even bigger bits of what I've seen of what my children haven't been and, let's face it, in this place, *can't* be taught.'

Accompanied by an equally red-faced woman, invisible until now, he strode across the parquet floor and out of the door at the other end: his feet and the woman's echoed, with the intermittent squeaking of a pram, in the corridor beyond.

'Any other inquiries?' The Headmaster looked round the room less with a smile than a grimace.

A man got to his feet and, with the aid of a walking-stick, set aside one of the two vacated chairs now visible in the centre of the audience, and declared, 'I, too, was in the war. Not in the manner of our previous speaker, nor were my experiences in any way like his. I am not even a native of this country, and haven't even fought for it.'

Round-shouldered, squat, he gazed at the back of the person in front.

'Most of the war years I spent in a camp. I grew up used to having someone standing over me, telling me to do this, do that. I have had two children late in life. They are both at this school. A boy and a girl. In answer to the previous speaker, and in answer to the gentleman there,' he pointed his walking-stick in Atter-cliffe's direction, 'I do not wish to have people standing over my children telling them what to learn and when. I want them to learn of their own free will, and the things I want them to learn are not derived from books, but from their contacts with their fellow pupils. These things are to do with friendship and equality. Nor do I want them, in the evening, to come home burdened with work which they have to sit down to, and over which I have to stand in order to make sure they do it. I want them to come home to freedom. I don't want them to look back on their childhood as on a purgatory in which they were obliged to do things they had no wish to. There are many things in life that we are obliged to do, and I see no point in insisting that our children toe the line when they are at a stage when to enjoy life is still the one privilege they have, a privilege which, the way the world is at present, will be over for them far too quickly. No homework, no racialism, no corporal punishment, no learning by order. Life, and our children, are not for that.'

He sat down to a burst of applause which started, as before, at the back and spread to the front.

The Headmaster, smiling, raised his hand.

'Any more inquiries?' He took out his pipe, sucking at the stem before, getting out a lighter, he flicked up the flame and applied it to the bowl. He, too, like Miss Harrington, had crossed his legs: one thick, wool-stockinged calf was contrasted with her booted one.

'I don't see why,' Attercliffe said, 'a more formal approach wouldn't be beneficial to our children, bearing in mind the two extremes we've been presented with.' Adopting the accent, even the intonation, of the previous speaker, he added, 'How can they exercise their gifts if they haven't been provided with the means to do so? I have here one of my children's exercise books. It has an exercise corrected not by the teacher but by my son and, on the teacher's instructions, he has awarded himself twelve marks out of twelve. Eight of these twelve answers are incorrect and, not only that, contain serious syntactical errors. My son is unaware he has made them. I can illustrate this example from his schoolwork over and over again, and it seems to me, in respect of the supervision of classwork, as well as in the setting of homework, the school is absolving itself of its educative function in order to embrace a more accessible sociological one.'

'Fascist,' came a call from the back, and 'Gestapo,' came a cry, if less audible, and less sharply pronounced, from the figure with the walking-stick seated near the front.

'As Miss Harrington and I have already mentioned, I don't think we can generalise,' the Headmaster said, 'from one specific instance. If,' he went on, 'there are no further questions, I'd like to thank you all for providing us with an evening which I hope has been as illuminating to you as it has been to Miss Harrington and myself, and to which I can only add,' he took out his pipe, 'coffee and biscuits are available on the librarian's desk at the back.'

'What I don't understand is why you bother with it,' Wilkins said.

Elise stood at the window, gazing out, while Wilkins, standing at the door, the baby in his arms, shook his head at her and added, 'I keep telling your father but he doesn't listen. He hasn't cottoned on,' he concluded, 'to what this society is all about.'

'What is it all about?' Elise inquired.

She had come over from college, at lunchtime, in order, Attercliffe imagined, to borrow money: no sooner had she arrived, however, and gone into the kitchen to put on the kettle, than Wilkins tapped at the door and, after opening it, came inside.

'This society,' Mr Wilkins said, 'is one which, in its decay, wills everyone in it to grab all they can. That is what each one of us is doing, presided over by the unions – who want their share before the cake is finished – the well-to-do – who hold on to what they already have – and people like us who scrabble for the crumbs and end up under the table. Your father,' he gestured with the baby's dummy, 'is a moralist. He tries,' he went on, 'to see the decent angle, the one which, in his opinion, will do most people good.'

Elise had a painted face – so uniformly covered in white (with nothing but the orifice of her mouth and the darkened apertures of her eyes to relieve it) that, when Attercliffe had answered the door, he had failed to recognise her, inquiring, 'Yes?' before she, with the same fatuous expression, had responded, 'Can't I come inside?'

'I don't think he's very moral,' she said.

Mr Wilkins inserted the dummy in the baby's mouth; its eyes closed: it sucked. 'He goes on about your education as if any of it matters.' He gestured to the window. 'All this talk of social concern. The only thing,' he went on, 'that turns this world around on its pivot is the same thing that prompts you to eat your food, get up on a morning, go to bed at night, defecate, breathe. In short, chemical necessity.'

'Even love.'

'Love,' Mr Wilkins answered, 'has nothing to do with anything except self-interest.'

Elise, behind her apertured mask of cream and paint and powder, frowned.

'What's the most terrible thing in life?' Mr Wilkins eased the baby to his other arm.

'Dying,' Elise suggested.

'To be more precise,' Mr Wilkins listened to the squelching of the baby's dummy, 'pain. In order to obviate pain, mental or physical, spiritual or material, personal or communal, we make ourselves as comfortable as we can. One of the methods we use is love. Love gives us gratifying feelings. The opposite to everything we're seeking to avoid. Consequently we ascribe to it a significance which exceeds the significance we ascribe to any other feeling. It takes us out of ourselves. It relieves pain. We give it, even, a divine status.' He raised his one free hand. 'But all it amounts to is an impulse to take us away from ourselves and, by so doing, to obviate our feeling pain. It has no significance other than as a characteristic of the species, like, for instance, the colouration of a leaf, or the spots on an animal's back.'

Elise put her finger in her mouth.

'Life,' Mr Wilkins continued, 'is an egotistical exercise. Some achieve their absolution by self-sacrifice, some by offering no sacrifice at all, but, in the final analysis, their motive is the same: to distract themselves from pain, even if,' he raised his hand again, 'it involves, and, for some, particularly if it involves, an absorption in the pain of others.'

'Loving and caring for someone,' Elise inquired, 'is just the way we are?'

'Precisely.'

Mr Wilkins sat, the baby's head couched against his bicep; perhaps for the first time Elise was aware of his apron, a flower-patterned garment which covered his trousered legs like a skirt.

She smiled and, crossing from the window, sat down herself.

'If our need to love is biological it doesn't mean we have to dismiss it,' Mr Wilkins said. 'It lays us open to all sorts of possibilities. Everything becomes clearer.'

His gaze remained fixed on Elise's painted face – the scarcely-visible brows, the buttoned pupils, the colourlessly-painted mouth – then rose to her fanged and spirallingly-convoluted hair, sank to her shoulders, her scarcely-buttoned blouse, her tightly-fashioned jeans, her denimed waist, her tie-dyed, splatter-patterned denimed calves, the fringe of denim threads and tatters around her ankles, the fluorescent pink of her socks inside the unlaced fronts of her patterned plastic ankle-boots – and, taking all this in, he added, 'Life without illusions.'

His laughter, shaking his arm, woke the baby which, with a bolt-like opening of its pale-blue eyes, a spasming of its tiny hands at the ends of its wool-sheathed arms, suckled more fiercely on its dummy: its eyes closed, one less slowly than the other, a glimmer remaining beneath each lid; it sneezed, the dummy dropping out, its head rising before, without looking down, Mr Wilkins retrieved the teat and slid it back inside the mouth.

'That's the tea,' Elise said. 'I'll go and make it.'

She disappeared to the kitchen.

'I'll have to be going.' Mr Wilkins rose. 'I have to cook lunch for one of the young 'uns.' He added, 'A remarkable daughter. I can see great things for her in the future.'

'What as?' Attercliffe asked.

'Qualities like that,' he said, 'don't need a label. My home study course,' he continued, 'is enough to tell me that. I'm reading

The Poor Man's Guide to the Universe at present.' He closed the door.

'What a horrible man,' Elise declared as she came back in.

She set down a plate, sat, then rested the plate on her knees. From the pocket of her jeans she took out a knife and fork: a mug of tea she placed on the floor beside her.

'Did you want a cup?' she asked.

When Attercliffe didn't answer she looked up and said, 'I'll get you one if you like.' Her feet were turned towards one another as she balanced the plate on her knees: a mixture of tinned beans, cold meat, coleslaw and spaghetti.

'Did you come to borrow money?'

'A pound,' she said, 'if you've got it.'

'Hasn't your mother got any to lend you?'

'She hasn't.' She ate quickly, her gaze, half-abstracted, turned to the window. 'I didn't understand a word he said.'

'He's a self-educated man,' Attercliffe said.

'Like you.'

'No. Not like me,' Attercliffe said. He added, 'Not exactly.'

She ate noisily: the sounds of mastication were not all that different from the suckling of the baby on the dummy.

From below came the sound of a television set.

'You don't sound as bad as that.' She chewed again. 'I think everything he says comes out of a book.'

'What do you do,' he asked, 'if, at the age of forty-five, you find you've another thirty years to live and you haven't any occupation to perform that will be of any use to anyone?'

'Do what Mum does.'

'He's chosen to study books.'

She dug her fork into the mound on her plate, raised the food to her mouth, chewed, then declared, 'She was asking Maurice for money.'

'Who was?'

'Mum. She said he owed her it. She was using your phone in the bedroom.'

'It's not my phone,' he said.

'That's how she sees everything at present. "Your father's furniture". "Your father's house". "Your father's telephone". We can hardly sit down without her telling us how much it's going to cost.'

'It does cost money,' Attercliffe said.

'And how.'

She wiped her knife around the plate, licked the blade, smacked her lips, put the plate down, picked up the tea, sipped, frowned, then drank more deeply.

'She said he'd promised her everything and given her nothing. I don't think she knew I was in the house. Are you keeping her short on purpose?'

'I'm not keeping her short at all,' he said. 'What's happened to your allowance?'

'I'm spinning it out.' She finished her tea, set it by her feet, wiped her mouth on the sleeve of her blouse, and asked, 'Until the house is sold we're broke, is that the situation?'

'Not broke,' he said, 'but will be.'

She crossed her legs, sat back, and picked a piece of food from between her teeth.

'I'll have to look round for something smaller.'

'Wilkins won't be pleased.'

'He won't.'

'Strange seeing a man behaving like a woman. Well, like you are, too, as a matter of fact.'

'It's the price,' Attercliffe said, 'we have to pay.'

'The denaturing of men and the reinvigorating of women, though I don't think Mum would agree with that. She says liberation's a con put up by men to get women off their backs and turn them into the whores they really are.'

'It's not,' Attercliffe said, 'what she says to me.'

'It's not,' Elise said, 'what she says to the boys, but what she tells us when we're on our own.'

'Did she get any money from Maurice?' he asked.

'A hundred pounds. She sent it back.'

'Changed her mind,' he said, 'or because it was too little?'

'Because it was too little she changed her mind.'

He laughed; she laughed herself: leaning back in the chair, she added, 'It's an object lesson to her daughters.'

'Don't you feel you can help her?' Attercliffe asked.

'We belong to a different generation, Dad. She talks to Cathy and me as if we were all in this together.'

'You could suggest,' he said, 'that she looked round for a job.'

'She'd never leave the house. It's all she's got. She tells us that

202

more often than she tells us about how much everything costs.' She kicked out her legs, her body arched, her hips thrust up, her head flung back, her face, with its peculiar powder-and–cream-and-paintwork, turned towards the ceiling: she laughed. 'I can scarcely believe she's Mum at all. I look at her and think, "Did I come from that? And Cathy, and Keith, and Bryan and Lorna?"' She straightened in her chair. 'You must admit it, Dad. You've screwed her up no end.'

She knocked the plate with her foot, pushed it to one side, then said, 'You've lost your job, you're too old to play football, you've lost Mum, you'll soon be broke. No one out there,' she indicated the window, 'cares about anything any longer, like that awful man said. It's materialism gone mad, and, day by day, it gets shoddier and shoddier. How do you keep going?'

'I thought you'd come,' Attercliffe said, 'to cheer me up. Apart from borrowing money.'

'Despite everything that's happened you don't seem either to get depressed or even to disapprove. It's as if you're teaching us a lesson, but one which neither Mum nor I, nor Cathy, nor the boys can understand. Cathy was astonished by the way you didn't react when she was taken in.'

'What do you believe in, Elise?' he asked.

'Having a good time.' She ran her hand through her hair.

'You don't strike me as a good-time girl,' he said.

'Not good time in a frivolous sense,' she said. She added, 'But good time in the sense that working for a living doesn't matter. Now that it's cheaper to use labour in poorer lands to make the things we used to make ourselves, the only value left is to spend our energy in living every minute. Like that man said: everything takes on a different meaning.'

She thrust herself up, crossed her legs and, glancing down, picked at a thread on her blouse: she drew it out, her chin pressed against her chest, her eyes closely focused; smoothing the cloth, smiling, she announced, 'Having a good time places a value on what you are. That's the dilemma Mum is in.' The lower lip was pouted as she examined the blouse again. 'It's why you never like my music.' She laughed, got up, and concluded, 'I'll have to be going.'

'Will a pound be enough?'

'Unless you've got two.'

'That puts you in the same state of dependency as the one you say you despise in your mother.'

'That's your moral nature speaking,' she said and – as he got up – took the pound and then the second, kissed him on the cheek, turned to the door, opened it, and was already running down the stairs by the time he reached the landing.

19

The school, academically, is badly run. Below you will find an account of work that has never been marked and, leading on from this, of errors that have been persisted in through a lack of supervision.

He put the pen down and speculated on whether it might be better to type it out: he picked up the pen again.

Keith has played for the school at football. On each of the occasions that I've gone to watch there has been no teacher from the school to sort out the intermittent squabbles, to offer the team advice, or even to cheer it on. I have taken this duty upon myself but the prevailing feeling that the children have is that the school is as little interested in encouraging them as they are in representing it. From a team which, on its first outing, played with spirit, enterprise, and not a little skill, it had, by the end of the third game, degenerated into a quarrelling rabble – greeting my own intervention, as a parent, with a mixture of contempt, disinterest and disbelief: 'If the school isn't interested,' was their attitude, 'why are you?' I've endeavoured to counter this reaction on subsequent occasions, and I think to some effect, but the point I wish to make is that the same lack of involvement on the part of the staff is reflected in this same staff's attitude to the academic work done throughout the school: marking is intermittent, the setting of homework non-existent, the supervision of classwork perfunctory. If your own child were at the school would you be content to leave things as they are?

*

'I was hoping we could settle it without solicitors,' Attercliffe said. 'We've managed all this time.'

'I've already consulted mine,' she said.

'What does he suggest?'

'You'll be getting a letter shortly.'

From the furthest distance came the moan of engines as the diggers and the tractors toiled in the chasmed recess of the opencast mine.

'Even this,' she went on, 'is bad enough, but I'm prepared to accept it and make it work.'

'It'll only work,' he said, 'if I don't have a home at all.'

'Two or three rooms can be a home,' she said.

'I can't afford two or three rooms,' he said. He added, 'A bed and breakfast at the best, or a room in someone's flat.'

'That needn't be so bad,' she said.

She still maintained her 'wifely' position: back straight, head erect, hands clasped, feet and knees together: the only concession to emotion that she allowed – and one, Attercliffe reflected, she probably couldn't arrest – was a flushing of her cheeks and brow.

'When you've a job you'll feel better,' he said.

'I don't think I could take a job,' she said.

'Why not?'

'Any work that's available to someone in my situation is either unskilled labour of a demeaning nature, invariably underpaid, or involves working in a subservient capacity to a man.'

'What do you propose to do?' he asked.

'I propose to bring up the children. I don't intend,' she went on, 'to allow the break-up of my marriage to reduce me to working as a skivvy.'

'Why a skivvy?'

'What the proverbial woman is compelled to do when she insists,' she said, 'on going out to work. I propose,' she went on, 'to work in the house and, in that respect,' she concluded, 'you have a duty to support me.'

'How?'

'By providing a suitable home.' She glanced at him directly. 'In respect of what I've been used to in the past two and a half years, Frank, it's a considerable compromise on my part.'

'In terms of what I've been used to, it's a greater compromise on mine,' he said.

'We all have sacrifices to make,' she announced. 'I've made most of mine already.'

'How?'

'By being a wife. By being a mother. Even, if it comes to that, by being a mistress.' She smiled. 'Men,' she continued, 'despite the myth of female liberation, and largely, I might add, as a consequence of it, can go on doing precisely what they like – shaping the world, directing it, manipulating it, commenting upon it – work, art, science, philosophy, religion: it's all the same. In no area,' she concluded, 'is it not dominated, exclusively, by a masculine interest.'

Leaning forward, she drew her cup of coffee to her: lifting it, she drank.

'I'm accepting a realistic assessment of our situation which, necessarily,' she waved her hand – thin-boned, white-skinned (the nails, like Elise's, painted red) – 'takes into account the world out there.' The hand fluttered by her shoulder, paused, then descended to her lap where it was clasped inside the other. 'Being a mother is something I've been cut out for. It's a job I shall continue to do to the best of my ability.'

'I can't support you,' Attercliffe said.

'You'll have to.'

'I'll look after two of the children, or even four, but I refuse,' he continued, 'to live in the circumstances I would have to live in if you insisted on living here.'

'It's all set out in my lawyer's letter.' Her gaze remained fixed on the wall behind his back.

The house, he had to admit, was unusually tidy; even the mound of clothes which, if neatly folded, was invariably waiting on the bookcase to be ironed had been removed: the fireplace glistened, the grate gleamed, the hearthrug bore only the imprint of his and Sheila's feet in its freshly-vacuumed pile. A bowl of fruit – apples, oranges and bananas – stood on the sideboard.

The doorbell rang.

She said, 'You're not expecting anyone, are you?'

'A purchaser,' he said.

'You never said.'

'I told you I'd come over,' Attercliffe said, 'to make arrangements for someone to see it.'

She got up and, before anything else could happen, went out to the hall, rushed to the door and, beating on the glass, cried, 'Go away!'

Attercliffe, having followed her out to the hall, turned to the kitchen and, opening the back door, set off down the drive: the agent, in a dark suit and a long-winged collar, was standing on the lawn at the front of the house; a woman in a two-piece suit and a feathered hat inquired, as the door was battered again from the other side, 'Have we got the right address?'

'There you are, Mr Attercliffe,' the agent said.

'My wife,' Attercliffe said, 'is disinclined at the moment to let us in, but if you don't mind her opposition,' he added to the woman, 'I can show you round.'

'If it won't be too much trouble,' she said as a two-fisted figure could be seen assaulting the door from the other side – the figure itself, amplified in some parts, attenuated in others – distorted by the irregular texture of the frosted panels – expanding and contracting to the accompaniment of engines moaning on the open-cast mining-site.

'If you'd like us to come back,' the agent said, 'another day.'

'She has to get used to the house being looked at,' Attercliffe said. He smiled at the woman – young, tall, slim-featured (judiciously made-up around the eyes, the cheeks and the mouth) – and added, 'We can, if you like, go in by the kitchen.'

Leading the way, he reached the back door as Sheila – trapping his foot – endeavoured to close it: pressing the door open as she retreated, he indicated to Mrs Samson that she and the agent might step inside.

The agent stooped, leaned forward, and peered in; a tensing of his shoulders, then a perfunctory straightening, indicated that the way was clear and, turning, he smiled, stepped in and, gesturing to the space around him, announced, 'The kitchen.' He led the way to the hall, pausing in the door, glancing out – and pausing once again while Mrs Samson, still in the kitchen, perused the washer, the cooker, the fridge, the working-top, the cupboards and the sink – then, with a smile (surprisingly even teeth between lightly-painted lips), she followed him to the door of the living-room, stepped in, glanced to the window – took in the 'executive' fireplace, the three-piece suite, the bookcase, the dining-annexe, the sideboard, the bowl of fruit – and was about to return to the hall – the agent already poised on the stairs – when, from the landing, came a cry, 'Not here! Not in this house! This house is my house and belongs to me!'

A shoe flew past the agent's head.

It was followed by a second: it thudded against those panels of the door on which, only moments before, with a peculiar venom, Sheila had been beating.

'This house,' came the cry, 'is not for sale!'

The agent tried the front door handle, found it locked, turned, then, with Mrs Samson, retreated first to the living-room then back inside the kitchen.

A second shoe in the mean time, together with a book, had landed in the hall; they were followed by a shoehorn, a mound of bedclothes, then, finally, by a brick – one used to prop up a plank of wood used as a bookcase by Catherine's bed.

Attercliffe climbed the stairs in time to identify a second brick standing on the floor by Sheila's feet and, as she stooped to pick it up, he brought her down with a tackle which, on the football field, might – seventeen or eighteen years before – have stood him in good stead.

The back door of the house had already closed and a cackling of voices came from outside followed, after a moment, by the sound of a car door slamming, then of a second, then of an engine starting and, finally, moments after that, by a screech of tyres.

'I'm not having people looking at my house.'

Sheila, her skirt above her knees, her head pressed against the wall, her shoulders hunched, called, 'This house is not for sale!' and when Attercliffe announced, getting up, 'They've gone,' she remained in very much the same position, flushed – her arms flung out – and, extending a hand to pull her up, he added, 'I'll have to arrange for people to come when you're not here.'

'I'll always be here.' She ignored his help.

'That,' he said, 'we'll arrange with your solicitor.'

'Not even he can get me out.'

She got to her knees, panting, then, leaning to the banister, drew herself up.

She staggered, righted herself, then started downstairs.

He sat on the edge of the landing, his feet on the stairs, and watched her tidy up: bedclothes, pillows, shoes, shoehorn, brick; finally, in a neat pile, she carried them up, edged past him and, humming, moved around the bedrooms.

A thump, a bang, the sliding of a plank: she vanished into the bathroom.

As he arrived in the door she was gazing into the mirror, adjusting her hair.

'You'll have to come to terms with it,' he said.

'I already have done, Frank.' She wiped the corners of her mouth with her finger, turned, came past him – re-entering her bedroom – and announced, 'I don't think that that will be a problem.'

'Why not?'

'I'll not allow them.' She came back out and went downstairs: when, a short while later, Attercliffe followed her down, she was tidying the kitchen – clearing up what evidently had been cleared up several times already. Humming to herself, she added, 'Don't let me keep you.'

'I thought you looked upset.'

'I don't think so, Frank.' Before he could respond, she added, 'That woman. Have you ever seen anything so ridiculous?'

'I thought,' Attercliffe said, 'she looked quite pretty.'

'A woman like that,' she said, 'is a godsend. Her husband must be happy. Knows she'll be twittering around all day. She may even have a job herself. A corollary of his, but not as important. "The money comes in useful." You can see it on her lips.'

'I'll see her on my own when she comes again.'

'She won't come again.' Her arms stretched out on either side, she leaned against the sink. 'Can you imagine what she'll tell her husband as she grovels by his feet tonight? "She *threw* things at me."'

'I thought it was the agent,' Attercliffe said.

'Him as well. He won't come back. Agent's fee or not.'

She folded her arms, her head on one side.

'You have to fight,' she said, 'for the things you want. I learnt that first of all from you, but I learnt it even more from Maurice. "Having got what you wanted, Sheila," he told me, "you've to fight even harder to keep it."'

'What's he got to keep?' he asked.

'Money. Prestige. Position. A Rolls. A Bentley. A Jaguar. A magnificent house. He makes more money in one month,' she added, 'than you could make in a lifetime.'

'Is that why he tired of you?' he asked.

'I made demands which he couldn't respond to. Just as he has his integrity so,' she continued, 'I have mine. On some things you can't compromise. Doctor Morrison made it plain. I had to show integrity. I had to say that this is where I stand and, just as a man – any man, if he's a man at all – is uncompromising with his values, so a woman has to be uncompromising in the things she will not accept within herself. Women may be slaves in everything but name, but from some things, Frank, they can't withdraw. The moment they do,' she went on, 'they cease to exist. They cease to exist for men but, more importantly, they cease to exist for themselves.'

'And your clinging to this house,' he asked, 'is where you've drawn the line?'

'I am simply,' she said, 'making a statement. This far and no further. Beyond this point I refuse to go.'

As he turned to the door, she added, 'It's your duty, Frank, to keep me here. Just as it's mine to be a mother to your children.'

'You've left it too late,' Attercliffe said. 'By approximately two and a half years.'

'We have to accommodate the world as best we can,' she said. 'Your obligation is to go out there and earn a living, mine is to supervise the children.'

She followed him out to the drive and, before he reached the car, she added, 'I'm a realist. I always was. If I can't change the world, I'll make the best use of it I can.' Glancing round as Attercliffe opened the car door, she announced, 'Everyone will think you're visiting me on purpose, when the children are at school,' gesturing at the houses and giving him, as she did so, a ravaged grin.

*

Of course, I can appreciate there are domestic difficulties where Keith and Bryan are concerned. These may well have influenced their attitude to their work. Frequently, when parental problems get out of hand, the school becomes a convenient distraction from the more intractable situation prevailing at home. I can only remind you, if you are dissatisfied with the education your sons are receiving, you are free to remove them to another school. Yours sincerely, E. Mainwaring (Headmaster).

Dear Atty,

The last time we met was one murky winter's afternoon in the second half of a match at Morristown when, amongst other things, you gave me a cauliflower left ear which, to the disgust of my wife, the Jenny Donnington that was, I haven't been able to get rid of. Which is by the by except to say that it hasn't stopped me reading your report on the education – so-called – provided by Walton Middle School (Mixed).

The recommendations put forward by my committee include: the setting-up of a homework timetable; the provision of facilities within the school for those children who are unable to do such work in any other place; the supervision and the marking of schoolwork and homework to become the direct responsibility of the Heads of Department and, through them, of the Headmaster and the Deputy Headmistress; and that this responsibility should involve a regular scrutiny of work done throughout the school in regard not only to its presentation but its content and its style; there should be a regular, supervised rostering of out-of-school activities.

Apart from coming up from positions where you were least expected – your main contribution to the game, as I recall – I can't say, when I saw the signature on your letter, it caught me entirely by surprise. Nor could I say, were I to meet you at the back of Morristown mainstand one dark and windy night my first inclination wouldn't be to give you a bloody thick ear – and hope, as I did nearly twenty years ago, to get away with it – yet, notwithstanding, I sign myself, yours fraternally, 'The People's Friend', and present Chairperson of the Morristown Metropolitan District Council Education Committee.

20

He turned the key and found the back door bolted; the agent smiled: the tall, slim-featured woman (this time in a high-crowned hat with a bevelled brim, sweeping down above one eye) smiled as well. 'We'll go round to the front,' Attercliffe said.

Their feet echoed in the drive; the morning sun lit up the fronts of the houses opposite. A curtain stirred: a figure was silhouetted against the reflected light of a mirror.

The front door, too, was bolted.

'That's odd,' Attercliffe said when, a moment later, there was a distortion of the light behind the frosted glass: a key was turned and the door drawn back.

Sheila stood there, in a dressing-gown and slippers.

'I thought you were out,' Attercliffe said.

'I was.'

'I thought Elise and Cathy were taking you shopping.'

She smiled at the woman behind Attercliffe's back; she smiled at the agent. 'I didn't feel well. I thought I'd come back. I'm just changing upstairs, as a matter of fact.'

She smiled more engagingly than ever.

'Come in.' She addressed the woman and then the agent. 'You've come to look at the house.'

'If it's not inconvenient, Mrs Attercliffe.' The agent had, with the woman, taken one pace backwards to the lawn and, with this inquiry, took an additional step to one side.

'Not at all.' She held the front door wider.

Attercliffe entered. The woman, preceded by the agent, followed.

'Is it all right?' the woman inquired. 'We can easily come back another time.'

'Not at all,' Sheila said again.

She closed the door behind them.

'Go into the living-room. I'll make some coffee.'

They stepped ahead of her and entered a living-room in which the principal upholstered chairs were covered in washing; in front of the fireplace the hearth-rug had been replaced by a blanket which was used, in frosty weather, to cover the engine of Attercliffe's car.

'I shan't be a minute.' Singing to herself, she went through to the kitchen where, after the rattling of innumerable pots and pans, a tap was turned and a kettle – or, presumably a kettle (it might have been a cauldron) – was filled.

'You saw down here before,' Attercliffe said. 'Why don't we look upstairs?'

'I'd prefer to leave, if you don't mind,' the woman said, but already Sheila had re-emerged from the kitchen, passed, fleetingly, across the hall and the sound of the front door being locked was followed by her cry, 'I shan't be a minute!'

She passed by the living-room door once more and the clattering of pans resumed in the kitchen.

'We might as well look upstairs,' Attercliffe said. 'The next time you come,' he added, 'I'll guarantee to have her out.' He gestured round. 'All you have to do is remove, mentally, the impression she's created. The house itself,' he concluded, 'is sound.'

They followed him to the stairs: he allowed the woman to precede him and observed she wasn't wearing tights but stockings. They were halfway up the stairs, the agent, too, in front of him, smoothing down his hair, when Sheila, her head raised, her eyes bright, emerged once more from the kitchen. 'It's not very tidy,' she announced. 'But you'll get,' she declared, 'a fair impression.'

The beds, in Catherine's and Elise's room, had been pulled back: the mattresses as well as the blankets, the sheets, the eiderdowns and the pillows, together with the contents from each of his daughters' drawers and cupboards, had been flung across the floor.

It was impossible to enter the room itself and they each looked in in turn, the agent as briefly as Attercliffe himself, the woman, if anything, more quickly: on one wall, in red, had been printed, 'THIS HOUSE IS NOT FOR SALE'.

Only in the main bedroom, Sheila's own, had the effort to dismember the drawers and the cupboards – as well as the desk – been interrupted, possibly by the sounds of their arrival. Clothes and bedding were strewn across the floor, but one or two of the drawers, though pulled out, were undisturbed. What appeared to have been more broadly disseminated about the room, scattered over the floor as well as the cupboards, the desk and the drawers, and the bed, were the remnants of Attercliffe's scrapbooks – yellow newsprint and photographs – the majority of them torn.

'NOT FOR SALE' was written on the dressing-table mirror. In the bathroom, the bath was full of discoloured water; the basin appeared to be stacked with mud. Sheets of newspaper were screwed up in the toilet: they too appeared to have been discoloured.

When, preceded by Attercliffe, they returned downstairs, Sheila, a tray in her hand, inquired, emerging from the kitchen, 'Do you want to see the kitchen?'

'We've seen all we need to see,' the agent said behind Attercliffe's back.

'Coffee won't be a minute.'

'We have to leave, Mrs Attercliffe,' the agent added, but already Sheila had returned to the kitchen.

'It's a bit cluttered,' she called. 'But make yourself at home in the lounge.'

Stepping around Attercliffe, the agent approached the front door: he tried the handle.

Attercliffe took out his key and fitted it in the lock.

'I've locked the front door,' Sheila said behind his back and he turned to find her standing there, the tray – containing what looked like a plate of biscuits, three cups of coffee, a bowl of sugar and a jug of milk – held before her. 'I'll just find somewhere to put it down,' she added as she disappeared into the living-room, 'I've changed the front door lock.' Reappearing an instant later, without the tray, she announced, 'A woman, living on her own, with young children,' she smiled at the woman, 'has only herself to look to for protection.'

'Have you changed the back door lock?' Attercliffe asked.

'I find,' she smiled to the woman again, 'with so much violence about, a woman, particularly with young children to protect, can't be too careful. Do you find that, Mrs . . . ?'

She waited for the name to be announced.

'Samson,' the agent said behind Attercliffe's back.

'You must have your coffee before it gets cold.' Sheila indicated the living-room. 'I've put some biscuits out as well.'

'No, thank you,' the woman said.

'We might as well,' Attercliffe said.

'No, thank you,' the woman said again, and added, 'I'd be very grateful if you'd unlock the door.'

'And I'd be grateful too,' Sheila said, 'if you wouldn't keep coming back to my house. This house,' she concluded, 'is not for sale.'

'Your husband, Mrs Attercliffe,' the woman replied, 'has said it is.'

'My husband is not its sole owner,' Sheila said. 'Without my permission,' she added, 'he has no right – nor will he ever have the right – to sell it.'

'Your husband, Mrs Attercliffe,' the agent said, his hand on the door, 'is within his rights to put this house on the market.'

'If,' Sheila said, 'you don't want your coffee, perhaps you wouldn't mind if I had a cup myself?'

She returned to the living-room; there was the sound of the tray being thrown on the floor or even – the sound was repeated – against the fireplace.

She reappeared, a cup in her hand.

The woman flinched.

'Don't you find that men are arrogant, Mrs Samson?'

Raising the cup, she sipped from the rim.

'The way things are at present,' the woman flushed beneath the brim of her hat, 'I find they have a great deal to put up with.'

'I find,' Sheila said, 'they've scarcely anything at all,' and added, 'You, on the other hand, because you submit to the humiliation of pandering to a man, take the masochistic line of "do whatsoever thou wishest unto me for it'll only show I love you."'

'I'd appreciate it if you'd unlock the door,' the woman said.

'I'll unlock it in my own good time,' Sheila said, and added, as Attercliffe stepped towards her, 'I've hidden the keys. Though you can,' she continued, addressing the woman, 'climb out of the window. Crawling, with your philosophy, should come as second nature.'

'Couldn't we ring the police?' the agent said.

'That'll look good,' Sheila announced. 'Two able-bodied men molested by a woman.' To the woman, she added, 'It's not you I'm attacking, but him.' She indicated Attercliffe. 'One day you'll see how all you've taken for granted has been mistaken and how all the women around you are slaves. Even those who believe they've achieved their liberation and have been given a token place by men. Only, this time, instead of taking them for granted, the men, like him, and no doubt like him,' she indicated the agent, tall, dark-eyed, dark-haired, 'will laugh, as they're laughing now.'

'Isn't that paranoia?' the woman said.

She was looking for an alternative exit from the house and had glanced down the hall to the recess and the cupboards at the other end.

'It is paranoia,' Sheila said, 'as long as you're a man.' She added, 'If you're a woman, it's common sense. They give us children, respect our potency, then put us out to grass.'

To stress this final declaration she threw her cup – not at Attercliffe, nor at the woman, nor even at the agent (who, like the woman, raised both arms and cowered) – but through the doorway at the fireplace in the living-room.

It shattered.

'You fill me with contempt,' she said. 'Titivate yourself up to complement an odious image of you engendered by a man. Come to look at a house you will never own yourself. Fit in. Collaborate. Where's your spirit?'

Sweeping her arm in the direction of the living-room, she said, 'At least my daughters will never turn out the way their father wants.'

Glancing first at the floor and then at Attercliffe, the woman said, 'It seems to me you're sick.'

'I am sick,' Sheila said. 'Of seeing your silly painted face and your ridiculous hat and stockings.'

She returned to the kitchen, rattled several pans, then shouted, 'The back door's open, if you want to leave.'

Stepping over a bucket, several pans, the contents of an up-turned drawer and of several emptied cupboards, they emerged in the drive at the side of the house.

The woman, her handbag suspended loosely from her hand, walked briskly to her car, got in and, with a glance behind, to see that the road was clear, drove off.

The agent paused by the gate, said, 'I'll be in touch,' crossed the road to his own car, got in, and followed her.

'That seems to have gone well,' Sheila said in the still open door behind Attercliffe's back.

'Very,' Attercliffe said.

'Given her something to think about.'

'It has.'

'You have,' she said, 'to make a strong impression. It's first impressions,' she went on, 'that count.'

'What happened to Elise and Cathy?' Attercliffe asked.

'I left them in town,' she said.

'Did they know you were coming back?'

'I told them,' she said, 'I was going to the toilet. I thought when they suggested going shopping it sounded very odd.'

'Odder still when they come back here.'

'I'll soon have this straightened.' She touched her hair. 'Ready for the next lot,' she added, 'should you choose to bring them in.'

'I shall have to have a key,' he said.

'I'll get one made.'

'Haven't you had one made for the children?'

'Not yet.'

'How do they get in?'

'I'm always here,' she said. Taking hold of the door from the other side, she added, 'Anything else?'

'Nothing for the present,' he said.

'I'll have them ready when you come at the weekend. Sound the horn,' she called through the vibrating panes of the door as she closed it. 'It'll save you coming in.'

'People in our situation,' Benjie said, addressing his remark to Tiny, 'don't stand a chance.'

Slight, slim-featured, he leaned back in the chair and laughed; Tiny, too, leaned back, his fisted hands on his knees.

'It's all to do with colour. If you're black, people treat you as if you're scum. Or, if not, they condescend.'

'They condescend.' Tiny turned his head in Attercliffe's direction: he had, Catherine had announced, on their arrival, got 'a stiff back'. ('A copper fell over me' – laughter.)

'It stands to reason,' Benjie announced.

'Why did you ring me up and tell me,' Attercliffe asked, 'that Cathy had been taken in?'

'I thought I should.' He stamped his foot on the carpet, laughed again, and added, 'There you go again. Suspicious.'

'I'm trying to find out,' Attercliffe said, 'what it is in me you thought you were responding to.'

'Suspicious,' Benjie said again.

'He thought you'd care,' Catherine said, 'what happened to your daughter.'

Even the room, Attercliffe reflected, they treated with suspicion, unable to understand, for one thing, why he should have come to live here and, now that he had, what it was that kept him.

'If you imagine that I care about her, then you must care about her, too,' he said.

'Sure.' He dug his heel at the carpet.

'If you do,' Attercliffe went on, 'why do you involve her in things which won't do her any good?'

'What things?'

'Giving her clothes that are stolen. Giving her records. Giving her books. If she's a receiver of stolen goods she could,' Attercliffe went on, 'be sent to prison.'

'She won't go to prison.' He glanced not at Attercliffe, nor at Catherine, but at Tiny.

'Why not?'

'None of them are nicked.'

'I thought they were.'

'I borrow them.' He laughed; the larger figure beside him laughed as well.

'Borrowing without permission amounts to stealing,' Attercliffe said.

'They were stolen from me in the first place.'

'How do you reckon that?'

'The British exploited the empire. Part of the empire,' he went on, 'is us. When we were aboriginals we let you do it. Now we're taking back some of the things you took from us.'

'Such as?'

He spread out his hands. 'You name it. We nick it. Wealth from the Commonwealth is what made this country, and wealth from the Commonwealth,' he added, 'is what we're taking back.'

Tiny turned his foot on one side; he turned his other foot on its outer edge as well: the ribbed soles of his shoes confronted one another across several inches of threadbare carpet.

'All this is clapped out.' Benjie gestured at the room, but intended to indicate, Attercliffe imagined, not merely the flat, the house, and the town, but the country. 'It lives on its glorious past and suffers,' he said, 'from delusions of grandeur.'

'If you've been arrested for a crime which you confess privately you've committed, why do you lie about it when you get into court?' Attercliffe said.

'What court?'

'Of law.'

'What law?'

'The country's.'

Benjie frowned.

'I don't belong to this country, Mr Attercliffe,' he said.

'What country do you belong to?' Attercliffe asked.

'His country.' He dug his finger at Tiny's chest.

The two of them laughed, kicking their heels at the floor.

'I thought you lived round here,' Attercliffe said.

'We live in our own land,' Benjie said. He added, 'I don't ask you to live in it. Why should you ask me to live in yours?'

'You wear clothes like I do,' Attercliffe said. 'Live in a house like I do, go to the same schools, visit the same doctors, pay with the same money, go to the same prison if you break the law, do the same sort of work, pay the same taxes. How can you say,' he went on, 'you live in another country?'

'Our land isn't this land,' Benjie said.

'What is your land?' Attercliffe said.

'Our land,' he said, 'is all around you. Only, if you're not in it, you can't see it. And if you can't see it, you're not in it.'

'What about Cathy?'

'She makes up her own mind.'

'The only difference between us,' Attercliffe said, 'is that, whereas we can both see my land, I'm not allowed to see yours.'

'You can see my land any time you like.' He laughed, spread out his hands, and kicked his feet once more at the carpet.

'Does your father live in your land, or does he live in mine?' Attercliffe asked.

'He doesn't know where he lives. All I can say is,' he added, 'I don't live where he lives. I've emigrated,' he concluded, and laughed again.

A little later they got up to leave, going out to the kitchen, rinsing the mugs they had used, laughing, banging down the stairs.

'See you,' Catherine said, as she started to follow.

'That didn't go down too well,' he said.

'You don't understand a scale of values that's based not on having but on being,' Catherine said. 'What they're telling you happens to be true. Everything they do,' she continued, 'has a proper scale of values. For instance, how can you say they pay the same taxes? They can't get any work. How can you say they live in a house like you do? The place they live in is almost a ruin. How can you say they visit the same doctor? The doctor you have wouldn't touch them with a barge-pole. How can you say they go to the same prison? The law they break is not their own. How can you say they go to the same schools? The curriculum they're taught has been made up by whites.' Her name was called and the panelling on the door downstairs was banged. 'Black is white, and white is black. It's the world,' she continued, 'they have to live in. It's the land,' she concluded, 'you'll never see,' and, yelling, 'I'm coming,' she started for the door.

'Won't you come at the weekend?' Attercliffe said.

'I'll see,' she said and, closing the flat door, skipped down the stairs, several at a time, calling from the hall below, 'See you, Mr Wilkins.'

Attercliffe reopened the door of the flat. 'It's getting to be a habit,' Wilkins said, as he reached the top of the stairs.

'Do you object to them coming?' Attercliffe asked.

'I don't object,' he said. 'They have a great deal,' he went on, 'to put up with.'

He looked round, standing in the door as Attercliffe, turning to his desk, sat down.

'No one can disguise we live in a racialist society,' he continued. 'On a personal basis,' he paused, 'there's little prejudice at all.'

Taking the cover off his typewriter Attercliffe started to type.

'On a community basis,' he went on, 'it's an entirely different matter.'

'My daughter,' Attercliffe said, 'is going to end up in prison.'

'She has her head screwed on. I could see that at a glance.' He added, 'You're proud of her taking a stand with the disadvantaged. I can see that in your eyes.'

'I have to get back to work,' Attercliffe said.

'Anything I can get you?' Wilkins asked.

'No, thanks,' Attercliffe said.

'I'm free for five to ten minutes.'

'No, thank you.'

'I'll go downstairs and pacify the baby. It was jolted awake by all that noise.'

He left the flat door open; a moment later, from below, came the squeaking of the pram.

'It's fresh, innovative, and shows, above all, an intuitive grasp of theatrical effect.'

Towers sat back, his hands locked together on the top of his head: his chair creaked.

'The dynamic is maintained by a constant flow of feeling. Everything,' he went on, 'is implicit. Nothing is stated.'

He tapped his hand on the script, examined the title, *Players*, which he read aloud, and said, 'I never would have thought of setting a play in a football changing-room, with all the events you might assume to be of interest taking place off-stage. I like the idea of challenging people. This play, in that sense, is a challenge to me. It's bigger than anything I've previously undertaken. I shall schedule it,' he continued, 'right away. There'll be one or two problems with the nudity. The committee to whom I am accountable take a conservative view, but I'm sure,' he added, 'I can straighten them out.'

He called, 'Meg,' leaned over his desk, in the direction of the door, and when, a moment later, Meg came in – dark-haired, slim-featured, jeaned and denim-jacketed – he said, 'I want you to prepare a contract. A good 'un. Make it,' he continued, 'so that, if it's a success, he can afford to write another. One of many,' he added to Attercliffe. 'I can see a long line to follow this.'

'Congratulations,' the assistant said. 'With Harry behind you I'm sure we'll win.'

'With me in front of him, an' all,' the pneumatically-featured figure replied.

Attercliffe gazed not so much at Towers, as he talked, as at the posters and the photographs on the wall, at the other scripts piled, some on a table, others on the floor: he gazed up at the window, out of which – on the top floor of the Phoenix – nothing was visible but the sky above the square.

'You'll come in for casting?' The director set his feet on the desk. 'I couldn't cast it without your support. To have a touchstone would help me no end,' and, leaning forward to gaze past his feet – two metal-studded boots with metal-capped toes – he added, 'It's extraordinary, with no experience of the theatre, that your instincts as to what can go on on a stage are so specific. It's as if,' he continued, 'you'd been writing plays for years.'

His metal-capped boots were tapped together.

'If I wasn't here I wouldn't have believed it. To have plucked' – he raised one hand above his head – '*something* out of the air.' He laughed. 'A once in a lifetime chance!'

'She can make it difficult,' Norton said, 'for a very long time.'

His hands clasped on the top of his head, he sat behind his desk in a manner reminiscent of Towers – though without his feet propped up before him.

The clatter of a typewriter, together with the ringing of a telephone, came from the outer office.

'Her solicitor,' he went on, 'will advise her to stall for as long as she can. The debatable point being how much and to what degree a redundancy payment constitutes an income. That,' he lowered his hands to the folder before him, 'could take as long as a year.'

Attercliffe said, 'By which time I'll be broke and she'll have to leave the house.'

Folding back his hair – a frothy mass through which the light from the window shone (a view of the street leading to the eponymous Norton Square) – he said, 'It pays her to procrastinate in the hope you'll get another job.' He added, 'And in the know-ledge that, the longer she stays there, the more difficult it's going to be for you to get her out.' He tapped the folder. 'She's suggested, for instance, you could easily travel the country looking for work while she looks after the children.'

'Aren't you going to argue on my behalf?' Attercliffe asked.

'You know her situation. Although she's agreed to give you a key she is in her rights not to allow anyone to come to the house with a view to buying it without her permission.'

The telephone rang on his desk; he picked it up, said, 'Excuse me,' and, turning in his chair, still speaking, gazed directly to the window.

'She's a very determined woman.' He replaced the receiver. 'She's acquired a great deal of your obduracy,' he went on. 'I suppose you shouldn't complain.'

'Her occupation of the house,' Attercliffe said, 'increases her morbidity. She sees herself sitting there, being kept by me, until the children have left. Which, in Lorna's case, will be another fifteen years.'

'Divorce her.'

'Divorce,' Attercliffe said, 'is not what I wanted.'

'You'll have to make your mind up,' Norton said. 'Something you haven't done for the past three years.'

Voices came from the outer office.

'The sooner we finalise that,' he added, rising, 'the sooner you can get her out.'

21

The floor of the room was marked out with tape; it ran off in two directions: a girl, stooped, in jeans and a sweat-shirt, was cutting a last strand of it with scissors, and sticking it down.

A table and chairs were arranged along one side of the room: it was from here Attercliffe had watched Towers rehearsing with Phyllis Gardner; the interior was a windowless crypt, with a trampled yard outside.

There were twenty-two actors and three stage-staff: a square-shouldered, close-cropped figure wearing a corduroy skirt and a cardigan who was sitting beside Attercliffe at the table writing notes in a script, the girl in the sweat-shirt sticking down the tape, and Meg, in jeans and a sweater.

Towers could be heard in the hallway speaking on a telephone, his voice obscured by the roar of the traffic since, evidently, the outer doors had not been closed.

The actors, moving around the chairs, came to the table, inquired about the text, consulted the corduroy-skirted assistant, talked to Meg, and drifted off to the alcove at the side where the sweat-shirted girl, having completed her taping of the floor, had started to supervise the making of coffee.

Towers came in; he was wearing, in addition to his metal-capped boots, a pair of corduroy trousers, a three-quarter-length jacket with a fur-lined hood, and, beneath the jacket, a Fair Isle sweater.

'The designer won't be here for us to look at the set. His car has failed to start this morning.' He shook Attercliffe's hand and added, 'Have you had a cup of coffee?' then called to the room, 'Gather round and we'll look at Jenny's floor-plan.'

A chart was opened on the table: the items drawn on the plan were pointed out by Towers, a grubbily-nailed finger indicating the entrances and exits, the position of the masseur's table, the benches, the bath. He crossed to the tapes on the floor, paced along each one in his metal-capped boots, suggested where the principal playing-areas for each of the scenes might be, returned to the table, took off his jacket, took off, also, one of his boots, felt in the sole, then, receiving a cup of coffee from the sweat-shirted girl, invited the actors to sit in a ring of chairs set around the table and proposed that each one of them, in turn, should announce his name and the character he was playing. He introduced himself, his corduroy-skirted assistant, whose name was Jenny, the sweat-shirted girl, whose name was Ann – and finally Meg who, picking up a file, called, 'If there's nothing else I'll go back to the theatre,' at which point Towers, leaning over the table, took up a script, opened it and began to talk about the play.

He described the action – before and during and after a match – the nature of the game itself, the characters it attracted, the attitudes of mind it encouraged, asked if there were any questions – several of which he invited Attercliffe to answer – and, replacing his boot, suggested they might open the scripts and begin the play's first reading.

As they read, Towers gazed to the space behind the actors' backs, and at the area of the floor between the taped-off sections of the set itself. The largest and the oldest of the actors, a dishevelled-looking man with tiny eyes and a minuscule nose, appeared, as the reading continued, to fall asleep; periodically, his head jerked upwards.

When it came to the occasion when he was obliged to read, the voice of Jenny called, 'Felix,' and as his head came up and a script – much creased and thumbed and folded – was opened on his knees he called, ' "Hope I'm not intruding, Danny. Thought I'd have a word." '

The actors laughed; the assistants laughed: Attercliffe laughed himself.

Phlegm rattled in the speaker's throat: the intonation of his voice was deep.

' "Chilly in here. That fire could do with a bit of stoking." '

The actors laughed again; Towers laughed: Jenny and Ann joined in.

' "Just to wish you good luck, lads." '

' "Thanks," ' several of the actors said together.

' "Fair play, tha knows, alus has its just rewards." '

The actors laughed again.

' "Play like I know you can play." ' The mouth, as tinily-featured as the nose, was pursed. ' "There'll not be one man disappointed." ' The reddened eyes glanced up. ' "Any grunts and groans? Any complaints? No suggestions?" '

' "No, sir," ' several of the actors answered.

' "The club secretary here'll be in his office afterwards, if there's anything you want. Play fair. Play clean. May the best team win." ' He raised a small, short-fingered hand and revealed the frayed cuff not only of his overcoat but of the shirt beneath. ' "Good luck." '

Lowering his hand, he thumbed through his script, found a passage, inserted his finger, closed his eyes - and appeared once more to fall asleep.

'What I like about your play - I am speaking, I take it, to the author? You are the man who wrote it? You must tell me if I've been misled - is the variety of its characters. You don't often get that in contemporary drama, which goes in much more for social types - young, old, rebellious, and so forth. Whereas all yours, as far as I can see, first and foremost, are human beings.' He leant on the bar: folds of fat projected from beneath his sharply-pointed chin and above the velvet collar of his overcoat.

Other figures jostled at the bar, including, further along, the bulky figure of Towers talking to Meg, Ann and Jenny, but Attercliffe's companion appeared as oblivious to them as he was to his surroundings.

He belched, tapped his chest, and added, 'Richness is the key to life. I am speaking of cash as well as the theatre.' He belched again, drank and, as he emptied his glass and Attercliffe offered him another, announced, 'I could see you were a sport when you came in the room. I'm not often wrong on first impressions.'

Workers from the nearby offices of the Metropolitan District Council pressed to the bar, or sat at the crowded tables in the space between the bar itself and the door.

Felix, his overcoat unbuttoned and revealing a stained, double-breasted, pin-stripe suit, a light-grey tie and a wrinkled shirt, the collar of which – obtruded upon by his swelling neck – was dark with grease, replaced his empty glass and, picking up a full one, said, 'I made a fortune once, and lost it, not in a day, but in under a year. That was when I was young and idealistic. I ran a theatre. In the provinces. Actor-managers went out of fashion. The ones that could manage could never act, and the ones that could act could never manage. I – my name is Mason – fell between.' He lowered his glass, took a drink, took a second, took a third, swallowing loudly, and added, 'Whereas I could act as well as I could manage, or, conversely, manage as well as I could act, I could never do the two together: "To beer or not to beer", and all the time I was gazing at the stalls: "Twelve in the ten and sixpennies, sixteen in the eight and nines, and twenty-four in the five and eights. That comes to how much altogether?" and afterwards, in the manager's office, instead of adding the accounts, I was giving notes: "Too close in that scene, and too distant in the other", whereas what I should have been doing was seeing how much was not left over from twenty-five pounds, sixteen shillings and twopence threefarthings when my expenses came to twenty-seven pounds, two shillings and eight.'

He drained his glass, set it down and announced to the barman, 'Same again for my friend and me,' and, to Attercliffe, continued, 'My wife was an actress. She was a demon.' He tapped his head. 'Mentally afflicted.'

He turned to the bar, looked along it, tapped a coin on the counter, and called, 'Over here, barman, when you've got the time.'

'We lived,' he added to Attercliffe, 'like cat and mouse for twenty-five years. I tried to kill her seventeen times. Once with a knife, twice with poison, three times with gas, four with electricity, and a countless number of occasions by strangulation. The problem was, I have very small hands while she, unfortunately, had a very thick neck. Once,' his gaze reverted to the ceiling, 'I hit her with a bottle, another time, having wrapped her in a carpet, I drowned her in a bath. I had just rung up the police to inform them she had had a serious accident when she walked into the room and shouted down the telephone, "He tried to kill me." I had a hell of a job explaining that.'

The barman approached along the counter; the drinks were poured: the coin in the actor's hand was laid on the bar.

The barman repeated the price.

'That's all I've got on me, steward.' The actor's hand was fisted now beside his glass.

Attercliffe laid a note on the counter.

'My friend,' the actor said, 'has come up trumps. It's a good job,' he went on, 'I had him with me,' and added, 'This is the well-known playwright whose name I can't recall but whose reputation you will hear about in a very short time,' and, signalling with his glass to Attercliffe, drank, laid the glass down, gasped, belched, and declared, 'The murder of one's wife is the easiest crime to get away with. Opportunity? Always there. Alibi? Always loved her. Gain? Immeasurable. 99.9 per cent of all domestic crime is husbands murdering their wives yet, because of the circumstances, you never hear a word about it.'

Walking beside Attercliffe, rapping his metal-tipped toes on the pavement, Towers said, 'Been telling you about his wife?' and added, 'It's all part of his one coin tapped on the counter routine. "That's all I've got, barman." Quite a card.'

'Isn't he too drunk to work this afternoon?' Attercliffe asked.

'I won't get to him till the end of the week. That's why he's started. He'll have sobered up by then.'

'Has he killed his wife?' he asked.

'She died a few years ago. In a car crash. Felix himself was driving.'

They re-entered the crypt where the actors who started the first act were drinking coffee.

The scripts were reopened; the play began: the club-cleaner came in and prepared the jerseys. The first of the players arrived to change for the match.

He woke in a sweat; the air, nevertheless, was cool, the top of the window was open.

The flat was small; how small the quietness of the night made clear: he could hear the children breathing – the stuffiness of Lorna's nose, the murmur of Keith as he talked in his sleep.

The telephone rang downstairs; he heard the banging of a door, and he had already reached the landing when a figure emerged from the flat below: crossing the hall it lifted the receiver, called, 'Yes?' and, aware of Attercliffe approaching on the stairs, added, 'You know what time it is?'

Wilkins's daughter, clad in a nightdress, laid the receiver on top of the coin box and, returning to the flat door, shouted, 'It's not me they're ringing but your friend upstairs,' whereupon a light went on inside the flat, followed, a moment after that, by the sound of the baby crying.

'Is that you?' Sheila's voice inquired as the door slammed behind Attercliffe's back. 'I've just had a call from Cathy.'

'Where?' he asked.

'Some place she's gone to live at.'

'What place?'

She said, 'That's why I'm ringing. She's gone with Benjie.'

'Did she give you an address?'

'She says no one is to go there.' A sheet of paper rustled at the other end.

'I haven't got a pencil,' Attercliffe said. 'I shan't be a minute.'

As he went upstairs a further altercation took place inside the flat: crockery ricocheted across a floor.

'What's all the noise?' Sheila said when he picked up the phone again.

'That's the disturbance,' he said, 'caused by your call,' and as she dictated the address he added, 'Did she say she was leaving school?'

'She says she will live exactly as she does at home.'

'What about school?'

'She says she intends to go on with that.'

'I'll go and see her tomorrow,' he said.

'She asked that you didn't.'

'She prefers you to go?' he asked and, to the sound of someone colliding with the back of the flat door – at which the banisters, the stairs and the wall of the house vibrated – he repeated the question.

'Neither of us is to go,' she said.

'What does she expect us to do?' he asked.

'Understand.'

'I do understand.'

The voices of Wilkins and his daughter, together with those of several others inside the flat, obliterated Sheila's answer.

'Has she taken her pills?'

'What pills?'

'Her anti–reproduction pills.'

230

'She's taken everything,' she said, 'apart from her clothes.'

'If she hasn't taken her clothes she can't be serious in leaving,' he said.

'She's not interested in clothes,' Sheila said, her voice drowned, once more, by the voices from the flat. 'She's taken what she wanted.'

'Perhaps he'll steal any clothes she needs.'

'That's likely.'

'And food. And books. And medication. Even the money she needs at school for dinners. If it's a depressed area there must be plenty of old women knocking about. Probably the best day to visit her is pension day, then Benjie might be busy and not present to distract her.'

'Are the children safe?'

'What children?'

'*Our* children!' her voice screamed at the other end. 'What are they *doing*?'

'The children are asleep,' he said.

'Can't you find somewhere else to live?'

'It's difficult,' he said, 'so long as my wife insists on tying up all our resources in a house, the occupation of which she reserves exclusively for herself.'

There was silence at the other end: there was silence, too, in the flat behind.

'What's going on, Dad?' came Bryan's voice as, pyjamaed, flat-footed, he appeared at the top of the stairs.

'It's all right,' Attercliffe said, at which Sheila said, 'What's all right?'

'I'm talking to Bryan,' he said.

'I thought he was asleep!' her voice wailed from the other end.

Attercliffe said, 'He's woken up.'

'If anything happens to those children I shall hold you responsible,' she said. 'They've told me about that horrible flat and the horrible people who live downstairs.'

The door behind him opened; Wilkins came out – dressed in his shirt, his trousers and his coat, and carrying a pair of shoes.

Opening the outer door, he nodded, drew on the shoes, closed the door, and set off down the street.

'Elly's asleep,' Sheila said. 'I've no one here to talk to.'

'Call up Maurice,' Attercliffe said.

There was no answer at the other end.

'Or Gavin.'

There was still no answer.

'I'll ring you in the morning,' he said as the light went out beneath the door of the flat and in the glazed panel which formed the upper quarter of the hall partition.

'Are you going to see her?'

'I shall.'

'Who'll look after the children?'

'I'll leave Keith and Bryan in charge.'

'Of Lorna?'

'She'll be all right.'

'My God. What are you doing to our children?' she cried. 'Someone, somewhere,' she beseeched, 'must understand.'

'I'll get in touch tomorrow,' he said.

'Please bring Cathy home. I'll do anything she asks.'

'She'd soon grow tired of that,' he said.

'Just say we'd like to talk to her.'

'You talked to her on the phone.'

'She refused to discuss it. She said she'd made her decision, just like I'd made mine and you'd made yours.'

'All I've done,' Attercliffe said, 'is to accommodate the wishes of everyone around me.'

'I can't stand the thought,' she said, 'of her coming to any harm.'

He said, 'She won't come to any harm.'

'With criminals!' she cried.

'With evangelists,' he said.

'Is she religious? She's not religious? She's not become religious!' Her voice rose, once more, to a wail.

'I am talking of their sense of vocation, rather than the content of their doctrine,' Attercliffe said.

'It's like a nightmare. It is a nightmare. I can't believe it's happening,' she said. 'We're the only family I know who has had anything to do with blacks. Why,' she went on, 'does it have to be us?'

'It's because,' Attercliffe said, 'your children have more spirit.'

'More desperation,' she said. 'More *despair*.'

'That's not how anybody else would judge them,' Attercliffe said.

'How will it look if she's arrested again?'

'She wasn't arrested before,' he said.

'She was taken in!' she screamed. 'Why are you so *perverse*?'

'You'd better calm down,' he said.

An argument, conducted in screams, erupted in the flat behind. He waved Bryan back upstairs.

'If anything happens to those children I shall never forgive you,' she said.

He put the phone down, knocked on the flat door, and, after an interval of silence, during which he knocked again, a voice inquired, 'Who's that?'

'It's Mr Attercliffe,' he said.

The flat door was shaken.

A latch was turned.

Mrs Wilkins, dressed in a coat with its collar drawn up, barefooted, nightgowned – a grey-haired, thin-featured figure without an upper set of teeth – looked out.

'Sorry about the telephone,' he said.

'Robert's gone out,' she said and, aware, suddenly, that she had no upper teeth, she covered her mouth and added, 'I shan't be a minute.'

Attercliffe gazed into the minuscule hall of the flat – a passage from which several doors opened out: from one shone a light; a face appeared from inside another. After glancing out, it vanished.

Mrs Wilkins returned; she smiled.

'On the next occasion it rings in the night,' Attercliffe said, 'I'll answer it, Mrs Wilkins.'

'I don't mind.' She smiled again.

'Or,' he said, 'we can leave it off the hook.'

'That's no problem at all, Mr Attercliffe,' she said as a baby's crying started in one of the rooms, followed, an instant later, by the screaming of her daughter.

'I'll tell Robert you called,' she said. 'He went to get some air.'

Later, as Attercliffe lay in bed, he heard the front door close downstairs, then a creaking on the stairs themselves: he got up in time to forestall Wilkins tapping on the door.

'I went out for a spot of air.' His neighbour's figure was silhouetted on the landing. 'Not back in prison is she?'

'No,' Attercliffe said. 'Sorry about the telephone.'

'What's life for,' Wilkins said, 'if you can't call on a friend?' and, murmuring, 'Where would we be without it?' he returned downstairs, turning to his door where, stooped, he paused, before inserting his key.

22

The interior of the shop was filled with wooden crates – most of them dismembered – and a number of wooden benches, the metal legs of which had been removed. A door, at the rear, leaning from its hinges, led into a darkened passage.

There was a smell of damp; wooden laths showed through the ceiling.

A door, on one side of the passage, gave access to a flight of stairs; paper, peeling from the wall, released a cloud of dust: a banister, at the top of the stairs, was propped against a wall.

In a room scarcely broad enough to take a single bed a figure stooped over a knee-high table: on the table stood a metal stove; a smell of gas obscured the more prevalent odour from the floor below.

The figure looked up: its hair long, its feet bare – skirted, bloused – it inquired, 'Have you come about the money?'

'What money?' Attercliffe asked.

'Aren't you the man from the council?'

He shook his head.

'What do you want?'

'I'm looking for Catherine Attercliffe,' he said.

'She's out.'

She returned her attention to the stove: it comprised a hot-plate and a tiny oven.

On the hot-plate stood a segment of dough.

'Is Benjie here?'

'He's out.'

Though younger than Catherine, her figure – crouched,

shrouded in the skirt and the loose-fitting blouse – might have been, Attercliffe reflected, that of an older woman.

Beside the stove, on the knee-high table, stood a mound of dough which, discoloured, the girl picked up, tore in two and rolled into balls.

'Cooking?'

'Baking.'

She beat the dough with her fist; the table rattled: the stove shook.

The girl's eyes were dark, her hair black, her cheeks – apart from the smears of dust – red: picking up a knife, she prised the dough from the table.

'Is Tiny here?'

'Who?'

'Benjie's friend.'

'Through there.' She directed the blade of the knife along the landing.

He was aware of music and voices as he entered a dilapidated room on his left: a hole, caverned out of the brickwork, led into an equally dilapidated room in the adjoining building.

A voice called out: several black faces scrutinised his arrival as, having scrambled through, he glanced about the room the other side.

'Is Benjie here?' He straightened.

A figure, leaning from a window, turned, withdrew its head, and asked, 'Anything you want?'

'I was looking for Benjie,' Attercliffe said.

Several of the figures moved to the door.

'Are you from the council?'

'I'm unemployed at present,' Attercliffe said.

A cassette-player, removed from the room, was pitched to a higher volume on the landing outside.

'Or Tiny?' Attercliffe asked.

The remaining figures left.

'Who's Tiny?'

'Steve?' Attercliffe suggested.

'Who's Steve?'

'I don't know him by any other name.'

'Benjie I never heard of.'

The youth was bald, his head glistened.

'How did you get in?' he asked.

'Through the shop.'

'Hey,' he stepped out to the landing, 'the shop's left open.' Turning back to the room, he added, 'You can't come in without permission.'

He closed the door behind him.

A moment later, reopening it, he said, 'Anything you want?'

'I was looking for Catherine Attercliffe,' Attercliffe said.

'Not here.'

'Perhaps,' Attercliffe said, 'I could leave a message.'

'Next door.'

'Anyone in particular I should talk to?'

'Do you speak English?'

'That's right,' he said.

'I only speak Arabic.'

'I understand you perfectly,' Attercliffe said.

'In that case,' he said, 'why don't you piss off?'

He closed the door again.

Attercliffe returned through the hole in the wall.

The girl, crouching to the stove, was taking a bowl of food from the oven.

'Do they think I'm the police?' he asked.

'I've no idea.' She turned to a sink set beneath a window at the end of the room.

She turned a tap; a pipe shuddered on the wall: stooping to the sink, she rinsed then lifted out a number of pots and pans.

'Are you a friend of Cathy's?'

'I know her.'

Her figure was stocky, her feet black, her heels blistered; through crouching, the backs of her calves were red.

'Did you come through the shop?'

'How else can you get in?' he asked.

'Through the yard.' Thick, unwashed strands of hair were flicked across her shoulder.

'Do you have a name?' Attercliffe said.

'Selina.'

'Do you have a second name?'

'No.'

'Are you at school with Cathy?'

'Yes.'

'Are you still attending?'

'Yes.'

A figure appeared in the door: black, wide-eyed, it surveyed the back of Selina then, without glancing at Attercliffe, inquired, 'Anything you want?'

Dressed in a black, low-crowned hat and a simulated leather overcoat, it leaned in the door: to the crown of the hat was attached a brightly-coloured feather.

'I'm looking for my daughter.'

'This her?'

Attercliffe shook his head.

'What you doing, girl?' the figure asked.

'Cooking.'

'Looks like washing-up to me.'

'I'm washing-up as well.'

'Don't want to see no dirty pots.'

'That's right.'

'Looks good.' The figure smiled. 'You leave that door unfastened?'

The girl didn't turn; nor did she pause in her washing-up: one rinsed pot, followed by another, was inverted on the draining-board beside the sink. 'I've been cooking.'

'What you cooking?'

'Baking bread.'

'Smells good.'

'You can have some.'

'Later,' the figure said. 'As soon as your visitor leaves.'

He stepped back to the landing, turned, and disappeared, not to the room at the back, but up the stairs: a moment later, from overhead, came the sound of a door being fastened.

'Do your parents know you're here?' Attercliffe asked. When she didn't answer, he added, 'Are they worried about you being here?'

'How should I know?'

'Have they been to visit you?'

'Why should they?'

'I thought they might.'

'I don't see why they should.'

Pulling out the plug in the sink, she picked up a discoloured strip of cloth and began to wipe the pots.

'Do you want a hand?' he asked.

'No thanks.'

She squeezed past him and, the cloth in one hand, a pot in the other, opened the oven door, looked in, closed it and, squeezing past him once again, returned to stand at the sink.

'Where does Cathy sleep?' he asked.

She gestured to the wall.

'A room like this?'

'Bigger.'

'How did you come across the shop?' he asked.

'I heard about it.'

Setting each pot upright, beside the sink, she added, 'You ask too many questions.'

He answered, 'Wouldn't you be better off if you lived at home?'

'This is my home.'

'How old are you?' Attercliffe asked.

'Sixteen.'

She went out to the landing and, turning to her right, closed a door behind her.

A banging of boxes came through the wall.

The one chair in the tiny kitchen, the back of which had been broken off, stood against the door, the edge of which it was propping open.

Attercliffe sat down.

A street-lamp came on in the road outside.

Down the flight of stairs a door was banged.

Dancing upwards, her hair flung up at each quick step, Catherine's head appeared.

'Shopping?' Attercliffe asked.

'That's right.'

Carrying a plastic bag, she shouldered past him.

'Everything going all right?'

'Perfect.'

She was wearing a skirt and jacket; her hair had recently been washed and, still wet, was drawn back from her face by a ribbon.

'Selina's in there.'

He indicated the adjoining room.

'How long are you staying?'

'As long as you like.'

'I'd prefer you to go.'

She was removing the contents of the plastic bag: a cupboard, lined with paper, and attached by hooks to the wall, shuddered as each item was placed inside.

'Where does the money come from?' Attercliffe asked.

'The usual place.'

'Where's that?'

'My pocket.'

She folded the plastic bag into four, squeezed past him, turned to her right, opened the door of the adjoining room, stepped in, closed the door behind her and asked, in a voice loud enough for Attercliffe to hear, 'How long has he been here?'

'Not long.'

'Been asking a lot of questions?'

'That's right.'

'Has he talked to anybody else?'

'He went next door.'

The sliding of the boxes continued.

Attercliffe stepped out to the landing and knocked on the door. When Catherine called, 'Come in,' he pushed the door back. Windows, curtained by blankets, looked out to the street.

Wooden cases had been arranged around a table. Two mattresses lay side by side on the floor, an open suitcase beside each one.

The floor was pitted; wooden laths showed through the plaster both in the ceiling and on the walls.

Catherine was kneeling by a suitcase: from it she was extracting clothes, folding them, and laying them on the mattress furthest from the door.

'I'll watch the bread,' Selina said and, without glancing at Attercliffe or Catherine, stepped outside, closing the door behind her.

'Perhaps we could talk about it,' Attercliffe said.

'All you want.'

As she went on folding the clothes, he said, 'There's nothing we can do to stop you living here. Nor,' he added, 'if this is what you want, am I here to persuade you to leave.'

'You couldn't,' she said, 'if you wanted.'

Her eyes were bright, her cheeks pale, her lips taut.

'It's not a battle,' Attercliffe said.

'It is for me.'

'Why should it be?'

'We've been through this before.'

'Not in a place like this.' He gestured round.

'This place is no different,' she said, 'from any other.'

'It looks a good deal different to me,' he said.

'Looks,' she said, 'aren't everything.' She leant back on her heels.

'It's only natural that your mother and I should feel concerned.'

'Just as I feel concerned,' she said, 'about the things that you do.'

From the room next door came the sound of dough being thumped against the table.

'Which is a concern your mother and I share with you,' Attercliffe said.

'I doubt it.'

She got up from the floor, dusted her skirt and, taking care to avoid a number of loose floorboards, crossed to the window.

'What do Selina's parents think of it?'

'Her father's abroad and her mother,' she announced, 'lives with another man.'

'Aren't they concerned with how she's living?'

'Her mother lives in a place very much like this. It's why,' she continued, 'she gave us this address.'

'Isn't she concerned about the friends you have next door?'

'Her boyfriend,' she said, 'happens to be black.'

'I see.'

'We've been through this before.' She folded her arms and, turning away, gazed at the darkening street.

'It's not their colour but their criminality that disturbs me,' Attercliffe said.

'Their criminality,' she said, 'is their colour. Their criminality,' she went on, 'is their cultural response to living in a consumer society.' She added, 'The goods mean nothing in terms of possessions, no more than a toy or a piece of food or a garment means anything to a child.'

'You see them as children?' Attercliffe asked.

She said, 'I am making an analogy, Dad. The only one you understand. I see them as people whose values are punished by the world we live in. To me, those values are more to do with living than those you cling to in your pathetic attempt to stay attached to your children, and your even more pathetic attempt to stay attached to Mum. My coming to live here is more real than my living anywhere else. I prefer it to the values of Walton Lane.'

Having unfolded her arms and turned to the room she gazed at Attercliffe directly.

'All I want you to know is that whatever happens I'll still be around. Walton Lane or not,' he said.

She sat on one of the boxes.

'Do you need any money?'

'No thanks.'

'Is Benjie living here as well?'

'On and off.'

'And Tiny?'

'In the other building.'

'Are they separate habitations?'

'They're supposed to be two.' She added, 'They punched a hole in the wall. Before that,' she gestured off, 'they came across the roof.'

There was the sound of someone calling from a window, then a rush of footsteps across the landing followed, from the bowels of the shop, by the calling of Selina's voice.

The same voice and that of one other person came from the stairs; a moment later, a short, bulky figure, dressed in a robe, was followed by Selina into the room: dark-eyed, dark-haired, red-cheeked, it gazed round at the room with a look of pleasure.

'Cathy!' the figure said.

'This is my father,' Catherine said.

From embracing Catherine, the figure turned; from inside the robe an arm appeared: a hand was thrust in Attercliffe's direction.

'This is Selina's mother,' Catherine added.

'No formal introductions here,' the woman said, and to Attercliffe she added, 'If we can't meet here on equal terms I don't know where we can. I'm Rose.'

Selina, carrying a basket, called, 'I shan't be a minute,' and went out to the kitchen.

'My father's name is Frank,' Catherine said as the woman shook Attercliffe's hand.

Testing one of the boxes, the woman sat down. 'Frank,' she said, and added, 'I've just dropped by for supper.'

A pair of reddened knees protruded from the hem of a darkly-patterned skirt: thick calves ran down to rope-soled sandals.

'The smell of cooking's inviting,' she said, and added, turning to Attercliffe, 'What do you do, Frank?'

'My father's unemployed, Rose,' Catherine said and, taking a seat on a box next to the mother, added, 'He used to be a journalist.'

'A journalist.' The woman flicked back her hair. 'I used to be one of those.'

'I didn't know,' Catherine said, and asked, 'What sort of things did you write?'

'I was a travel-writer, Cathy.' She said, 'Mainly in the Dutch East Indies. Where, for my sins, I met the man by whom I had my only child. Enlightenment,' she smiled, 'didn't come in my life, Cathy, as early as it's come in yours.'

The daughter returned from the kitchen; she was accompanied by the overcoated and feather-hatted figure who had appeared in the kitchen before.

'How good to see you,' the mother said, rising. 'I hope you're going to share our supper, Gary.'

'Not tonight, Mrs Johnson.'

Gary allowed himself to be embraced.

'Not tonight,' he said again.

'Tomorrow.'

'Tomorrow is another day.' He examined a watch. 'I shall have to leave.'

He touched the brim of his hat which, in his embrace, had been dislodged, added, 'See you soon, Rose,' and, with a pounding of wooden-heeled shoes, disappeared not down but up the stairs.

'That's Gary,' the mother said. 'A friend of mine from the old days.'

'Gary's an old chum of Rose's,' Catherine said.

'Old! Old! How time passes,' the mother said. 'What have we got for supper?'

'It depends what you've brought us,' the daughter said.

'I was hoping to savour some of your cooking,' the mother said. Smiling at Attercliffe, she announced, 'These girls have a lot to learn.'

'Let's get it ready, Catherine,' the daughter said, and added, 'Is there anything you'd like to drink?'

'There's a bottle of wine in the basket,' the mother said and, as the two girls went out and their voices, speaking simultaneously, came from the kitchen, she asked, 'You'll have some supper, too?'

In order to scrutinise the room more closely, she drew her box to a fresh position.

Attercliffe said, 'Aren't you concerned about them living here?'

He indicated the collapsing ceiling, the fragmenting walls, the crumbling floorboards, the blankets hanging at the broken windows.

'They'll soon lick it into shape.' She smiled. 'Selly has a knack of making herself at home. It's how I brought her up.' She waved her arm. 'She was born in a tent, with the nearest doctor four hundred miles away, and most of that,' she went on, 'was over mountains.' Glancing at the single beds, the debris-littered floor, the patches of light and shadow thrown up from a lamp in the street outside, she added, 'It's good to see young people on their own. It's what life, after all, is all about. If you're not fulfilled within yourself you're not in a position to relate to other people. Today, with all the pressures to conform – far more than there were when you and I were young – it does the heart good to see young people taking their chance.'

The sound of laughter came from the kitchen followed, a moment later, by the rattling of a pipe on the wall.

'What about the neighbours?' Attercliffe asked.

'That's the beauty of the place. Most of the properties round here have been abandoned.'

'I mean next door.'

Her nostrils flared; her eyes expanded. 'There isn't anyone next door.'

'It's full of youths,' Attercliffe said.

'You mean the boys?' She laughed; strong white teeth were revealed between thickly-fashioned lips. 'Gary keeps an eye on them. In addition to which they're Selly's friends. Lots of them I know. Going back to the old days.'

'In the Dutch East Indies.'

She laughed again. 'That,' she said, 'was a very long time ago. My husband had a job out there. He had to give it up and we came back here, which was when I gave up journalism. I still,' she went on, 'write occasional pieces.' Indicating that Attercliffe might take a seat on the box adjacent to her own, she added, 'The boys are what living in a place like this is all about.'

'Don't they get up to trouble?'

'What sort of trouble?'

'Theft. Assault. Attempted murder.'

'They're full of mischief!' She drew her sandalled feet together. 'None of them,' she continued, 'means any harm. It's what the authorities fail to understand and why a place like this is a godsend.'

'Cathy's friend, Benjie, has been to Borstal.'

'They always exaggerate their misdemeanours. It's what outsiders,' she continued, 'never understand. What appears to be non-conformist behaviour is merely the expression of a nature which a society like ours condemns.'

'Like attacking old-age pensioners.'

'I don't blame the youngsters, but those,' she said, 'of our generation who, when they see a spirit of adventure, try to crush it. What they crush, of course, are the elderly, the infirm, and those incapable of looking after themselves. I blame the authorities entirely. Assaults on the elderly are a consequence of suppressive action.' She breathed in, expanding the front of what he could see now was a darkly-patterned dress. 'Here, at least, they can be themselves. It's a curious phenomenon,' she went on, 'that the victims of a repressive society are seen as its culprits, and the culprits are seen as the custodians of justice. It's the inversion of traditional values,' she concluded, 'that lies at the root of violence.'

'I thought,' Attercliffe said, 'it was the other way around.'

'Each child is born into this world uncorrupted and in a matter of hours it is subjected to a society whose goals are achieved by a constriction of its spirit. Disciplining our children to suit the technological requirements and not,' she explained, 'the other way around.'

They sat knee to knee in the darkening room while, from beyond the door, came the sound not only of Selina but of Catherine singing: pipes rattled, water gushed, crockery was clattered.

She added, 'You'd have thought, after the Victorians, society would have learnt its lesson. Not for as long as I recall have the young been persuaded to accept suppression as a universally recognised goal in life.'

'Supper's ready!' came a cry from the room next door.

Selina's mother got to her feet.

As she turned she took Attercliffe's hand, and they arrived at the door of the adjoining room with both their hands buried in the folds of the mother's robe.

Four bowls had been set out on the draining-board beside the sink.

'We never got our drinks!' the mother cried and, squeezing between her daughter and Catherine, she stooped, sniffed, and called across her shoulder, 'Just what the doctor ordered!'

They returned with the bowls to the other room; a candle was lit: wine was poured.

'I've just been telling Frank,' Selina's mother said, 'of how, when I was young, I would have given so much for a chance like this.' She glanced at her daughter, then at Catherine and, finally, at Attercliffe himself and, as each of them delved at their chipped bowls with their variegatedly-patterned spoons (Attercliffe's with its stem twisted like a corkscrew and imprinted with the legend, 'Stolen from British Rail'), she added, 'Our true responsibility to our children rests in a place like this. So much awaits to be discovered, so much to be achieved. But not' - with her own variegatedly-patterned spoon, Selina's mother gestured round - 'in the manner prescribed for us by more conventional spirits.'

23

'I don't understand how you can be so complacent,' Sheila said. 'Living in a ruin!' She stooped, shielded her face, and cried.

'Mrs Johnson is pleased by their enterprise,' Attercliffe said.

'That woman is a lunatic.' She beat the arm of the chair.

'You're giving way to prejudice,' Attercliffe said.

'I'm giving way to anxiety about my daughter,' she said. 'Your daughter. The one you went to fetch.'

'I went to see how she was,' he said.

The room was bare; as much of the furniture as could be moved she'd taken into the hall: the remainder, including the two chairs on which they were sitting, as well as the floor, was covered by sheets.

A stepladder, on which he had seen her standing when he'd got out of the car in the road, was arranged against one wall: on a ribbed platform, at the top of the ladder, was set a can of paint; a paintbrush was laid across it.

Sheila wore a smock; paint was flecked across her chest, across her headscarf, and across her shoes – a bespattered pair of plimsolls.

The backs of her hands, too, and her wrists were flecked with paint: a solitary fleck animated the pallor of her cheek.

One half of the ceiling and two walls were painted: a pale green, on the two walls, displaced the pale cream which had been their previous colour.

'Unless you wanted me,' he went on, 'to bring her back by force.'

'By anything!'

'How?'

'Reason with her.'

'You approved,' Attercliffe went on, 'like Selina's mother, of your daughter's independence.'

She brushed her wrist beneath each eye and, aware for the first time that she was visible to the occupants of the houses opposite, straightened, felt in the sleeve of her smock, got out a handkerchief, examined it – chose a clean patch amidst the paint – and blew her nose. 'I suppose you'd just abandon her.'

'Why?'

'She's abandoned me. She's abandoned you. She thinks of nothing,' she added, 'but her own interests.'

'I'm proud of what she's done,' he said.

The nose was blown again. 'Ruining her life. Ruining her chances. That child,' she continued, 'is only fifteen.'

'She is nearly sixteen. She often tells me.'

'What difference does one year make!'

'You've often commended her common sense and stressed the freedom she needs to discover her femininity.'

'This isn't her femininity, this is her depravity.' She got up, stiff-backed, from the sheet-covered chair and gazed over a half-sheet of newspaper attached to the lower half of the window: only the top of Attercliffe's car and the upper storey of the houses opposite were visible and a patch of sky, the scene animated by the flecks of pale-green paint that had dried in diagonal splashes on the unprotected glass. 'I'll go and see her,' she added.

He said, 'It won't do her any good.'

'It'll do me some good. In addition to which,' she glanced back, 'I see through all this feminist crap.'

'I don't think it's crap,' Attercliffe said, 'with Cathy. Far more, it's to do with her disturbance at what,' he went on, 'goes on between her father and mother. The reason,' he gestured round, 'she has found a new home, however decrepit, is her disillusionment with this one.'

'I knew you'd blame me,' she said, 'in the end,' and, coming past him, scrambled up the ladder, retrieved her brush, dipped it into the tin of paint, slashed at the ceiling, and added, 'I'll no more accept it from you than I will from her.'

The ladder creaked; she dipped the paintbrush back in the tin, leaned back, examined the area directly above her head then, brush still in hand, descended the ladder and, with one hand and the back of her wrist, endeavoured to move it to a fresh position.

Attercliffe got up.

'I need no assistance, thank you.'

The ladder groaned: Attercliffe caught hold of the tin of paint as its contents cascaded on to her smock, on to her arms, and on to her shoes.

'Damn,' she said, but added nothing further and when he stooped to pick up the brush she turned, examined her hands, then her smock and, stepping over the pool that had formed at the foot of the ladder, kicked off her shoes and went out to the kitchen.

He folded the sheet, saw several drops of paint scattered on the carpet and, looking for a fresh sheet, laid it down.

'I am quite capable,' she said, reappearing, 'of clearing up. When,' she added, 'you've wiped your own shoes perhaps you'd leave. I can't work,' she went on, 'with people *hovering*.'

He took off his shoes and went out to the hall; she followed him to the kitchen where, having opened the back door, he set his shoes on the step outside, returned to the sink, and asked, 'Would you like a cup of coffee?'

'No thanks.'

'Mind if I get one?'

'I do mind,' she said, and added, 'If you didn't live like a sponger, and earned a living, we could afford to have someone decorate the house.'

'I'll come and do it myself,' he said.

'No thank you.'

'Why not?'

'I'm quite capable,' she said, 'of doing it myself. On top of which I prefer to keep the house free of all intruders.'

He dried his hands on a towel, wiped off a fleck of paint by his mouth, turned – found her gazing at him (eyes distended, cheeks flushed, forehead pallid, lips tightly flexed) – and said, 'It could all be amicably arranged if you didn't feel this need to score off me all the time.'

'Men score off women effortlessly,' she said, 'merely by being what they are. I am, as it happens, securing my assets. I'd be foolish to do otherwise. You act in a way that society determines, I act in a way which, to a woman in my predicament, makes sense.'

Having taken off her smock, she dropped it in a bowl, set it in the sink, turned on the tap, stepped back, then, glancing round, continued, 'If you'd leave me to get on with my job. You've made

249

it plain,' she turned off the tap, 'that you've no intention of counselling Cathy, in which case I shall have to do it myself.'

Attercliffe said, 'You'll make it worse.'

'I shall insist,' she said, 'that she comes back home.'

'How?'

'I'll beg her.'

'You'll throw a fit.'

'I shall throw anything that's necessary,' she said, 'to get my daughter back.'

She opened the kitchen door to the drive.

'If you want to clean your shoes there's a rag in the garage.'

'I'd advise against hysterics,' he said. 'Cathy sees through it, on top of which it sets her a bad example.'

'Example,' she said. 'We're back to that.'

'She is influenced by you a great deal,' he said.

'By me?'

'By you especially. Far more than she is by me.'

Her gaze shifted to an inspection of his shoes and, turning back to the kitchen, she announced, 'She doesn't give *me* much sign.'

'It's because she is that she doesn't,' he said.

'Is it?'

'The best thing you can do is to encourage her to go on with what she's doing. After all, you left home for a better life and if, in the long run, you came back she may see that as the inevitable course for her.'

'Pickersgill said you were good at manipulation. He said at the very beginning, "Why," he said, "do you allow Frank to put you in the wrong? Don't you realise he creates these situations and you're only responding to what he does? He's as much a cause of what's happening as you are, even more so, for a man is always in a better position in these situations, yet you always end up by feeling guilty." '

She indicated the door again.

'I shan't encourage my daughter to stay where she is. I shall insist she comes back home at once.'

'What if she refuses?'

'I shan't allow that,' she said, 'to stand in my way.'

She closed the door behind him.

As Attercliffe, a short while later, stood in his stockinged feet wiping his shoes on a rag in the garage, he heard music coming from the house – one of Elise's or Cathy's records – and when he returned to the car he saw Sheila through the upper half of the living-room window, back up the ladder, this time in an overall, slapping at the ceiling.

He sounded his horn as he drove away.

'What I like about the part,' Felix said, 'is the way it shows up the man for what he is.' He got up from his chair – his script rolled in his hand – and, while Towers manoeuvred the actors into fresh positions at the opposite end of the windowless room, he crossed to the coffee alcove, nodded at Ann, glanced across the floor to see if, from this angle, the interior of the alcove could be observed by Towers, took out a bottle – squat and bevelled – unscrewed the top, drank, screwed the top back on, turned, picked up a plastic cup of coffee, recrossed the room, sat, groaned, examined the coffee, set it by his feet, and added, 'A drunkard.'

'Could you keep it quiet, Felix?' Towers called, pacing the floor in his stockinged feet.

'People like me are a dying breed. Praised for our artistry on the one hand and condemned for our self-centredness on the other. Yet if you aren't self-centred how can you hold a company together, direct its actors, take the leading parts and, at the same time as you head the billing, keep an eye on the till? The till – where all enterprises start and where all but a minority of them founder. Subsidised theatre.' He waved his hand. 'I don't think I told you, by the way, on the first occasion that we met, how in a very unfortunate accident I came to kill my wife.'

'Could you keep it quiet, Felix?' Towers called again.

'We were in a car. I scarcely need to tell you, to an itinerant artist, driving comes as second nature. I could no more not drive a car than not know how to raise a curtain, strike a set, deliver a line which I have rehearsed if not performed a thousand times, "*Give me some light – away!*" or sit on a stage in such a position that I am not aware of all the sight lines. Though she is the dear-departed, she was, by any standards, a pain in the rectum, although, when I first met her, she was a beautiful actress of considerable charm.'

He drew out a wallet, removed a photograph and, having straightened it, held it out: placing his face beside Attercliffe's in order that the two of them might examine it together, he added, 'Ophelia.'

'Was that her name?'

'It was where we met. I was playing Claudius. I was scarcely twenty-one. She was two years older. When she died and I looked at her birth–certificate I discovered it was nearer three.'

The photograph was folded down the middle: a creased line obscured the centre of the face, leaving, on either side, a solitary eye set in a cheek drawn back by a smile.

A horizontal line amputated the body in the region of the waist, leaving a tiered skirt suspended above a centrally-fissured bosom.

'Pretty.'

He refolded the photograph and returned it to his wallet.

'Hamlet she was very keen on. He was twice as old as me. The audience used to applaud at the end of my scenes, and at the end of the duel scene they called out for me to kill him. Him!' He stabbed at the wallet. 'Finally, when she lost her beauty, she turned to drink.'

He picked up his script, turned to the pages he'd marked with a pencil and, muttering under his breath, closed his eyes, reopened them, and added, 'In those days it was one week's rehearsal and two weeks' playing. The mind,' he stabbed a finger at his temple, 'was chock-a-block. Rehearse all day, perform each night.'

'Can you keep your voices down?' came Towers's shout, his stocky figure propelled once more across the floor – returning, a moment later, and calling, 'Your cue, Felix, in a minute.'

'Ready,' Felix said, and added, 'On a bend and, overtaking a car, I realised there wasn't one car there but several, while, on my side of the road, coming directly towards me, was a lorry. "If," I thought, "one of us has to die, should it be someone with their talent still intact, or someone whose talent has expired beneath the ravages of drink?"' He smiled. 'I explained to the spectators – mainly the drivers from the other cars – that I'd intended crashing into the lorry with that half of the car in which I myself was sitting, only, to the driver of the lorry, it looked as if I'd turned his way on purpose. My distress, I can assure you, after all these years, has not abated, particularly since the coroner pointed out that I was to blame for the crash entirely, and no one, to the present day, believes me when I say I loved my wife, despite the tribulations of her failed career, and that if I had the choice again – which I'd welcome – I'd drive the car as I drove it then.'

He turned in his chair, knocking over, as he did so, his cup of coffee, and, addressing Attercliffe directly, asked, 'Do you think there is a part of us which wants the worst for us when we only want the best?' – rising, as he identified a signal from across the room, and calling, ' "Hope I'm not intruding, Danny. Thought I'd have a word." '

Slumping in the chair beside him, Towers said, 'I'm trying to clear each actor before he speaks, so that he's not endlessly emerging from behind the others. With twenty-two characters on a stage, which isn't much more than twenty-five feet across, it isn't easy. Mason, when he's on, has to have a central position. Can't lose him in a hurry, not that he'd let me, but the whole of it has to be arranged in terms of the text. When I look at it, it's very strange; the groups and the positions emerge naturally. I've never known it happen before.'

He took a cup of coffee from Ann, handed it to Attercliffe, took the other she was holding, shook his head over a tin of biscuits, drew, with his stockinged feet, a chair before him, gazed off across the room to where the tapes and the chairs and benches marking the set were surrounded, on the parquet floor, by the dusty imprint of the actors' shoes and, gasping at the heat of the coffee, continued, 'If you see a move that doesn't look right I hope, after all these weeks, you'll say so.' Placing his feet on the chair before him, and glancing off to where Mason, head and shoulders above the rest, was talking to several people at once, he asked, 'What was he going on about?'

'His wife.'

'Again.'

'He talked of a perversity,' Attercliffe said, 'that drove him one way when he wished to go another.'

'What it all boils down to,' Towers said, 'is that he's no one left to blame but himself.'

He got up, called, 'Let's try again,' and, as the figures drifted back across the room, and the stage-manager came back to sit at the table, to realign her coloured pencils, to reinspect the alterations, the transpositions, the lines and diagrams she'd drawn on her script, Attercliffe got up too, stretched and, conscious of the stuffiness of the room, went out to the yard – with its parked motor-bikes, chained bicycles, and cars – and, gasping, took in the air.

'Even if you'd found a purchaser,' Sheila said, 'you couldn't do anything about it.'

Her voice crackled by his ear.

'At least,' Attercliffe said, 'it would bring matters to a head.'

'They were brought to a head a long time ago. I thought,' she added, 'you'd got my message.'

The Buckingham Bar was crowded; amongst those sitting at the tables he identified Booth and Attwood, Morgan and Davidson-Smith, Dougie Walters and Phyllis Gardner, and even, curiously, Heather.

Also sitting there was Freddie's nephew.

'I am not redecorating the entire house in order to hand it over to someone else.'

He turned in the box to examine the nephew more closely: he was sitting with the woman with whom Attercliffe had seen him walking out of the Buckingham Bar on the day he had told him he was giving up his claim to Fredericks's will: a small, sharply-featured, dark-suited figure, sitting at the same table as Morgan and Davidson-Smith.

'Cathy told me about your visit.'

'Have you seen her?'

'She rang me up.'

'What on earth for?'

'To tell me that you weren't to go again.'

'Where on earth are you speaking from?'

'The Buckingham Bar.'

'I thought it was your flat.'

'I'm ringing from here,' he said, 'because, unlike the hallway of the flat, I can't be overheard.'

'I've heard Fredericks talking in that kiosk,' Sheila said, 'when I've been sitting the other side.'

'That's because there was no one but you and Freddie there.'

'The days of romance,' she said, 'are over. I've added up what has to be added up, and taken away what has to be taken away, and the only thing I'm left with is the house.'

'Whatever you said to Cathy has made her more determined to stay,' he said.

'How much money have you got?'

'I've two coins more.'

'I shouldn't waste them.' She put the phone down.

Redialling the number, he found the line engaged.

He stepped out to the bar. The nephew nodded his head, the gesture acting as a signal to the woman sitting beside him: turning, she smiled, and, leaning across the table, made a comment which Morgan and Davidson-Smith responded to by glancing up.

'How are you?' the nephew said. He pushed back his chair, stood, and added, 'You haven't met my wife.'

The woman extended her hand.

'I was telling Connie,' the nephew said, 'of our previous encounter.' He gestured at the bar, waiting for Attercliffe to shake her hand, and, indicating they might move away, continued, 'Could we have a word? Outside might be better.'

As he allowed his wife to lead the way, the door to the street was opened from the other side.

Elise came in. 'Hello, Dad,' she said. A tall, white-jacketed, white-trousered, plimsolled, slim-featured and fair-haired figure followed her inside.

'This is my daughter,' Attercliffe said, and added, 'This is Mr and Mrs Fredericks, Elise.'

'Any relation to Mr Fredericks?' his daughter asked.

'His nephew and his wife,' he said.

The nephew extended his hand.

'We were coming in for a drink.' Elise shook his hand, shook the wife's and, indicating her companion, added, 'This is Alex.'

'How do you do?' the tall, white-jacketed figure said.

'Have you been here often?' Attercliffe asked.

'When we can afford it,' his daughter said.

'Who's affording it now?'

'Alex.' Smiling from within a mask of make-up, she squeezed past, nodded to the Frederickses, called, 'See you,' and, her arm in that of her companion, disappeared across the bar.

'I didn't catch her name,' the nephew said.

'Elise.'

'Full of character.'

'I'm surprised you could see it.'

'And her friend.'

'Really?'

'Youth,' the nephew said, 'it leads the way,' and, indicating they might move to the street, added, as they stepped out to the pavement, 'What we wanted to talk about was Uncle's play.'

'Uncle's?'

'Freddie's.'

'Freddie's?'

'*Players*.'

'*Players*,' Attercliffe said, 'happens to be mine.'

'He must have had a hand in it.'

'None at all.'

'You didn't find it,' he said, 'amongst his papers?'

Attercliffe shook his head.

'You'd swear to that in court?'

'If I have to.'

'It's only a natural precaution,' he glanced at his wife, 'in the light of the fact that you were his literary executor.'

'That's right.'

The door to the bar reopened.

Amongst the figures that emerged was Elise's tall companion, followed by Elise.

'It's pretty dead in there,' his daughter said.

'Shouldn't you be at college?' Attercliffe asked.

'Free period,' she said, 'but we're going back.'

He watched her cross the road and, accompanied by her friend, set off along the pavement in the direction of the college.

'Is she still at school?' the nephew asked.

'Another year.'

'You must be proud. Both ours are lads. We miss not having a daughter,' he added.

'If we thought Freddie had had a hand in *Players* we wouldn't hesitate to pursue our interests,' his wife announced.

'I'm sure you wouldn't,' Attercliffe said.

She took her husband's arm.

'Didn't Uncle play in the old days?' she asked.

'No,' the nephew said. 'He didn't.'

He offered his hand to Attercliffe, waited for him to shake it, then, turning to his wife, set off, his arm in hers, in the opposite direction to that taken by Elise.

Attercliffe himself turned back to the bar, pressed open the door, recalled he had insufficient money to buy a drink, and, returning to the pavement, stood there for a while, his hands in his pockets, gazing off along the street.

24

The sea was calmer than on their previous visit. On this occasion only the boys and Lorna had come with him: Sheila herself had stayed behind; Catherine, to whom he'd sent a letter, hadn't troubled to answer his invitation; Elise, who'd shown no interest, had gone out with her friend.

It was cold; the sky was overcast: it looked like rain.

The children at first sat in a tiny group, with only two other pairs of figures visible along the beach, its width reduced by the incoming tide. A warship was anchored some distance from the shore: it was this which, on their arrival, had attracted the boys' attention and some time later, while Lorna, mournfully, played in the sand, they had wandered down to the water's edge and, their hands in their pockets, gazed out at the low-slung shape.

'Daddy?' Lorna looked up. 'Mummy says she'll never be happy.'

'When did she tell you that?'

'She told Elise.'

She rested back on her heels.

'Some people are only happy when they're complaining,' Attercliffe said.

'What's "complaining"?'

'Whining.'

'I'm always whining,' she said.

She scooped at the sand and called, 'There's water,' while, from further along the beach, came the protesting voice of Bryan, 'Give over!'

Having exhausted his interest in the boat, pursued by his brother, he was running along the water's edge.

'You'll have to cheer your mother up,' he said.

'Audrey says she's mad.'

'Why?'

'Because she's been in hospital.'

'It wasn't because she was mad,' he said.

'What was it for?'

'Because she needed a rest.'

Her back turned to him, she scooped up the sand more quickly, flicking it above her head, and he called, 'Watch where you're throwing it,' to which her muffled voice replied, 'I've got to the water.'

Finally, sitting on the edge, she stamped her feet in the bottom. The side caved in.

'If you help your mother by cheering her up she'll have more time to spend with you.' He indicated the boys. 'They're old enough,' he went on, 'to look after themselves.'

'Will I look after myself?'

'One day.'

She gazed off to the sea: arrested by its anchor, stern-on, the warship swung in their direction.

She got up from the hole and, coming to where he was sitting, got into his lap, lowered her head to his chest, curled herself against him, set her thumb in her mouth and, her gaze abstracted, stared in the direction of the harbour.

'I don't want to look after myself,' she said.

She removed her thumb from her mouth.

'One day,' he said, 'you won't be able to stand the sight of me.'

'Why?'

'Ask the boys.' Now the only figures on the beach, they had reached the opposite edge of the bay.

'I like you more than they do.'

'In a different way.'

'Why in a different way?'

'Because,' he said, 'you're not a son.'

'Do you like me?'

'I do.'

'How much?'

'A lot.'

She thrust her shape against his chest.

'It's cold.'

'That's why it's better you dig a hole.'

'I don't like digging one,' she said.

'I'll dig one with you,' he said, 'and when the boys come back we'll hide inside.'

She climbed out of his lap and, handing him the shovel, stood by the hole as he dug it out.

'How about a castle?'

She shook her head.

'Or making a boat?'

'A hole,' she said.

Occasionally she dropped in and patted the side, scooped up sand, and precipitated further falls as she scrambled out.

The beach, in the direction which the boys had taken, was now deserted.

'Shall I get in?'

'I can't see them coming back,' he said.

She looked along the beach herself, said, 'There they are,' only, the two figures walking along the road, above the beach, turned out to be a man and a woman.

'I'm cold,' she said.

'Let's find somewhere we can eat,' he said.

He dusted down her legs, cleaned her feet, looked back along the sand, then, packing their possessions, lifted her in one arm and, with her arm in turn around his neck, set off in the direction of the harbour where, on the quay, he'd parked the car.

The road at the back of the beach was devoid of traffic, the shops on the other side white-shuttered: she hummed to herself as they walked along, pointing at the warship.

'It's moving.'

'It isn't.'

'I thought it was.' Indicating first one white-shuttered front and then another, she said, 'Where will we eat?' and finally, wriggling in his arms, 'I want to go.'

He took her to a women's toilet adjoining the quây. After stepping, wide-eyed, into the darkened entrance, she returned and said, 'I can't work it,' holding out the coin he'd given her, and adding, 'Can you do it for me?'

Along the quay there was only a handful of men working in the fish-sheds: the road above the beach was still deserted.

He took her hand; inside the toilet, the door to a cubicle stood ajar: the toilet seat itself was broken. He dropped the coin in the slot on the adjoining door; a voice on the inside said, 'It's taken.'

He tried the adjacent door, found it locked, dropped another coin in, and the door sprang back.

Toilet paper and refuse were strewn on the floor.

They returned to the street outside.

'Where are we going?'

'We'll do it in the gutter.'

She drew down her pants, he held her up and, as she crouched in this position, he saw the boys coming along the road, one some distance behind the other.

'There's Keith and Bryan.'

Water jetted by his feet.

A car went past.

'I'm finished.'

He set her down; she stooped, drew up her pants, and added, 'We can hide behind that building.'

She indicated the fish-sheds which, adjacent to the car-park, lined the harbour wall.

They waited by the corner, Lorna stepping out, dashing back, quivering, clutching his leg, stepping out again – only to cry out as, laughing, the two boys came around the corner, calling, amidst their laughter, 'We saw you!'

They went to a café adjacent to the quay; they ordered a meal, gazing out at the harbour, at the strands of cloud above the bay – at the back of the car, inconspicuous amongst the backs of several others, parked against the harbour wall. 'Shall we go back?' Keith said. 'There's nothing to do.'

'It'll soon brighten,' Attercliffe said.

A column of cloud drifted in to the land, approaching the headland, absorbing it, passing on.

'It's cold.'

'We'll run about and get warm.'

'We have run about,' Bryan said.

'We can run about again.'

'I wish we hadn't come,' Keith said and Lorna, preoccupied with eating, glanced from his face to Bryan's then back again.

Attercliffe said, 'You can go back on the train if you like.'

Their faces brightened.

'You'll know the way home from the other end.'

Already they were standing up.

'Can't you hurry, Lorna?' Keith said, gazing at her plate.

'I have,' she said, eating more slowly.

'It's safer,' Attercliffe said, 'if she stays with me.'

The boys stepped back from the table. 'Come in the car,' Keith said, 'when you've finished. We can walk up to the station and meet you there.'

'They are only obligations, and what you are obligated to,' Catherine said, 'is something that no one else can see.'

The floor, in addition to having been swept, was covered here and there with rugs. Other material hung from the walls: curtains of varying lengths were suspended from the windows.

'Your relationship with your parents, otherwise, means nothing at all,' Attercliffe suggested.

Sitting on the floor, her back straight, her hands dipped in her lap, her feet bare – a skirted alcove formed by her cross-legged thighs – she said, 'It means as much as you want it to.'

Music reverberated through the building: it throbbed from the room above their heads.

It was growing dark: in a room in one of the houses opposite, level with their own, several men, their coats discarded, their heads stooped, their shoulders hunched, were playing cards at a table.

'You've been brought up to assume it does mean something,' Attercliffe said.

'Things change,' she said. 'It doesn't mean I have to go on with it. Furthermore, things can be changed. That, for me, is the most important thing of all.'

'You don't have to disown the past,' he said.

'I might go back to acknowledge it,' she said. 'But not to propagate its values. This is my progress.' She added, 'The rest I can do without.'

The floor shook; feet trampled overhead: dust filtered from the ceiling.

'I dread families.' She gazed at her feet. 'I can't see anything in them. Nothing in Mum, nothing in you, nothing in Elise, nothing in Bryan, nothing in Keith. Nothing in Lorna. Flesh and blood.' She shuddered. 'It makes you creep.'

The sound of singing came from the kitchen.

'I've finished with Benjie.'

262

She raised her head.

'What was his reaction?' Attercliffe said.

'He made a beeline,' she said, 'for someone else.'

Rising from the box where, having eaten the food she'd offered him, he'd been seated, he went over to the window.

'I've changed my mind, not about his predicament, but,' she added, 'about his significance as far as I'm concerned.'

A car drew up in the street below; a van was already parked outside the shop: plastic cones had been set along the pavement.

There was the sound of breaking glass: the music wavered, stopped – and was superseded by the sound of someone shouting. A moment after that the door was flung open and Gary, or a figure not unlike him – long-coated, feather-hatted – called, 'It's the fuzz,' and, closing the door behind him, ran swiftly off upstairs.

Catherine, still sitting on the floor, glanced up. She said, 'Do you want to be taken in?'

'What for?'

She shrugged. 'Hash. Stolen property. Evidence,' she went on, 'of prostitution.'

'In here?'

She said, 'Honestly,' and added, 'Hardly, Dad.'

The door opened; a peak-hatted, uniformed figure came inside: he was followed by Selina.

'You live in here?' the figure inquired.

'My friend and I do.' Selina, a teacloth in one hand, a plate in the other, added, 'We've just had dinner. I'm washing up.'

'All Selly likes doing is cooking.' Catherine laughed as a second, peak-hatted, uniformed figure stepped inside and asked of Attercliffe, 'Who are you?'

'I'm visiting,' Attercliffe said.

'Who?'

'My daughter. And this,' he went on, 'is my daughter's friend.'

A torch lit up the unmade beds; it lit up the boxes and a makeshift desk, a set of drawers and a cupboard.

'Any means of identification?' the second policeman said.

Attercliffe got out his wallet and as Catherine said, 'Don't show him it unless he's got a warrant, Dad,' he got out his driving-licence and added, 'I have my car outside.'

'Name?' The second policeman glanced at Catherine.

'Jones,' Catherine said.

'Attercliffe,' Attercliffe said. 'The same as mine.'

'Your name?'

A torch was turned on Selina.

'Selina,' Selina said.

'Selina what?'

'Jones, as well,' she said.

The driving-licence was opened.

'Address?'

'Walton Lane.'

'Number?'

'Twenty-four.'

'Played for the City?' the first policeman said.

'At one time.'

The torch was flashed on to Catherine's face, then Selina's, then back to Catherine's, then, returning the driving licence, the policeman said, 'Don't leave the building,' and, preceded by the first uniformed figure, went upstairs.

'Why are you so co-operative?' Catherine stood up. 'So obliging.'

'Why are you so cantankerous?' Attercliffe said.

'It has its place.' She gestured to the door. 'They were aggressive, and without any cause.'

'There are some things worth being unco-operative about. This,' Attercliffe said, 'wasn't one of them.'

'I'd have thought,' she said, 'it was.' She crossed to the window, leaned out, and called, 'Leave those people alone,' and added, 'Why don't we go down and stop them?'

There were shouts from the street, the revving of an engine, and shouts from the windows of the house next door.

Attercliffe watched his daughter Catherine's face gripped by a frenzy not unlike the one which, from time to time, had overwhelmed her mother.

She ran to the door, padded across the landing and, a moment later, her voice was raised, not in the street, but in the room above their heads.

'Are you going up?' he asked Selina.

After glancing out of the window she sat down by her bed; from beside the pillow she picked up a packet of cigarettes, took one out, struck a match, ducked her head to the flame, blew out the match and said, 'They'll be up in a minute,' and added, 'No

264

sooner said than done,' when, a moment later, illuminated by the beam of a torch, a dog, secured on a lead, appeared inside the door and, restrained by a uniformed figure, proceeded to her bed.

It thrust its nose at the blankets.

It smelled around the walls; it smelled inside the cupboard.

It returned to Selina's bed.

'Do you mind?' its handler said.

Selina, dusting down her skirt, stood up.

The dog pursued its course to Catherine's bed, returned to the walls, the cupboard, thrust its muzzle – as the policeman opened them – inside the drawers, and – straining on the lead – went out, once more, to the landing.

A second, uniformed figure came inside, followed, in the beam of a second torch, by a uniformed woman.

A light was flashed on Attercliffe's face. 'Do you mind,' the policeman said, 'turning out your pockets?'

Selina, already, had raised her arms.

Attercliffe emptied his overcoat pockets; he emptied those of his jacket; he turned out those in his trousers: he allowed the policeman to feel his chest, to run his hands beneath his arms, along his sides and down his legs.

'Is there any legality in this?' he said.

Turning to the uniformed woman, gaunt, dark-eyed, the policeman asked, 'Anything there?', adding, 'Don't leave the room,' as he and the woman departed.

Selina sat down once more by the bed.

'You don't seem as disturbed by it as Catherine,' Attercliffe said.

'It doesn't bother me.' She added, 'If you live like this you must expect the harassment.'

Attercliffe sat down on one of the boxes.

There was a padding of feet at the door: Catherine, her pigtails loose, her hair dishevelled, stepped inside.

'They have a job to do. I have mine. The two,' Selina continued, 'are not in conflict.'

'Have they looked in here, Selly?' Catherine asked.

'That's right,' Selina said.

'Did Dad say anything?'

'He asked,' Selina said, 'but wasn't answered.'

'They've taken eight away.'

'Only eight.' Selina smiled.

'And are searching the house from top to bottom.'

Sounds to that effect came from the floor above their heads.

'Shouldn't you have a light in here?' Attercliffe asked.

Selina struck a match; from beside the bed she picked up a lamp: a yellowish glare lit up the room.

Catherine, having gone to the window, turned, came back, and sat on a box.

'Do you want a fag?' Selina asked.

'No thanks,' she said.

'Have you started smoking?' Attercliffe asked.

'Now and again.'

'On top of taking drugs.'

'What drugs?'

'Whatever the police came here to find.'

Feet clambered up the stairs; feet clattered across the ceiling: a car started up in the road outside.

'Hash is no more potent,' Catherine said, 'than alcohol or tobacco.'

From below came a murmur of voices: feet shuffled on the pavement.

In the house opposite the men playing cards were standing at the window.

'Will you go on living here?' Attercliffe asked.

'As long as I can.'

'How much longer is that?'

'I've no idea.'

The light from the lamp glistened in her eyes and he realised, in her rage, she must have been crying.

'Why don't you come and stay with me?' he asked.

'What for?'

'I can give you a home.'

'With a family.' She added, 'I'd have to share with that.'

'Are Elise,' he said, 'and the boys, so bad?'

'Not bad. But there,' she said, 'I'm only a part. Here,' she went on, 'I'm everything.'

Music broke out from the room below.

Looking at a watch on her wrist, she added, 'I'd like to go to bed.'

'I'm surprised you can sleep,' Attercliffe said, 'with all that racket.'

'I never notice it,' she said.

'Aren't you going to the party?' Selina asked.

'I might.'

Attercliffe got up from the box and went to the door.

'Can you lock this door?' he asked.

'What for?'

'To stop intruders.'

'There aren't any intruders,' Catherine said.

'Can anyone come inside?'

'We're the only ones who sleep in here,' she said, and when he paused, she added, 'You have a peculiar sense of virtue, Dad.'

She came out to the landing, after he had called, 'Good night,' to Selina, and said, 'Despite what you say, you can't help trying to persuade me to leave. The more you do,' she added, 'the more determined I am on staying.'

She remained on the landing as he descended the stairs, and it was this image of her standing there, at the head of the stairs, that Attercliffe took with him to the street, for, in looking up, finally, as he got in the car, he saw her once again – at the window – caught by the lamp – slim-featured, dark-eyed, wild-haired – and when he waved she smiled, glancing down, her hand raised briefly in acknowledgment.

25

It was a girl Elise had brought or, rather, as the figure in the light-coloured coat and a headscarf turned, a woman – one young enough, nevertheless, to be a friend, and excited, Attercliffe thought, as was Elise herself, by the pressing-up of the crowds to the door: it was only as he stepped towards them – avoiding one incoming group and then another – that he recognised his wife.

'I hope you didn't mind,' Sheila said, and when Attercliffe said, 'Not at all,' she announced, 'It's more an evening for you, after all.'

'I thought you didn't care for me,' he said.

'There's a first time, Frank, for everything,' she said, and added, 'It is, after all, a part of our past.'

'You're not going to argue about it?' Elise inquired.

'I'm glad you've come,' Attercliffe said and, taking his wife's and his daughter's arms, he guided them inside.

'I've never seen so many naked men. Not simultaneously,' she said.

'You don't mind seeing so much of it?' he asked.

'Not at my age, Frank,' she said.

'Particularly,' he went on, 'since you see so little at present.'

'Just because I'm at home doesn't mean,' she nodded at Doctor Morrison across the bar, 'I'm not extremely busy. I merely re-marked,' she nodded at Butterworth and his wife, 'on the quantity, not the quality.' Aware of Towers, propped at the end of the bar, she added, 'How did he come to put it on?'

'It was his own initiative entirely,' Attercliffe said.

'How did you come to write it?'

Attercliffe said, 'At Freddie's suggestion. He didn't mention it again, however, until just before he died.'

'He never liked you,' Sheila said.

'I thought he did.'

'He was envious of you,' she said, 'as a player. He was even more envious of you,' she added, 'as a man.'

'He got me a job on the *Post*,' he said.

'After he lost you one on television.'

'It was he,' Attercliffe said, 'who took me on.'

'He got you a job, saw you were about to succeed, and dragged you down to his level.' She was thrust against his arm, her glass spilling and, wiping down his sleeve, she added, 'It was why I went to Maurice. With him, at least, there was never any question.'

Attercliffe glanced across the bar, saw the face of Fredericks's nephew – saw, in a peculiar way, the face of Fredericks – not unlike, in a curious way, the face of Towers, or even, he reflected, that of Felix Mason, or – the thought for an instant made him smile – that of Pickersgill himself – and, glancing back at his wife, he said, 'Why did you never tell me?'

'The man sitting next to me was writing for the northern edition of a national paper and described it as the best new play he'd seen in months.'

She leaned forward in her chair, her knees and her ankles drawn together, her elbows on her thighs, her hands clutched around her glass of wine.

Elise had gone to bed; there had been the murmur of her radio overhead, a call from one of the boys, then, when Sheila had gone to the kitchen and returned with a bottle of wine, declaring, 'I bought this to celebrate,' the house had grown silent but for themselves.

Her forearms, like her knees and ankles, drawn together, she said, 'You must be feeling pleased.'

She had, in the past few weeks, lost weight – having, when she first went off with Pickersgill, put on a great deal: a leaner version of her original self confronted Attercliffe across the hearth.

She set down the glass by her feet. 'I wasn't going to go, as you know, then Elise said it had been her intention all along to ask me.' She turned her look to the window with its undrawn curtains and the darkness of the road outside. ' "As your eldest daughter and your first child I thought I should." That girl has got her head screwed on.'

She leant back in the chair and crossed her legs: her gaze went up to the ceiling, to the over-painted plaster, to the striation of cracks she hadn't filled in. 'What will you do now?' she asked.

'Go on,' he said, 'as I was before.'

A faint creaking came from overhead as one of the children stirred.

A car went past in the road; from a further distance came the sound of trucks on the line that ran across the river.

From the region of the castle came the hooting of an owl.

It was the first time he'd noticed anything at the back of the flat – the gardens he'd noticed, and the configuration of the houses, identical to the one he was in; but, above the roofs, he recognised for the first time the profile of the valley – the line of the hills, the woodland, the hedged incision which marked the cutting in which a railway line ran off to the south.

'What,' Wilkins said, 'have you learnt from the past few months?'

'More than I might, at one time, have imagined,' Attercliffe said.

'Whatever the success of the play at least it's given you that. On the other hand, if,' Wilkins said, 'you look at the reality, as opposed to the fantasy which absorbs the majority of people's lives, you can only come to the one conclusion. Having destroyed the world in theory, the practice can't be far behind. Nevertheless, I get your point – specifically with your children. Even with your wife. Bleak, but – how should I describe it?'

'Promising.'

'Promising.'

From below came the sound of the baby crying but Wilkins's attention was focused not so much on that as on the view outside the window: his gaze had been caught by a distant glimmer – the sunlight, perhaps, on the rails in the cutting – flashing once – a single beam – before it settled and, with a strange persistency, shone out above the town.

MORE ABOUT PENGUINS, PELICANS
AND PUFFINS

For further information about books available from Penguins please
write to Dept EP, Penguin Books Ltd, Harmondsworth, Middlesex
UB7 0DA.

In the U.S.A.: For a complete list of books available from Penguins in
the United States write to Dept DG, Penguin Books, 299 Murray Hill
Parkway, East Rutherford, New Jersey 07073.

In Canada: For a complete list of books available from Penguins in
Canada write to Penguin Books Canada Ltd, 2801 John Street,
Markham, Ontario L3R 1B4.

In Australia: For a complete list of books available from Penguins in
Australia write to the Marketing Department, Penguin Books Australia
Ltd, P.O. Box 257, Ringwood, Victoria 3134.

In New Zealand: For a complete list of books available from Penguins in
New Zealand write to the Marketing Department, Penguin Books
(N.Z.) Ltd, Private Bag, Takapuna, Auckland 9.

In India: For a complete list of books available from Penguins in India
write to Penguin Overseas Ltd, 706 Eros Apartments, 56 Nehru Place,
New Delhi 110019.

David Storey in Penguins

A PRODIGAL CHILD

David Storey's first novel since his Booker Prize winner, *Saville*.

Growing up in the 1920s, Bryan Morley, the second son of a farm labourer, knows he has a special destiny. Alienated from his family he sees a world full of possibility through his friendship with Margaret Spencer, the daughter of his father's employer. Then one day he meets Margaret's aunt, Fay Corrigan, and falls under the spell of her reckless sensuality . . .

Echoing the themes and cadences of Lawrence's *Sons and Lovers*, this moving novel truly catches the nuances of working-class family life and the obsessive ruthlessness of the relationship between an older woman and a prodigal child.

'Storey's own powers are displayed with a vivid solidity throughout the engrossing pages of this richly satisfying book' – Peter Kemp in *The Times Literary Supplement*

Also published:

Novels

FLIGHT INTO CAMDEN
PASMORE
RADCLIFFE
SAVILLE
THIS SPORTING LIFE

Plays

EARLY DAYS/SISTERS/LIFE CLASS
IN CELEBRATION/THE CONTRACTOR/
THE RESTORATION OF ARNOLD MIDDLETON/
THE FARM
HOME/THE CHANGING ROOM/MOTHER'S DAY